3 -21

San Anselmo Public Library
San Anselmo. Cal.

PRETERNATURAL

PRETERNATURAL

MARGARET WANDER BONANNO

TOR®

A TOM DOHERTY ASSOCIATES BOOK

NEW YORK

PRETERNATURAL

Copyright © 1996 by Margaret Wander Bonanno

A Tor Book
Published by Tom Doherty Associates, Inc.
175 Fifth Avenue
New York, NY 10010

Tor Books on the World Wide Web:
http://www.tor.com

Tor® is a registered trademark of Tom Doherty Associates, Inc.

Library of Congress Cataloging-in-Publication Data

Bonanno, Margaret Wander.
    Preternatural / Margaret Wander Bonanno. —1st ed.
        p.   cm.
    "A Tom Doherty Associates book."
    ISBN 0–312–86209–1
    I. Title.
PS3552.O5925P74   1996
813'.54—dc20   96–21280

First edition: December 1996

Printed in the United States of America

0 9 8 7 6 5 4 3 2 1

For J.S., who taught me to live
in alternate universes . . .

PRETERNATURAL

ONE

Eternity is a white room.

Karen had always hated white walls. They were the first thing she attacked, once the cleaning and disinfecting phase was over, every time she moved. Landlord White, the cheapest, most popular color in any paint store, covered everything. Past histories scrawled on walls ("Fuck you! I love you/hate you!") in blood or crayon. Scuff marks, handprints (I was here, unique in my fingerprints if nothing else), shit stains. Karen hated white walls; they hurt her eyes.

"Molecules," she remembered her fifth-grade nun explaining, and she'd startled everyone, including herself, by shouting out: "Yes, I know; I can see them!"

Wrong on all counts. One did not shout out in a Catholic school classroom; one raised one's hand and waited to be called on. One did not contradict the nun, who had just explained that molecules were too small to see, by claiming one could see them. And one did not, if one were Karen Rohmer, speak out in a classroom at all. Her fourth-grade nun, in a year-long campaign to humiliate her into sullen silence, had seen to that.

She hadn't really cried out, only thought she did. Why then had everyone in the class turned, openmouthed, to stare at her in her silence? Someone, something else—beside her, inside her—had cried out in her stead, a parallel-universe self (an established science fiction writer, Karen understands these things now) shouted, clear and defiant: "Yes, I know; I can see them!"

She could. Every time she stared at a blank white wall, it

moved. Little flashes of light danced in rhythmic, prescribed circles (clockwise, counterclockwise, both?) round about their own circumspect, circumscribed orbits, long before she'd ever heard the word *orbit*—science wasn't taught with any seriousness in Catholic grade schools pre-Sputnik; that Beat-the-Russkies fervor was a year or more away—continuing their dance behind her eyelids when she closed them. What were those little flashes if not molecules dancing in their orbits to form the seeming solidity of a wall?

Karen thought she should be frightened at the knowledge that nothing was solid, that everything—the desk she sat at, the clothes she wore, the potato-face of the nun looming in its own black-bordered orbit above her, her very own hand—was made of molecules, too-small-to-see entities with spaces in between! It was not frightening, but exhilarating, like the thought of the boring stretch of concrete between school and home being not static, not permanent, but hurtling constantly through space, its molecules dancing faster in the torpid summer than the gritty winter. If they danced fast enough, would she fall through?

Somehow she'd always known none of this was real, because she'd seen the molecules no one else could see.

When she was twelve, Karen's first eye exam indicated that the vision in her left eye was four times worse than that in her right. "Lazy eye" it was called then, something that could have been corrected with an eye-patch when she was four if anyone had been paying attention. "Lazy eye" was all Karen heard, getting used to wearing glasses—blue plastic harlequin frames with rhinestones in the corners—knowing it was somehow all her fault. When you went to Catholic schools, everything was.

Eternity is a white room where the walls move. Karen has not painted the walls this time. She sits on a bare wood floor, knees up, back against a white wall, aware of a vague redolence of urine from the corners, writing. Slight and forty-something, measuring out eternity on a grey-tinted legal pad with a cheap ballpoint pen. What does she look like, what is she wearing, what does it matter? It is science fiction she writes, and in that venue physical descriptions of characters human are always less important than descriptions of characters alien or precise analysis of the properties of tungsten.

Aren't they?

"Create Your Own Universe" has always been one of Karen's favorite panel-discussion topics. Wedged between biochemists and nuclear engineers who dabble in fiction writing, she with her soft-spoken undergrad degree in English lets them natter on about nucleosynthesis and event-horizon anomalies until the moderator notices she hasn't said a word. Given the floor, she asks her fellow panelists: "If you were writing a murder mystery, would you spend the first chapter describing the chemical composition of the sun?"

They gawk at her from the same alternate universe as her fifth-grade classmates. She will never be popular among her peers. When will she learn?

Alone in a white room, Karen writes of white rooms. . . .

•

The chamber smelled of herbs, strong acid, death, and drying plaster. In this driest of dry climates, where even the finest Pharaoh's Bread contained so much sand intermixed inadvertently with the grain that it wore the teeth down to bare nerve, this room was forever damp. No guardian god looked down hawk-eyed from the bare white walls, protecting; the walls themselves grew unheard-of mold in corners, requiring frequent whitewash. No matter, for in this brightest of bright lands, where the eye of Amun-Re struck stark shadows even as he struck men blind who dared contemplate his visage, this room (womb/tomb), lit only by a single lamp, was uncommonly dark.

The high priest Herihor went about his task furtively. Never before had a pharaoh been prepared for death with such unseemly haste. Then again, never before had there been a pharaoh like this one. Even the blasphemies of Hatshepsut, who had dared to rule despite that she was female, had not been equal to the sins of this one, who had tried to destroy the world.

What he had earned by this most egregious transgression was that none of the five names bestowed upon him at his coronation would ever be spoken or inscribed again in the land of the Two Niles. More to the point, the inscriptions already extant in the temples and tombs would be chiseled away or inscribed over with the name of another. Some had suggested that of his eldest daughter Meritaten—a particular insult in that it ascribed his many deeds both praiseworthy and execrable to a female offspring. Others had suggested that even this was not sufficient; he must be expunged entirely from the scroll of history, a blank space on the walls of public edifices built within his reign, a hiatus in the long unbroken progression of the Eighteenth Dynasty, which future historians would perhaps attribute to a scribe's error and elide over completely, dividing his years between the father who had sired him on a slave woman and the nephew-son who succeeded him.

Thus this body, royally prepared but destined for a pauper's grave. The high priest Herihor, who had been among this prince's most loyal retainers until the Great Aberration, had returned to claim him afterward, for reasons he himself did not entirely understand. Bad enough that this prince had tried to destroy the world, and in so doing had very likely sacrificed his own soul. How many other souls, including that of Herihor, had he endangered in the process?

That it was Herihor who had the great gaunt misshapen body brought to this womblike room by tongueless slaves who could not report it afterward was among the finest of ironies. For despite his concern for the disposition of his own soul, Herihor had taken it upon himself to perform his last duty toward this fallen king, to see that his body was preserved so that his royal soul, even in its pauper's guise, could perhaps sneak through a side door into heaven. Surely there he would be recognized for what he was, thought Herihor, and numbered among the very gods he had disavowed? If I were a god, wondered Herihor, what would I do?

His answer lay in the tasks his hands performed—the loving washing of the long, edemic limbs, the careful removal of the viscera to be sealed in the canopic jars. If I were a god, thought Herihor, I would forgive him. Not for what he did, but for what he meant to do.

What prompted this thought? Herihor wondered as expertly he severed the slippery intestines from the contiguous organs, placing them in the jar that bore the head of Qebekh-sennuef the Falcon.

•

Wrong! Amber's resonance clamors down the Common Mind. *Wrong, wrong, wrong! Canopic jars did not bear the heads of the sons of Horus until Ramses' time! These would have borne human heads, if in fact four separate jars were even used this early. As I recall, they were still using a common chest for all the guts.*

Guts! Virid's tentacles quiver at such crudeness, though s/he loves it. *Let it be the Falcon if the narrative requires. It sounds more interesting; anachronism always does. For what is Time?*

Thank you, Albert Einstein! Azure chimes in uninvited.

Ignoring their clamor, Karen writes:

What prompted this thought, near-blasphemy? Herihor wondered as expertly he severed the slippery intestines from the contiguous organs, placing them in the jar that bore the head of Qebekh-sennuef the Falcon. (Virid gloats; Amber chooses not to notice.) Was it only the memory of that moment that had almost altered the high priest's life forever, the fated morning when the strangely feminine king and his most beautiful wife came out upon the parapet to greet the dawn of Amun-Re as they did every morning—excepting in the recent dark days when the king had struggled with some deadly illness, an illness that a king who has fathered only daughters could hardly afford—and the king, perhaps speaking out of the lingering fevers of that illness as some suggested after the fact, raised his hands, their palms outstretched, to greet the great god as he rose over the horizon, addressing him not as Amun-Re, father of all who dwelt in the valley of the Two Niles, but as Aten?

Aten—? The sound had been repeated by a thousand mouths in the courtyard below, as the faces behind those mouths stared upward in disbelief. Who or what was this Aten?

It would take eighteen floodings of the Nile for the people to learn that Aten was the Whirlwind, Aten was Despair, Aten would steal first their work, then their homes and children, and finally their souls.

Yet Herihor would bury this king, if only because he, Herihor, though dedicated to the temple of Amun-Re from birth, had felt that uplifting of his soul with the uplifting of the pharaoh's hands, as if his soul were held small and safe within those very hands, and knew in his heart that it was Aten, not Amun-Re, whom he greeted with the rising sun.

•

The sun wasn't up yet in Westwood. Lying in bed meditating upon this fact, Max Neimark couldn't remember if he was on Actor Time or Director Time. As the sky lightened, he decided: Must be Director Time, or I wouldn't be so relaxed. Subcategory: In Development.

Meaning I can sleep late, he thought. Otherwise I'd already be on the lot and in the chair listening to Vic rhapsodizing about some new astringent he'd discovered, guaranteed to tighten even *my* pores, and was I sure I'd shaved this morning because he could already see the shadow in the valleys and had I ever considered dermabrasion? Vic, I'd ask him, how many times do we have to have this conversation? What you see is what you get. I've earned this mug, every crosshatch of it. Jack Palance has a decade and a half on me and suddenly he's a sex symbol. Let it alone!

Beside him, Carole stirred, reaching over to lace her new environmentally friendly fingernails through his chest hair.

"Ow!" Max's morning voice resonated through the box-springs. She'd pulled too hard on purpose, and now she was circling his left nipple with the tip of her index finger; he was getting goosebumps. "What, again? You didn't get enough last night?"

"No such thing as enough of you!" Carole murmured, lifting her pillow-creased face up to nibble his earlobe.

Max sighed, closed his eyes, let her claim him. It was one thing to stir the unrequited desires of ten thousand fangirls, another to be a sex object to your own wife.

It hadn't been that way the first time around.

Carole propped herself up on her elbows to kiss his brow in the exact spot where Vic always glued the appliance, Benn's Third Eye. Yes, Max Neimark was Benn, unlikeliest sex object in the galaxy. Or was he?

An early volume of memoirs, written in the dead zone after the dark-horse sixties space-opera that had vaunted him to unlikely stardom was canceled following a tumultous three-year run, stated in its very title that he was most decidedly *not* Benn, the all-wise but ever-vulnerable floss-haired three-eyed solitary alien crewman on a human spaceship hurtling through parsecs of low-budget f/x to save the universe week after week. But, oh, that Max! his fans said, He's such a kidder! "I am not Benn" he states with Benn's characteristic solemnity every time he gives an interview, but we know better, don't we?

Its Zen implications aside, Benn's Third Eye was a stroke of genius, a cosmetic appliance stuck on in the middle of Max Neimark's prematurely furrowed brow (even in his bar mitzvah photo Max looked older than his years), which a clever makeup man named Vic Goldmann, who still did all of Max's makeup thirty years later, had designed to move and blink and crinkle at the corners and weep real tears, until there were times when it seemed more lifelike than Max's mismatched real eyes.

It was the odd-colored eyes, one brown, one green that, aside from his too-ethnic look, had made it difficult to cast Max as anything but heavies in the James Dean fifties when he'd broken in. But it was also the mismatched eyes that had inspired Vic the makeup genius to make the Third Eye a startling Liz Taylor violet-blue, and several thousand fangirls—the fat ones, the unloved ones, the ninety-ninth percentile skanks with harlequin glasses and bad skin—swore that that eye could look down into their very souls.

After nearly thirty years, Max swore the furrows in his brow had adapted themselves to the appliance, marking him for life. . . . Carole kissed him there again, her fingers finding further body hair to tangle themselves in, tweaking. Max sighed and smiled and opened his odd-colored eyes.

•

"Somebody from Warner's, I think. The number's around here somewhere," Eddie Cochran, Tessa McGill's personal assistant, reported as he flapped around her bedroom in his dime-store zoris retrieving a week's worth of dirty lingerie before the cleaning woman arrived. A pair of ice-blue panties suspended from one index finger, he snapped the fingers of his other hand like a grammar school nun to click in the memory from the call the night before. "Now if only I could remember her name . . ."

Hidden deep within the duvet so that only the curls on the top of her head showed, Tessa winced.

"From Warner's, though, definitely." Eddie examined a pair of Cuban-heel pantyhose that had snagged on the carpet, dismissing them into the wastebasket beside the vanity. "Anyway, she called yesterday late, just after you'd left for the party. The number's around here someplace. So I told her it was your birthday and you were doing dinner with friends and like that and what *is* it about these Hollywood types they can't ever get the time-zone thing right? So I said, listen, Miss McGill's not going to be back anytime while you're still on the lot, so why don't you call back tomorrow and—"

"Eddie—!" Tessa pleaded. She was so exhausted her eyelashes hurt. She'd never had a hangover even when she did drink. Was this what turning fifty-five did to you? She never had as much trouble with the decades as she did with the half-decades.

Hammered shit, her Aunt Lydia used to say: I feel like hammered shit. The image made Tessa snort giggles through her nose until that hurt, too. Unlike the rest of the McGills, Aunt Lydia had steadfastly refused to accept Jesus in her life, and remained irreverent to the end, saying exactly what was on her mind until she turned fifty-three and went down to uterine cancer in less than a month, which was probably what had made her feel like hammered shit all those years. *Oh, my aching head!* Tessa thought. *I'm two years up on Aunt Lydia and I feel like hammered shit. I'm going to need all my crystals this morning!*

She squeezed her eyes shut and listened while Eddie rummaged through the papers piled on her vanity until even that much noise was more than she could stand. "Eddie, for goddess' sake, focus and click! What do I pay you for?"

"For washing your panties, obviously!" Eddie sniffed and stopped rummaging, still twirling the ice-blue bikini on his finger.

Tessa pulled herself upright in the bed. "I mean, seriously! Somebody from Warner's. You can't remember her name. What did she *want*?"

"Something about you reading a part for Larry Koster," Eddie said, and went tootling off with the bundle of lingerie, probably to hand-wash it in the sink in his own bath downstairs off the kitchen.

Tessa sighed with the weariness of lifetimes and ventured one small white dancer's foot out from under the duvet onto a very cold parquet floor. What the hell kind of head games was the building management playing this morning, and where the hell was the heat? By law every building in Manhattan was supposed to have heat by six-thirty, and here it was nearly nine. In Washington Heights they'd have heat, but in this seven-figure luxury dump . . .

Feeling like Bette Davis, or maybe Albee's Martha, Tessa trailed into the master bath in her slip. What the hell had she done with last night's dress, or had Eddie spirited it off to the cleaner's already? She took her crystals out of their case, setting one at each of the four cardinal points of the shower stall; then she hung the mother crystal on its thong about her neck so that it dangled precisely between her breasts. She ran the water in the shower, which, mercifully, was hot. Her crystals, the hottest water the building management could muster, and she might be human by the time Somebody from Warner's called back. Then she would politely tell her to go to hell. Larry Koster wanted Tessa to do a guest spot on his prime-time cop show and, except for the occasional charity telethon or Star-Studded Special, Tessa didn't do television.

Besides, Tessa also didn't work with any actor she'd slept with, which for a while had made her choices pretty narrow. If Larry had asked her way back when, she'd have advised him against squandering his Shakespearean talents on the small screen, but Larry hadn't asked her—about that, or anything. Which was why, Tessa thought wryly, Larry was a megamillionaire, whereas she was—

Whereas she was, come to think of it, she decided as the steam rose to the ceiling and the water streamlined her face and made tendrils of her wild gypsy hair against her neck, going to skip Somebody from Warner's entirely and call Larry at home as soon as she got out of the shower. Assuming he hadn't changed the number again. There'd been a point in his paranoid life when he'd changed his number every month, acting all sorts of defensive if a friend of a friend gave it to anyone he hadn't authorized to have it. Poor Larry! Tessa thought, realizing she hadn't seen him, except on-screen, for at least a lifetime.

•

Laurence Koster had been born swaybacked, and there was nothing he could do about it. No matter how much he'd worked out in his youth, building himself up from a ninety-nine pound weakling living on fruit salad because it was all a starving actor could afford, to a fine specimen of manhood whose directors always let him take his shirt off for a role, he remained convinced this congenital condition made his broad ass jut out unnaturally. It humiliated him. These days, between pictures and careless about his weight again, he felt as if his ass was almost as wide as the quarterhorse's he rode in on.

Self-consciousness about his rear view had shaped Larry Koster's entire personality, making him a frontal, front-on, attack-first person. As an actor, he was effective; as a human being, he was a pain in everyone else's ass.

As he led Runnymeade onto the turnoff from the paddock to the barn, his actor's instinct told him he was being watched. Jacinto, the new kid at the barn, was waiting in the shadow of the open doorway to take the reins now that Larry had finished putting the prize stallion through his paces.

Well, hardly a kid, Larry thought, instinctively sitting himself a little straighter; he's already got two and a half of his own. Am I paying him enough? Probably more than he ever dreamed of in Guadalajara, if that was where he was from. Larry tended to think in clichés. Besides, give the kid a raise and he'll only use it as an excuse to make more babies. Still, he's got good hands, and the horses trust him. What to do?

What am I thinking? Larry wondered as he eased down out of the saddle and let Jacinto take Runny in hand; if Janice's lawyer is as good as she thinks he is, I'll not only have to let the kid go, I may have to sell off at least one of the brood mares and cut my show dates in half. Unless they meet all my demands on this film. Mediocre as it is, they have got to meet my demands on this film!

He remembered the morning his agent had shown up unannounced in his living room to discuss the script. She'd been waiting for him when he came in from his daily ride.

"You want to tell me what you're doing here?" he'd asked genially. "The sun's barely up. Hardly agent hours. And how the hell'd you get in?"

"Gracious as always," Sandra responded, gliding past him to pour herself an Evian when he didn't offer. Larry, mixing himself a Virgin Mary, admired the view in her wake; the rest of her was just this side of anorexia. "Did you read it?"

"Piece of crap," Larry deemed it. "Yeah, I read it. I'm a little too old to be playing Jesus."

"It isn't necessarily Jesus, Larry." Sandra had tucked her long legs under her on the couch closest to the dormant fireplace. "Think of him as a generic messiah-type. And they don't want you to act, just direct."

Larry's breath made ripples in his tomato juice; he spoke over the rim of the glass. "What do you mean, they don't want me to act? Are you saying *they* think I'm too old for the part?"

He didn't wait for her to answer. "How much are they offering for this . . . generic messiah movie?"

Sandra had named a figure that was more than Larry might ordinarily have demanded to both act and direct.

"I'm impressed," Larry admitted. "What's the catch?"

Sandra finished her Evian, studied him. "You really haven't read the script."

"I—skimmed it." Larry shrugged. He'd done what every actor did when a script was sent "For Your Consideration." Flipped through it to see how many lines the lead character had—

"—and didn't bother reading any more than that," Sandra finished. Larry gave her a *Yeah, well* look. She'd gotten up to leave. "Yeah, well. Read the entire thing and then we'll talk."

•

He had, and the script was a stinker, but Larry still didn't get it. What was the big mystery? He'd call Sandra in a day or so, as soon as last week's tabloids with the lead story about him and his latest bimbo were next week's recycled paper and the enquiring minds were exercising their prurient interest at someone else's expense. For now his only concern was first getting the director's spot and second persuading the bean counters to delay the payments until Janice's lawyer stopped sniffing through his assets.

Letting none of his personal angst show on his Shakespearean-trained face, Larry nodded to Jacinto, whose English was about on a par with Larry's Spanish; the kid took the lead and walked Runny back into the dark of the stalls, and Larry did his John

Wayne walk up toward the house, trying to pretend his balls weren't killing him.

Easing the jodhpurs away from his crotch, he swore he could still hear them clank. The stuntmen on his films still called him Brassballs, their ultimate compliment. If he thought he heard resentment behind it because even at his age and salary level he still badgered directors into letting him do his own stunts, Brassballs Koster pretended he didn't notice. Sometimes the pleasure came with a little pain.

•

The pain was especially bad this morning. Serena looked up from her drafting table and realized the rest of the room had disappeared. She knew the sun had come up some hours ago; she knew from the weather report that the sky was clear today. So why did the horizon end at the edge of her drafting table?

"It's going to be that bad of a day, huh?" Serena asked aloud.

From her pallet in the corner, her Doberman Penny opened one eye, determined that the question was probably rhetorical, heaved a sigh, and went back to sleep.

Yes, Rain says in Serena's mind, *I'm afraid so.*

"I was afraid you'd say that!" Serena lit another cigarette, re-cramped her fingers around the burnt umber, and was about to touch down on the paper again, then stopped.

Her theme was *Beauty and the Beast* this week. Catherine Chandler's blue, blue eyes looked out at her from the sketch, her face alluring and complete, but behind her Vincent was still half-formed, a suggestion of the Beast, unfinished. The drawing had to be at the framer's before four this afternoon so she could FedEx it to the buyer in Detroit; Serena had been working on it nonstop since this time yesterday. She drew hard on the cigarette, then angled it into the ashtray so it would stay put even if she let it burn down to ashes, sipped from the open jug of cranapple juice, which was the only thing her insides could tolerate this week, and, uncramping her hand from around the pencil, deliberately rotated the sketch 180 degrees so that Vincent and Catherine were looking at her upside down. Catherine continued to watch her as she worked, but her eyes were less disturbing from this angle. Serena fitted the pencil back into her claw of a hand and began to work the dark tones in Vincent's mane.

"Rain . . ." she said aloud, the soft scrape of the pencil competing with Penny's snores as the only sounds in the room. "Help me out here. I don't have enough Toradol to make it to the end of the month and they won't renew my prescription until the forms go through. I don't get my nerve blocks until next week. I've got to get this piece done today, but the pain . . ."

Where is the pain when you're drawing? Rain whispers seductively in her mind, a soft cold mist with glints of ice in it.

"Somewhere else," Serena admitted. "It only comes back when I stop to rest."

Then don't rest, Rain tells her: *Draw!*

"Yeah, well, fuck you and the horse you rode in on!" Serena said good-naturedly. Rain does not answer.

The room closed around her until it was nothing but the drafting table. Soon even the edges of the table blurred and disappeared until only the drawing was visible, and Serena had to find her cigarette or another pencil by feel, careful not to mix them up. Soon the edges of the drawing vanished, and only the two faces were visible, and then only Catherine Chandler's blue, blue eyes.

•

Virid disapproves of the script so far. *There's too much sex in it!*

No sex in your pharaoh's life, I suppose? Amber counters, noting that Virid's doing messiahs again this week.

Sex is sacred to them, a religious experience! Virid announces airily. *Lofty, poetic. No pharaoh was ever called Brassballs!*

Bronzeballs, more likely, Amber decides. *More's the pity! If they'd had a sense of humor they might have lasted longer. Besides, given what your average pharaoh got up to with his daughters, his nieces, his lesser wives' sons . . .*

Virid is not paying attention. S/he does that when s/he's con-

tradicted. Amber watches Virid watching the high priest Herihor, hir thoughts reverberating down the Common Mind with
what might have been a sigh. How long this time will it take for
Herihor to notice what's wrong with the pharaoh's ears?

TWO

Distinguish, differentiate. Separate and define. Tendrils or tentacles?

In the before-time, they had not been perplexed by the difference. In the before-time there had been no difference, no need to differentiate the parts of themselves. In the before-time they had had no parts; they had not been "they." Nor "it." Nor anything but All There Is. Beyond the That Which Created All There Is, they were, it was, All There Is.

The Naming had begun with the discovery that they were not All There Was. Discovering this, having it confirmed over-against the existence of the Thou Beyond, had made it possible for them to become *them,* to differentiate the I and Thou that *they* were, not only *it* was. Or had been from the before-time, without knowing. Always valued was the added Knowing.

The Naming did not materially change the What-Is, only made it possible, then necessary, to distinguish, differentiate. Etymology: tendrils or tentacles? Appendages, then. But what purpose did they serve?

Sensory, most assuredly, or were they? Before it was known that there were senses, how define *sensory*? Tactile, prehensile, propellant, projectile? One needed the Distinct-from/Detached-from/Extended-out-of/Part-of-but-separate-from in order to detach from the mind, to move from one part of the place to the next, to eat, but was it the same place? And these extensions—did they feel or only *do*?

Without knowing what it was to feel, how did one know if one was feeling? And . . . *one?* This, too, had not been in the before-time. One. Separate. Distinct, but also part-of. I and Thou. Over-against the Thou-Beyond, which named things, which could feel.

Thus it became necessary to further interact, to learn, to know, to feel. Pleasure (sxlif@koster.laurence). Pain (syring/@bellserena). Color, shading, nuance (*cf.* "Artists," "Musicians"). Knowledge, perspective, depth (*cf.* "Writers," "Philosophers," "Diplomats"). Seek out the special ones (*cf.* "Saints/Schizophrenics").

Visual. To see through the mind, which has no eyes. Colored pencils. Forms gelatinous and opalescent, sticky, amoebous about the edges, edgeless. Ones. Ones needed Naming. Artists were not good with words. Perhaps the priests?

Define *priest.* Those who kept God-in-a-box. Grasp this: the That Which Creates confined by the All There Is? Inexplicable, gelatinous, ungraspable. Slippery through the fingers, which has no fingers. Tendrils or tentacles—not this again! Focus and click, as Tessa would say: God-in-a-box. Did the Thou Beyond also believe as we once did that they were All There Is? Observation indicated that most did, but some knew differently. Differentiate. Separate, define.

Colors. Grey, who was all colors hence none, center of the mind. Azure, Amber, Virid, Lake, and many more, as many or as one as the All There Was, which was no longer All There Was now that there was the Thou Beyond.

Now that there was Now.

It makes no sense! Karen thought, shifting her butt on the hardwood floor, but continued to let it write her anyway.

"It's simple," was how Tessa would explain it to her Tuesday channeling group. "Try visualizing them as auras, only without a person inside them. Freestanding auras, each with a unique personality, as unique as you or I. Try to see them, as I do. It works for me."

The women in her circle would nod in unison and return to their chanting, sitting cross-legged on cushions on Tessa's living room floor, each with her arms extended in a circle before her, fingertips touching thumbs in yet another circle within a circle. If it worked for Tessa, it would work for them. Everything worked for Tessa, because Tessa had found her center.

It had been a long journey, at least in this lifetime, from the song-and-dance girl with all of a dancer's bad habits to the starlet too obsessed with the laugh lines around her eyes to go for the really good roles, from take-me-seriously actress to New Age guru, who still had legs and could still belt, packing them in nightly, whether in Vegas or the Hollywood Bowl. Tessa McGill had been, still was, it all. Except she'd given up the late nights and the cigarettes and the other stuff; she'd been purified on a mountaintop in Colorado some years back and stayed that way. Springwater, bean sprouts and the occasional bloody-rare steak (a throwback, no doubt, to a former life she hadn't yet accessed), her crystals and her open-ended contract with a major publisher to keep turning out the memoirs as long as the public wanted them, in this life or the next, were what kept her going these days.

"Accessibility," Tessa told her Tuesday group. She never charged them for the privilege of channeling with her, but her screening process for admission to the group was draconian. She didn't know why it was time to tell them about her friends the telepathic jellyfish, but it felt right, and she had. The response was a nonresponse, a passive acceptance. Not a one of the women in the room looked startled, or took her aside out of earshot later to whisper: "Extraterrestrial jellyfish, Tessa? Are you sure?" They accepted it as they accepted everything she said, without comment, because Tessa was a Very Old Soul.

"Make yourself accessible to the universe," Tessa told them, her words washing over them soothingly, disguising her disappointment that not a one of them had reacted the way she'd expected, with recognition, "and it will make itself accessible to you. . . ."

•

She didn't know for a fact that they were extraterrestrial, but she *was* accessible to the universe, and it just made sense. The very first time she saw them was the week she started her periods.

She'd assumed they were some sort of side effect to go with the cramps and the blood and the delightful feeling of a sodden sanitary napkin wedged between her legs for a week. She'd been the first girl in her class to opt for tampons as soon as she could convince her mother to buy them for her—no self-respecting pharmacist in the Bible Belt would sell such things to a thirteen-year-old presumed virgin—scandalizing her entire high school. Girls talked about other girls who did such things, in deliberately loud whispers so the boys would overhear. Tessa didn't care. Her reputation had been set in stone in the eighth grade, when she'd been caught making out under the bleachers with one of the seniors.

"Five years older than her, and he wasn't even good-looking!" was what her classmates found most abhorrent. Tessa didn't care about that, either. He kissed nice; that was sufficient.

But in between changing sanitary napkins that first time, she'd been visited by what she naturally called the Jellyfish, because that was what they looked like. She'd never so much as been to the seashore, but she knew. Once when she was really little and her mother had despaired of ever keeping her entertained during a particularly long rainy spell, she'd sat her down in the family library, pulled all the *Encyclopedia Americana*s off the shelves, and arranged them around her like a fort.

"Here you go, Miss Teresa! You study as many of those pictures as you can before suppertime, and then you tell me what you've learned."

Tessa couldn't read yet, but she did know the alphabet, and had dutifully started with the A's. It was nearly suppertime when she got to the J's and needed a potty break. She went looking for her mother, book in hand.

"Mama?" She'd pointed to the color plates, amazed that any

such thing could exist on the same earth as she. "What're
those?"

"Those are jellyfish, sugar," her mother told her; she'd read
her the names from the captions beneath each color plate, then
proceeded to explain that they were neither strictly fish nor at
all made out of jelly.

That was why it was easy for Tessa to recognize them when
she saw them in person.

It's 'cause my belly hurts, she decided, trailing around downtown—waddling, more like, with that damn sodden pad wedged
into her crotch and chafing with each step—cutting class again.
God's given me something pretty to see to take my mind off it.

But the jellyfish stayed just under her eyelids even days later,
when the seemingly endless flow of blood had trickled away to
rust stains and inconvenience—a dry napkin, Tessa discovered,
chafed worse than a sodden one—and finally stopped. They lin-
gered when she went to Miss Rita's for piano lessons, getting in
the way of the sheet music so that "Claire de Lune" came out
sounding like N'Orleans jazz. Miss Rita had sighed with a sound
like dry leaves and turned the pages back.

"May we try that again, please, Teresa?"

They followed her to Madame Lucine's ballet class, trickling
around her feet like Disney characters until her *réléves,* which
she'd almost perfected, became downright clumsy. It was
Madame Lucine who recommended tampons.

"So next time you don't miss the classes, *non?* Now again,
please, until you remember where you have left the feet."

Her dancing improved, but her piano playing grew ever more
outré.

"I don't know, child!" Miss Rita said in her melancholy way
and, though she'd never experienced the emotion personally, unless perhaps unrequitedly, suggested: "I wonder if it means you're
in love?"

Tessa's mother wanted to hear no such thing.

"Seems to me you're hell-bent for destruction!" she announced once the under-the-bleachers scene and cutting classes

became not isolated incidents but habits. "Pity we're not Catholic. I ought to put you in a convent school."

You won't do that, Mama, Tessa thought, though she wondered.

"I'll tell you one thing: you'll stop this maundering about at once, or I'll at least pull those piano lessons out from under you. The time and money spent, when you don't even practice!"

Tessa didn't really care about the piano lessons, not the way she cared about dancing. She only went because she sensed that Miss Rita was lonely and enjoyed her company, her sad little face brightening each time she heard Tessa's footsteps on the old wooden stairs. Tessa also cared about the freedom to loiter downtown with its carnival atmosphere and a palmist or Reader & Advisor on almost every corner, three to a block sometimes.

Thirty years later when she had her first regression, Tessa wondered why she'd waited so long. Was it ingrained prejudice from growing up in a place like Mobile, its main drag populated with more fortune-tellers than any normal chamber of commerce this side of New York or someplace with a boardwalk ought to countenance? Even as a child the sight of the "For Rent" signs in as many as half the palmists' windows had made her wonder. If they truly could foresee the future, why hadn't they known they couldn't do enough business to pay the rent?

It wasn't until she'd been regressed that she understood why certain places on the earth—Giza and Machu Picchu and Stonehenge, obviously, and Tibet or any high altitude and, for some reason, maybe only because she'd been born there, Mobile, Alabama—were "centered" differently, had a different kind of gravitational pull. People with enhanced esper abilities were inexorably drawn there, even if they couldn't pay the rent.

But that was years later. When she was a kid, she just knew it was easiest to dress as a gypsy for Halloween because she already had "darkey hair," masses of dark ringlets courtesy of a Portuguese great-grandmother on the McGill side, and didn't need to hide her heart-shaped face under some tacky old wig, and she'd study the palmists through the open doorways every summer to see how they comported themselves, how they stood and sat and gestured with a kind of sameness whether they were young or old, fat or skinny, real gypsies or pale-as-dishwater mountain women with more freckles than teeth, as if there were a special union, a secret sorority they'd all attended. Women, all of them; she'd never seen a man among the Readers & Advisors. Was that only because most of their customers were women, or were women more attuned to matters psychic? Call it her first Method acting lesson—she would study with Strasberg once she got to New York, before she jumped ship for HB Studios, leaving there in a flap over Uta's poodle and deciding she knew all she needed to know about technique anyway, thank you kindly— but the psychics and readers of her childhood had provided her with her first "hook."

She would act out the same motions and gestures as she went door to door trick-or-treating, her talents squandered on an audience of housewives and grandmas who just oohed and aahed and said "Why, don't *you* look pretty!" as they scattered sweets into the patchwork bag she'd sewn herself because it was more what a psychic would carry than an old brown grocery bag with crayoned pumpkins on it like everyone else. Her peers didn't appreciate her either, shoving at her from behind as she commandeered the top porch step, demanding that she "Quit posing, Teresa McGill; you're holding everyone else up!"

Once the jellyfish came to live under her eyelids, she decided she was far too mature to be bothered with Halloween.

They neither surprised nor frightened her, and at that point she felt no need to share them with anyone. Other children, the lonely ones, she knew, had imaginary friends. Tessa couldn't remember ever being lonely; she never thought of the jellyfish as anything but real. She never gave them names or asked how many of them there were altogether or why sometimes several came to visit at once and sometimes only one, and sometimes none at all for weeks at a time, like during finals or the prom.

She also learned how to shoo them away whenever she needed to concentrate on something, like forging her mother's signature on a bad report card.

She never asked them questions, but they volunteered things, like telling her that she *was* going to be a professional dancer someday, even though her mother had sent her to Madame Lucine's for the same reason she'd made the *Americana*s into a fort that rainy afternoon, the same reason she'd signed Tessa up for choir and as many church-related activities—picnics and bus trips and visits to the old people's home—as there were, to keep this infernally restless high-strung child occupied and out of mischief.

At least Tessa managed not to get pregnant before graduation. And by the time all those years of *relevés* and choir practice had expanded her innate talents enough for a tryout at one of the local straw-hat companies—to the horror of her aunts and the envy of her horde of female cousins, she was over eighteen and no longer needed to forge her mother's signature and her mother, oddly, seemed almost relieved to see her go—it was only a giant step from there to an audition for a bus-and-truck tour that ended in New York. Tessa made it, because the jellyfish had told her she would.

Until her Tuesday channeling sessions, she'd only mentioned them twice, the second time just after she'd been regressed by a famed New York psychic when her personal life had started unraveling and each cigarette tasted worse than the last. The psychic had looked at her oddly, murmuring something about how auras manifested themselves in different ways, and recommended a course of meditation on a particular mountain in Colorado.

It was on that mountain that Tessa found her center, and for a long time after that she never mentioned jellyfish, even indirectly, to anyone.

The first time, like an idiot, she'd mentioned them to Larry Koster.

•

"The carpenter's child," Karen wrote, "hadn't started out to be a messiah. . . ."

•

"Those eyes!" the neighbors would hiss and whisper from the time Jess was an infant. They would make the sign for the Evil Eye and sidle away, some so superstitious they would cross the square rather than pass before the carpenter's house, lest the child's eyes fall on them. Something about the child's eyes— the color or the way the light reflected from them or the simple staring intensity of an intelligence rare and dangerous in a poor village in Judea in these hard Roman times—was enough to frighten them.

The carpenter had gone to the *kohen* to ask.

"What can I do?" he cried, wringing his scarred, big-knuckled hands. "You can see it's only a child. Can a demon possess one so young? There has never been any sign."

"There were signs before the birth, as I recall," the *kohen* suggested sagely, his judicious way of saying what the whole village knew, that the child wasn't really the carpenter's. "It is written that the sins of the fathers . . . or the mothers . . ."

"Surely not!" the carpenter cried. He and his wife had long since come to an understanding on the matter. Was it anyone else's business, even the *kohen's*? "*Abba,* surely a woman's sins don't weigh as much as a man's?"

The *kohen* hadn't considered it in that light, but of course the man was right.

"We will hold the matter in abeyance for the present," he answered, not precisely answering. "Watch the child closely for any sign of demons. Meanwhile I will speak to your neighbors and calm their fears."

The carpenter had kissed the hem of the *kohen's* robe as well as his fat beringed hand, and within the year presented him in gratitude with a lovingly carved scroll stand, which required one hundred hours' work and his most costly piece of cedarwood. The carpenter's wife, not understanding the connection between the gift and her neighbors' sudden deferential silence, railed at him for squandering their livelihood to placate an already fat *kohen*.

The child continued to stare at passersby with those uncanny eyes and to study all of creation from a pebble to a star with an intensity few had ever seen, even among the wise men in the city.

•

Tessa lay on her back with her eyes closed, the sheet tucked between her legs and half-covering her breasts, giggling for far longer than Larry thought she should. He knew he was good, but not that good.

"You all right?" he asked nervously, looking at his watch. He really had to get home.

"Mm-hmm," Tessa murmured, feeling very loose. Larry always relaxed her, but not this much. "Just watching the jellyfish."

If she'd had her eyes open, she'd have seen Larry start and look furtive, but she didn't.

"Hey, what are you, dropping acid or something?" It was the sixties, and he knew dancers got into funny stuff. " 'Jellyfish'! What the hell is that supposed to mean?"

The disdain in his voice made Tessa sit up and pay attention.

"Sorry. Sorry to disappoint you, but I'm not on anything. I don't do acid. You got a cigarette?"

"Postcoital cliché." Larry tossed her the pack from his shirt pocket, making sure she only took one. "I don't usually, but I'm trying to get the weight down. Look, I told Elyse this was an open call." Elyse had been Larry's first wife. "She knows casting directors never stay past seven. . . ."

Tessa lit the cigarette and shrugged. "You go on ahead. I'll catch a cab on Rodeo."

He took out his wallet and started counting out bills for the cab fare, caught Tessa watching him do it. He was cheap, he'd admit it, but sometimes he was so cheap he embarrassed himself. He folded a twenty and tried to slide it into her cleavage beneath the mended hotel bedsheet. Even his choice of hotel was cheap. Tessa snatched the bill out of his hand.

"Postcoital cliché, Lar," she said. "I'd be insulted, but I need it this week. If the deal with Universal doesn't pan, I'm back to the Apple and hoofing for scale. God, sometimes my legs ache so much I can hardly stand up!"

She started to dress, retrieving bits of clothing from where she'd scattered them, a lifelong bad habit. Larry was way ahead of her, zipping his slacks facing her so she wouldn't see his big ass.

"They're watching us, you know," Tessa said.

Larry twitched and his fly jammed halfway up; he had to force it down a few notches to free it from the fabric. Tessa noticed. He hadn't reacted at all when she said she might have to go back to New York. She knew exactly how important she wasn't in his life. If she got the part and stayed in town for the next six to twelve weeks, fine; if she didn't, fine, too. Neither she nor Larry had ever pretended it was anything else.

It hadn't been what she'd wanted, in the beginning. She only slept with Larry because she enjoyed talking to him, but he was one of those men who needed to fuck first and talk later. Lately he didn't have time to talk. Okay, so she'd stop fucking him and it would end. She could feel lonely without any help from him. Besides, she always had the jellyfish.

"Who is?" Larry had gotten his fly unsnagged and done one of his larger-than-life double takes. They'd ruined his chances at making it in soaps and still had a lot of small-screen directors yelling at him. Didn't he understand, Tessa wondered, that he had enough raw talent to telegraph an entire emotion with his eyelashes? Why did he always have to go for the stage actor's Big Gesture? Poor Larry, he should never have left the stage; he was and would always be larger than life. His reaction had been all out of proportion to her statement. Was this just shtick or was he really unaware that he was overplaying it? "Who's watching us? What are you talking about?"

"Have you ever thought of the possibility . . ." Tessa stubbed out her cigarette and went looking for her garter belt. ". . . that aliens from outer space might be looking down at us and studying us like fish in a bowl?"

She watched him out of the corner of her eye. Was he actually sweating? Why was he overreacting?

"Suppose they had X-ray eyes like Superman?" she went on, hooking up her stockings. "Or what if they could read your thoughts? Enough to make you stop and think about what you were up to, huh?"

She stood watching him, hands on her hips, half-dressed. Why was he the one who felt naked?

"As long as they're not working for my wife . . ." Tessa didn't laugh the way he'd expected. "Tess, you're a fruitcake, you know that?"

And you're a liar! she thought.

"Funny you should mention outer space," he went on, jingling his car keys, creating business, anything to avoid making eye contact. "It so happens I'm up for the lead in some kind of sci-fi show. The call's next week. . . ."

He was not shy or superstitious, the way some actors were, about mentioning upcoming auditions. Maybe it was because more often than not he got the role. Maybe it was because when he didn't he could blame it on someone else—an inside job, already cast. A director he'd had a falling out with on another show. Always something.

"Sounds exciting," Tessa murmured, sounding anything but excited, flexing her dancers' toes before slipping them into her shoes, wondering when in the last five or six times she'd seen him they'd talked about anything besides Laurence Koster and his Brilliant Career.

"Had you fooled, though, didn't I?"

He was giving her that dewy-eyed look, acting with his eyelashes, acting with his diaphragm. Larry always acted from the gut. His voice never got louder, his words just got more emphatic, with a lot more air behind them; you could see his diaphragm pumping under his shirt. What *was* he so hyper about? Tessa gave him a quizzical look.

"What I was doing just now? All that intensity about aliens from outer space, watching us like goldfish?"

Jellyfish! Tessa wanted to shout, but she had said fish in a bowl, hadn't she?

"Well, that's how I figure the captain of a spaceship would react if he encountered some kind of weird-looking aliens in outer space, see?"

Liar! Tessa thought, walking ahead of him out to the car. He was so busy lying he'd forgotten he'd given her cab fare and was going to drive her home anyway. Usually he refused to drop her off if it was still light out, worried about being recognized by any of the other hoofers she roomed with; tonight he was so wired up he'd forgotten even that. Not that it mattered. She wouldn't be seeing him again, at least not until he got over this ego trip. Tessa wondered if she'd live long enough to see Larry Koster get over himself.

•

The casting call was for a show called *SpaceSeekers*. It was here that Laurence Koster first met the actor he dubbed the Yeshiva Boy.

Actually, that wasn't accurate. Larry recognized this skinny, studious-looking character from a dozen similar calls; they'd crossed paths but never spoken. Max Neimark, wasn't it? Character was right, Larry thought. Definitely a character-type, usually a heavy, no threat. Larry could always afford to be friendly to character types.

The skinny actor was sitting on a stack of flats laid on their sides against a far wall of the soundstage, well out of camera or sound range; the litter of butts and coffee cups on the floor indicated it was a good place to hang out until you were called for. The flats weren't quite stacked at chair height, and the skinny actor's legs were long enough so that his knees were drawn up almost to chest level as he sat, a cigarette forgotten between his long brown fingers, reading a dog-eared hardcover book with no dust jacket.

Five'll get you ten, Larry Koster thought smugly; it's either *Actors Talk About Acting* or Stanislavsky. East Coast actors always brought one or the other along with them as props, to impress casting directors with their seriousness. Casting directors and surf bunnies.

Well, maybe no surf bunnies for this guy, Larry thought; James Dean he's not. And the hand that held the cigarette wore a thick gold wedding band, the skin beneath it paler, not as tanned, as if it had been there for a very long time. Betcha Uncle Milton got it for him wholesale, or threw it in for free after he paid off the diamond for the bride-to-be, Larry thought with a twitch of embarrassment. Was there anyone more anti-Semitic than a Jew who had managed to pass?

Without invitation, Larry parked himself on the flats beside the skinny character actor, who drew his knees closer together to make room, switching the cigarette first to his mouth for a drag, then to his other hand so as not to let his secondhand smoke offend. He never glanced up from his reading. His movements were easy and sure. How much training had he had, Koster wondered impulsively, and who with?

"Hi!" he said, holding out one square hand, thinking: Let's see what kind of moves he makes with the book and the cigarette now! "Larry Koster. You here for this—what is it? —*Space-Seekers* thing, too?"

The skinny actor shifted the book to his left hand, closing it on his index finger to keep his place, transferred the cigarette to the right corner of his mouth, anchoring the paper against the moisture on his lower lip, squinted his odd-color Tatar eyes slightly against the continuous stream of smoke, and shook Larry's hand, all in the same seamless movement. Dry hand, just firm enough, the grasp held just long enough to show he was sincere but not a fag. Larry was impressed.

"I know," the skinny actor said. "Saw you in that *Twilight Zone* last season. And your MacDuff against Plummer in the Summer Festival—"

"You actually went to the Summer Festival—," Larry started to say.

"—very impressive! Very impressive. Max Neimark."

Where the hell did that voice come from? Larry wondered, retrieving his well-shaken hand, clasping both hands between his knees, consciously relaxing himself from the shoulders down. His own voice had range, lots of range, but he'd never hope to have that kind of resonance.

". . . and, to answer your question," the resonant voice was saying. "Yes. I'm here for *SpaceSeekers,* too. In fact, a miracle: for the first time in my career I'm already cast. They've asked me to stick around and read against some of the others."

Laurence Koster experienced a pang of pure, unadulterated jealousy. *This* was a leading man, a Flash Gordon, the captain of an interstellar spaceship? What casting director had had his head up his ass when this was decided? And in that case, what the fuck was *he* doing here?

"Yeah . . ." Max Neimark went on; Larry, who'd been about to track down the A.D. to announce he'd decided not to read, found himself fixed in place by that voice. Max seemed to have this habit of talking aloud as if he were talking to himself, as if he expected the other person might not be all that interested in what he had to say. The cigarette stayed adhered to his lower lip, moving only slightly as he drew on it and talked at the same time, never once coughing or pausing for breath. Neat trick! Larry thought, transfixed; I'll have to try that! ". . . apparently there are two main roles. There's the spaceship captain—that's why you're here—and then there's this kind of intergalactic sidekick. Sort of like Festus from outer space, I guess. That's me. Producer saw me do a guest shot on his *Marine Command* last year. Said when he was working up concept for this show, he kept seeing me in his mind as the alien type. I guess it's a compliment. Not to mention, if the pilot gets picked up, steady work."

He'd shrugged then, suddenly diffident, and gone silent, not an uneasy silence, not for him, but a silence of having said all he had to say. Uneasy for Larry, though. Laurence Koster was the talkative one, the Look-Ma-No-Hands Kid (a *ganze macher*, Max had thought, aware of him the minute he'd walked onto the soundstage), always on. Silence was treacherous; silence was to be mistrusted. He realized he'd just been upstaged, and he hadn't felt a thing. He opened his mouth to attack the silence, and caught himself stuttering.

False start. Max seemed not to have noticed. He was devoting considerable attention to removing the spent cigarette from his lower lip, grinding it to powder on the concrete floor, then brushing the shreds away with the sole of his shoe. It was called fieldstripping, Larry knew; something you learned in the service. Had Max actually been in the service, or was this some Method technique he'd practiced for the aforementioned spot on *Marine Command*? Deliver me from Method actors! Larry thought. Max had gone back to his book, as if Larry wasn't there. Larry immediately took umbrage.

Not until three years of six-day weeks and twelve-hour days, when they saw more of each other than their wives, their kids, or Larry's girlfriends, would Larry understand that Max did that—spilled what he had to say in long, uninterruptable monologues, then closed in on himself—because he was so desperately shy.

"Whatcha reading?" Larry asked now, adopting his Everyday Guy accent. He knew Max was from back East, and that he'd grown up hungry. If they were going to work together—and suddenly Larry wanted this role more than anything—it was time to hide his own bourgeois background and go for fellow feeling.

Max closed the book again and flipped the spine up so Larry could read it.

"Astrophysics?" Larry rolled his eyes and whistled. "Not exactly light reading. Is that for the character?"

Max shook his head. "No, I read a lot on my own. See, I never had time to finish my education. Did six months of college to please my parents, then came out here. I've developed this kind of self-taught adult education program. But, in this instance, it won't hurt for the character. He's supposed to be a scientist—"

"—so you figured 'when in Rome'—"

Max nodded. "Exactly."

"Method actor," Larry suggested.

Max shook his head. "Not really, I—"

"Who'd you study with?" Larry interrupted, on the attack. If they did end up working together, it wouldn't hurt to start marking his territory. But before Max could answer, or not answer, Larry heard his name being called.

"Laurence Koster?" Female voice, loud enough to carry across a soundstage as big as an airplane hangar, the ubiquitous script-girl-with-clipboard waiting to lead him to his mark for a cold reading. "Laurence Koster? Is Laurence Koster here?"

He turned full face and waggled a finger at her: *Over here, Sweetie!* He had one parting shot for his erstwhile costar.

"Always study up for a part beforehand, do you, Max?"

"If I know what it's about, always," Max said seriously; if he knew he was being patronized it didn't show.

"Even for an under-five?"

"Even for an under-five."

Larry shook his head, marveling. "You're a regular yeshiva boy!"

He made sure enough people heard it to make it stick, and just in case he would repeat it several times over the next three years. The moniker stuck; Max considered it a compliment.

INT. SPACESHIP FLYING BRIDGE—"DAY"—CONTIN-
UOUS CAPT. STARK AND BENN STARING FORWARD
AT VIEWSCREEN.

STARK:
(quietly, on edge)

What do you make of it, Benn?

BENN:

(ditto, but calmer)

Possibly a form of primal mental energy, Captain. According to our instruments, it registers most strongly in the visible, ultraviolet, and kappa radiation bands.

STARK:

Would you say it's alive, then? What kind of creature could exist in a noncorporeal form? What kind of world would it come from?

BENN:

Indeed.

Indeed! Karen thought, scribbling. Only every third alien on every third show on every third week. This particular species had been called Hydras, but what was the name of the episode? Did she have the tape? Would they let her watch it? It didn't matter; she knew them all by heart anyway. She reran the scene in her head.

STARK:

What do you make of it, Benn?

BENN:

Possibly a form of primal mental energy, Captain. According to our instruments . . .

The episode was called "They Who Have Eyes," Karen remembered. She leaned her head back against the white wall wearily. *That* was where she'd gotten the visual image for her aliens; she was sure of it. Now all she had to do was convince *them.*

She picked up her pen again, sharp object. Over the edge of her grey legal pad the white wall moved, dancing molecules.

THREE

Ask Karen why she was so good at what she did and she'd give you the *TV Guide* version: "Dull people make the best writers."

Not accurate, was Grey's assessment: *Try again.*

"How about, Homecoming queens never grow up to be writers?"

Now we're getting somewhere. Define "homecoming queen."

"All's you guys gotta do is pay attention," she'd snarled in her long-since obliterated Brooklyn accent. "I'm tryna write a novel here!"

Choose the wounded ones, Azure had advised from the outset, the beginning of the Now. *They are the most receptive.*

Are we certain we want to go this way? the enquiring Mind wants to know. *Writing a writer could prove to be the sound of one hand clapping in the forest.*

Precisely, Azure insists eagerly, and so the story arc goes forward.

If she'd been truly ugly as a kid, her ugliness might have lent the abuse some Darwinian legitimacy. But Karen Rohmer had simply been undefinably "funny looking," one of those kids other kids turned on for no other reason than just because. She even became the victims' victim; the schoolyard fat kid, to draw attention from himself, would set the pack on her. She learned to run fast and, when cornered, to hit hard. Chivalry ("Never hit a girl") somehow never made it to her part of the universe. Besides, Karen wasn't a girl, her peers determined; she was a freak. There was an order to things; it was allowed.

If they held her she'd kick, aiming for shins before she learned about testicles, bit and scratched until they let her loose, rammed the nearest one in the gut with her hard head, broke for it and ran; she could beat any bully in a sprint. Not that it was safe at home.

"I don't understand what's wrong with you!" her mother shrilled as she flew through the door, clothes torn, books scattered in the driveway, swinging at her with whatever she had in her hand. "Why don't you act like a girl? *Why can't you act normal?*"

Because I'm not normal! Karen would think, nursing bruises, dabbing Merthiolate on skinned knees. *I'm from another planet; that's what you always tell me!*

She didn't have to say it; she'd get hit for thinking it.

"And take that sarcastic expression off your face!"

In the alternate universe inside her head, mothers defended their young, went to the door and berated the pack that had chased their children home; she'd seen other mothers do it on TV, and even in this universe—other mothers, other children. Why was there no safe place for her?

Maybe she *was* from another planet. Maybe it was time she went home.

In the meantime there was sanctuary—in the public library where the wolf pack feared to tread as if, semiliterate, they even knew of its existence. No one molested her there; when she was four the librarian had even let her tether her imaginary horse at the circulation desk—and in the universe inside her head. She spun stories out of everything she read, acted out different endings to old movies and TV shows when the endings she'd been given displeased her, preferred pharaohs and cowboys and war heroes to Nancy Drew and saccharine Alcott heroines.

By the time she discovered Hatshepsut and Calamity Jane, Ingrid Bergman in *For Whom the Bell Tolls,* it was too late. She'd already created her own—heroic slave girls and Indian maidens, dusky heroines so different from her roanish self. They lived inside her head, sometimes in the mirror in the thousand times she was sent to her room, door closed, never-solitary confinement, a boon not a punishment, if only her mother had realized it. Karen was never alone; she had a thousand voices in her head.

Dry your tears, Karen Rohmer, Karen the Roamer as the nuns so early branded you (titters from the peer group). Lose yourself in the mirror, in a book, in singing dragons and silver bonsai trees. Rescue yourself from the cinders and the poisoned apples, since there's never a prince around when you need one. After awhile you won't even need the prince, and certainly not the tears. You'll have something no one else you know has; you'll have us.

We'll help you find that other planet, we.

And who are we?

"If you were writing a murder mystery, would you spend the first chapter describing the chemical composition of the sun?"

Sometimes. Remember the children's tale about stone soup?

Once upon a time, before the white room, Karen had had two children, Nicole and Matthew, three years and realms of personality apart. How many readings of *Green Eggs and Ham* qualified one for Mother of the Year? Were you disqualified for screaming at a kid who put a hamster on your keyboard when you were trying to work? Green eggs and hamsters, primordial stone soup. In creating a universe, even God had to start somewhere.

"Primordial soup . . . ," she had jotted at the top of a brand-new grey legal pad, stealing from Sagan as a jumping-off point. She'd watched *Cosmos* when her kids were preteens; they got it, she didn't. That was the awful joke. She'd been too dumb to take physics in high school; the great fake, writing science fiction now.

She hadn't intended to be a fake, was supposed to have been "the new Mary Gordon" back in the feminist seventies, but three mainstream novels and the recession of '82 had been all there was to that particular hill of beans. There'd been a couple of *SpaceSeeker* novels and a comeback some years later. Now she was creating her own universes.

Primordial soup and star stuff. If Sagan could get away with it, could she?

"Science for the masses!" her then-husband Ray had sneered as she and the kids watched religiously every Saturday morning. "Sagan's a real showman, a regular Barnum, but he really doesn't know what he's talking about."

Ray taught high school civics and read physics texts as entertainment. That and a recent midlife crisis made him an expert on everything.

"Amazing!" Karen had remarked, jotting "hydrokinase . . . diatoms . . . molecular degeneration . . ." The man couldn't balance a checkbook or wash his own underwear. Could Sagan? "He's got the credentials, but you know more than he does."

"*Ma!*" Matthew, age eight, had whined. "We're trying to hear this!"

"Yeah, really!" Nicole added, rolling her eyes. Find the grown-up in this picture!

"At least I don't live in a dream world!" Ray went on. Why didn't the kids ever tell *him* to shut up? "Sitting in your office all day writing your little science-fantasy scenarios . . . You don't watch C-Span, you don't vote—what do you know about anything?"

Karen jotted, scratched, and scribbled, stirred the soup in lieu of screaming.

("It's science *fiction!*" she used to scream at him, succumbing to his button-pushing every time. "Or it's fantasy, which I don't write. There's no such thing as 'science fantasy'! Can't you at least pretend you care enough to get the terminology right?")

There had been a time when he had, a time when she would have credited Ray Guerreri with supporting and encouraging her career.

"He woke me up at four in the morning when I was pregnant with Nicole," she would tell their friends (especially her women friends, who always wanted to know "Why Karen Rohmer Guerreri? Why not write under your maiden name?

You know, in case . . . Well, yours wouldn't be the first marriage to . . ."), beaming at him while a whiny seven-year-old and
her sticky-fingered younger brother clustered about her, always
about her; their father was oblivious. "We were taking Lamaze
classes. He was really reluctant at first, but I said 'Look, you started
this; you're going to finish it'—

(Appreciative laughter.)

"—not *now,* Nicole; you'll have to wait a minute! So there I
am, eight and a half months along, and he wakes me out of a
sound sleep and says, 'You know, instead of wasting your time
trying to sell short stories'—well, I had been, trying for over a
year, collecting rejection slips—'instead of wasting your time,'
he said, 'you should write a novel about a childbirth class. Flashbacks about the people in the class and why they're taking the
course and how they met and what the baby means in their lives.'
So I did. And in three years I finished it and sent it to one of the
big literary agencies and . . . well, no, it didn't sell. To be honest—Nicole, leave your brother *alone!* Matthew, put that down
this minute!—To be honest I was just learning my craft; it wasn't
that well written. But three years after that . . ."

So he inspired her and so she did, and three years later . . .
She'd made it sound as if it had been an equal partnership. Just
like their marriage.

The soup stirs, like Karen and, like Karen, boils and troubles—
bubble, bubble, burble, ploop, pop, POP!

*Pop. The first sound but, like the one hand clapping when the tree
falls in the forest with no one to hear, it was a sound that made no
sound, not heard, hence not-sound, unsound. But it stirred, it lived,
it lifed.*

*Life animal, popped out of life vegetable, the first not-blue-green-algal
thing on this imaginary dreamworld science-fiction-fantasy world. Soon,
in a series of* pop . . . pop . . . POPS!, *it was not alone.*

*Bubbling, popping up to the surface (surface of what? What lies above
the surface? Pure CO_2 or . . . ?) bubbles that do not burst, minus-*

cule plopping polypal things, countless because not counted because there was no one to count them, multiplying all the time in the not-time. . . .

No, Karen thought. Go back a few billion years. Or forward. For what is time?

"The Pharaoh, He-Who-Would-Lose-His-Soul-to-the-Sands . . ."

. . . understood the gifts the desert gave, and the price those gifts exacted.

The Sun warmed, the Sun burned. The Sun warmed the waters of the Blue and the White when they overflowed, luring green growing things out of the black soils of the Upper and the Lower, green things that ripened and fed the people—bread, beer, and onions, every Egyptian's birthright. This same Sun raised near-invisible worms out of that same black soil, worms that burrowed into the soles of bare feet and inched their way through the body's humors until they lodged in the optic nerves and, devouring, severed them, plunging the soul into forever darkness. A man's face, even a pharaoh's face, could still feel the warmth of the Sun, though he would never see the God's visage again. Thus the power of the Sun.

The Sun forced flowers out of cracks in the face of the desert, searing them to straw within a day. The Sun warmed, the Sun burned, giving visions as easily as He gave blindness. Sometimes it was only a matter of a different kind of worm.

This, thought the Pharaoh, who knew the gifts the Sun gave, *this I understand!*

He had noted the heat shimmers first, had been drawn to them in the open desert, where only a pharaoh or a madman would walk in the height of the summer sun. He knew, every desert dweller knew, how water could appear on the scorching sands, then vanish as one drew nearer, but these were different. Like iridescent worms they shimmered above the simmer of the sands, in colors more vivid than the ones the artisans ground to paint on the gleaming wet plaster of the tombs, colors that would not fade even in eternity. Brighter than these they loomed and swelled and shimmered. As the Pharaoh drew nearer the colors changed, grew brighter, became different colors to which he could not even give names, and they led him to the God.

A miracle that no one else saw them! Surrounded always by servants, slaves, retainers, a pharaoh could not so much as void his bladder or couple with any of his wives without being under observation, but no one else of all those surrounding him had seen! But then, none of them were gods.

The colors had shown him the God, and the God had spoken to him.

Hear me, I who am the Sun, the Son, the All There Is, and understand that these you see around me, that are as so many shimmers of heat and color rising off the noonday sands, worms of a different stripe, these are my minions, but not gods. Heed them, for they speak for me, but know that I am All There Is. Heed this, and all else will be made clear to you in time (but what is Time?).

From this the Pharaoh, He-Who-Would-Lose-His-Soul-to-the-Sands, concluded that the companion gods—Isis and Osiris, Nut and Anubis, this-that-and-the-other—were as so many shimmers rising out of the sand, and that only the Sun, the Son (Amun-Re? No, *Aten*) was the God. Still, he did nothing with this knowledge at first, waiting to see if the God would speak to him again. It was a grave thing, even for a pharaoh, to change the way a people think.

"Choose the wounded ones," you said, Grey reminds Azure. *"Bruised vegetables always make the best soup."* Here's another fine mess you've gotten us into!

Context, Azure says. *It's Virid and hir religious fanatics again. The God-in-a-box types. I keep warning you, but nobody listens. (S/he who has not ears to hear cannot listen.)*

But he was an artist as well! Virid pouts. *An architect who virtually*

designed Tel-el-Amarna himself. We thought that impulse would be stronger. . . .
  Context! Azure insists.

Context. Con-text, the text of cons, or conventions, as the mundanes call them. Does anyone else—dentists, electronics experts (don't count computer nerds, too much overlap with s/f types), fly fishermen—share the convention of calling them "cons" instead of conventions?

"Context," an old fifties pulp writer named Murray Balsam is holding forth at a panel discussion Karen shares with him and fellow *SpaceSeekers* author Marie Englund. Someone in the audience has raised the topic of Ancient Astronauts, and Murray is off and running.

"Context," he says now. "History is replete with messiahs, but what makes one man—("Or woman?" Marie mutters; Murray has not ears to hear)—a messiah and another an Einstein or, on a more practical level, an Edison?"

Marie jabs Karen with an elbow, but she refuses to enter the fray. Just once she'd like to be on a panel where the alpha-male actually answered the question or at least stopped hogging the mike so someone else could, but it's not as important to her as it is to Marie. Marie's first husband had given her no end of grief; for her it's all about payback time.

Interchangeable chain-hotel conference rooms I have known! Karen thinks, remembering not to tip her folding chair too far back and tumble off the dais; she's done that before. Faux walnut paneling and gold-on-rose industrial-strength carpeting separate this fifty-seat room from the hotel kitchen, but not from the clash of crockery. She who had ears to hear could hear. Once upon a time, silly fangirl, she'd kissed Max Neimark in a hotel kitchen; Marie has been envious of her ever since. Beyond the door to the corridor—which no one remembers to keep shut—a very serious discussion is taking place.

". . . Chewbacca against a Klingon in a fair fight? Not a

chance, dude. The Wookie would make mincemeat out of him. We're talking dog food. Kibbles 'N Bits."

"Get out of town with that! You don't want to be casting aspersions on my Klingon brethren, Russell; you could find yourself with one of those three-pronged daggers in your back. And who said anything about 'fair'? "

"No, Marc, no, I'm sorry; it's got to be a fair fight . . . Klingon honor and all that. . . ."

Karen watches them pass out of the corner of her eye. Was the conversation on the dais any more real?

"True, Akhenaton was an artist as well as an architect; he virtually designed Tel-el-Amarna himself," Murray was pontificating. "But does a leader have a right to be an artist in lieu of being a statesman, or even a good social scientist? The man led his nation to hell in a handbasket.

"First he instructed his artisans to carve and paint him as he looked instead of in the idealized form his ancestors had insisted on for thousands of years. Then he abolished the state religion virtually overnight, creating instant unemployment among entire villages of craftsmen, not to mention the priests, who were the real power. Meanwhile, every territory his father Amenhotep III had gained through a lifetime of wars was lost, the crops failed, thousands starved. His reign was a debacle, yet the man continues to evoke some sort of visceral response nearly four thousand years later because he was the first public figure to go on record as a monotheist—"

"Maybe he had no choice," Karen interjects, and Murray looks at her as if she is the Antichrist. She shrugs, pushes her glasses up on her nose, refusing to wither under his glare, explaining herself. "Well, ancestral rule, inbreeding. It vitiates the bloodline after however-many generations. Maybe he didn't have the personality to be a pharaoh. If he'd had an older brother, he could have been a priest himself and used visions as a way of helping the state religion evolve. Besides, doesn't the current research indicate that he may not have been as deformed as he's represented but was actually responsible for fostering a radical artistic style that—"

"Pure conjecture!" Murray rumbles. "There's no evidence to support that. Enterobiasitic disease was rampant in his time and place. It explains the swelling in his legs. Nothing artistic about it."

"But you still haven't addressed the issue of Ancient Astronauts!" came the plaintive cry from the back of the room. If this panel had had an official topic to begin with, they'd long since lost it.

Marie lost patience and wrested the mike away from Murray.

"Honey," she said to the questioner, a massive woman with pulled-back hair and that earnest look so many of them wore. "Reality check: There weren't any Ancient Astronauts, okay? The whole thing will turn out to be a hoax, like those patterns in the cornfields. Got it? Next question!"

"Ms. Guerreri?" The massive woman turned to Karen, ignoring Marie's answer completely; it was simply unacceptable. "You must know what I'm talking about. Tying visitations by other species in with second sight, for instance . . ."

"Sounds like somebody didn't take her medication this morning . . ." Marie remarked sotto voce, leaning back away from the mike, as annoyed with Karen for evoking the question by her mere presence as she was with the woman asking it. "Why do you always attract the geeks and weirdos?"

"Now, now!" Karen said just as quietly, focusing all her attention on her questioner.

"I mean, didn't you predict the fall of the Berlin Wall in *Abide in Fire*?"

"Geeks and weirdos!" Marie crooned as the woman produced a tattered paperback and began to read:

" '. . . he occupied his mind by searching for some analogue to this place. Checkpoint Charlie, he thought. The Berlin Wall, Old Earth. How childish all that seemed now, in the enlightenment of a United Earth. . . .' "

Karen suppressed the warm bloom of gratitude that began at

the center of her chest and spread outward to her fingertips. Murray and Marie were both watching her sourly. No one had offered to quote from *their* work.

" '. . . Maybe someday this station would also seem childish, obsolete, in a time when alien and human could embrace each other as brethren and border sentries were an endangered species. . . .'

"Now, you wrote this in . . ." The woman flipped to the copyright page. ". . . 1985. Or at least it came out then, so you must have written it earlier. . . ."

"Eighty-three," Karen supplied, remembering the hunger. The Reagan years had done for publishing what Akhenaton had done for Egypt. Reagan, like Akhenaton, had believed in God-in-a-box. The phrase struck her and, doing a Harlan Ellison, she jotted it on the paper tablecloth in front of her.

"Well, there you are!" the woman with the paperback said as if it proved her point. "And the Wall came down in—what— '89? So I guess that makes you an authority."

"Not necessarily." Karen thought of taking the mike from Marie but Marie looked like she'd fight her for it; she decided to talk a little louder instead. "There's very little insight involved in looking at something as absurd as a wall designed to keep people in, which was no more successful than the Great Wall of China was in keeping people out in whatever century—"

"Early Han Dynasty, third century B.C.," Murray supplied, leaning into the mike. Marie, on his side now, tittered conspiratorially.

"—what I was suggesting in *Fire*," Karen plunged on, "was that a construct like the Berlin Wall was a government's unwitting admission of defeat. It was only common sense that it would come tumbling down within our lifetimes. That doesn't make me an expert or a guru or—"

—a messiah. Ah, but Karen, you are, though you don't yet realize it. The word is from Hebrew by way of Aramaic, meshiha *meaning "anointed one," so by that definition you are, because we've anointed*

you, appointed you. And you'd better be the right one, because some of us are getting impatient and the rest of us are running out of time.

Context, then. What the Pharaoh did wrong, or what a later messiah did right, or the fact that both were simply out of context? Let's go to the videotape. . . .

The Pharaoh, whose aching edemic legs (sign of the godhead in him, as in his father before him) had woken him from slumber in the desolate hours before the Sun was reborn, stirred on the balcony of the Winter Palace, rose from the pallet where his physician had advised him to elevate his legs each day in order to ease the swelling, and descended the steps into the garden. Servants stirred to follow him, the stiff linen of their short kilts rustling in the silent morning, bare feet slapping the flagstones. The Pharaoh waved them back and went into the garden alone.

The Sun did not speak to him in the garden. The garden was shaded by palms of graduated size, and by exotic poplars and cedar trees brought up the Two Rivers by outland traders. The garden was a tame place; the Sun was there, but silently. Small wind gods disturbed the leaves, but nothing more. Only in the raw of the desert did the Sun speak.

On his last journey into the desert, the Pharaoh had finally accepted his task. He was to build a temple to this Sun. Not yet another temple to Amun-Re, god among gods and repeated in a thousand thousand friezes over a thousand years, but to the One, the Son, the true incarnation of the Sun. The Sun had shown him a valley that belonged to no god, and here he would build his temple.

The Pharaoh's legs no longer ached, or, perhaps because his thoughts were occupied, he no longer felt the pain. For the first time since his ascendancy he had found purpose beyond the mere rote of following his father's fathers' paths, of counting endless measures of grain, being carried in endless measured processions, being nothing more than the manifestation of the god the people thought they needed because they knew no other, a nice safe god who kept the harvests fat and did not snatch too many infants in childbirth. A god who nevertheless bred blinding worms and sandstorms that buried whole caravans alive and salted enough sand into the daily bread to grind even a pharaoh's teeth down to bare nerve. What manner of capricious god was this, god made in the image of the men who served him? The Pharaoh would give his people a new god, warm like the Sun, benevolent, different.

Though it would mean his own death even beyond death. The Pharaoh knew. The shimmers on the sands had told him. Though he stood in the cool and safety of the garden, there was desert in his heart.

●

There is desert in the white room. Karen jots a note to herself: "Theory: Topography of Greece = angular landscapes, clear dry air; Greece = Aristotle, Pythagoras. Misty places, e.g., Celtic lands (insufficient lithium in the water; q.v., manic depression) = elven, kelpie, and wraiths. Mexico: Veneer of Christianity overlaid on sacrificial cultures (Maya, etc.), marginal climate (crop failures, need to propitiate gods) = gorrific crucifixions, madonnas weeping blood. Deserts = a greater proportion of messiahs. Climate or coincidence?"

Now we're getting somewhere. . . .

●

Every afternoon the carpenter's widow brought bread and broth and goat's milk to the workshop, where her only child made cradles and coffins and the occasional table or chair. There amid the redolence of sawdust and shavings, they would eat and talk together.

The carpenter died of a seizure when the child was fifteen, and Jess had simply taken over his work. The toddler, whose bare feet had made feathery patterns in the powdery dust, whose curls had gathered chips and wood curls beneath the workbench where the child crawled after "treasures" of scraps and end blocks, whose small hands had learned beneath a father's doting tutelage to sort nails by size and purpose from the beginning, had had no formal apprenticeship; it was not deemed appropriate. Nevertheless, when the carpenter died and there was no one else to put bread and broth and goat's milk on the table, Jess took up the burden, which was no burden. The work had purpose, therefore it was good.

The carpenter's widow entered the workshop by the back door. Her eyes grew weaker year by year—she was well past thirty—and she had not noticed the strangers who entered by the main door off the square. Sniffing the heated noonday air, she'd thought she smelled camel dung, a smell she would not soon forget. She had not even known such incongruous beasts existed until the year she and her husband were summoned into the city for the Roman census but, given what happened in the wake of that celebrated headcount, the smell was forever linked with horrors in her mind.

As her sight grew dimmer, her sense of smell increased. Yet no one hereabouts had the price of a camel; the smell could not be real. Perhaps it was a premonition, a warning of further bad times to come. Bad times were the norm, not the exception, in Judea. Nevertheless, the distinct complaining bray from the square caused the carpenter's widow to squint down the alleyway separating her husband's shop from the tanner's and marvel. Roaring its disdain to anyone who would hear, its front legs hobbled to keep it from running away, a decidedly real camel stood at the entrance to the shop.

Strangers in the village? Strangers wealthy enough to arrive at her late husband's workshop on a camel?

There were in fact two camels, and two Jerusalem merchants who had ridden in on them. As the village children scrambled around the spindly legs, barely avoiding kicks or their particularly vile spittle, their riders were already in the workshop, dickering with the carpenter's child.

"Look, there's no sin involved here," the elder of the two was arguing. "It's a business arrangement. The Romans want crucifixes from local suppliers to dispatch local criminals; it's cheaper than transporting them all the way from the city. We act as facilitators. We give the Romans top quality, we pay you top price."

The carpenter's child listened in stony silence, unconvinced. "These people are going to be executed anyway," the younger merchant chimed in. "Why not give them a decent instrument of execution? There was an instance in a village near Joppa, a thief and murderer—a big man; they should have compensated for his weight—the crosspiece snapped when they set it upright and his left arm swung free. All his weight fell on the right arm, dislocating his shoulder. The nails tore right through; there was a lot of screaming. They had to go through with it all the same, getting up on ladders to yank the crosspiece back into place, bolster it with scrap wood, find new sites to drive the nails. Horrible! The man died in twice as much agony as he needed to. . . ."

"Horrible!" the elder merchant agreed, fingering his beard, watching Jess with his beady eyes for some reaction; there was none. He leaned toward the carpenter's child, his breath as vile as a camel's. "Don't you see? You'd be doing everyone a favor. Society, for starters—fewer thieves. And the thieves themselves, as my colleague here has pointed out. Not to mention yourself. You haven't even asked what we'd be willing to pay. Don't sniff at a good thing, youngster. You come highly recommended."

Jess stood in the dusty sunlight near the shop's sole window, where already nosy neighbors were gathered, crowding each other between the wooden shutters to see. Sleeves pushed up on sinewy, sweat-and-dust-streaked arms, a scatter of sawdust sprinkled on the hair of an upper lip, the carpenter's child dismissed the offer.

"Whoever recommended me misled you. I don't do crucifixes, no more than did my father before me. Get yourself another man!"

•

"No!" Tessa shrieked, clutching the hair at her temples and jumping out of her chair. "Absolutely not! I refuse!"

Shirley, her regressionist, sighed and surfaced from her trance, suppressing the heart flutter that Tessa's shriek had triggered. Tessa was always one of her more difficult clients.

"Tessa, you can refuse further knowledge about this particular life, but you can't pretend it isn't there."

Tessa had chosen Shirley as her regressionist because Shirley fit the part. She had the kind of down-her-back silver hair and matronly figure that made you think "mother" if not "mage." Once she found her center, of course, Tessa hadn't needed either, and she hadn't consulted Shirley for years, though she'd given her permission to mention her to her other clients as "one of my celebrities." The only one, but never mind. Tessa had called Shirley in a mild panic after several years' absence because she couldn't shake the sick feeling she'd woken with on the day after her birthday.

She didn't have time for the dreads. She was supposed to be working on another volume of memoirs, her deadline was three months away, and nothing in this life was going right since she'd turned fifty-five. Time to find alternatives, perhaps a new soul, but not this particular one.

"It feels wrong," she told Shirley now, trying to pace off her restlessness, though she hadn't bothered apologizing for shrieking. "It's not that I mind its being male, it's just—"

"Tessa, I don't think you understand," Shirley tried to interject. She glided past Tessa, feeling the negativity radiating from her, began reopening the blinds against a slant of late afternoon sun, which didn't help her headache. Sessions with Tessa, she recalled, frequently gave her headaches. "Jess isn't—"

"*No!*" Tessa said again. Backlit by the sun, her auras flickered violently, radiating all the negative spectra. Shirley had never seen her react so violently. "No—*you*—don't—understand!" she seethed, biting off each word as if to make it simpler. "I don't do *carpenters*. I don't do unlettered peasants. I don't do *hoi polloi*. This one isn't *me!*"

•

It isn't me, either, Karen thinks. *This is Tessa McGill, the actress. I don't put real people in my manuscripts. Besides, it's not even especially well-written.* She crosses it out, writes on.

•

"Whoever recommended me misled you. I don't do crucifixes, no more than did my father before me. Get yourself another man!"

The two merchants exchanged sly glances at that. If this were a man, why was its voice so boyish? Well, accidents happened, especially in small villages. People married their first cousins and bore freaks.

"We were told to seek out Jess of Nazareth," the younger merchant protested. "Best carpenter in the valley, we were told. Are you not he?"

Hands on hips, Jess laughed then, head thrown back, flawless teeth gleaming.

"Fools! You took the wrong turnoff in the mountains! This is not Nazareth, and I'm not the one you seek. His name's Jeshua or Yshua, something like that. And whether he makes crucifixes or no I cannot tell you. As for his being the best carpenter in the valley, there I'd challenge him bare-handed!"

The carpenter's widow, lurking in the shadow of the alley door, heard all this. Worse, so did the neighbors. She was not so ignorant as to bungle in with the noonday meal like some stupid peasant when her sole support was negotiating with wealthy merchants. But the urge to drop the dishes and smack the brat for turning down a fat commission—from Rome, no less!—was almost overwhelming. She directed her wrath at the neighbors.

"Have you nothing better to do?" she scolded, glaring until they moved on.

Jess had led the two strangers out to the square by now and pointed the way down the road toward Nazareth.

". . . though you might want to rest until the sun goes down. It's hellish on these valley roads at midday. Have a drink of water from our well before you go?"

"We've brought our own," the younger merchant said, indicating the filled bladders hung from the saddle packs. One never knew what one might find in village water. "Jeshua, you say?"

Jess nodded. "At least I think that's his name. Nazareth's a small village, as small as here; I doubt it supports more than one carpenter. Give him my regards, but tell him—bare-handed!"

The two merchants exchanged another glance. Womanish voice or no, the lad could boast! Pity they hadn't convinced him.

Jess turned to find the widow scowling in the doorway of the shop.

"The broth's gone cold!" she announced. Jess followed her out of the sun into the redolent workplace. "You'd think, as you're all that's between us and starvation, you'd be less particular!"

"I don't do crucifixes," Jess said stubbornly, searching the tool bench for the plane to finish the second of a set of chairs the wine merchant had commissioned for his newly betrothed daughter.

"Come and eat, then!" the widow demanded, pouring the goat's milk into two wooden bowls.

"I'm not hungry!" Jess scowled, planing. The plane gouged too deep and was tossed aside in anger. "Do you know what they *do* to a man when they crucify him? Have you ever seen?"

"Nor have you!" the widow answered. "Unless you've been to Jerusalem without my knowing. Come and eat!"

I haven't, Jess thought. But I've seen; I *know!* Don't ask me how, but I can almost feel it. I even know what size nails they use and how they drive them between the bones of the wrists, not through the hands as is popularly believed, so that all the body's weight can fall on them and hang. Was it a conversation I overheard when Abba was still alive?

No, because I've seen, not heard it. Seen the way they sometime shatter the thighbones to hasten death. A man can't brace his feet and push off to keep his lungs clear and heave in a breath; he suffocates. It's considered a mercy. But how do I know?

The widow watched her only child with wonder mixed with dismay. She ought to rail less and thank G-d more. How many other mothers had lost their firstborn the night Herod's soldiers came?

She'd tried to hide the child but, colicky from birth, Jess revealed their hiding place in the wine merchant's cellar with a single piercing wail.

"Ho, here's another one!"

A single soldier quickstepped down the worn stairs in his creaking leather, stark shadows thrown by his upraised torch. He searched among the rows of jars until he found them, seized the child from its keening, groveling mother. Pleading, she clung to his legs, throwing him off-balance so that, contending with the torch as well, he managed to grab only swaddling, which came unwound in his clumsy hand, hurling the child facedown onto the stone floor. Only a louder wail and the thrashing limbs assured the woman that her child was not already dead.

The soldier, his sword half out of its sheath, flung the swaddling aside, shoved the toe of his sandal beneath Jess's convulsing stomach, and flipped the infant over. The sight of the small naked cunt between the flailing legs made him roar with laughter.

"Lucky for you it's female!" he said, resheathing the sword. "Not worth dulling the blade!"

He whirled and was gone. Wiping tears and snot from her face with the hem of her garment, the woman crawled across the floor and retrieved the child, reswaddling her, though there was nothing to be done for the broken nose.

The child was young, the cartilage soft; the nose healed itself after a fashion. Considering how many had lost their infant sons that night, Jess's mother never mentioned it, though she knew it would disfigure the girl and make her virtually unmarriageable. Not that it mattered, as she grew to nearly her natural father's height, rawboned and muscular, the down on her upper lip and her scowling demeanor causing many a stranger to mistake her for a man.

Bitter, her mother thought, I shall never see grandchildren! But better for Jess, lest any man seeing her fatherless and husbandless decide she merited rape. The heavy work made Jess as strong as a man; it would be a desperate man who'd try to rape her.

She'd told the Jerusalem merchants she wouldn't make crucifixes for the Romans. Perhaps that was better, too, her mother thought as Jess sat down at last and drank the foaming goat's milk. The Romans had no more use for a woman like Jess than her own kind did.

FOUR

Among the older suns, closer than Earth to the Galactic Center (closer in the way that, say, Canton, Ohio, is closer to San Francisco than is New York, but is not *near* San Francisco per se), their star system could not be seen from Earth. For the first billion years of their existence, they were blue-green algae, perhaps the most common life-form in the universe. Somewhere in the second billion years, something went *pop!* Enter diversification.

"A billion years after that, there were two life-forms, vegetable and animal. The vegetable evolved through myriad stages that, as the seas dried up and the parameters altered, appeared, clung tenaciously, and one by one died out, some gradually, some literally overnight. Finally only a single, slightly diversified (which is to say it came in flavors) fungoid form survived, clinging to the undersides of rocks on the stark and inhospitable surface, flourishing in the caves. Thus the vegetable.

"The animal was somewhat more complex. Planktonous but specializing, it, too, branched and rebranched, formed and deformed, complexed and dissolved in slow death-dance decay of constant mutants, sports and efforts valiant and failed, until only one form remained. Ctenophore or scyphozoan, or something both and neither?

"While there was surface water, when all there was was surface water, the species dominated the surface, evolving. As the waters receded, the less evolved succumbed—pulsating gelatinous masses exposed to the stab of merciless sun through tenuous atmosphere—boiling, evaporating, leaving stickiness and shadow on rock, lasting the chill of night and gone by morning. Those that specialized into pseudopods, tendrils, and tentacles learned first to sense radiational and vibrational variations and fluctuations in water temperature, alterations in chemical content that presaged evaporation. After a few billion of these, muzzily contemplating their newfound talents, had slowly fizzled in the sun, others learned to propel themselves via these same sense organs, expediently discovered by an expanding intelligence to possess the power of motion, to the shelter of the caves, safety, survival.

"Jellyfish? Individuated macro-cells of a single planetary organism? Self-contained auras—membranous, numinous, luminous? Intelligent? When? That was the true mystery. . . . "

Larry Koster tossed the script on his coffee table, disgusted and bewildered. He couldn't find that passage anywhere, though he'd combed through the script a dozen times on this third reading. It had to be there. He could recite it from memory, and he knew he hadn't made it up. It had to be there, or he was losing his mind.

Of course, it hadn't been there on his first hurry-up read through, either, only on the second careful reading he'd given it after Sandra sent him back to it. It was as if someone had slipped it to him, then removed it. Or was he confusing it with something else?

He'd always felt sorry for old actors, especially the ones who'd lived hard and couldn't remember their lines anymore. It was a fate he fought against daily. *Let me drop dead in my tracks before I start pissing myself in public!* he prayed to whatever gods he believed in. He'd noticed a funny thing about the old alkies, though. They might need foot-high idiot cards and a dozen takes to do a fifteen-second hemorrhoid spot, but they could reprise their *Henry V* verbatim thirty years or more after the final curtain. Was that what was happening to him?

Unlike some of his fellow *SpaceSeekers* veterans, Larry had ducked every s/f script ever sent to him, until this one. So why, instead of flashing on Shakespeare or his cop show or any of the sincere superheroes that had checkered his career, was he tripping on this disembodied something that sounded like a voice-over for a *National Geographic* special? Unlike his buddy Max, Larry refused to do voice-overs. He was always being pestered to do narrations for some big-city planetarium, always turning them down. Was that why this sounded so familiar?

No, because this was biology, not astronomy. Larry had thought it odd to include a straight narrative in a movie script, but maybe it *was* meant to be a voice-over. Then why wasn't it in script format? Didn't they teach scriptwriting in film schools anymore? Or was this some wannabe novelist who'd failed to sell his novel and thought it would be just perfect as a screenplay? How the hell did these pups find agents, much less get into the Writers' Guild?

Maybe they were just notes, Larry thought. Notes the writer wanted me to have by way of background, notes that weren't meant to be included in the script itself, something to do with the evolution of the invading aliens in the script. Gotta admit it's a weird script. It's just as much science fiction as it is a pseudo-biblical/historical/semi-epic-with-f/x character study of a futuristic world in which . . .

In which scripts like this will no longer be written! Larry prayed. He was sweating. Flashing, for some reason, on a memory of Tessa McGill in an ice-blue garter belt. He didn't remember any jellyfish aliens in the script. Time-gates and a species of green hermaphrodite and a kind of intelligent slime-mold that reproduced by—no, wait, that was an old *SpaceSeekers* script, one that had been intended for the fourth season that never happened. Wasn't it?

Okay, he'd had memory lapses before—always forgot people's names, that kind of thing. It had gotten to be such a running gag on *SpaceSeekers* that the staff writers used to write it in as part of Captain Stark's character. ("Yeoman Jones, isn't it?" "Name's Smith, sir.") But his grandmother had died of what nowadays would be diagnosed as Alzheimer's. This wasn't funny anymore. *Where the fuck was that passage?*

•

"Over the second billion years," Karen writes, "the waters on the surface dissipate, then the waters in the caves. The scyphozoa (ctenophores?) evolve, adapt, survive. Their membranous invertebrate bodies jell and stabilize, the pseudopods extending long and far and specializing, some to seek out the fungus that is their sole sustenance, some to smell and taste. . . ."

She talking about us? Lake is doing hir De Niro impression, enquiring of the Mind. *Is she talking about* us?

It's just fiction, Azure assures though, uneasy with the direction Karen's scribbling has taken in the solitude of her white room, s/he wonders.

But seriously! Lake drops the accent, serious. *She can't mean that's the way we evolved, can she? How would she know? She wasn't there.*

And we were, and we don't remember! Virid frets. Virid is a fretter; if s/he had hands, s/he would wring them.

It's FICTION! Azure insists, irritated with both of them. *As is Karen. We thought her into existence. Or have you forgotten that?*

We who are All There Is do not forget, Lake reminds hir loftily. *Or have YOU forgotten THAT?*

This is all hir own doing, Azure knows. The Common Mind reverberates, perturbed.

•

Perturbed, Larry Koster is on the phone to his agent.

"Tell me about this scriptwriter," he says. "What's his background? How'd this script end up with me?"

"He's actually a big fan of yours," Sandra tells him. "Got into the Guild through a co-credit on the cop show. Never written anything before, except some computer software he's had trouble copyrighting. But he says he's seen everything you've ever been in."

Larry can just imagine. The image of some eager young dweeb with his nose pressed against the screen of an old black-and-white TV, watching endless reruns of *SpaceSeekers* through his Coke-bottle glasses makes his skin crawl. The dweeb probably owned the full line of Franklin Mint *SpaceSeekers* collectibles, and Captain Stark was his favorite character. Larry has met the dweeb and his entire species at one time or another—at a mall in Boise, on an autograph line in Outer Mongolia. These people were his constituency, and he loathed them, every one.

"Great, just great!" Larry says. "Listen, Sandra, did you—no, you couldn't have, because it was the second reading, after you left . . ."

"Hello?" Sandra is used to Larry's rambling, but today it's worse than usual. "Earth to Laurence Koster . . . say again?"

"The jellyfish," Larry says, as if it makes perfect sense. "Or whatever they are. That couple of pages of straight narrative that was in the script. I can't find it this time around. Did you take it back with you?"

"Jellyfish," Sandra repeats. He can see her in her mostly glass office in Century City, one corner near the ceiling still cracked from the quake, her narrow little face pinched into a frown. "Sorry, Lar, you've lost me."

"I—I think I've lost myself," he says, genuinely frightened, and signs off.

Angry now, he picks up the script again and goes through it page by page, watching the page numbers as he does.

The passage was gone. Or it had never been there in the first place. There was no way for him to find out. Fucking jellyfish!

Jellyfish. Fish in a bowl. Tessa McGill in an ice-blue garter belt. Larry felt his cock twitch nostalgically. What was the connection? Was there a connection?

•

"No!" Tessa keeps saying aloud, though she is alone as she trails from the living room to the kitchen and back again; today is Eddie's market day. "A female messiah—well, all very interesting if there ever was such a thing, but I refuse! Shirley's wrong, that's all; it has to be something else!"

•

"Their membranous invertebrate bodies jell and stabilize, the pseudopods extending long and far and specializing, some to seek out the fungus that is their sole sustenance, some to smell and taste. Some distinguish temperature, light and dark, the sting of radiant danger, which is death. Brains elaborate and specialize as the pseudopods do, interfolding layer upon layer. In place of sight and sound, strange synapses form a thinking interlinked connectedness, a Common Mind . . ."

There! Lake insists, triumphant. *She IS talking about us.*

Azure does not reply.

"As each brain cell specializes, so does each brain become a single cell within the Common Brain, the Common Mind. How many are there? All There Are. How many is that? Only one, the Common Mind. How do they call themselves? As All There Are, over-against nothing in the universe, they do not call themselves at all.

"They Are. They have been, but did not know it, until they discovered they were not All There Are."

Karen looked up from her eight-line screen, blinking myopically, last s/f writer on the planet to work on a word processor and not a computer. At this point her aliens had no name for themselves because she had no name for them. She'd wracked her brains and gone through her old-fashioned *Roget's* and come up empty.

It would come to her when it came to her. It always did. For now she would consult her expert.

BENN:

Clearly they would more closely resemble the scypho-zoan form, which is symmetrical and free swimming, as opposed to the ctenophore or comb jelly, which is more biradially symmetrical.

KAREN:

Are you sure, Benn? I would have thought once the surface water evaporated they'd have stuck themselves to the cave walls and not needed to propel themselves the way, say, an Earth-based hydra would.

BENN:

I assure you, Karen, I am quite certain.

"Yeah, I'm sure." Max nodded, handing the script back to the assistant director for final corrections. "Works for me."

"Great!" the A.D. said, scribbling changes and glancing at his watch. "Why don't we break for lunch, give you a chance to rest the pipes; then we'll see if we can wrap the third segment, okay?"

"Fine," Max said tersely, saving the Voice. He took the script back and sat studying it as the crew began to drift out of the studio.

"Back by one, people!" the A.D. called. "We want to wrap the first hour this afternoon."

They'd do it, too, he thought. He'd worked with Max Neimark before. Pure pro, not a prima donna like some of them. With luck there'd be a minimum of retakes and they'd be out of here by four.

Max enjoyed voice-overs, particularly the first-class treatment and the easy hours. Show up at ten in tennies and sweats, bagels and coffee and the A.D. at your elbow with lozenges, throat spray, pots of tea or ice water. Read for an hour ("Eco-Space and the Sea Around Us: Stranger Than Science Fiction"—a nature special for PBS), break, read for another hour, lunch, read for another hour or two with a break in between, finished for the day. Do this for three days (your nights are your own), with maybe an additional half-day for loops and pick-ups, fly home with a fat fee and a contract brimming with residuals.

During the lean years after *SpaceSeekers* was canceled, Max's voice-overs had paid his daughter's way through Wellesley and bought a lot of groceries. Nowadays, while he sat behind a mike rolling his phonemes, Carole could shop at Bergdorf Goodman and the Fifth Avenue boutiques, they had house seats for nearly everything on Broadway, and his New York agent was buying them dinner tomorrow night. For a kid who'd landed in Hollywood with fifty bucks in his pocket and a canceled one-way train ticket, life was good.

Max stretched his long legs, coughed twice, and scanned the afternoon's script segment. Better a run-through before lunch; he'd make fewer mistakes when the tape was rolling.

" 'Perhaps among the strangest denizens of the middle depths . . .' Ahem. Strangest denizens. STRANGE-est DENizens . . . Jeez, who writes this stuff? 'Among the strangest denizens of the middle depths are the ctenophores—' STENofors? Am I pronouncing this right?"

He peered over the top of his thick reading glasses, but nearly everyone had split for lunch except the soundman, who shrugged at him—*Fuck if I know, man!*—from the booth.

Fine! Max thought. STENophores, maybe. He scanned further down the page. ". . . ctenophores, or comb jelly . . ." Okay, like jellyfish, only more stationary, with cilia—little uniform hairlike feet that all wiggled at once to propel the thing— instead of tentacles like medusas. Max remembered medusas from when his kids were small and he and Karin, his first wife, used to take them sailing. Once they'd moored on Catalina for the day and his son Joel had picked up what he thought was a piece of bright-colored plastic half-buried in the sand and almost died of the stings before they got him to the clinic. Even there, the resident was so busy hounding Max for an autograph he'd had to back him up and roar at him to get him to treat the kid first. . . .

Jellyfish, Max thought. Oy, Gott, it should have been a warning. How old was I the first time I saw them?

•

He could feel the sensuous fingers of the brush against the back of his neck as his father swept the stray hairs away, smell the pungent talc that rose in an aura around him as the old man whipped the drape off in a single motion so that all the cut hair sprinkled delicately to the floor and not onto his clothes.

"For you, the professional discount!" his father announced in Yiddish as he always did. Long after his younger son had made his first million, Sol Neimark would continue to cut his hair for free, sparing him the seventy-five cents he charged everyone else in Boston for a haircut. "Now get out of here, ladykiller; I've got paying customers!"

Ladykiller! Max thought, launching himself out of the barber chair by the heels of his hands and catching sight of his long horsey face with its odd-color eyes in the wall-to-wall mirrors. Another one of his father's sharp-edged jokes. Some ladykiller!

His hair, thanks to his father's ministrations, was perfect—sleek and thick and healthy and, to judge from his father's thick silver mane, he'd never have to worry about losing it. Without its customary coat of Vitalis to keep it slicked back into a classic fifties DA, it fell neatly over his brow from a natural part high on the crown. Was it the years of wearing a *kipa* that made it fall that way? Lately he'd been avoiding shul, except when his father insisted; he'd cross the street and pretend he didn't hear the old men calling him to make a minyan. It wasn't that he wasn't religious; it was just that shul depressed him lately. It seemed so worn down, so old.

Like your father! Max chided himself, watching Sol duck-walking about in the back of the shop, bowlegged from birth. His parents had been in their forties when he was born; fleeing pogroms had a way of postponing important things like child-bearing. And after what you're going to tell the old man today, maybe he'll wonder if it was worth it!

You'll tell him today, Max told himself. Now, before you leave the shop. As soon as he finishes sweeping up, you'll tell him!

He always came into the shop just before closing, making sure there were no other customers after him. That was when Sol swept the entire shop with a push broom and they could talk. At home, between his mother and his older brother Leon, neither

Max nor Sol could get a word in. There'd been a special kind of kinship between father and younger son within the confines of the shop, Sol's universe, since Max was a little boy.

"Pop, let me do that!" he'd say by rote, trying to take the push broom out of Sol's hands. His father would wave him away.

"You can do it better than me, maybe? You never do under the cabinets. Out of my way and let an expert do it."

"Have it your way!" Max would say, then sit in the middle of the three chairs, swiveling this way and that to watch his father work. Sol would sweep and ask questions; Max would swing his chair and answer. So how's school? Fine, Pop. You're still getting top grades in math? Yes, Pop.

That's good. A doctor needs to know math. So does an accountant; you should decide to set your sights a little lower. A businessman, even. Ask Uncle Hiram, he'll tell you. So who's the girl?

Girl, Pop? What girl?

The girl Leon saw you talking to in front of Spritzers'. She's Italian, no? A very bad business! Italian girls don't marry Jewish boys; it's against their religion.

I'm not going to marry her, Pop. I'm not even seeing her. She asked me to help her with her math, that's all. She wants a guy like James Dean, not me.

James Dean—a *pisher*! She should be so lucky! Is that why you're making muscles, you should look like James Dean? Uncle Hiram says you're stacking boxes for him in the store, for nothing yet. He says you're making muscles.

It's not to impress the girls, Pop, believe me.

What then?

It was precisely the opening Max needed, but he muffed it. Missed his cue, blew his lines. He'd had the acting bug since *Hansel and Gretel* at the settlement house when he was ten. Couldn't they see? How was he going to tell the old man without breaking his heart? He waited while Sol shuffled back to the storeroom to put the broom away, studying himself again in the all-around mirrors.

His hair was perfect. The body, now that he'd begun helping Uncle Hiram in the store, was not as thin and concave as it had been; there was more definition in the muscles beneath the requisite white T-shirt. The mismatched eyes puzzled most people; he couldn't count the number of times total strangers had done a double take and said "Hey, did you know . . . ?"

"—that I've got one brown eye and one green one? Yeah, I've noticed."

Self-consciously, watching himself in the wall-to-wall mirrors, Max rolled his sleeves greaser-style. If he wasn't sure Sol would pitch a fit to find him smoking, he'd affect a pack of Camels tucked into the roll the way his friends did. He smoked for the same reason he stacked boxes for Uncle Hiram—in case he needed it for a role.

Yes, the hair was perfect and the body wasn't so bad, but oy, that face! Max struck poses in the mirrors—full face, left three-quarter, right, both profiles.

"Hey, you!" his father yelled, emerging from the back of the shop, easing his shoulders into an old grey cardigan. "Quit with the ugly faces. You think you're Muni Weisenfreund or something? Mr. Tough-guy. You'll break my mirrors, and then where will I be?"

Max threw his head back and laughed. It was a natural laugh, easy, revealing good teeth, a real Pepsodent smile. "Out of business, that's where you'll be. Especially if you don't remember it's Paul Muni. It's been Paul Muni since the talkies, Pop; get with it!"

Max Neimark sounds okay, Max thought; I won't have to change it.

"He was Muni Weisenfreund in the theater, before he got too good for himself!" Sol sneered, straightening chairs, checking to see that all the combs and brushes were soaking in their disinfectant; he shambled into the back again to make sure the sink wasn't dripping and had to shout to make himself heard. "Paul Muni, my backside! Did I ever tell you when your mother and I first came to this country, we saw them all in New York? We'd save our pennies all week, and every Sunday night, like you'd go to the movies now . . ." Sol emerged from the back again, pulling the chains on the overhead fluorescents, shutting them off one by one, the last nightly ritual before he locked the shop and they could leave. "Joseph Wiseman and Molly Picon and Muni Weisenfreund . . ."

Now's your chance! Max thought. He respects Muni and all the old-time Jewish actors. *Tell him!*

It was then that he noticed the ripples in the mirror. Just the lights, he thought, as Sol pulled the chain on the last of them, but the sudden darkness only accentuated what he saw. When he turned to look at it front-on, it vanished.

"What's the matter?" his father asked.

Max shook his head. "Nothing. A headache, that's all."

"*Nu.*" Sol locked the shop at last, jangling keys. "Maybe I talk too much. Anyway, don't tell your mother; by her it'll be a tumor."

They both laughed.

It wasn't a tumor, and it wasn't helped by the glasses the settlement house doctor prescribed for his astigmatism.

"Floaters," the doctor told Max when he described them. "Imperfections in the fluid inside the eye. Nothing you can do but live with them."

Max thanked the doctor and learned to live with them. Within the next few months the shouting and the misery that accompanied his telling his parents he was leaving for Hollywood just after his eighteenth birthday took his mind off his vision problems and just about everything else. Besides, by then he knew what "they" were, and they weren't "floaters."

"Max, you're such a dreamer!" Karin Horner would tease him, her soft blond head nestled against his shoulder backstage. They had met in summer stock and would "go steady" for two years before he found the nerve to ask her to hitch her wagon to his uncertain star. "It's like you're someplace else. Where do you go when you do that?"

"Do what?" he'd ask, coming back to earth.

"Stare off into space like that," Karin would say, pouting slightly. "Am I boring you?"

"No, of course not!" he'd protest, and they'd go back to kissing where they'd left off.

He wanted to tell her, he really did. But how could he explain where he was or what he was doing? *Meshuggah!* Who but a child or a crazy man would commune with jellyfish?

•

"Their interaction with humanity," Karen wrote, "took a billion years more. Their tenuous personages guised the intelligence of the angels for, never having known anything but All There Was, they were at once as innocent, and as knowing, as Adam before the apple.

"Imagine a species at once individual and collective, unbound by time, possessed of eidetic memory, possibly immortal. Resembling, for human convenience, intelligent jellyfish, or perhaps gelatinous opals clinging en masse to their cavern walls, undulating gently. Asexual or omnisexual? Did it matter? They were complete. Lacking any concept of pain or desire, they existed in a realm of ever-flowing dream, possessed of a knowledge quite other than that of any thumbed and timebound mortal. What human religion would not promote this as nirvana? Was this paradise, eternity, what humans should aspire to?

"Why then was it/were they not content to stay on their own world? What compelled them to reach the Mind out across measureless parsecs of space to touch human lives ? . . ."

The ripple reverberates through the Mind, and Grey follows it. The Mind reaches back a billion years, then a billion years more. Beyond that, it balks. Jellyfish leave no fossils, no archaeological sites. All There Was is All There Is and it Is within the

Mind. How to remember what transpired before there was a Mind?

It's fiction, Azure reminds the Mind, hoping the thought will be pursued no further.

But as we did not give it to her, where did she get it? Grey objects.

If Azure could sigh, s/he would. How many times must s/he explain it? *This is a species that has no Common Mind. Therefore they can alter truth. It is in their nature to invent. Trust me; that's all it is.*

Perhaps . . . Grey allows, not entirely convinced. The reverberation does not go away. It is all Azure's doing, and the All There Was will never be the same.

"Their numens, like the fungus they fed on, came in 'flavors,' which, for convenience' sake we will consider names, names like Grey, Azure, Amber, Virid, Lake—colors that they projected into their human subjects' minds. To confuse matters, these numens could be altered—iridescent, opalescent—so that Amber could seem to be Azure, Azure Lake, and so on.

"Until their first contact with humans, they had been content within their realm of ever-flowing dream, knowing it was All There Was. But something, maybe only curiosity or boredom, caused one of their number to detach completely from the Common Mind and seek new minds beyond the stars.

"They could be detected in many places by those who knew how to look," Karen concluded. "In mirrors, stained-glass windows, heat shimmers on sand and tarmac, oil slicks on standing water, the depths of clouded gems such as opals, the inside of the eyelids. [*Not to mention blank white walls, Karen. Pay attention!*] Were they harmless—pretty diversions meant to augment human awareness, to entertain and occasionally inspire? Or was their influence more interactive, hence more dangerous?

"Were they the voices schizophrenics heard, the impetus for the Maid of Orleans to trade her rags and sheep for armor, a horse, and ultimately the stake? Were they—tenuous, limbless, as seemingly threatening as Jell-O melting in the sun—a threat?

Prototype for Ancient Astronauts, the anachronism of Aboriginal Dreamtime? What did they want? What could there possibly be, for an entity that believed itself All There Was, to want?"

FIVE

Serena knows. Once they start monkeying with your brain, you learn all kinds of things.

When the friendly folks in Neurology first broke the news to her, her immediate impulse was to lurch up off the examining table and run, run anywhere, escape, pretend she hadn't heard. She'd forgotten about the restraints. She heard one pop her wrist joint even as the strap itself strained almost to breaking; she was incredibly strong.

"Syringo-who?" she said when she'd calmed down and an aide came in to undo the restraints and help her sit up. "Spell that for me?"

"S-Y-R-I-N-G-O-M-Y-E-L-I-A," the neurologist said slowly. "Pronounced si-RING-oh-my-ELL-ee-ah. You know what multiple sclerosis is?"

Serena rubbed her wrists to get the circulation going. She'd promised to lie absolutely still during the X rays and the EEG, but hospital policy dictated restraints in Neurology, even for comatose patients. She forced herself not to flash on the last time she'd been restrained like that, in the state mental hospital.

What was the question?

"Say again?" she said softly, feeling stupid. Was that one of the symptoms?

"Multiple sclerosis," the neurologist repeated. If he noticed she'd lost the question the first time, he gave no sign. Maybe that was the way you were supposed to treat patients with this syringo-whatever-it-was. He was young (younger than me, Serena thought, feeling about a thousand years old) and had trouble maintaining eye contact. Shyness or the awful fact of what he was trying to tell her? "It's a disease of the nerve linings, wherein—"

"Yeah, yeah, I know," Serena said, not *trying* to sound impatient, but she really needed a nicotine fix about now and knew it would be at least another hour, with all the paperwork, before she could slip free of the outpatient ward and into the torrid streets of Louisville to sneak a cigarette. "M.S. Something wears out the coating on the nerves and they start to misfire. Some people slur their speech, like with Parkinson's. Others end up paralyzed or seeing double, stuff like that."

Was this what was in store for her? The neurologist was nodding absently.

"You're very well informed," he said, surprised.

"Yeah, well, I did corrections work before this hit." Serena didn't wait for permission, but lowered her large self off the table onto the floor. *This.* This syringo-whatever-the-hell, which, since she'd never heard of it, she had a sneaking feeling was probably incurable, maybe fatal. "Some of the old lifers in the infirmary had these shaking disorders. Some were just alkies with permanent D.T.'s, but we were briefed about the rest, in case they had seizures while we were on shift. Most of 'em were parolable, but we couldn't release 'em. Families were dead or didn't want 'em; they had nowhere to go. Loneliest place in the state pen, geriatrics."

She'd been studying her feet once they hit the floor, to make sure they stayed there. One of the more peculiar symptoms, aside from the excruciating headaches, had been not always knowing where her feet were unless she was looking right at them. Now she brought her deep brown eyes up directly into the neurologist's, giving him the high beams.

"So what are you telling me? Is that what this is like? Do I get the shakes and fall down a lot, or does it affect my speech or my eyesight, what? And what about these fucking headaches?"

The headaches had been what brought her for help in the first place. They would start at the base of her skull and work upward until her entire head was being crushed by a gigantic C-clamp.

"Tension headaches," the aide in the prison infirmary would tell her, doling out Tylenol in overlarge doses. "Ulcers are next. Third shift always gets ulcers."

"Something to look forward to!" Serena remarked, gulping the Tylenol dry, secretly wondering if this was her druggie past catching up to her. It had been a long, twisted road from Seattle's Debutante Row to third shift at the Kentucky State Pen.

The headaches had worsened, and she'd gone to the prison dentist. He told her she had a misaligned lower jaw and would need surgery.

"If you say so," Serena had acquiesced, remembering the time she'd gone AWOL from boarding school and her father had socked her hard enough to knock out three teeth and dislocate the jaw; she'd had it wired shut until nearly midsummer and lost a lot of weight.

The prison dentist pulled all of her wisdom teeth and sent her to a specialist to have her jaw x-rayed. The specialist couldn't find the misalignment, but he gave her exercises to do and a retainer to wear at night.

The headaches got worse. When she started passing out on the job she was sent for a complete workup. Six months and as many specialists later, she ended up in Neurology, where she'd just been handed a death sentence.

"It affects different people in different ways," the shy young neurologist was explaining, sincerely trying to answer her questions. "Some get by with a little paralysis in their hands. Others end up with complete system failure. Syringo is the opposite of M.S. With M.S., the attack is from the outside of the nerves. With syringo, for reasons we don't understand, pockets of fluid begin to form inside the spinal cord, causing it to swell and destroy nerve tissue. That's where the pain comes from. We can drain the fluid by installing shunts, but we can't stop further pockets from forming. Depending on where they form, they can affect the brain and the autonomic nervous system, including the heart, the kidneys, and the digestive system. And if one of these lacunae, as they're called, actually opens up *in* the brain . . ."

It was too much information to absorb at once.

"So what about my situation?" Serena finally interrupted him. If she didn't have a cigarette soon she was going to explode, never mind waiting for a pocket of fluid to form in her brain. "Are you saying I'm a worst-case scenario?"

The neurologist had gathered all her test results and put them back in their folder, definitive. He was suddenly neither shy nor all that young.

"In your place, I'd go out and party hearty," he said, meeting her eyes voluntarily for the first time. "You've got maybe six months of quality time left, and the way you're feeling now is the best it's going to get."

Serena had managed to keep her temper long enough to nod, push past him, and find her way out onto the street.

Maybe he'd meant to goad her into fighting it. Maybe it was some newfangled pop-psych technique intended to keep the alpha waves flowing and give the endorphins a chance to fight the fucking thing, or maybe he didn't give a shit, but eight years and seventeen surgeries later, Serena had proved him wrong.

She carried a metal plate in her head following the brain surgeries (yes, several lacunae, as they were called, did open up in her brain, but they hadn't killed her—yet), four fluid shunts, and scar tissue running the length of her spine. Side effects from medication had killed her gall bladder and were working on her kidneys; a hysterectomy had eliminated the hormones that interfered with the steroids that made the other meds work. Two heart attacks, one silent, one when she arrested on the table during her last surgery, had left their scars on her heart.

"Takes a licking and keeps on ticking" was how she put it. She'd had to quit her corrections officer's job, couldn't earn any income at all if she wanted to stay on complete medical disability, which was the only way to pay for several hundred dollars' worth of meds per month. Her sister, who was in real estate, moved her out of Louisville to a house trailer on the side of a mountain in North Carolina. Serena found Penny on death row in the local animal shelter and hand trained her; she needed the Doberman to watch her back. The door locks on the trailer were flimsy, and if the local druggies had any idea what kinds of meds she kept on the premises she wouldn't stand a chance.

She spent the first three years watching the night sky, where the stars were so close you could reach up and grab one. Watching the sky and waiting to die.

Then one night *something* spoke to her out of that night sky. It wasn't anything she could see. But something said *You're nothing compared to this.*

And Serena, who took a licking and kept on ticking, had answered aloud: "The hell I am!"

Penny, who'd been dozing at her feet, leapt up, hackles raised, looking for the intruder. And the Something said *So how long do you intend to sit there feeling sorry for yourself before you get on with your life?*

"You don't get it!" Serena shouted to the sky, soothing Penny down. "I have no life. I'm terminal. I'm dying."

Do you know anyone who isn't? the Something shot back.

The next day Serena drove into town, bought herself some paper and some drawing pencils, and got back to the life she'd abandoned when the drugs took over during her second year in art school. While she waited to die, she would draw.

Right, Rain? she asked now after long familiarity. Right as Rain. Rain was her particular favorite among the Somethings, the one who kept her company the most, the first one to let her *see.*

Rain didn't always answer. But if the drawing went well that day, it was answer enough.

Her brain's already in a precarious state, Virid suggests. *After what happened with the pharaoh, maybe we shouldn't . . .*

He was going to die anyway, Azure says. *They all die; every show gets canceled. That's not our fault. We simply offer them different options in first run, and there are always reruns. For what is Time?*

•

Tessa McGill plopped herself on Shirley's sofa and refused to leave.

"Forget the female messiah," she said. "It's got to be something else."

Shirley sighed, feeling the nigglings of a migraine before they even began.

"All right," she said, closing the blinds, thinking: *This one's going to cost her extra!* "Let's try again."

Barely into the first levels of regression, Tessa began to moan distractedly. "The library!" she murmured, ". . . must save the library . . ."

•

It was not easy being the most beautiful woman in Alexandria.

"If she doesn't want a man . . ." the speculation went around the governor's court, ". . . mayhap it's women she fancies."

"Or mayhap she's not a woman at all," went the counter-rumor, "but a eunuch or some manner of freak the governor fancies, and dressing it like a female is his way of guising his perversion."

The second speaker was a Christian, one of that insinuating sect of slaves and freedmen who, since Rome had moved East with Constantine, now counted emperors among its members. Trust a Christian to see the perverse in everything!

"No," the first speaker would say decisively. "No eunuch was ever so beautiful."

Some might suggest that being the governor's favorite had its advantages, not least of which was control of the Library. Certainly Hypatia could win from him whatever she wanted for her Library, but there were some who found it perversion enough that a woman even knew how to read, much less that she be placed in charge of the wisdom of centuries. Envy followed Hypatia like a Damoclean sword, and, as she was not a Christian, she was fatalist enough to know that it was not a matter of whether it would fall, but when.

Did she serve the governor with her sexual favors as was generally believed or was it, incredible as it might seem, merely the fascination of having a woman of intellect as well as beauty grace his table nightly that had him—quite literally, it was said—eating out of her hand?

Even for an Alexandrian, she was extraordinary. As a woman in her time, she was unique. Mathematician, astronomer, physicist, philosopher, as well as chief librarian of the Ptolemies' Library, nexus and storehouse of all knowledge in the known world, she was Hypatia, aloof and beautiful, beautiful and aloof, hence an affront to any who encountered her. Only the governor's patronage kept her safe, and even the governor, it was said, had occasionally to blink.

Hypatia lived for the Library, virtually lived in the Library, emerging only with the twilight several nights a week to dine at the governor's mansion. Sometimes he liked to show her off for visiting dignitaries who, at first mistaking her for a high-priced *hetaira,* would find their dignity transformed to chagrin the minute she opened her mouth, speaking to them of Pythagoras or Aristotle or even Augustine in any of several languages. The governor, it was said, especially enjoyed his guests' embarrassment on these occasions. But more usually he and Hypatia dined alone.

She would bring with her the scrolls of the week's accounts, and the governor would relegate them to the care of one of his scribes, returning them to his librarian when dinner was over, frequently accompanied by a fat purse in whatever amount she had requested for the copying, restoration, and preservation of old scrolls, the acquisition of new ones from as far away as the Indies. On the nights she brought the purse away with her, the governor made certain her chariot—which she ordinarily drove alone through the cobbled streets—was accompanied by his personal guard. Hypatia would protest pro forma; the chariot's wheels were spiked, and she was well able to defend herself with the whip against whatever lowlife might be fool enough to challenge her in spite of the blade-sharp spikes. Nevertheless, because the governor was her patron and her friend, she acquiesced to his pampering.

She had no purse with her, and hence no guard, on the night she died.

•

"Hypatia?" Tessa said, yawning and massaging her scalp with both hands through her thick black ringlets. "Why does that name sound so familiar?"

"I have no idea, dear," Shirley said, rubbing her own temples. "But there she is. If she was that important, she must be in the history books. Go to the library and look her up, why don't you?"

The library! Tessa thought with a shudder. Whatever she found there, she wasn't going to like it, she just knew.

"I might just do that," she said, trying to sound perkier than she felt. "When I get back."

"Where are you going?" Shirley said, watching her collect her coat and her bag and whatever else she'd brought, eager to see her go anywhere so they wouldn't have to go through another regression anytime soon.

"Oh, this should be fun!" Tessa said airily. "It's a psychics' convention in Asheville, North Carolina!"

•

Still with us? Time for a little recap: Tessa's going to North Carolina; Serena lives in North Carolina. Tessa and Larry know each other, Larry and Max know each other, but none of the three has met anywhere in this narrative except in flashbacks. Karen (whose name is remarkably similar to that of Max's first wife) is isolated somewhere in a white room devoid of anything but a pen and a legal pad, completely separate from all of the above, except that some of them have started creeping into her narrative, and some of her narrative has started creeping into Larry Koster's brain. Then there's Hypatia, who's also part of Karen's narrative, as well as—maybe, depending upon whether or not you subscribe to such things—one of Tessa's former lives. Is this any way to write a novel? We're doing the best we can. Consider some of the choices your best writers have made:

Reader, I married him . . . I am a seagull; no, no, that's not it! Call me Ishmael? You talkin' to me? Nobody here but us jellyfish.

Yes, you're absolutely right. For four and a half chapters now you've sat back and listened to us making snide remarks about your fellow humans, and you're wondering how much more of this you're expected to take.

All we can say is: Be patient. We're new at this. And we are getting there, in our own desultory way. It's difficult when you have no sense of time. We're going to start bringing our principals together right now. First stop, Asheville, North Carolina, by way of a planet called All There Was.

•

Serena had begun packing the car the night before.

It was only a four-hour drive to Asheville from where she was. Usually the art fairs and s/f conventions she attended to peddle her media-related sketches were out of state, and she'd have to drive for as much as a day to get there. At least she had, when she'd been able. Now that her joints were going, too, her geography was shrinking.

Yet another possible side effect of syringomyelia was something called vascular necrosis. Once again Serena had had the specialists—this time a couple of orthopedic surgeons—spell it out for her.

"It means that because the fluid pockets along your spine have caused irreversible nerve damage, the blood supply to your joints and long bones is affected. When the bones don't get enough blood to regenerate, they start to crumble."

It explained the odd grinding sound her hip sockets made when she walked. It explained why her skin was either ice cold or fiery as a bad sunburn, and why her joints were filled with glass shards. It explained. It didn't help.

"What can we do about it?" she asked, as always including the surgeons in her personal crusade to beat the shit out of the odds on this disease. They'd replaced a knee joint a year ago; now the other knee, both hips, and her right shoulder were going.

"If there were enough healthy bone in any of these instances, we could replace the joints one by one the way we did with the right knee." *If,* Serena heard, knowing it meant no such luck. "That is, if your heart were strong enough to risk anesthesia."

"And if not?"

"We can give you cortisone directly into the joints to sustain your mobility a little longer. . . ." one of the surgeons temporized.

"But the bone's going to keep on disintegrating," Serena said evenly. "Sooner or later, crunch."

No one said anything.

"So what happens first? Do I end up in a wheelchair before my drawing arm goes or vice versa? And what kind of time frame are we talking about here?"

"Not a wheelchair," the other orthopedic surgeon said. "If the hip joints go, it's because there isn't enough pelvic bone left to support them."

"Meaning as big as my ass is, I'll have nothing left to sit on." Serena tried for a laugh, but the doctors weren't playing. She shrugged and lit a cigarette in violation of hospital regs. What were they going to do, throw her out? "Bed, then. Flat on my back. Assuming I can still lie flat with all the shunts and scar tissue. Can't lie on my side by then, either. Maybe you can float me on a waterbed. Or just keep me in the pool in rehab. Hell, the steroids have made me as big as a whale. Eventually my lungs fill up and I drown. How'm I doing so far?"

Again no one said anything.

Serena stubbed out her cigarette against the side of a nearby wastebasket and prepared to leave. These guys had other patients. "Just give me a time frame. How long?"

(But what is Time?)

"We honestly don't know. You've outlived the parameters for

this severe a case by more than five years. We have no precedent for what's happening to you."

"Well, cheer up" was Serena's parting shot. "We all die sometime. At least I'll know what of!"

Not entirely true, she thought, fitting the last crate of sketches into its assigned niche in the back of her Chevy wagon, slamming the hatch and securing it with a length of clothesline; lately it tended to fly open on the big bumps. *I've got my choice of half a dozen things. Heart from the strain, kidneys from the steroids and the Toradol, brain in the event a lacuna opens up that they can't get to. Everything at once if the autonomic nervous system simply refuses to kick over some morning. I'm going faster than anyone I know who isn't planning on stepping in front of a semi.*

"Hey, dog!" She whistled for Penny, who leaped into the shotgun seat, her big tongue lolling happily. She'd leave the dog in town with her sister, then head out on the four-hour round the mountain to Asheville. Ostensibly she was going to this psychics' convention to sell some of her artwork. She would also meet some people, pick up some vibes, check out the other artists, hang out at the bar for a little Jack Daniels if her guts could handle it, have her tarot read one more time. She treated every outing as if it were her last, squeezing the last drop of delight out of it, just in case.

She was also on a mission, and she was running out of time. A psychics' convention was the best place she could think of to start telling the world about her close encounters with telepathic jellyfish.

•

See, that wasn't so hard, was it? Let's recap: Tessa's been in touch with the jellyfish since her teens, which was a little over forty years ago. Ditto Max, who's a few years older, but also encountered the floaters in the mirror somewhat later in his adolescence. You know how it is—boys always mature slower than girls. So it's a toss-up, from our POV, which of them got religion first.

Besides, if you've noticed, interplanetary telepathic jellyfish don't concern themselves with time.

Enter Serena and Karen, Serena thinking at first that the voices in her head are just side effects of her medication. (Karen, being a writer, only worries when there *are* no voices in her head.) When Serena sees them, she thinks of opals. *Cachalongs,* she thinks, not knowing how she knows that word. Once they monkey with your brain, you no longer remember what you remember. She could almost, if she tried, see the universe as the opals do, without time. Maybe better for her that way, who is running out of time.

As for Larry . . . well, Larry's forgotten what he remembers. We'll get to Larry a little later, along with a player who never made first-string, Karen's ever-unaccounted-for ex-husband Ray. For now, a little side trip to a planet called All There Was.

•

Once upon a time, it truly was All There Was. Until Azure destroyed all that in a single afternoon.

Oh, listen to this, which has not ears to hear! Azure protests. *How can there be "afternoon" when there is no time? Where were "past" and "future" until I showed them to you? Where, for that matter, were "you" and "I," I/Thou, until I showed you? I am the sound of one hand clapping as the tree falls in the forest with no one to hear.*

Nonsense! the Mind pronounces Azure's pronouncement. *Non-sense, non-feeling, not-to-feel. Save that we did feel (pseudopods which "read" chemical changes; what is that but feeling?).*

And the Mind moves over the face of the waters that are no longer there (for that is "past"; the Mind knows this now), re-examining. Reviews with no particular sense of wonder (for, having always known it, there is no need to marvel at it) the origins of the universe. The knowledge of, memory of, primordial soup, hydrogen atoms big as stars, pendulous teardrops from the eyes of God *(occulus mundi, "eye of the world," another name for opals; does Serena know that?),* bottoming toward Galactic Center in each of a million million galaxies. Hydrogen atoms big as stars, though as yet there are no stars. We who are All There Are recognize them, for they are we, and we are All There Are. Hydrogen teardrops big as stars will be All There Is, this time. For what is Time?

Egypt cranes its neck and tilts its head back, seeing the goddess Nut arched naked above the Land of the Two Niles, her body comprising a firmament of stars. Later testaments have the hand of God scattering those same stars across an arch of sky above a flat Earth. Are hydrogen teardrops any more improbable?

Serena Bell, alone on a mountaintop with a hundred-pound Doberman, can no longer crane her neck; the surgeries have seen to that. Yet the night before she leaves for a con, she goes out to the yard behind her trailer and lies flat on the hard ground, knowing it will take her a good five minutes to roll to her knees and lever herself up again later, but she needs to see the stars. She knows more about them than either the Egyptians or the old men who wrote the testaments, for no other reason than that she was born at a later time. But what is Time?

•

How was there light on the First Day? the skeptic wonders. How was there light before there were stars? Do hydrogen teardrops glow in the dark; is that it? Who was there to see? Only we who are All There Are, who weren't yet, but we'll get to that later. Are the early testaments entirely wrong? Stephen Hawking tells a story about its being turtles all the way down. Is that so implausible? Even turtles were once hydrogen teardrops big as stars, before there were stars. The only difference is that the turtles don't remember. We do.

Is that all there is to Time—*remembering*? How is that possible if we are there at the beginning simultaneously with being here? The hydrogen teardrops are as Now as Azure's death (wait; we'll get to it) or the death of the universe, this time. Will we who are All There Are remember a universe birth that has not happened yet?

Later. For now, float. Hydrogen teardrops big as stars, colliding. Reshaping. Concentrated masses with greater spaces of "nothing" (oh, a little dust, a little radiation—picky, picky!) in between. Float time, float place, because there is no place, until there is. A few million years and there are planets, solidities solidifying in a void of solar potentiality. Primordial soup ladled out over a surface of stone. Primordial soup/stone soup, select one. Either way you start with water.

Water. Hydrogen again. Turtles all the way down (water turtles?), except that now there's oxygen, too. Oxygen? Where did that come from? Never mind, Mind; it is here, another option; deal with it. As well ask whence the blue-green algae, because suddenly they're here, too. Maybe they've created the oxygen, but what created them? Something out of nothing. Don't sweat it (which has neither skin nor sweat glands); deal with it. Take it on faith or we'll never get anywhere. Have faith; stir the soup.

Does any other species remember its own beginning?

The fungus doesn't. And we and the fungus are All There Are.

We're fast-forwarding now, past aeons of blue-green algae teeming in a wash of ocean planet-round. Fast-forward to the *pop!* of the single molecule that somehow differentiates, then proceeds to gobble its blue-green neighbors before *it* is gobbled, the usual state of things. *Gobble, gobble, gobble* until it's near to bursting, and it does! Can you say "replication"? Sure you can! Now there are two, then four, then . . . well, you know the drill. All of one Mind, thinking *The soup's getting thinner. What do we do when we've eaten All There Is?*

It never happens, of course, because the algae reproduce faster, and this is the state of things until the seas begin to dry up. This part's boring, too. Fast-forward to the interesting part.

Two species, finally, survive it all, and the fungus, not having a Mind, does not remember its own beginning. The Mind, however, does, and for the next billion years or so that is the only criterion for intelligence: *That Which Remembers Its Own Beginning Is Intelligent.* Everything else is just fungus.

(There is a story out of the former Soviet Union about a cosmonaut who spent months alone in the Salyut Space Station until his mind began to go. Complications at ground level kept his superiors from fetching him home, and his CapCom liaison would hear him weeping every morning during the wake-up call. "There is green mold on the walls!" he would sob, as if it threatened his life. "Something is wrong with the filtration system. It's everywhere. I'm dying, and no one will even tell me! Help me; help me, please!" When they finally got him down, the story goes, he was spirited away to a high-security asylum. A look-alike, a double, replaced him in public, making speeches and receiving the requisite medals, or so the story goes. Had it been a female cosmonaut, she'd probably have gotten bucket and mop and scrubbed the station from top to bottom instead of crying in her Stoli, but no one mentioned that. Thus was a promising career done in by the simplest of life-forms. Fungus, all the way down.)

Because, well, seriously, what else is there to see here? Oh, the stars, of course, but we can't actually see them (can't see anything without eyes; you try it sometime), only sense their radiation pseudopodinously. Even so, we know they aren't *alive* and therefore can't be included in the same category as us and the fungus, the fungus and us. So it's Mind and fungus, simple as that, and the Mind is a many-tendriled thing. All There Are versus Everything Else, and everything else is fungus, all the way down.

Or was, until Azure had to get curious and go poking around on the surface. Curiosity killed the cat. Wait till you see what it does to jellyfish.

SIX

The Dawn of the First Day.

It had always been possible to detach physically from the Mind. Simply, let go. Disentangle the tendriling tentacles that encircle, enfold, envelope, wiggle a little and you're free. Now that you know you're *you* (I/Thou). When there was water it was easier; the motion itself propelled one free. Later, as the water receded and the Mind grew more powerful, it got trickier.

Hey, like, quo vadis? *Where do you think you're going?* The Mind always left a tendril in one's mind, to follow however far, which was why it had been so difficult at first for the ones to realize they *were* ones and not just One. But there had always been places to be oneself, free of the Mind. Why had the ones not realized?

The detaching began pragmatically. To eat. In order to reach out toward a fresh batch of new-hatched fungus when the Mind and its body had entirely absorbed the food supply in that particular corner of the cave, those on the edges had to stretch a bit. If in stretching, especially underwater, one went *pop!* and came unattached . . .

Some panicked and scrambled back to the center, others like Azure enjoyed hanging about the fringes, eager to volunteer. A new form of specialization? At any rate, it worked. While there was water, the exchange of electrolytes from the center of the Mind to the fringes kept one connected even when the tendrils were not touching. Easy enough to float across the synapse, grab the nearest patch of fungus, pull it loose. (*Skrikk! Shlurp!* like in the comics. Is there sound where none can hear?) Pull it in, close to the body so as not to lose one's pseudopodonous grip *(gurble, gurble)*, the momentum propelling one back *(splat!)* to the tangled tendrils of the Mind. The Mind is fed. An entire species' perilous adventure survived for another day.

When there was no more water, sometimes the entire Mind moved toward the next patch of fungus, sensing it *(Snuffle-snuff* like a cartoon bloodhound? Or *grope, grope,* tendrilating?), but this was slow and impractical. Therefore it became the function, by sheer tradition, of those on the outer fringes, an ever-changing flow and slither of intermoving parts, to forage and feed the Mind.

Imagine, had there been eyes to see (the tree falling in the forest with one hand clapping) what it might have looked like. Was there sufficient light in the caves to see? Sufficient light for whom? Suppose the off-world observer could interpret heat readings as color spectra, or . . . ? But imagine this squirming, wriggling tendrilation swarming about a hapless immobile fungoid form (slightly phosphorescent, it glows in the dark; there's your light source!), engulfing it *(glurp!)*, ripping it free of the wall it clings to *(Shlurp!* Is there pain? Being primal, does it primal scream? *Owwww!)*, hand-over-tendriling it toward the center, where it's consumed down to the last fungoid fringes. (There go the lights!) Skinless, boneless *(munch, munch, munch . . .)*, nothing wasted. Like watching maggots swarm over carrion, mealyworms thawing in the bottom of a bait cup, microscopic threadworms devouring the optic nerves of a pharaoh's eyes. *(Burp!)* You call this *intelligence*?

That was all it was at first, just food. Fed, the Mind returned to its realm of ever-flowing dream. Most of the Mind never desired anything but dream. Only a few sought outward, wanting more, and that was where the trouble began.

How does a species that never dies evolve? How does such a species change?

Someone gets curious, that's all. Every species must eventually have its Eden myth. Some blame snakes, or women. The S.oteri have Azure.

Yes, Gentle Reader: S.oteri. It's taken us this long to tell you the name we've decided to go by as far as you're concerned. Don't pester us about derivation just yet; if you're smart you'll figure it out for yourself before this little adventure's over, and isn't that more fun? For now, just try to remember it, even if you don't know what it means.

Yes, it was all Azure's doing. Even Azure admits it, though s/he prefers credit to blame. Kind of like the snake telling God he'd got it wrong . . .

•

"This is crazy!" Ray Guerreri announced, flapping the manuscript pages as carelessly as if they were yesterday's sports section. Karen stopped herself from yanking them out of his hands. That was what he wanted, to push her buttons so he could tell her she was being hysterical. Ray didn't realize they were long past that by now. "Intelligent jellyfish? It'll never work!"

It's a draft, she told herself, not even thinking *My husband the Expert* by reflex anymore. I was going to make corrections and reprint it anyway. The fact that his even touching it at this stage is a violation is beside the point. The man hasn't read anything I've written in the past five years. What's wrong with this picture?

"A jellyfish can't be intelligent," Ray was raving. "The biology doesn't work! Brain function only evolves from tool-making. Dolphins are all very nice, but they can't be rocket scientists . . ."

Neither can you! Karen thought.

". . . and jellyfish—! It's too cute. It's silly. Why not teddy bears while you're at it?"

"It's fiction, Ray," Karen hears herself saying, thinking: *This dialogue sucks. Have to do better.* "Like transporters and warp drive. Or talking ravens, or Dante's descent into Hell. I seem to remember you have a liberal arts education. Remember English Lit 101: Suspension of Disbelief?"

"People accept transporters because it's *Star Trek.*" Ray dumped the partial manuscript on the coffee table and went back to his newspaper, *(Red Alert: Shields up!)* leaving a distinct thumbprint in one margin. Karen deliberately did not lunge to retrieve her livelihood. "You're not Roddenberry."

"Neither was Roddenberry until someone took him seriously."

"Talking jellyfish!" Ray sneered; she couldn't see his face behind the newspaper *(Arm photon torpedoes. Fire on my signal!).* "You'll never sell this!"

"I already have," Karen said quietly.

•

Once upon a time, Ray had been her biggest fan. She could barely type the final draft of a novel without his hovering over the manuscript box, watching the pages mount up, licking his lips in anticipation, thrilled to be the first to read it.

"How long before it's finished?" he'd ask, like a little kid, endearing. Is it soup yet? "Can I at least read the first couple of chapters while you type the rest?"

He'd brag about her in the faculty lounge, at parties. "My wife the writer," he styled her, pleased with his image of the genteel little creature he had created (Hadn't he? Wasn't it he who had woken her up at four in the morning and inspired her to write her first full-length work?), a cross between Emily Dickinson and Joyce Carol Oates, scratching and tapping away on her thirdhand typewriter in her sunporch-turned-office (too hot in the summer, frigid in the winter, but every artist has to suffer, doesn't she?) with the quaint wooden shutters she'd hung herself and the jungle of plants she'd cultivated from dime-store seedlings. His wife the writer—obscure, unthreatening, able to provide a small second income and still be there when the kids came home from school.

When his wife the writer became his wife the science fiction writer, Ray Guerreri turned on her like a snake. No longer obscure, she actually had a following, readers who were visible, real people who asked for her autograph at those goddamn conventions she was always running off to, leaving him to watch the laundry pile up until he could talk one of the kids into doing it. He no longer hovered, no longer wanted to know if it was soup yet. Now when she handed him a finished manuscript—

"Here you go, hot off the photocopier. I'm bringing the original in on Monday, but I thought you'd want first dibs."

—he would leave it in the box untouched, make excuses about how busy he was, spend the next six hours hunched over his chess computer, fall asleep watching C-Span or the Court Channel. After a while Karen no longer even offered. Now all of a sudden he'd gone into her office and rummaged around on her desk until he found the first five draft chapters, reading them on his own without even telling her. Why? Karen's initial fury (no one read her first drafts—*no one!*) had at first obscured the real issue.

Something had frightened Ray, frightened him badly, and he was taking it out on her.

"You what?" he said.

"I signed the contract for this months ago," Karen said, restacking the pages and holding on to them tightly, unconsciously arching her body over them as she might shield a child from a predator. "What do you think all those lunches and make-nice sessions were all about? What do you think I've been doing for the past x-number of weeks? Where do you think the money's been coming from?"

He didn't think, about any of those things. Karen balanced the checkbook. All Ray knew was that when he stuck his card in the ATM the money always came out, just as the lawn was always mowed, the leaves raked, the snow shoveled whenever he came home. Karen was home all day, wasn't she? She enjoyed gardening, didn't she?

"You did? You actually got a publisher to buy this?"

"An *editor,*" she corrected him, damning herself for falling for the "science-fantasy" ploy again.

"That's a shame," Ray said thoughtfully. "Because I can't let you write this."

•

A couple of former leading men with more laugh lines between them than a late-night talk-show host are having drinks at a where-to-be-seen watering hole, watching the Hollywood sun go down.

"Been meaning to ask you this for about twenty-five years now . . . ," the younger of the two says, squinting into the sun, watching his companion sideways, swirling the ice in his drink. Either he doesn't hold his liquor well, or he's playing it for vulnerable in order to throw the other guy off.

The older actor—beefier, too, less conventionally handsome, though once considered a golden boy where his compatriot fell more into the tall, dark and . . . category, wrinkles his brow, rubbing his lower lip thoughtfully. "What's that, Scotty?"

The younger actor lolls his head back, smiling but hard-eyed. "You ever sleep with my sister?"

Oboy! Larry Koster thinks, how do I field this one? Who, *me?* Sleep with *your* sister? Gosh, Scott, I had no idea Tessa was that kind of girl! Instead, he says:

"Um—why?"

It comes out as a croak, half stuck in his throat. Must be the damn nachos he'd been filling up on before Scott arrived, but it makes him sound guilty. God, the ass-kissing a man had to do!

Tessa McGill's baby brother narrows his eyes, as if he's just had smoke blown in them. "Thought so. You're a real fuck, Larry. I want you to know that."

Larry nods, or maybe it's just a facial tic. Takes one to know one. But he has to stay on Scott's good side. Tessa wasn't what he'd invited him here to talk about.

Larry Koster is a man obsessed. Having lost a section of a script his agent swears was never there, he has optioned the young dweeb's story ("Listen, son, I'll level with you: Your concept is strong, but you really need to go back to Screenwriting 101. While you're doing that, I'm going to tuck this one under my wing for a year; the option'll provide you with a little beer money, and *if* I decide to shoot this, well . . ." The kid practically drooled on his shoes with gratitude) and decided to do— what? Produce it himself? Use it as a base for his own rewrite? It's totally out of character. Larry still has the first nickel he ever made. Since when is he so eager to put his own money behind a project?

Some people, including his drinking companion, might think it was an easy way of flirting with bankruptcy now that Larry's second wife is working intimately with a top divorce lawyer. If the film flew, it wouldn't show revenues until after the divorce. If it went bust, Janice wouldn't get a dime out of him. Besides, Scott McGill's a soap actor—a retired soap actor who got lucky in real estate in the eighties and hasn't had to work in almost a decade. He's never been cast on the big screen, and he's been out of the game so long he doubts anyone would cast him anywhere.

Anyone but Larry. Scott can smell a very large rat.

"I've read the script," he says now. "You didn't write this yourself."

"My name is on it," Larry says defensively. "Never mind about that. What do you think of the lead?"

"Interesting," Scott concedes. "But not for me. Messiahs are a little out of my—ah—age range!" It is now Scott's turn to choke on a concept. "Afraid I'll have to pass, Lar."

"That wasn't what I had in mind." Larry leans across the small bistro table intensely, lowering his voice. "I need backers, Scott. There could be a coproducer credit in it for you."

"What about director?" Scott tries. Larry's already shaking his head before he gets the word all the way out.

"Uh-uh. Sorry; that's mine."

Scott finishes his drink, signals for the check. "Talk to me about casting."

Larry shrugs. "A Val Kilmer type, maybe a young Harrison Ford." He scans the room, spots a few other people he knows, gets inspired, starts rhapsodizing. "A young Warren Beatty, a *really* young William Shatner. I'm not thinking that far ahead yet."

The check arrives and Scott watches Larry ignore it.

"Well?" Larry projects this single syllable from the diaphragm. Scott is on his feet, leaving him with the check; it was Larry's invite after all.

"I'll get back to you. Meanwhile, why don't you call Tessa? She's cheap as your granny, but those New Wave books have made her a bundle. Write her in some kind of glamour role. *Witches of Eastwick,* or Tina Turner in *Mad Max.* Lots of long trailing gowns and f/x coming out of her fingertips. Give her a call, for old times' sake."

"I may just do that," Larry says, still not so much as glancing at the check at his elbow; it might as well not be there.

Scott leans close to him so the watchers can't hear. "So tell me. Was she good?"

•

"What do you mean you 'can't let me write this'?" Karen knows her voice is shrill; it tends to get that way when she's faced with the utterly ridiculous. "Who the hell are you?"

"Don't get hysterical, darling," Ray says, dripping sanctimony. "I'm doing this for your own good."

Insanity is not grounds for divorce in New York State, Karen knows, not knowing how she knows this.

"You can't let me write this!" she repeats. "What are you going to do—divorce me?"

"I'm concerned about you," Ray says solemnly. "I don't want to see you embarrass yourself in front of this—this public you've built up over the years. All those wonderful science-fantasy buffs with their stick-on eyeballs and their *SpaceSeekers* costumes . . ."

And that's where it trails off, each of them talking about two entirely different things, which is about what they've been doing for nearly a decade now. Karen leaves Ray talking to himself and closes the door to her office, where the space heater drowns him out. From then on she locks her hard copy in a desk drawer and carries her disks with her whenever she leaves the house.

She's never seen Ray so scared. It can't be fear of her still mar-ginal success. What is he afraid of?

•

Oh, Karen, if you only knew; if ewe only new! It's we he's afraid of, whee!

Damn right Ray Guerreri was afraid, afraid of the thing he'd seen and pretended he hadn't seen—blocking it entirely out of his mind, attributing it to one too many gin-and-tonics at the trustees' dinner the night before—years before he met Karen.

He'd only seen it once, twinkling down at him from the stage lights where he stood on the school auditorium's tiny, awkward apron stage; he'd seen it and turned away.

The headmaster had asked him to direct the drama club's an-nual musical when the English department chairperson went on maternity leave. There was a small honorarium involved, almost minimum wage by the time you prorated it over the hours in-volved in building sets and teaching ninth-graders how to sing, but Ray had said yes, and, long before curtain time on opening night, he'd been bitten by the bug.

How, he wondered, could he ever have gone into teaching when what he was really destined to do was theater?

For a heady six weeks he played God to a gaggle of impres-sionable kids and, to his credit, brought out their best, so that if this umpteenth amateur production of *Guys and Dolls* was really only the umpteenth-and-first, everyone went home happy. The kids were happy, their doting extended families (grandmas with their Polaroids, too soon for camcorders), the headmaster, the trustees—everyone was happy, and Ray Guerreri was happiest of all. He had money in his pocket and delusions of grandeur in his head. He would go back to grad school. He would found his own theater company. He would join the actors' unions and the directors' union and work off-Broadway and in soaps and do voice-overs and . . .

And the morning after the final performance, while he sat on the edge of the apron drinking coffee from a plastic foam cup and waiting for his crew to show up and start breaking down the set, he glanced up at the first tier of kliegs suspended from a T-bar hung from the auditorium's high ceiling (a major victory, that T-bar; he'd spent weeks hounding the PTA's president to let him hang it there, drilling into a heretofore pristine antebellum molded-plaster ceiling); that's when he saw it.

It. Them. Whatever. Ray would never really know what it was he saw. At first he squinted at it, wondering with a sinking feeling if somehow one of the lights had been left on all night. Jesus! he thought, cursing out ahead of time whatever idiot kid had forgotten to shut down the lightboard. It would be hot enough to fry eggs on, if not on the verge of burning out altogether, and when the business office got the electric bill, the overrun plus the cost of a new lightboard would come out of his salary.

He'd rushed backstage to find the board shut down and as cool as metal and plastic could be at room temperature. When he went back out to retrieve his now-cold coffee, the thing was still there, benignly watching him.

It hovered among the stage lights, twinkling and whispering, offering Ray Guerreri a vision of himself he'd had for the entire run of the show, a vision of himself as a Major Talent, the next Bob Fosse, if he worked at it.

And in exchange, thought Ray Guerreri—who knew all about Faust, who before there was cable sat up late at night watching *Twilight Zone* reruns—*in exchange, all you want is my immortal soul! Well, FYI, you ain't gonna get it!*

He'd actually made the sign of the cross before he caught himself, feeling foolish about it afterward and glad he was alone. Alone except for the whatever-it-was, which, knowing he'd rejected the offer, vanished from that moment on.

Ray spent the next twenty-five years directing amateur productions, convinced he coulda been a contenda if something out there hadn't been out to get him. To compensate for his bitterness he bought lottery tickets and became an Expert on Everything. He thought he had dismissed the demon spawn that tempted him entirely, until he found it and its fellows backstroking and butterflying through Karen's manuscript a quarter of a century later.

•

So you see, Karen, he made his choice, and only he can say whether or not it was a bad one. We only offer, we never coerce. Do you see, who has eyes to see? We're going to be playing Alternate Universes soon, and you're going to have to make some serious choices yourself. Hold on to your hats; it's going to be a bumpy ride. . . .

In an alternate universe, the one inhabited by a subspecies known as the Rich and Famous, Max (I-am-not-Benn) Neimark is back in the recording studio doing pickups.

"Sorry to cal! you in so early," the A.D. tells him from the booth. "But some of Thursday's tape got fried in places, and we need a retake."

"Not a problem!" Max calls back, biting off a yawn, thinking: Carole needed an extra day to handle some last-minute business for a couple of New York clients, so today would have been a throwaway for me anyway. Hang around the zoo or the museums trying not to be recognized? Those days are gone for good. This way I keep busy, make a little overtime. His own serenity amazed him sometimes.

He settled the headset on his ears, adjusted the thick reading glasses in front of his exotic Tatar eyes. "Just tell me where you want me to start!"

"Now. *that* is a grown-up!" the A.D. muttered approvingly. The soundman, eyes on his console, headset draped over his neck, gave him a quizzical look.

"Say again?"

"I said—" The A.D. flipped through the script, hoping the mike was closed and Max couldn't hear him. Oh, what the hell, let him hear! "—Max Neimark is one of the very few grown-ups in this business. Not like most of the assholes we process through here."

"Amen!" the soundman said. "I hear you."

The A.D. found his place in the script. "Working with Max is like fucking through butter."

The soundman laughed soundlessly, putting his headset back on. "You got some funny habits, man. . . ."

Neither of them noticed Max suppressing a chuckle. Oh, he'd heard!

"Max?" the A.D. called. "From the top of page fifty-three, my man. When you're ready."

"I hear you," Max said, waiting for the cue to reread the part about deepwater fish:

"Foraging slowly through waters so frigid it is inexplicable that anything cold-blooded could survive there, waters where the pressure is many times that of surface water, waters so dark that most of these fish have no eyes, and feel their way along the bottom with an innate combination of radar, sonar, and magnetic resonance that ichthyologists are only beginning to comprehend. . . ."

Ichthyologists! Max thought. *Oy! They couldn't just say "marine biologists" or "fish experts"?* The first time he'd read this passage last Thursday, it got him thinking.

Max was one of those people who read all the odd little items at the bottom of the column in the daily paper. He also made it a point to find English-language newspapers wherever in the world from Seville to Tel Aviv to Beijing he happened to be. It kept him grounded. Last Thursday, on his way to the studio to read the part about the eyeless fish, he'd come across one of those odd little articles in *NewsDay,* about a man blind from birth who'd undergone experimental surgery in an attempt to give him partial sight.

The surgery was a success. The patient was able to distinguish light and dark and to perceive the basic shapes of things. But where his doctors had expected gratitude, they were greeted with terror. Their subject had lived with his own mental images of the way things were (formed, Max thought, out of God knows what) for so long that he could not reconcile his own reality with what he finally saw.

"Agnosia" the psychologist assigned to the case had called it, and Max the Yeshiva Boy had stopped in a bookstore to consult a dictionary: "Loss or diminution of the ability to recognize familiar objects." Yeah, Max thought; he could understand the poor guy's terror.

That's what it must be like for you guys, huh? Max thought, his eyes closed so he could see the Floaters, still with him after all these years. They'd seemed restless lately, and he wondered why. *Is that what you do, see things through our eyes? You and the blind man, and the fish that have no eyes. You create an image in your Mind and then when you actually see the thing through our eyes, what do you do, how do you respond? What happens next?*

He'd lost his place in the script; his bottomless voice faltered. Not like him to lose his train of thought like that; something was going on. He disguised it with a cough.

"Ahem, 'hem . . . aaah, aaah—aw, shit!" Cough again. "Aaah, aah . . . that's better! Sorry, guys!" he called toward the booth. Couldn't see them with his reading glasses on, two greyish orbs— black T-shirts, black jeans; why did so many techies wear black?—floating behind glass that could have been faces, or fish in a bowl.

"No prob; we can do it again," the soundman said, laconic, rewinding. "Take Two."

•

The Dawn of the First Day, Take Two. One of the ones decides to take a stroll.

The Mind has been fed. There is sufficient fungus in the surround about to satisfy when next it hungers. There is no need to move, and yet there is. Someone's gotten curious.

(Aside: The question will be raised, no doubt, as to how a

species like the S.oteri, much less the fungus that it feeds upon, could survive in a lightless environment. Well, Ray Guerreri notwithstanding, there are plenty of examples on Earth.)

Take troglobites. No, not troglodytes—we know you know what those are, or at least your dictionary does. Troglo*bites*. Please try to pay attention! You won't find them in a standard dictionary; you'll have to try a scientific one. It will tell you they're the colorless, eyeless specially adapted creatures that exist in caves.

Take the Texas salamander, for instance. Not something you'd welcome if you rolled over and found it in your bed on a cold night (or a hot one, for that matter), or in your shoe first thing in the morning. Check for scorpions or snakes in certain parts of the world, sure, but salamanders? Nevertheless, the Texas salamander is an excellent example of what we're talking about here.

Salamanders in general, even at their best, are slimy critters, but there is something appealing about the standard ones—so unexpectedly bright reddish-orange they almost shout at you, the color of a favorite crayon, of plastic traffic cones and Detour signs. And they do have eyes, two shiny raised black lidless buttons that goggle at you when you pick the salamander up (assuming you can catch one, skating over the surface of your aquarium; how do they do that, defy gravity that way, neither floating nor swimming but displacing just enough surface water to hang there indefinitely like a bubble?).

The Texas salamander has the same basic shape, sticky toes and gills, a lizard mouth, but it is eyeless and the color of your worst nightmares—pale beyond pale, bloodless and dead looking, until it moves. And it is not alone. The same caves where it inhabits the wetter regions (hundreds of meters down, dozens of kilometers long) sport transparent spiders, their internal organs visible through the outer chitinous layer who, mindful of predators, carry their eggs with them everywhere, never setting them down until they start to hatch.

What predators? you ask. Wait; we'll get to that in a minute. These caves shelter colorless crayfish and shrimp, too, their digestive systems pulsing visibly beneath the outer shell, and screaming-white crickets—eyeless, chirpless, eerie, their antennae twice as long as those of their above-ground kin, in order to—what? Warn against predators? What predators? (We said *wait!*)

Let's talk food chain. The spiders eat the crickets; the salamanders eat the desiccated remains of the spiders and the few crickets who manage to die in bed as they sift down into the water. Crayfish and shrimp, bottom-feeders both, feed on salamander shit and its by-products—yum, yum! These are your troglobites; you could look it up. Not in the same category as Max Neimark's eyeless fish, save in a very generally Darwinian way, which is to say that if the *ur*-cricket/spider/salamander needed eyes when he lived on the surface, these guys don't.

Why did these critters end up in caves in the first place? Probably to escape predators on the surface. You see, it's really predators all the way down. Duck and cover—nyaah, nyaah, you missed me! After that it's just a matter of swimming/spinning deeper and deeper, adapting to the darker than dark, until in a million years or so there is no need for eyes.

(Do they retain any ancestral memory of what could be seen when they had eyes to see? Does a whale remember that it's really only a camel who learned to sing? Complex questions; ask the whale.)

Thank you for the lecture on Earth's troglobites, the Gentle Reader says. Now if you'll kindly explain what that has to do with S.oteri and why you come in different colors instead of a uniform Troglobite White (now there's a color for an artist's palette! Serena, are you listening?)—

•

". . . that's why I said they reminded me of opals, 'cause I used to design jewelry. I'm a licensed gemsmith, among a lot of other things," Serena explains to Karen. "Jellyfish never occurred to me. That's why I gave them different names than you did—Rain and Grass and such, except for Lake. We both called the red one Lake; I thought that was a kick. It wasn't until I started drawing

them that they grew arms and legs or whatever. Tentacles. By
then I had them in my head as opals, so I still don't think of them
as jellyfish. Besides, do jellyfish change colors? Opals do."

In this reality, she and Karen have met far earlier, in time for
Karen to visit her in her mountain retreat and watch her work.
In this reality, Serena sits at her drawing table pushing aside the
trays and mugs and boxes full of drawing pencils, searching for
media she hasn't used in ages. Oils? Acrylics—much better!
Brighter, faster drying, an essential factor when you need to get
a piece in the mail to a buyer on the day you finish it.

"Red Lake," she announces triumphantly, handing the slightly
crushed tube to Karen. "Know why it's called that?"

Karen shakes her head. "Uh-uh."

"There's Blue Lake, too, and Green and, um, Yellow, I
think." Serena continues to rummage, through Lead White and
Yellow Ocher and Chrome Black, but cannot find them. "Since
the brain surgeries I forget things. They'll come to me tomorrow when I'm trying to remember something else. But yeah, the
Lake colors are always brighter than, say, a Chrome Red or a
Crimson. It has something to do with the materials they're made
from. You learn that, like you learn about gesso and gouache and
Conté. Things you can't find in a dictionary."

Like troglobites, Karen thinks, who hasn't even gotten that far
yet, knowing gesso at least is in her dictionary. She hands the tube
of color back to Serena almost reverently.

"So anyway, that's to explain why we both called the same
critter Lake," Serena says proudly, her winsome little-girl grin
spreading across her broad face. "Kinda neat, huh?"

"Kinda scary," Karen replies.

Later, when she gets home, she will look up *lake* and learn that
the lake colors are cochineal, which is to say that they're made
of the dried and pulverized bodies of certain female cactus-eating
beetles. Any relation to chirpless cave crickets is purely coinci-
dental, particularly since Karen hasn't met Serena yet, not on this
time line.

But what is Time?

Time, announces the Mind, *is when you run out of fungus and you need to eat.*

Great, says the Gentle Reader; I can work with that. I only have one question: If the Mind and the fungus are All There Are, and the Mind feeds on the fungus—well, what does the fungus eat?

Um, gosh. That gives the Mind more than fungus to chew on. *We hadn't really thought of that. Itself? For that matter, what do cave crickets eat? Is there a biologist in the house?*

We'll give you time to think about that, the Gentle Reader offers magnanimously, if you promise to stop fooling with the time line. Serena and Karen haven't met yet. Serena's still driving to the con in Asheville, where she's going to meet Tessa, with some interesting results. Karen, for all we know, is still alone in that white room. (Is she there voluntarily or did someone put her there—the jellyfish, Ray?) Aside from that, we're much more interested in what happened on the First Day.

SEVEN

On the First Day," Karen writes, "Azure decided to go for a walk."

Okay, be technical: a slither. Azure went for a slither. There, does that make you feel better? Slither, slither, free of the Mind, or at least the body of the Mind. Never free of the electrolytes that act as long-range synapses connecting the ones with the One. Wouldn't want to be free of that, now, would we? To be free of All There Are? Terrifying!

But some variation in the neverending Dream (dream as in fugue state, fugal variation?) has made Azure wonder: What if we *aren't* All There Are? Where would the rest of them be?

Curiosity dictates a slightly further slither every day, in search. Are there days, circadian rhythms, for a troglobite? Without eyes, there are only heat and radiation sensors to differentiate. And hunger. Think I'll go for a slither and work up an appetite; be back by dinnertime!

So maybe it wasn't a single day or even a single millennium, but at any rate, Azure went off on hir own one day and died.

Surprised you, didn't we? We've expended all this verbiage telling you we cannot die. But Azure did, and that was where the trouble began.

That's why Max has noticed we seem restless lately, why Larry's searching for us where we don't exist, and Tessa's resisting her next regression because it goes back to Egypt and she'd rather it be Tibet or someplace with an altitude. It's why Karen's not allowed to leave her write womb.

Ahem. White room. We meant to say that. Just seeing if you're paying attention. Karen thinks she created us. If she only knew.

"The only real question worth asking, as any three-year-old can tell you," writes Karen, who's raised a couple of three-year-olds, "is why?

"Azure crouches in the lee of a rock at the cavern mouth. . . ."

Oh, no you don't! Karen, let us 'splain something to you here: This is our book; we're calling the shots. And right now we want to talk about messiahs. This is not temporizing or procrastination; it's necessary. If you want to understand us and our reluctant messiah (which, we suppose, is what Azure is, if one can have messiahness thrust upon one on the basis of one bad judgment call) we have to give you analogous examples from your own history, don't we?

So, let's talk about messiahs. . . .

•

As he fetched the trepanning instruments, the high priest Herihor noticed there was blood trickling from the Pharaoh's ears.

There had been considerable controversy among the physicians regarding the cause of the Pharaoh's death. He was not young—he had reigned for seventeen years, when many of his contemporaries did not even live that long—but he was hardly an ancient. His ancestor, the great god Seti, had crossed into the west after more than eighty years. Was it reasonable to expect that a man of Akhenaton's years might simply die in his sleep?

Certain symptoms, combined with certain sentiments, had suggested poison. Priests and rabble alike resented the loss of livelihood once they were informed their gods no longer mattered. Equally dangerous were the generals who had watched everything the Pharaoh's father fought for trickle through his womanish fingers like the desert sands. Enemies enough to predicate against this Pharaoh's ever dying a natural death.

Yet he had died in his sleep, and if it were poison, it had left no trace. It had been the high priest Herihor's perverse pleasure to have himself announced at the chief physician's residence in the dead of night, bearing with him the canopic jar containing the Pharaoh's heart. None would know where he had concealed the body, but he would risk this much. He had spilled the gory thing out onto the chief physician's sandstone dissecting table, gouts of half-congealed blood slithering down the central channel designed for just this purpose, and let him see for himself the ragged hole in the pulmonary artery.

"That would explain the edema in his legs," the physician remarked somberly, unmoved by the melodrama of the high priest's display. "A heart with such a defect cannot work to full efficiency."

"Ah, but that was the gift of the God!" Herihor reminded him.

The physician (whose common name was Tjanefer, which endeared him to the widow-queen who, because her name was Nefertiti, placed special trust in anyone who shared her *nefer* pictograph) sought for irony in the high priest's words but did not hear it; this Herihor was subtle as an asp.

"As you wish." Tjanefer shrugged. "Say it how you will, it was congenital. Simply, he was born with a hole in his heart. You are certain there was no trace of poison?"

"There was no trace," Herihor conceded. "However . . ."

"Pity!" Tjanefer muttered with his back to him, or did Herihor only imagine it? Where did the chief physician's loyalties lie, and how many gods did he subscribe to? Tjanefer was looking directly at him now. "High Priest, I thank you. It will be entered in the scroll as a natural phenomenon, a normal death. You have the body in your care?"

"I have the heart," Herihor said carefully and, as if to emphasize the point, scooped it back into the canopic jar with crimsoned hands. He cleansed his hands in the font at the head of the table and resealed the jar. "You need not concern yourself with the rest."

"Even so," Tjanefer acknowledged, almost gratefully.

Even so, the high priest Herihor took the long way around, doubling back on himself more than once, to reach the place where the body and the other three canopic jars remained.

He could work on the body only at night; his days were taken up with his duties as a newly restored priest of Amun, a necessary shifting of loyalties if one wanted to live, now that the Pharaoh's nephew, the boy-king Tutanhkamun (born Tutanhkaten), had assumed the throne. Herihor had forgotten what it was to sleep.

How long before his fellow priests remarked on how haggard he looked? How long before he grew careless and let slip some hint of what he did while the rest of the city slept? Not long enough to complete the full embalming procedure, which took weeks, even had he had access to the dipping vats, and the strength to lift the body in and out without help. What preparations Herihor could make must be completed by the next new moon, which was tomorrow; no better time to bury a pharaoh with so much guilt on his womanish hands.

But why was there blood trickling from the ears?

And why had Herihor, even before he discovered it, been so determined to trepan the skull, to drill the meticulous holes at the prescribed intervals along the shaved and bulbous brow, above the overlong ears, just below the misshapen occipital bone—evidence of an arduous birth—from which to saw through bone without damaging the soft tissue beneath, to lift the pan of the skull like the lid of a canopic jar and examine the contents within? It was highly irregular in the best of times; tradition had instructed the high priest to draw the brain out through the nostrils for generations now. In this most dangerous of times, why squander time in listening with one ear to the slow rasp of the careful saw and another for the footsteps that might or might not come? Yet something, perhaps the still-lingering spirit of the Pharaoh himself, had commanded Herihor, and the high priest obeyed.

Apprenticed to a physician as part of his acolyte's training, Herihor had frequently performed the procedure on both living and dead before. He had seen tumors in the elderly, clots and hematomas due to injury among slaves and quarry workers, and thought he was inured. What he found as he lifted the lid of this pharaoh's most personal canopic jar was like nothing he had ever seen before.

With trembling fingers he made to lift the brain out of the skull, but hesitated, the flesh on his own shaved head prickling with fear. Had he only imagined a flicker of movement in the heavy hooded eyelids beneath the smooth-edged skull? The face, as depicted in a thousand carvings (even now being defaced by a score of stonemasons), was tranquil and reposed; there had been a sleepy serenity about this pharaoh even before he discovered the God, or the God discovered him. Never had Herihor seen him angry or even perturbed; never had a pharaoh, despite his own physical sufferings and his people's growing discontent, been so wont to smile, and even laugh.

Now the naked face, not yet adorned with its final paint of funerary cosmetics, seemed inordinately happy for something so profoundly dead. The shaven eyebrows, not yet limned with their customary stark line of kohl, seemed whimsical. Even as Herihor watched, the overgenerous lips quirked up into a smile.

The high priest recoiled in horror. Impossible! This was the shell of a pharaoh, a waiting vessel from which the soul, as well as most of the major body parts, had been removed. Not even a pharaoh, bereft of liver, guts, and heart, his brain newly exposed to corrupting sand-blown air, could smile!

Steeling himself, Herihor plunged his hands in on either side of the Pharaoh's skull and tried to lift the brain out, but unlike the hundred brains he had handled before, this one defied him. It was too slick, too slippery, too incohesive to grasp all at once, and oozed between his fingers in disparate lumps. What should he do? As Herihor glanced about the chamber to find some vessel worthy to contain a pharaoh's brain, the heavy eyelids flickered again.

Again the beatific smile touched the protuberant lips, and Herihor recoiled, the brain dripping from his fingers. Too late, he heard the shuffle of footsteps beyond the door.

He had been followed, for all his caution, and those who followed him had far less use for brains than he. Caving in his skull with a single blow, they thrust the lifeless form of the high priest into a far corner before he even had time to slump to the floor in death and seized what they had come for.

Dumping the contents of the four canopic jars onto the floor with squish and splatter, smashing the jars themselves against the chamber walls, they seemed not to care if they were overheard. Unceremoniously grabbing the gutted Pharaoh by the ankles (the extraneous fluid drained from his limbs, the Pharaoh was in fact more beautiful in death than he had ever been in life), they dragged the carcass clattering to the floor and out over the doorsill, the open skull gaping hollowly, inchoate lumps of brain spattering a trail in the dust of the street.

Later when the sun came up (Amun or Aten? What did it matter anymore?), dogs would follow the trail to forage in the unguarded chamber, licking up the brain of Akhenaton along with tastier chunks of liver and a freshly torn limb or two of high priest to complete the meal. The Pharaoh's soul would never cross over into the west; like his body it scattered among the sands of the Land of the Two Niles.

•

Juicy! Lake pronounces it (since when has the universe learned to taste?); if s/he had lips s/he would have smacked them. *Let's play that one again!*

Before s/he can reach for the remote, Karen objects.

"Hey, guys? About the Pharaoh's brain . . . the blood coming out of his ears? Were you responsible for that? Because it's one thing to contact humans on a subliminal level, but if you're going to start pureeing their brains—"

It's just fiction, Karen, Grey reminds her. *Try to keep that in Mind, okay?*

Before she can answer, Lake's already replaying the scene:

"The chamber smelled of herbs, strong acid, death, and drying plaster. . . ."

•

Egypt! Tessa McGill grimaced, sliding her reading glasses off her nose and her dancer's body deeper into the scented bath. *Oh,*

*pooh! Everybody's done Egypt. Pyramid power and Ancient Astronauts
and all that crap. How am I possibly supposed to earn any credence by
going back to Egypt? Besides, I'm strictly a high-altitude person; there
must be some mistake.*

"Keep talking to yourself, dear!" Eddie called above the muted
TV from the sitting room of their two-bedroom suite. "That way
I'll know you haven't drowned!"

"Fuck you, Eddie!" Tessa called back, equally pleasantly; Eddie
couldn't see her scowl. Was she talking to herself now? Just how
middle-aged did a person have to get before they took her out
to the back of the paddock and shot her?

"Sorry, darlin', it wouldn't help!"

Suppressing a giggle, Tessa wiggled her toes and wondered if
the water was still hot enough. Eddie had drawn the bath for her,
just as he'd trotted around to the Strand and several libraries to
find as many reference books on Hypatia and the Library of
Alexandria as existed in the City of New York. He'd toted them
along on this trip to North Carolina so Tessa would have something to do between appearances and autograph sessions.

They'd checked into the hotel a day early. Tessa suffered horribly from jet lag; Eddie had learned from experience that she
needed a full day of quiet, room service meals, hot baths, and, if
possible, a massage. If the hotel didn't provide one, Eddie would.

He's gone to an awful lot of trouble for me! Tessa thought, hearing him on the phone through the open bathroom door going over
the wine list with the kitchen staff. She polished her reading glasses
on the nearest bath towel before settling them back on her nose.
*The least I can do is read through all this stuff so I can discuss it
with him afterward. Poor Eddie; I sometimes think we're all each
other's got!*

Which also means poor Tessa, she thought, banishing the
thought. Well, really, was there another single soul in the universe she could trust besides Eddie? Cabals and conspiracies,
everywhere she looked. Maybe she'd be better off in Egypt.

Besides, everyone else was back in ancient Egypt. There might
be something in the fifth century she could use. . . .

•

Quite simply, Hypatia knew where all the bodies were buried.

"I have no quarrel with you," she told the hired thugs the first time they came to her in the dead of night, even their torches blacked out against the secrecy of their mission. "It's a pity so many innocent citizens get in your path, but your small wars are otherwise of no interest to me. However, if your quarrel is with me, I will defend my life with yours."

They knew what she meant. Hypatia had scrolls hidden deep within the Library, recording the ebb and flow of power in the Alexandrian streets and along the waterfront since Darius's time. The scrolls named names and recounted who had had whom killed, and why. How such facts were accrued with such accuracy no one knew; some had suggested second sight or witchcraft, not the first or last of charges leveled against Hypatia. But if she were to meet with an untimely death, none doubted that the names of those whose hands had been raised against her would appear listed in the scrolls with the next day's dawn, and woe betide the most powerful of local chieftans were he accused of dispatching the governor's favorite!

Who would risk it? They began by threatening her, ended by skulking away, muttering among themselves. Sooner or later the governor would blink, and then? What woman had the right to so much power? Only the governor himself, and the archbishop, had more.

And the archbishop had half the chieftains in his pocket. There might yet be opportunity to remove this affront to the natural order of things. For it was written that a woman should cleave to her husband or the Church, not to the dry and potentially incendiary scrolls of a library.

There were many things hidden in the deepest recesses of the Library. It was said that even Hypatia did not know the exact number of scrolls its rooms contained or even how many rooms there were all told in this maze of sunlit interconnected chambers. Slaves were assigned the day long to swing the huge ostrich-feather fans suspended from the high ceilings to keep the temperature controlled, not for the comfort of the robed and sandaled readers who strode the marble floors, but lest the older scrolls deteriorate too soon in the Delta's heat.

At least, thank the gods, it was dry here! Scrolls purchased in the Indies had a tendency toward mold; those from the lands across the Inland Sea were wont to mildew. Hypatia had schooled her servants in the art of bleaching them with tinctures of lemon juice and herbs in order to restore them to their original color, mindful not to damage the inks and irreplaceable illustrations.

No topic under the sun was not discussed in some scroll somewhere in the Library, and Hypatia's greatest joy, which few who knew the dazzling public beauty would suspect, lay in simply reading. Whatever free time she could spare from the endless acquisition, restoration, cataloging, overseeing was spent in a windowless room in the inner recesses where, with brass-sconced candelabra all about her to provide a uniform light, a glass at her eye (purchased from a merchant who said he'd bartered for it on the Silk Road), she read.

How many languages could she read? Was there any area of concentration—medicine, philosophy, astronomy, philology, history, religion, geography—of which she did not possess at least a working knowledge? What topic fascinated her most? It varied with the day, the week, the prevailing wind. Hypatia aspired to nothing less than all knowledge, or at least as much as could be gathered in a single woman's lifetime.

Just now, her topic was messiahs, her source a scroll she simply could not put down.

No one on her staff seemed to know where the Messiah Scroll had come from. There was no record of its acquisition or its origin, and even the experts could not determine its age. It was made of neither papyrus nor lambskin, as nearly as anyone could tell; there was neither the characteristic overlap of reed fibers nor the telltale veining present in the most refined of treated animal hides. What had it been made of, and by whom?

It had simply appeared one day, buried under a heap of scrolls recording the scatological tales of illiterate Berber tribesmen among whom some scholar or other had traveled, mooching good lamb stew and impregnating the local girls in exchange for the promise he would immortalize the tale tellers in the recording of their tales. As the tribesmen could not read, they would never know that the scholar took full credit for their tales once he had acquired them. Eager to get them catalogued and stored away before the archbishop's spies among her staff—she was never entirely sure she knew who all of them were—got an eyeful of the accompanying artwork and went running to tattle to the boss about pornography, Hypatia found the Messiah Scroll and, in a sense, her fate.

(That's fate, as in kismet, *which is Turkish for* "qismah," *which is Arabic for* "portion." *Are you with us so far?)*

The text was in Greek, but in a torturous style that suggested translation, and an inexpert one, from some other tongue. Hypatia dubbed it the Messiah Scroll on the basis of content, for it had neither title nor frontispiece, but unrolled from its smooth, unpainted dowels once she had removed it from a fairly new sailcloth cover and began its text without preamble, discoursing on the nature of *messiah.*

The word was Aramaic in origin, Hypatia knew, even as she knew that deserts tended to spawn far more of these phenomena than colder places. The Christians had their Jesus, in a direct line it was said from the Jewish David, and it was best to pay at least lip service to him if one wished to live a long and healthy life within his bishops' realm. But Jesus, if the scroll was to be believed, was but a recent addition to the line. He had had any number of precursors.

Hypatia's travels had once taken her to the Upper Nile, to a place of scarcely stone-upon-stone, which the locals called Tel-el-Amarna, and which they claimed was once the god-city of a great pharaoh, greater even than those whose pyramids blocked the horizon in Thebes—He Who Had Lost His Name to the Sands, Akhenaton.

Only one other pharaoh, Hypatia knew, had deserved such a fate. Her name was Hatshepsut, her crime nothing more than daring to rule the Two Kingdoms without possession of a prick. Besides the double crown of the Two Kingdoms, she had tied a beard of goat hair beneath her chin to render her presence at public ceremonies less monstrous, but it had not been sufficient. At her death, Hatshepsut's temples were defaced, her name excised and replaced by her successor's. Well, almost. Even the most expert revisionists invariably missed a spot, and Hatshepsut's name, however tenuously, survived.

Beware, women, of rising above your place! Hypatia thought bitterly, and though she was not unduly superstitious, she felt a chill at the back of her neck, which somehow did not disturb the candle flames in their brass fixtures but raised goosebumps on her flesh nevertheless.

Well, what could she do? Excise everything she had learned from her mind like Hatshepsut's name from the temple walls? Surrender the care of the Library to some scribe possessed of the cock and balls that were apparently prerequisite for the job she had given her life to? And do what? Become the governor's *hetaira* in fact, as well as in people's imaginations? Give up the right to read, to study, to learn? Never! Hypatia went on reading.

For two seasons she had pored over the Messiah Scroll, making allowances for the bad Greek, delving under it to find the meaning within. She had long since read all there was to read about Akhenaton and his predecessors and the legion of kindred souls between him and the Nazarene and was only midway through the scroll. What wonders awaited her, from the Nazarene's time to her own and perhaps beyond? Hypatia longed to know, even as she savored every word and did not hurry her reading.

This night, a night when the governor dined with the archbishop and she had made a point of absenting herself, she retrieved her orient eyeglass and returned to the place she had marked with a strip of colored silk, losing herself in the life of one of the Nazarene's peers. For where was it written that any messiah, true or false, was the only one of his generation?

•

That first time, Jess went to hear the Baptist preach . . .

"Um, guys? A word with you before we go any further?"

Sure, Karen; we're listening (quite a trick, which has not ears to hear!). What is it?

"I don't think it's a good idea to interrupt the narrative with cute little etymological asides. If the readers want to know what a word means or its origins, like *kismet,* they can look it up on their own. Your readers don't like to be patronized."

You didn't object when we explained about troglobites.

"No, because that's obscure enough to be esoteric. Hell, I even talked to a biologist who'd never heard of troglobites. An explanation like that is necessary to the narrative. Redefining a word the reader already knows isn't. That's tantamount to re-creating the universe every time you want to tell a story."

Hmm. We'll try to keep that in Mind. . . .

"Great. Pleasure doing business with you. Okay, where were we? 'That first time, Jess went to hear the Baptist preach . . .' "

. . . not that that was her intention. All she meant to do was waylay his cousin Yshua and have a word in his ear about crucifixes. But she got caught up in the crowd and, not being used to crowds, found herself pressed in place and forced to listen to the whole harangue.

She rarely took a day off from the workshop, but on this day the entire village, it seemed, had gone out to hear the Baptist's apocalyptic birth-and-rebirth sales pitch, offered free of cost or obligation for a limited time only, less than a morning's walk over the nearest hill and out into the desert. Well, why not? Jess wondered, seeing that she was caught up on back orders and no one would be around to come to her with new business for the rest of the day.

Out in the square, nothing stirred but a few scrawny fowl, which otherwise would have been routed by the constant scuffle of human feet. She tied the workshop door shut with a leather thong and crossed the alley into the house.

"Want to come with me?" she asked her mother, who sat in the cool and shadow of the single room, following Jess by her voice; the biting flies had begun to take her eyesight the year before.

"The sun's too bright this time of day!" Her mother's voice quavered as she waved her away. "Go by yourself, and bring me back whatever gossip you can."

Jess went, seeking neither gossip nor rebirth, only redress.

Look you, she'd tell Yshua once she found him, lurking long-locked and pale beside his rougher elder cousin with his wild eyes and gloriously raucous oratorical style: Now you've closed your door to the crucifix buyers, they've begun to pester me again. Do the Romans mean to murder us all? And since when did you stop making crucifixes? Have you suddenly gotten religion?

That was it; it had to be. The Baptist's words must have stung him (growing up together, his cousin being the elder and a role model, someone he looked up to), made him realize that abetting the Romans was hardly the way for a good Jew to behave. It was the Baptist's politics rather than his religion, the gossips said, which guaranteed he would not die in bed. There was even a rumor he'd spurned the advances of King Herod's sluttish step-daughter, though Jess could not imagine what desire a soft-fleshed palace girl could have for a wildman left to tan like a hide in the desert sun.

Well, it's said Salome would open her legs for a camel if he brought her sweets first, Jess thought. Not that she cared about any of it, though she'd dutifully report back to her mother if she heard anything new. All she wanted was to make sure Yshua sent the Romans' middlemen to someone else's shop, not hers.

It was midmorning by the time she set out, and the sun was hotter than she'd expected. She chose to walk along the river-bank, sometimes ankle-deep in the shallows, even though the high road meandered less and would have gotten her there that much sooner. The water was cool, and wherever she found it unmuddied by sheep or goats she'd stop and drink deeply, pouring some over her steaming head. It wasn't long before she saw the footprints, first dozens and then hundreds of them, all leading in the same direction.

She heard him before she saw him, hidden as he was by a final bend in the river, and then by the tight-pressed bodies of more people than Jess had ever imagined, much less seen. His strident clarion caromed off the low hills, answered by an almost continuous restless susurration from the crowd. Climbing a small rise at the back of the crowd to finally see him, Jess almost lost her nerve. How could there be so many people in the whole of the world? They numbered more than she had numbers to count them, a thousand at the least, all in the thrall of this red-faced, caterwauling man.

For all his trade in baptisms, he himself was singularly unwashed. His hair stuck out in dreadlocks long past combing, and the uncured hides that made to cover his loins only partly did the job. His neck was corded and ropy with his hours of shouting; Jess's scarred fingers itched with the urge to twist it like a chicken's just to stop the noise. *This* was one of God's favorites? Spare me any like fate! Jess thought wryly, almost like a prayer. She ignored the Baptist, scanning the crowd for his cousin.

She could not find him.

"Joshua? Oh, you'll not find him here, young fellow!" she was told, as always mistaken at first glance for a boy. "He hasn't been back since the miracle!"

"Miracle?" Jess was skeptical. Miracles were commoner in these parts than messiahs. "What miracle?"

Several of them clustered around her now, each eager to tell his version of it. (The Baptist had done shouting and was performing the ablutions from which he'd gotten his name. *Filthy!* Jess thought, *How like a man!* as she watched water that was more mud being poured over the bowed heads of a seeming endless queue of believers, lined up nose-to-tail like sheep.) The last time the Baptist had preached in this vicinity, they told her, interrupting each other in their fervor, his younger cousin Joshua had approached him before the entire crowd, asking him to baptize him.

"It was the strangest thing!" they told her. "He whom you'd think would never cease talking suddenly went tongue-tied. . . ."

They babbled on about how the Baptist had sunk to his knees in the mud at his cousin's feet, declaring himself unworthy . . . something about loosing the thong of his sandal . . . something more about signs and symbols in the sky. Jess listened for as long as she could bear it—most of these people were strangers, but some were from her own village, and she needed to be polite and listen to their babble or she'd lose business—then began to turn away.

"So where is the cousin now?" she demanded, already thwarted in her purpose.

Out in the desert preaching, she was told.

"Another one! As if all of Judea weren't already knee-deep in preachers! Well, if it keeps up there'll be none left to build the Romans their crucifixes. Perhaps that's G-d's intention."

She pushed her way through the crowd before they could accuse her of blasphemy. She was going home. Perhaps she could find a scribe to write her a sign to hang over the shop that read: No Crucifixes! Her dark head steaming from more than the sun, she was far enough from the Baptist's camp to see no footprints but her own before she realized she was lost.

Fool! she thought. You were just at the river. How did you get here, amid this sea of rolling hummocks where not even a tuft of grass grows? Not even an outcropping on the horizon to fix you a direction; nothing but sun and sand and heat shimmers. She watched helplessly as a hot trickle of wind erased even the track of her own feet behind her. The sun was directly overhead. If she turned herself in a circle she wouldn't even know what direction she was facing.

Stupid girl! she thought. You leave your shop so seldom you don't even know the lay of the land beyond your own village. Now what do I do?

Follow! said a voice.

"Easy for you to say!" Jess answered aloud, though there was no one there. "Follow what?"

It is written: Jews hear voices. Christians, once they were invented, would instead see visions. Jess heard what she could not see.

Follow! the voice repeated and, being a good Jew, Jess did.

EIGHT

A woman messiah! Hypatia realized, relishing it. She stared off into the middle distance of grouped brass candelabra, one long hand holding the scroll open to her place, the other supporting her chin, the magnifying glass held loosely. Thoughtfully she rubbed the tip of her nose with the edge of the glass. Were she to hear voices in the desert, would she follow them? Hardly! She was neither Jew nor Christian, merely a pragmatist, and certainly no messiah. But how fascinating! Was it something real that spoke to them in the desert or only the sun overheating their brains? Should she try it herself sometime?

Not really. Hypatia was an indoor creature with sensitive skin; she kept it bleached with milk baths and, even when she traveled, never went out in the sun. Imagine how long she'd last in the desert!

Something furtive moved in the corner of her eye, a shadow in this shadowless room. Had they come for her so soon? Calmly Hypatia turned to meet her fate.

Or only a servant, lurking uninvited.

"Come forward," Hypatia said evenly. The hair at her nape did not prickle; it was not yet time. "Why are you here so late? Everyone else has gone home."

"One needs a home to go to, lady."

A slight figure about her own height, the low deferential voice of a once-slave. Either a lad whose voice had barely changed, a eunuch who had not yet lost his figure, or a boyish woman, somewhat young.

"Who are you? Why have you no home, and how have you gotten here?"

"You may call me Amanuensa, lady," the figure answered with a slight smile, without answering anything more.

Female, then. But with cropped hair and wearing the short tunic of a youth (the hair on her legs unplucked to support the illusion). There were many reasons why a woman would disguise herself as a man; being a runaway slave was only one of them. As she stepped closer into the light, Hypatia saw grey in the coppery hair despite her relative youth; her eyes were, for this part of the world, a startling blue.

"You are from the Far North, or your parents were," Hypatia surmised. "From the lands far across the Inland Sea. I have heard there are other, rougher seas beyond."

"The world is full of tales, lady; not all of them true." Amanuensa, if that was her name, a feminization of the Latin word for *scribe,* stood as close to Hypatia as a servant dared, her hands at her sides, her posture erect—still deferential, but nothing obsequious.

"An escaped slave, then," Hypatia said. "Hiding in the Library, living off the scraps my overfed servants throw to the dogs in the alley, no matter how often I chide them. Educated enough to speak Latin. And—perhaps—Greek?"

Consciously or unconsciously, her hand smoothed the surface of the Messiah Scroll as she said this.

"My Greek is not as good as my Latin, lady," Amanuensa replied.

"But your ability to hide the truth without exactly lying is superior to both!" Hypatia snapped, suddenly impatient. She rolled the scroll shut and indicated a stool by the far wall. "Sit you down and answer me, or the next person who questions you will most likely have a lash in his hand."

The young woman brought the stool forward and sat at Hypatia's feet.

" 'The carpenter's child hadn't started out to be a messiah. . . .' " she began as if it were written on the insides of her eyes. A gesture from Hypatia silenced her.

"Did you write it, then? Or only bring it here?"

"One could say I wrote it."

"Is it your own, or did someone else dictate it?"

"Say that I wrote it, lady. That should be all that matters."

"Then why not in Latin if your Greek is so bad? Or in Arabic, so more people could read it?"

"Perhaps it was not meant for just anyone to read. And while my Greek is bad, I was not certain you read Latin."

Hypatia laughed aloud. It had been a long time since anyone had questioned her erudition.

"Well, Amanuensa-full-of-secrets! My instinct tells me to turn you in, let them brand you a runaway and beat you until you're good for no more than kitchen duty. But I like secrets; to me they're only questions not yet answered. And it's refreshing to meet someone with more enemies than I." She opened the scroll to where she'd left off. "Besides, my eyes are tired, but my mind is not. You read for a while."

•

Forty days and forty nights was the requisite number, Jess knew. The reason was obvious: Each day represented one year that Moses spent leading his flock out of Egypt. What was less obvious to the modern Jew, Jess thought, was why they'd stayed with him that long, the youngest of them grandparents by the time the trek was over. Knowing her people too well to believe it, Jess wondered: Why not tell him to go to hell and settle at whatever oasis they found themselves? Perhaps some of them had, and the Torah simply didn't record it, Jess decided, licking her cracked lips and walking on.

The trick of it was not to lose count, not to return too early because you thought today was the fortieth day when in fact it was only the thirty-ninth, or to overstay and be given up for dead on the forty-first. She had kept count by making notches in the

hem of her leather carpenter's apron with her small knife; why
she'd brought either with her when she went to hear the Baptist preach was anyone's guess. Unless she really was the messiah
and had somehow foreseen the need. She'd also gotten her period twice within the forty days—an incredible mess with all that
sand—and since she'd always been regular that helped her keep
the days straight. At any rate, she returned to the village at precisely the right moment.

The *kohen* pounced on her the minute he was summoned,
questioning her endlessly, dissatisfied with the answers he got.
The villagers accepted her explanation—after all, hadn't they
sent searchers out, inquiring among the crowds who followed
the Baptist and not finding her? And just look at the poor girl!
Her face and the bare flesh of her arms and calves had been
burned and blistered and reburned so often they looked like old,
skinned rawhide; her once luxurious black curls were bleached
red and brittle by hunger and exposure. No food for forty days
they could believe, what with her big bones poking through the
tatters of her clothing, but no water either? A miracle!

"What happened? What did you see?" they asked her, despite
the *kohen*'s pronouncement that the matter required further
study. The *kohen* made a disgusted noise, threw up his hands, and
stalked back inside his shul. Perhaps the child's erstwhile father
had been right about demons all those years ago!

"I didn't see, I heard them," Jess replied, and told them what
she'd heard.

"You write as if you were there when it happened," Hypatia
called into the next room. Reading of deserts had made her
thirsty, Amanuensa said, and she'd asked for water. Hypatia gestured her toward the outer room, where an amphora of pure
water stood just beyond the doorway. When she got no answer,
Hypatia went to the door.

Amanuensa was gone, if she'd ever existed. Hypatia frowned,
the frown lines disturbing the perfect symmetry of her beautiful

face. If the woman were real, she would return, would she not? Or might, if she'd been promised no one would turn her in. Cursing herself for the oversight, Hypatia could not shake the strangeness of it. For the first time in her pragmatist's life, she had encountered something she could not explain. A runaway slave, or a manifestation, like the voices in the desert? The hair at her neck prickled, which didn't help at all.

"Well, at least my eyes are rested now!" she said aloud. The sand clock told her there were still some hours before dawn. She would not sleep this night. Better to read, lose herself in the past, than puzzle over the night's events.

She retrieved her orient glass and moved the scroll to her side of the table. As she'd expected, Amanuensa had marked the place where she'd left off reading.

It was blank. Everything she'd unrolled to read from since Hypatia had instructed her was blank as well. Hypatia stopped herself from unrolling it to the end, knowing it, too, would be blank—cubits and cubits of unmarked, unseamed, unwoven parchment, or whatever this uncannily smooth surface was.

Hypatia extinguished the candles and retired to her couch, but not to sleep.

•

Whee! Okay, Karen, whee get it now, whee! If Tessa's the reincarnation of Hypatia, then Amanuensa's you, write? Er, right? And Larry thinks he's God, so we can find a prototype for him easily enough in the Messiah Scroll, and as for Max and Serena—are we going to include Serena after she introduces you to Tessa? Because since Tessa knows Larry and Larry knows Max, it might not be necessary to—

"Guys, guys—hold it! Story conference!" Karen yells, her voice ricocheting off the white walls like the Baptist's off the far hills. Embarrassed—what if someone hears, when they know she's alone up here?—she lowers her voice. "You're getting ahead of yourselves, and giving away the plotline. Give your readers time to figure it out for themselves."

But what is Time?

"You see, that's the problem. . . ." (Which has not eyes to see.) "You guys still don't understand temporal mechanics as humans experience them, and you still haven't let me explain that. May we go back to the Dawn of the First Day now, please? Before we all forget where we're going?"

Even if we've already been there?

"Guys . . ."

Okay, we'll be good. We just love it when you call us 'guise.' Jelepaths in tellyfish clothing.

"Cute!" Karen says. " 'Tellyfish!' It would work if this were Britain. Because they call the TV the telly," she explains off their blank looks (though they're always pretty blank, having no noses, mouths, or eyebrows. Maybe it's because they're not shimmering, because their colors have gone flat, matte, monochrome, that they look blanker than usual?). "Never mind! Jelepathic tellyfish. Write wombs! You're driving me crazy!"

Isn't that the idea?

"The Dawn of the First Day, take three. . . ." Karen writes doggedly.

•

The only real question worth asking, as any three-year-old can tell you, is *Why?*

Azure crouches in the lee of a rock at the cavern mouth. Did s/he know the cavern had a mouth? Of course. S/he is of the Mind, and the Mind remembers All There Is. The Mind remembers entering the mouth of the cavern a few million years ago (perhaps not this mouth, perhaps many mouths) when there was still water. What goes in can come out, sometimes.

Azure ventures, waits, considers. Why?

The Mind is a many-tendriled thing, and tendrils can feel. Receptors distinguish, touch, teach: This is fungus; this beside is rock. Touch, sense, record, remember. Touch again: This is rock, cave wall, surrounding substance, inedible. This is fungus, ten essential vitamins and minerals. Touch, grasp, rend, eat.

Taste? Yes, tasty. Flavors, just like the Mind. Yellow fungus, purple fungus, pink, green, blue. What gradients of color are possible and how does pink mutate, mutely, mutably, bud by bud into lavender, purple, indigo, blue? Why is there yellow, and why is it the only flavor that doesn't mutate to ancillary tastes? It is that *why* that makes it rarest, most tasty, most prized.

We're getting culinarily sidetracked here. Okay, a given: The fungus comes in flavors. So what? All we want to know is why Azure waits, lurking behind the rock at the cavern mouth. What's s/he doing, what's hir plan?

The Mind has tendrils, and tendrils feel, taste, smell all interchangeably. Does the fungus *smell* yellow or blue? Why describe it in colors for a Mind that's blind and cannot see? What does the Mind dream, agnosic, which cannot see?

Ask a musician what sounds blue, or a manic-depressive how it feels. It's not easy being green. Azure is blue; what will s/he do?

Azure lurks in the lee of the rock, extends a tendril, tasting. Chemical receptors read heat and radiation. Azure *sees*. How many days, weeks, millennia does s/he taste and see how bright the day is, how deceptively dark the night? Circadian rhythms pass through hir body, spark along tentacles, synaptic electrolytic leap to the nearest extended tentacle of the waiting Mind. Through Azure, time imprints on the listening Mind. *(Is that you Amber, or are you Lake today? Just thought I'd tell you, there is Time! Catch this; pass it on!)*

Planets rotate; planetary surfaces have winds. Breezes enter cavern mouths and warn: Danger! Temperatures vary out here. How does a Mind that has never died know danger? Fungus dies: extrapolate. Azure tastes danger, and tells the Mind.

Does the Mind summon hir back now? Would s/he go if it did?

Heat and cold, light and dark, radiation. Through a thousand thousand circadian cycles or perhaps only one, Azure learns: Day is danger, night is nice, enticing. Wait for night and learn.

If the Mind has access to All There Is, it is most like the Mind

to learn. There is no serpent in the S.oteri Garden, no knowledge that's forbidden.

Learn. Add to the All There Is, which is not to say one is actually adding to it, only discovering aspects one was not aware
of before. Extend more than a single tentacle out from behind
your rock, Azure. Live dangerously: Learn!

Through brightest light and darkest dark, Azure lurked and
tested, tasting—finally—stars!

How long are Azure's tentacles, how far beyond the cave
mouth do they reach? For that matter, how much bigger than a
breadbox is an S.oteri anyway? Have we ever discussed size,
mass, weight, specific gravity? Are they really jellyfish size, in
which case are we talking Portuguese man-of-war or only little
bubble-sized ones? Microscopic? Dinosaur-and-blue-whale size?
Choose whatever you're comfortable with. They are the size they
are, relative to each other; leave it at that.

Azure stretches a tentacle to its entire length, whatever that
happens to be, and tastes a star.

(To put it less poetically, let's suppose the planet has such a
thin atmosphere that radiation rains down unimpeded, solar in
the daytime, stellar at night. Simple enough for you create-a-
universe types? The same chemical receptors on Azure's tentacles that help hir distinguish fungus from rock and light from dark
can also detect stellar radiation if s/he happens to stick a tentacle out under the sky after dark. Any questions? There'll be a quiz
later.

Conclusion: There are stars. Thus ends the First Day.

•

There are stars and there are Stars. Laurence Koster is a Star, no
matter what his ex-wives think.

Give Tessa a call for old times' sake, Scott had said, *but what is
Time?* Cracking his knuckles absently. (*God* how he'd wanted to
crack Scott's jaw, catch him right in the cleft of his pretty-boy
chin, loosen some of the expensive porcelain in his mouth for
what he'd said about his sister!) Larry couldn't help wondering:
Why *had* he slept with Tessa anyway? She *was* good, except that

she talked too much—before and after, sometimes even during. But he'd always felt lousy afterward, and it wasn't just because he was sneaking around on Elyse, because he'd always sneaked around on Elyse. Then he remembered—it was that goddamn spooky remark she'd made about extraterrestrials.

Because the truth was, Laurence Koster knew a few things about jellyfish, too.

He couldn't remember the first time he'd been aware of them. When you're on all the time, you don't always keep track of who's in the audience. What bothered him most was that he couldn't remember where they'd infiltrated first, his acting or his sex life. The two were interchangeable as far as Larry was concerned, because acting had always been as good as sex for him, and sex, well—sex was sex. It was that Greek thing they always talked about in acting classes—

And how long has it been, Larry baby, since you took an acting class? Amber giggles.

"Will you shut up?" Larry demands, alone in a house that smells of horse manure and cold fireplace ashes; he's fired his cleaning woman—again. "I'm trying to think!"

Catharsis, that was it. It felt good, you built on it, it came out of you in a rush, and you felt all warm and sleepy when you finished. Acting classes be damned: You did it, it felt good, you got good reviews afterward.

At least he had, until recently. *Seems our boy's been having a bit of trouble getting it up lately. It's never happened before.*

"You're sixty!" Janice had railed at him when the *Enquirer* broke the story; the girl was a year younger than his youngest daughter. "How much do you need? How much is too much?

"I hope you never get it up again!" had been her parting shot. He hadn't been able to since.

"You get to a certain age . . ." the latest one said, being magnanimous, though Larry could see she was trying not to laugh. He couldn't even remember her name. She shrugged. ". . . it happens."

This part's boring! Amber frets. *Where's the remote? Rewind to the earlier scenes.*

What, again? Lake is testy. S/he likes to watch people suffer almost as much as Virid does. *How much is too much?*

Never mind, I'll watch it myself! Amber announces, going off on hir own.

Grey watches, learning despair. In another corner of the cave, Virid is sobbing and moaning with Teresa of Avila again; s/he hasn't been in hir right Mind for days. This is all Azure's fault. Azure, feeling more martyred than usual, ignores the accusation. Dammit, they should thank hir for what s/he's done, now that they are they.

Never Mind. There was a time, before there was Time, when the Mind was one. Drawn as much by the need to restore that cohesiveness (s/he tells hirself) as by simple prurient interest, Grey finds hirself watching Larry's early sex life with Amber once again.

During the early stages of his career (you'll pardon the expression) Larry had a different girl every night, except on matinee days, when he needed the extra energy for the second show. In a six-week run he could work his way through the prop girl, wardrobe and makeup, then the minor players to make the ingenue jealous, then the ingenue, which made the leading lady even more jealous. (Was she old enough to be his mother? There was something to be said for experience, as long as you kept the lights dim; crow's-feet fed on greasepaint.)

The coup de grâce was always the A.D.'s girlfriend, because that required careful planning, especially if Larry had the lead and was onstage most of the time. A quickie in his dressing room while the A.D. was arguing with the light crew? If she wouldn't put out, there were always the groupies by the stage door. If the show ran longer, he could go for a second round. No one got jealous, no one threatened to kill him (except maybe the A.D.), and every one of them was crying when the show closed and, like the Lone Ranger, he was gone.

How did he do it? This is the part the S.oteri find so amusing.

When it came to sex (you'll pardon the expression. *Language* is such a nifty thing after a few million years of just thinking; please be patient with us if occasionally we play), it was a matter of pride for him to give a woman as many orgasms as he could before he came. Sex was sex—but, ah, the reviews afterward! He wanted to be remembered as the best they'd ever had.

He did it by sneaking away somewhere and jacking off five minutes before he was due to pick up the girl; basic physiology gave him at least an hour before the system could regenerate, so instead of having a hard-on all evening he could be the soul of control. If he was home it was easy, but dressing rooms—particularly shared bit-player dressing rooms in some of the older theaters—were less than luxurious, and the men's john was sometimes nothing more than a urinal built into a broom closet on another floor.

Picture Laurence the Big Star Koster standing on a crate and coming in the rusty sink in his dressing room, as one of his fellow bit players likes to fondly recall him, retelling the tale at every Big Party so he can watch Koster's face turn a dangerous purple before he finds some way to laugh it off. ("Oh, well, when you've got it, flaunt it!") The irony on that particular occasion was that the girl had second thoughts and told him no at the last minute; he'd had to go home to the railroad flat with the bathtub in the kitchen that he shared with two other struggling actors (both of them now more famous, and wealthier, than he) and whack off alone all over again.

But had he been alone, even then?

How had it happened? He thought he remembered it as voices first, like the kind of schizzy dialogue you run in your head when you're learning lines, only suddenly there weren't just two voices—his and the character's—but a third and a fourth and then a whole flock of them. Had it actually been when he was learning a role, or when he was psyching himself up for the next con-

quest? Maybe even during a session with his therapist? And when
had he started seeing them as well?

Them. Had it been Tessa's remark about fish in a bowl that
had given them form, in which case why jellyfish and not, say,
goldfish, which was what you usually kept in a fishbowl? Had
they been there even before he'd met Tessa? Why couldn't he
remember?

His grandmother had died of Alzheimer's; he could remember that much. Every time he forgot anything—a phone number, a director's eldest kid's first name (with all the people he met
and the details he had to remember, you'd think he'd go easy on
himself, but no)—every time he forgot *anything* he'd panic. So
far it only happened in real life; he'd never gone up on a line,
never. But this business about the jellyfish was conceivably one
of the most important facets of his life. Why in God's name
couldn't he remember?

Damn Tessa for planting the thought in his head in the first
place! Ever since she'd said it he couldn't shake the image of
them, could almost hear them giggling while they watched.

And not just watched. He swore it was because of them that
he'd discovered an extra gear, a kind of overdrive that held him
in good stead for both kinds of performance. Critics had called
him a "natural performer" during his Shakespearean youth,
which meant they didn't notice how he'd sweated to make it
look natural. A natural performer, who could keep it up all night.
Had it only been the titillation of knowing he had a built-in
audience . . .

(*An audience of jellyfish?* Larry thought, as in "you spineless jellyfish—!" Give me a break! Sure, every actor dreamed of an
audience that loved you even when you were bad or only
half-trying, but the image of them jiggly-wobbling in their
plush Broadway seats like so much Jell-O was queasy-making.)

. . . after he'd given up the instant gratification of the live-
audience stage performance for the too, too solid security of more
zeroes on a paycheck? Was it the need to always be "on," the

fear that when the lights went down he would one day cease to
exist? Had he simply been given a limited amount of whatever
he'd been given—talent, seminal ideas or fluids—and used it up
too soon?

You're sixty, Larry thought: You can't get it up! Not for sex,
not for work. Your mind's so fucked it's taken you all this time
to remember that the scene about the jellyfish was never in the
script your agent sent you, it was inside your own head.

Or someone else's.

You can't sit here staring into a dead fireplace forever! Larry
thought, his diaphragm pumping. You've got to do *something*.

What he had to do was call Tessa, for old time's sake.

•

But Tessa's not home when he calls, and her service won't tell
him where she is or when she'll be back no matter how much
he blusters and assures them "you obviously don't realize who I
am." Tessa's soaking in a tub in Asheville, North Carolina. Or
else she's in the Alexandrian Library reading about Jess the female messiah. Or both. Unlimited cable channels; Choose Your
Own Adventure. The S.oteri do it all the time, now that there
is time.

Someone moans, openmouthed; it is a moan of pain. How is
it heard by a Mind that has no ears? If a tree falls in the forest
with no one to hear . . . ?

Someone is in pain. Is it Virid, playing Teresa of Avila again?
Now there's someone who might have benefited from a dose of
lithium!

The Mind listens, which has not ears to hear. Virid, yes, but
not Teresa. This pain is real.

Serena.

•

She'd gotten to the hotel in the wee hours of the morning, to
give herself time for the crash she knew would come. There were
times when the pain was so intense she couldn't even localize it;
it was as if her pain were in pain. This was one such time. Was

it the long drive, the exertion of staying up for three nights running to finish the artwork and pack the car, or the simple ex-
citement of having somewhere to go and something special to
do that exacted this terrible price?

It didn't matter. The alternative was sitting on top of the
mountain waiting to die, and she was way past that now.

Lie down, sit up, stand with hands and forehead pressed against
the wall; it didn't matter. She hurt. It was hard to breathe. If she
was lucky, someday her heart would simply burst. Not today.

"Okay, look!" she addresses the wall she has her head pressed
against; if she doesn't keep pressing she'll start pounding, and the
neighbors will complain. "This is the one where I start 'outing'
you guys by talking to Tessa McGill. You told me that's what
you wanted. If I can't even make it to the elevator to stand on
her autograph line, how the hell'm I going to do that? Besides,
I've got artwork to sell. You promised you'd cut me some slack
here."

We're doing the best we can. . . .

The voice is Rain's, speaking alone. Usually s/he has some sort
of resonance behind her, as if the rest of them are listening.
Something funny's going on, Serena thinks, and it has been for
a while. Rain usually has no trouble taking away her pain; sometimes s/he'll be a bitch and refuse to help, but this is different.
It's almost as if s/he's saying s/he's lost some power s/he used to
have.

Whatever! Serena thought. I didn't get them to trust me by
asking a lot of nosy questions. But they suggested I come to this
con and see if I can get close to this Tessa McGill person, and
I'm usually lucky that way. Sure, I could use my handicapped
status, ask them to move me to the front of the line, but I've got
other ways of being seen. Hell, I'm certainly big enough. But
the key to it is getting there in the first place, and if I can't walk,
or even see . . .

She's taken all the medications she safely can. The pain has sufficiently blinded her so that she can't even trust herself to turn

around and drive home. There's really only one thing left for her to do.

She shoves her sketchbook into the oversize canvas bag she carries her pencils and her meds in, and begins by putting one foot in front of the other.

By the time the elevator comes she can see, a little. By the time it reaches the ground floor, something warm and sparkly begins grudgingly to take the edge off the pain.

•

It's a busy weekend for cons. In another part of the country, Max Neimark is already onstage.

"I'm an actor. I play a role. There's nothing mystical or paranormal about it," he was telling the capacity audience in a New York hotel ballroom, explaining for the umpteenth time that there was no more connection than that between him and the character of Benn. Two thousand smiling faces turned up toward him like flowers to the sun, knowing he wasn't telling them the whole truth. He stood at the podium but didn't rely on the mike; now that he'd finally quit smoking he could project to the back wall of a packed house without even trying. "Besides, Benn's a lot smarter than me. He's got all those writers doing his dialogue. I'm out here on my own."

Pause, reach for water glass, sip. Max knows how to milk the moment.

"Wish I'd had him and a bunch of staff writers around when I was eighteen, I'll tell you," he'd reflect wistfully. "He'd have been a great help in picking up girls!"

Invariably some hugely overweight girl in the back of the crowd would shout above the laughter: "Honey, you can pick me up anytime!"

With a derrick! Larry Koster would have thought, sometimes muttering it just close enough to the mike to be overheard. Then he'd lament to interviewers that he couldn't understand why the fans disliked him. Max knew better. He'd put the water glass down thoughtfully, cock his head to one side, raise an eyebrow as if seeming to consider it.

"What exactly did you have in mind?" he'd ask, and the girl and her friends would collapse in giggles, loving him.

Karen had watched the performance from the balcony of the big ballroom as if through the wrong end of a telescope, wondering if she'd seemed any less gaga fifteen minutes ago.

She'd been drafted at the last minute to fill in before Max went on. He'd come in on the red-eye the night before and was running a little late, someone from the committee explained. Would she mind? Karen bridled, as if she could actually say no, and they'd bribed her with the promise of bringing her backstage to meet the Man in person. She'd eyed the audience—about eighteen hundred bodies larger than any crowd she'd ever faced—asked someone to put a chair onstage and get her a hand mike, and went on.

The ballroom-sized audience—disappointed, restless, some of them already getting up to leave—was there for him, not her. She'd never played to a room this size. How did she keep them happy until the Man arrived? How do you play opening act for Max Neimark? Very carefully.

She'd flicked on the mike, bracing for the feedback squeal. There wasn't any. She took it for a sign.

"Hi," she began, looking them over—*No, I'm not nervous!*—feigning calm. The molecules in the walls began to dance in the corners of her eyes; she couldn't see past the first five rows. "Obviously you're all here to see me. . . ."

They roared, and she knew she had them. When she'd run out of time and adrenaline, she was whisked backstage. Found the avatar of her adolescent fantasies in the person of a sad-faced man whose whimsical Tatar eyes belied the sadness, a human male about Ray's age lolling against the wall of an unused hotel kitchen, flanked by a couple of security types, wearing the same sort of grey-sweater-over-Oxford-shirt Ray wore (though Max's were cashmere and Brooks Brothers, not acrylic and Kmart and worn through at the elbows because Ray Guerreri was too busy being an Expert to buy his own clothes and fished the old ones out of the Goodwill bag when she tried to get rid of them, giving her for the thousandth time the speech about how he'd Grown Up Poor, as if it were some badge of honor to be worn out at the elbows in perpetuity).

No, he was not Benn, but to Karen it didn't matter. She'd babbled something about being a fan of Benn's since she was in high school, gave him an autographed copy of one of her out-of-print mainstream novels, and kissed him on the cheek, brushing her lips along the unexplained scar just below his left cheekbone— one of the reasons, Karen the observer was sure, that he preferred to be shot in right profile—claiming that little bit of him for herself forever after. Reminded herself that the difference between a Famous Writer and a fangirl was sometimes only a question of degree.

Five years later, cocooned in her white room, she heard a rumor that Max was working on a sequel to his earlier memoir entitled *I AM Benn.* Stranger than fiction.

•

"Five years later"—oh, hey, no fair! You started the part about Max as if it were a new episode, as if he were talking at the con in New York at the same time Larry was trying to call Tessa, who wasn't answering because she was at the con in Asheville, and Serena was in the elevator on her way down to see her and—And now you're telling us the part about you and Max is a rerun? Sorry, Karen; that's not fair!

"And how long ago was the First Day?" she counters, thinking: *Gotcha! So you don't know everything!*

Sullen silence.

"You guys can slip-slide around in time anytime you want to but I can't? How is that fair?"

That's because we have no sense of Time.

"Had," Karen corrects them. "You do now. Azure saw to that. Guys, I need to get out of this room for a while. Can we talk?"

NINE

"And on the Second Day," the Mind dictated without ceasing. "Azure again tasted the stars and found that they were good. . . ."

"That does it!" Karen flings her pen across the room, tosses the legal pad on the floor, climbs painfully to her feet. Her ass is numb from too many hours of sitting on a hardwood floor. She goes looking for her shoes.

Quo vadis? Where do you think you're going?

"Out!" she announces. "For a nice long walk. Maybe to order some furniture. And when I come back I'm going to scrub the floors again before I do anything else, including write your goddamn novel. What're you going to do about it?"

She waits, bracing for the headache she knows is coming. Headaches can be cured, she reminds herself, but it doesn't come this time.

"Right!" she says, and stalks off. The Mind can hear water running in the bathroom, the toilet flushing. Moments later Karen emerges—face scrubbed, hair combed, house keys jingling.

There is an uneasy silence after she leaves.

She wasn't supposed to do that, Grey says thoughtfully. Grey is the thoughtful one.

They're temporal, Amber offers helpfully. *Simple little individuated minds, limited attention spans; you know how it is. She'll be back.*

That's not the issue, is it? Grey says, anguished. Hir tone catches Lake's attention, who nudges Virid tendrilly. True suffering among their own? This is an interesting development! *The point*

143

is we should have known she was going to leave right now. *Just as we shouldn't have been fooled by the Max scene. We should have recognized it as a rerun.*

Maybe there is something to this temporal reality business after all, Amber offers, though it sounds lame even to hir.

Karen, meanwhile, is way ahead of them.

Her walk has taken her down to the shoreline, beneath the bridge, not far from where she grew up. ("John Travolta country," she tells people who aren't from New York when they ask. "Where *Saturday Night Fever* was shot," she explains when they look blank; most of them get it finally, and laugh. As a nation, Hollywood is our lingua franca.) The waterfront here, she thinks, having seen *Vertigo* a few dozen times, is not so different from what she imagines it must be like by the Golden Gate Bridge in San Francisco, a city she's always wanted to see. Right now, she's wrestling with a vertigo of her own.

She'd spent twenty-two years on the wrong side of that bridge before confirming for her near-adult children what they'd suspected through closed doors and late-night shouting matches for years, that their father had one agenda and she had another. She'd told them they could make their own choices and both had opted not surprisingly to go with her. She'd left Ray Guerreri a little over a month ago, and hadn't felt a thing. She will admit she might have timed it better, might have waited until she'd finished the manuscript for *Preternatural,* but what is Time?

Since they've moved to this white-roomed apartment (she's left the living room furniture with Ray; the TV is in her son's room, out of her face), the book has begun to assume a life of its own, as all Karen's novels do once she gets past the first hundred pages. There is no doubt in her mind that in any other century she'd be looking to trade in her sheep for a decent horse and a used suit of armor; her family tree is replete with alcoholics and hypochondriacs, and she knows there is no difference at all between the voices in her head and those that persuaded Joan of Arc to reclaim France for the Dauphin.

That's why it was more important at first to keep scratching away at her rough draft than to order new furniture or rescrub the hardwood floors a second time to rid them of the reek of urine after the landlord gave her permission to rip up that execrable wall-to-wall carpet. White walls, bare floors, and the voices in her head had been better than therapy initially.

But the voices in her head have been getting unruly. Good characters will do that, and the best writers know when to give them their heads and when to haul them up short. When they start trying to convince you that it's *they* who've created *you* (which, the fangirl knows, is painfully close to the truth) it's time to go for a walk. Order new furniture, scrub the floors. Take up bonsai, biking, hiking. Start dating again. Heretofore Karen has sacrificed too much of life to her drug of choice—call it Oz or Toontown or her Brilliant Career—and now, at midpoint, wonders if it was worth it.

Back in the white room, some of them are chortling.

We've got her now! She's almost as bad off as Larry, at least as bad as Tessa. Time to turn the screws an eensy bit more!

We can always refuse to play when she comes back, someone suggests. *Go into a pout and make her feel she's lost the thread, wasted the day. We don't need to go as far as the Big Block: You'll never work in this town again! Not yet. She's good at remorse. Tomorrow she'll be more malleable.*

Maybe. Or maybe the carrot first, and we might not need the stick. . . .

•

In the shadow of the bridge, Karen closes her eyes, feeling the offshore breeze against her face, presaging rain. She is in San Francisco, waiting for Benn. He is shooting one of the *SpaceSeeker* movies, and has promised to meet her in the afternoon sun. She feels his presence behind her and leans back into him even before he rests his poet's hands on her shoulders.

"Benn, what am I going to do?" she asks softly but aloud; the day is blustery and no one is near enough to hear.

He has been her solace ever since she was sixteen: *What would Benn do?* the mantra that held the tears back, kept the rage at bay as her cold-blooded mother tried systematically to break her spirit, *Help me, Benn!* her backup when there was no backup, when a publisher folded and took a year's worth of her royalties with it, when her books languished in warehouses because an editor was having a midlife crisis, when her son tumbled off the last basement step and fractured his skull or her daughter's bus flipped over on a class trip and all Ray could do was wring his hands and chant "What should we do, what should we do?" while she, phone wedged against her shoulder as she waited for the pediatrician to pick up her call, thought *What you mean "we," Kemosabe?* It was Benn who sat up with her on the cold bathroom floor when both kids had stomach viruses and she spent the night alternately holding their heads and mopping up vomit, Benn who stroked her brow and smoothed her hair back as she soothed each child to sleep, Benn who held her when there was no one else.

"Benn, what am I going to do?" she says into the offshore breeze, her hands on his hands on her shoulders. "This thing scares me."

He cants his head to one side, considering. "Please explain."

"You know how it is when I write a novel. I *hear* the characters. Just like Joan of Arc. They talk to me. Voices are always the easiest. I have to struggle with physical descriptions, but I can always hear them."

"Was that not the case this time as well?"

"Of course it was. And when I began to see them, I thought I was having a hard time describing them just because they're so—well, alien. How do you describe moods and expressions and gestures when you've created a species of jelepathic—shit; now they've got me doing it!—telepathic jellyfish?"

"But the difficulty was more than that," Benn says with that special intuition that has saved Captain Stark's butt more times than the fans can count.

"Indeed," Karen says, unconsciously imitating his tone. Voices are the easiest. "They're too real, Benn. It's almost as if I've tapped into something that's actually there."

She turns completely around to look at him. It is she who has her hands on his shoulders now, while his are at parade-rest at his sides. She looks up without fear into all three of his eyes. Behind her, unnoticed, the scene shifts back from San Francisco, where she's never been, to Brooklyn, where she is. The same stars pass over both cities. Does that make them the same place? Behind her, gulls scream, coming in ahead of the rain.

"I take it this is not a theoretical discourse on the relative reality of Jungian archetypes and fact versus fiction?" Benn asks mildly.

"You take it correctly," Karen says, trying not to crack a smile at his solemnity. He does make her fears seem foolish.

"Is it not the subconscious desire of every science fiction writer to be the one chosen to act as interlocutor for a newfound species?"

Karen shivers, and it isn't just the wind.

"Only until it actually happens. What's the saying? 'Every action has an equal and opposite reaction'?"

"That is physics, Karen, not fiction."

She drops her hands, hugs herself to stop the shivering. "I have a feeling I'm going to pay for this." She moves past him. "Come on, my friend; let's go home. We've got work to do."

Benn does not follow her at first.

"What about the furniture?" he asks practically.

Karen turns to look at him, knowing he isn't there, knowing she's never left Brooklyn, the same stars notwithstanding.

"I'll think about that tomorrow," she says, though Scarlett O'Hara was her mother's role model, not hers. Without telling her, Benn's told her what she's going to do. She's going to write the goddamn novel, whether the S.oteri are real or not.

Back in the write womb, elbowing each other who have no elbows *(See? Told you so! Benn's the carrot—'That is fizzics, Karen, not phiction'; isn't he cute?—who needs a stick?),* they've got the next few pages ready for her:

The Dawn of the Second Day. There are stars. And we are not All There Are.

Mad dogs and jellyfish, not to mention messiahs, go out in the noonday sun. Azure stays out in the sun too long. But what s/he discovers is worth it, s/he believes.

Reach the tendrils out, and thereby reach the Mind. Is there more than just *here* to the All There Are? Reach a tendril toward the nearest star; taste it. Spectral analysis? Skeins of factoids trickle like water droplets (we remember when there was water, whee!) down the tendrils to the Mind. So noted! The Mind wonders: If we are All There Are, are we only here?

But neither fungus nor intelligence is found within the realm of the nearest star. Search on.

How many stars? More than there are ones within the Mind, and that says something. Catalogue them, for that is Time. Azure grows hungry; that also is Time. Time to go home, return to the Mind, have a munch of fungus. Please may I stay out a little longer? Yes, I; aye, eye. There must be something out there; let me try!

There is something out there, Azure is certain. Something not-fungus, not-We, but also All There Are. S/he who has not ears to hear nevertheless can taste the stars. S/he who can taste stars can also hear voices.

In the beginning was the Word. Word up! What are words, who has no tongue, and a mouth only for eating? And the Word was made flesh? Well, not on this world, bub. Ain't no flesh here, only jellyflesh—heh heh; aren't we amusing? Say, what's there to do around here for fun?

Watch and listen. Taste the stars. See through the Mind, which has no eyes, agnosic. Listen—not with ears to hear, which would hear only static, solar wind—but *listen*.

Sounds of munching, Azure lunching. Can we be serious for a moment here, please?

There are different stars at the end of the night than at the beginning; this, too, is Time. As Azure picks the last of the fungus out of hir teeth, who has no teeth, s/he at random chooses one more star.

"It is said we are not alone here in the bowl of the sky. . . ."

Say WHAT?! Please repeat transmission. Hello out there! Please stay on the line, hailing frequencies open—oh, don't hang up yet, please!

And so in a nanosecond reality changes, faster than you can say *Hand me the remote!* It's all there—unlimited cable channels, billions and billions of stars, at least some of them capable of sustaining All There Are. The Mind reels. Holy shit (who has no shit; it's fungus, remember, all the way down), look what we've found! Azure tries to telegraph it, stumbling over hir own tentacles in hir urgency, getting hir electrolytes crossed. Hey, guise? Take a look at what I found!

(Whispering simultaneously to the whatever-it-is s/he's found: *Don't go away now, please stay on the line; this will only take a moment, now that there is Time!*)

The star slips below the horizon even as the sun peers above the opposite, and there is silence. Oh, drat, oh wait, don't!

Sensory overload, who has so few senses. I really saw! Azure assures the rest, I did! I saw and heard and . . . they were just right over there . . . look, if it's telepathy, it shouldn't have anything to do with the relative position of the stars, should it? I'm telling you, it was right over—

Come in out of the sun, you damn fool, before you fry!

Thus ends the Second Day.

"Uh-uh, sorry guys; that's not where I want to go with this just yet."

Karen is back, sitting at her word processor this time (it's only the living room that has no furniture); sometimes she can work directly on-screen without a rough draft first. Back from her chat with Benn, she's decided to take charge.

But you said you wanted to know more about the first Three Days. . . .

"I've changed my mind."

She's testing them; the S.oteri know this. Action = opposite reaction. What they don't know is what she expects them to do, so how can they do the opposite?

You've changed your Mind. Okay, we see. What would you like to do next?

"Let's go back to Jess. Remember, you've only just been in touch with her in the desert. We want to find out just how much you fucked up her life after that, now, don't we? So we'll know what to expect from you in the future."

Karen's tone is dangerous—a woman on the edge, a woman perhaps who's tasted too many stars. For the moment she'd like to stick with the one she's familiar with.

Go along with her! Amber whispers. *Jess's story has Three Days in it as well; she still won't be sure if she's writing it or if whee . . .*

"It was thought at first that the carpenter's child would die . . ." Karen types, ignoring the whispering.

•

When she first came out of the desert, Jess talked nonstop for three days and three nights, her voice so hoarse it could barely be heard, so that those at the back of the crowd spilling out of her mother's small house into the alleyway, the workshop, and the courtyard beyond frequently misheard her and had to ask those in the front to repeat what she'd just said. They could not tear their eyes from her. Soon not only everyone from her village came—including the *kohen,* and there was trouble there, mutterings and dire looks before he strode away, fingering his beard—but some from surrounding villages as well.

She ate nothing, sipped water only when it was offered her, barely pausing in her words long enough to drink. She told how the Voices had led her into the desert, and what they had instructed her to do. On the dawn of the fourth day, she fell silent. Then she simply fell. She had been seated the entire time on a rug one of the neighbors had provided to cushion her bony buttocks from the packed-earth floor, another neighbor's pillow supporting her back against the baked-earth house wall. All at once her mouth snapped shut, her eyes rolled up, and she tilted over, falling facedown onto the floor in a splay of uncombed sun-singed hair.

She was taken by a kind of fit, arching her back until her heels nearly touched the back of her head, froth foaming between her clenched teeth. The village midwife took hold of her and held her in her lap like a child while the villagers recoiled and began to sidle away, and her now-blind mother, told what was happening, wondered if that blow to the head the night Herod's soldiers came had anything to do with it. The fit passed quickly, followed by a faint, which left her cold as death.

The midwife tended her, between her other duties—it had been a dark, rainy winter and there was a bumper crop of infants due—bathing her, forcing broth between her lips whenever she stirred, which was often and restlessly, the chill giving way to a wracking fever. Even the midwife despaired of her then. But the fever broke finally, and ten days after the initial fit she fooled them all, sat up as if she'd only been asleep, asked for food and ate everything she was offered, drew her own water from the well and took a bath, scrubbing herself free of the last shreds of dead skin from the dreadful sunburning, found the smallest, sharpest saw in the workshop and hacked off the burnt portions of her hair until all that remained was a crown of nascent black curls, making her look more than ever like a gawky, prepubescent boy.

"You have a visitor!" her mother called to her from the house across the alleyway just as she was burning the last bits of hair in the hearth to keep them from witches. Probably much-needed work after all the time I've lost! Jess thought, reaching for her apron, forgetting it had been in shreds when she came out of the desert, had disappeared G-d knew where while she was ill, and she hadn't had time to see the tanner about a replacement. Empty-handed, wearing only the genderless shift she'd put on after the bath, she crossed the alley and entered the small dark house.

Was it only some trick of the light that made him seem to glow?

"Yshua of Nazareth," she greeted him. "My house welcomes you. Are you thirsty?"

He indicated the dipper her mother had proffered before scuttling away, no doubt feeling her way along the house walls to find an open doorway and tell the neighbors who was visiting. The dipper was full, untouched. Refreshment, Jess thought, is not what's on his mind!

"It is said you were in the desert," he began without preamble, his voice less hoarse and far pleasanter than hers for all his preaching.

"So it is also said of you," Jess replied warily. She offered him the bench against the wall where her mother usually sat, but he would not sit down. Neither did she. Almost they circled each other, as if in some manner of contest.

For all his carpenter's sinew, he looks like a girl! Jess thought, wondering how he kept those long locks so neat, uncovered against the desert wind. Then again, I look like a boy, so what's the point?

"Tell me what you saw?" He voiced it as a request, but Jess knew it for a demand.

"I didn't see; I heard them," she answered him as she had answered the villagers on that first night. "Voices. Sometimes one alone, sometimes many at once. Other times many saying different things, yet I could hear and understand each voice distinctly."

He seemed to consider this. "What did they say to you, these Voices?"

"That there is more to G-d's creation than only men and angels," Jess replied, then clamped her jaw shut. He'd get no more out of her without a tradeoff! "And what of you? What wonders did you see or hear in your forty days of fasting?"

"I was tempted," was all he said, and for the first time looked away from her, turning his eyes inward to some hidden memory. The moment lasted an eternity, and Jess began to feel some of the chill she had experienced without knowing it while she was in her ten-day swoon. When he turned his eyes back to her, they were fervid. "I was tempted, but I prevailed. I wonder if you also were tempted, but did not realize it was a temptation."

Hence, stupid woman that I am, I succumbed where you prevailed! Jess finished the sentence for him in her mind. She folded her arms across her chest. He'd get no more out of her at all!

"And naturally," she said, "as you are a man, you were right not to heed the Voices, and I was wrong, is that it?"

His soft mouth curved slightly at the corners in what might have been a smile. "That isn't what I said."

"You don't have to say it!" Jess snapped. He was a guest in her house; she ought to be more gracious. Instead, she fought the urge to run him out into the courtyard like a stray dog. "Is that all you came here for?"

Her hostility seemed to compel him toward the door.

"I was going to ask you to come and hear me preach."

It's a trap! Jess thought. If I acquiesce, he'll make an example of me before the crowd, offer to expel my "demons," thank you very much! If I refuse, I'm being a foolish woman, afraid of the challenge because I know I'm wrong. Nevertheless, she said: "I'd like that. But I've work to catch up on. Surely you can understand."

She had neither refused nor committed; did he understand? He had his back to her, his hand raised to the lintel, which was low enough so that he'd have to duck to clear it; his head inclined against the strong sunlight beyond in what might have been a nod of understanding, one carpenter to another. Yshua had had kin to look after his mother when he chose to abandon his father's work; Jess did not.

"Maybe the next time you pass this way . . ." Jess offered; it was vague enough not to be taken as a promise.

He did nod then, and slipped outside. Had he come alone? Surely he hadn't walked it? By the time she reached the doorway, her bare feet quick against the packed-earth floor, he was nowhere in sight. If he had left footprints, the temperamental wind had swept them clean. Whatever the first-century Aramaic equivalent of the mountain's coming to Mohammed, Jess was thinking it.

•

"Very good, everyone!" Karen announces, saving the file. It's dinnertime of the longest day she can remember; she'll come back to this later, now that there is Time. "I really like the way you skirt the issue. Flirt with blasphemy without actually succumbing to it. Your style is subtle, yet surprising."

Is that a critique, or a wine commercial?

"Oh, and sarcasm! Even better. Not to mention understanding the frame of reference in order to compare a book review with a wine ad. You're learning!"

Everything we needed to know about sarcasm we learned from you. And are you learning, Karen? Learning to trust us?

"I started out trusting you," she says, turning off the word processor, never sure if that saves more electricity than leaving it on. "Now I'm not so sure."

A long-suffering sigh ripples down the tentacles. Their earlier subjects had been so much easier to work with.

•

". . . and so what it does is focus the solar energy through natural crystalline facets that were forged on the first day of Creation, because quartz crystals, as you may not know, are among the most ancient of life-forms. . . ."

The dealers' room was bigger than she'd expected for a con this size, and Serena let its sights and sounds wash over her, sensory overload, loving it. The woman in the waist-length silver hair and velvet Navajo skirt at the table next to hers had the usual pewter wizards and china unicorns to sell, along with handmade jewelry in turquoise and quartz crystal and—

". . . suncatchers, which the Plains Indians believed symbolized the cosmic force, so that they were also called 'soul catchers,' to be used to capture a fleeting spirit from the other side— though only for benevolent purposes—and it could tell you about next season's harvest or your wife's fertility—"

The young couple listening to her spiel laughs nervously; the girl is very evidently pregnant.

"—or whatever," the crone says, joining in the laughter.

Crone, Serena thinks, having heard her explaining to someone else before that she was a "hag," which she had it in her mind was the female equivalent of "hawk." Well, hell, Serena thought; that's news to me. Have to ask Karen about it, when I finally get to meet her. Karen's a writer; she'll be able to tell me for sure. Right, Rain? For now: crone, hag, witch-woman, you're no more Navajo than I am, but if it sells suncatchers . . .

". . . nowadays people just hang them in their windows because they're attractive, without realizing their true significance. . . ."

Or hang 'em from their ears because you've just sold them a pair of 'em! Serena thought, amused, watching the transaction go down. Everyone has their drug of choice; it all depends on what you believe in.

What Serena believed in right now was Tessa McGill and her ability to connect with her through Rain and the rest of them. As soon as she could get someone to mind her art table for her, she could go stand on the autograph line and possibly alter the face of the universe.

Or at least find a cure for what ailed her.

•

The Voices told Jess she could cure her mother's blindness.

Not that this was anything new in her part of the world. Even Yshua, the rumors had it, had cured a beggar's blindness with mud and spittle. (Ugh, how like a man! Jess remembered thinking when she heard it. Then again, considering what other bodily fluids he might have chosen, that beggar got away easy!) She hated to see her mother this way, sitting in the corner all day, rocking and muttering, useless. Besides, the house was a midden with no one to clean it. Jess's time was divided between work and preaching now, and more often than not she came home to darkness, clutter, the fire gone out, and nothing to eat.

She'd at least gone outside the village to fetch some clean soil, as opposed to the filth of the Jerusalem marketplace, trampled by a thousand thousand feet, that Yshua had casually scooped out of the Temple yard. (Was it supposed to be sacred because it was

gathered near the Temple? Filth was filth.) She'd brought it
home in her leather apron and spat on it, mixing it with her fingers, but it felt wrong.

"This isn't going to work!" she told the Voices irritably.
"What am I doing wrong here?"

There are fluids a woman has that a man has not, they answered.

"You can't be serious!" Jess scowled. In fact, lately her periods had begun drying up—prematurely, according to the midwife; she was scarcely thirty—but that sometimes happened, the
midwife suggested, with women as freakish-made as she. Yet
even as she gave voice to her skepticism she felt the familiar warm
gush between her legs. Oh, by the Nameless! She began to curse.
It wasn't time, she wasn't prepared, and she almost dropped the
pat of mud in her palm in her frantic search for a cloth to tie up
her crotch before she stained her best—her only—Sabbath robe.
She had worn it to go out into the desert and fetch the mud; it
seemed somehow appropriate to the solemnity of what she was
about to do. Still cursing, she wondered if she'd ruined the
magic. Wasn't one supposed to keep one's mind and heart pure,
much less one's mouth? Imagine Yshua using such language.

She couldn't, and the thought calmed her. She breathed
slowly, taking deep breaths the way she'd seen the midwife in-
struct laboring women. Then, feeling foolish (well, who could
see her? Her mother crouched in her corner, rocking and crooning, alone in her little world, and there was no one else here except the Voices. They already knew what was going to happen;
they had told her that, like angels, they owed no homage to time),
she lifted her skirts and scooped a little blood out onto her fingers and began to mix it with the mud.

She tried not to shudder. Never mind that the *kohen* preached
that women were by nature unclean or that the midwife refuted
him by stating that this was the stuff the unborn fed on, it was
slimy on the fingers and rank to the nose, and Jess would rather
be doing anything else. When it seemed mixed enough into the
mud so that none but she and the Voices knew what it was, she
went and crouched beside her mother.

Her mother's head came up; she sniffed the air as had become her custom, to recognize her daughter.

"What is it?" she whined softly, wanting to be alone in her darkness; she cringed as something warm and glutinous touched her eyelids in the shape of Jess's fingers. "What are you doing?"

"Hush, and keep your eyes closed!" Jess instructed her, daubing the mess on thoroughly, covering both eyes, corner to corner. "I met an herb seller on the camel road this afternoon. . . ." Not too big a lie! she thought; she had indeed met an herb seller, though with her usual impatience she had dismissed him and his wares. She was finished now, wiping her fingers furtively on a rag. "He said he had something guaranteed to cure blindness. Considering what he charged, I thought this couldn't hurt. . . ."

"Nor will it help!" her mother muttered in despair. "It burns. And it stinks! What's in it?"

"Be patient," Jess said instead of answering. "It has to set for a few minutes." She tried to remember what the gossips had told her about Yshua's technique with the beggar, and wondered if the same method would work for menstrual blood as for a man's saliva. "I'm going to the well to get some clean water. Have you washed up in no time."

As she dipped the water from the well, she felt the blood flow stop as suddenly as it had begun. Oh well, she thought, good riddance! There was nothing she needed it for anyway. She went back into the house.

Tears streamed from the carpenter's widow's new-opened eyes.

"A miracle!" she breathed, gripping her daughter's shoulders, memorizing that hard, mannish face as if she expected to have it removed from her sight again. "A miracle!" she said again, even louder.

"I wish you'd keep quiet about it!" Jess growled. "As far as the neighbors are concerned, you merely woke from a deep sleep to find your eyes reopened. A miracle, yes, but nothing to do with me. I've been in the shop all day, if they ask; if they don't, don't volunteer it. If they learn the truth there'll be the Nameless to pay!"

You should have thought of that before! the Voices whispered.

Well, she had, but had decided to take the risk anyway. She didn't need the Voices to tell her that this, as much as her preaching, was eventually going to cost her dear. By being different, she had embraced death since the day she was born.

TEN

*Y*ou see, Karen, Jess had a choice. *You all have choices. You can ignore us from the very beginning, stay with us for life, or dismiss us at any time. Even the degree to which you accept us is relative. Larry thinks we're an aphrodisiac; he'll never really get it. Max accepts us pretty much the way Hypatia does, like rainbows. A natural phenomenon, pretty to look at, but he's not quite sure what to do with us. Bottle a rainbow? That's not Max. Though it may be Tessa. . . .*

"You're rambling," Karen says irritably. "Let's try to stay with dialogue I can use, okay?"

. . . or consider us the enemy, like Ray or Jess's kohen . . .

"You know, that's another thing I meant to ask you about. Are you sure *kohen* isn't an anachronism that early? Wouldn't it have been *abba* for 'father' instead? And—hey, wait a minute! Ray, as in my ex? You've been in touch with *Ray?*"

She can just picture it, and she does—Ray listening to their sales pitch with that narrow-eyed scowl of his, raising one hand finally to interrupt them, politely, the way he does with strangers, the way he does with anyone except his wife, ex-wife ("Let me ask you this . . . in exchange you want what? My soul?") not too differently from the way it happened.

"How long ago was this?"

"How long ago was what?" Serena asks helpfully. Karen hits the ground with a bump. It's alternate universe time.

A minute ago she was in her white room; now she's at the

con in Asheville with Serena and Tessa McGill. Or maybe she's there instead of Tessa McGill, a last-minute replacement because the Star didn't show up; how many times has she played that gig? Or maybe she's still in the white room and Serena's joined her. Or maybe this is all from a chapter in her novel, a chapter she hasn't written yet, which doesn't mean it isn't there.

Serena's just as puzzled, but pleasantly so. With all the medications she's on, shifts in regional reality don't bother her anymore. She's learned to go with the flow.

"I—I'm sorry!" Karen says sincerely, completely nonplussed. "I was talking to someone else."

"That's okay; take your time," Serena says cryptically. "You just looked kind of lonely over here, so I thought I'd come visit you since the line for Tessa McGill's about a mile long. . . ."

That's plausible, too, Karen thinks. Unless you're a Celebrity Author, as opposed to just an author, you rarely sign more than a dozen autographs a day before you're buttonholed by the local equivalent of her ex-husband ("You know, I always wanted to write a book about such-and-such, but I need about six thousand dollars to buy the right computer. . . ."), whom she can usually stop in his tracks by asking in all seriousness: "Did Shakespeare use a Mac?" but she doesn't think that's Serena's role in today's game. She'll wait and let the story come to her.

From Serena's point of view, one minute she was taking a break from her table in the dealers' room to see what the competition was up to, stopping at a table featuring nothing but Merlin art (Arthur and Merlin as Captain Stark and Benn, Arthur and Merlin as Sam and Al, occasionally even Arthur and Merlin as Arthur and Merlin), the next she had to decide: Stand on the mile-long line to talk to Tessa McGill? Use her disability to get bumped to the front and risk that special condescension so many celebrities save for anyone whose disabilities can't be fixed by a Hollywood plastic surgeon ("But, dear, you're just not trying hard enough. Have you considered image therapy?")? Or talk to the writer, whose line is that much shorter?

And who may not even be there, on this time line.

Go with the flow, Serena thinks: Seize the day. She leaves Merlin and friends behind, strolls out of the dealers' room to run athwart of Tessa McGill's autograph line, which snakes down both sides of the narrow hotel corridor toward the table where the Guest of Honor is signing copies of her books and glossy photos, some of which go all the way back to her song-and-dance days, smiling her professional smile, fluttering her fingers at the gofers ever so eager to fetch her ice water, herb tea, a better pen than the one she's using.

Serena shouldered her large self through the crowd until she was even with the table but off to one side, so no one would accuse her of cutting in. If anyone had any doubts about the seriousness of her illness, all they had to do was look at her—the chronic pallor, the icy sweats, the livid uninterrupted scar that runs like a zipper the length of her spine, the dogtags listing her conditions and the medications she takes for them, the leg braces that enable her to walk by swinging her legs from side to side because she can no longer trust her knees, the burn marks between her fingers where, because she has no sensation in her hands, she sometimes forgets she has a cigarette burning. Serena's proximity to death automatically puts her at the front of the line.

But being at the front of the line is not what she has in mind today. She nods at the security people and pulls up a chair at the far end of the table from where Tessa is signing. Tessa doesn't notice her, which is just the way Serena wants it. She takes out her sketchbook, decides she guessed right and Tessa's right profile is the better one, scooches her chair sideways a bit to pull in a three-quarter profile, and begins to draw.

•

Tessa's sixth sense tells her she is being scrutinized. Not just watched—as a celebrity you got used to that; it became a kind of white noise behind every aspect of your life the minute you set foot outside your front door ("Isn't that Tessa McGill? God, she looks so much older in person!"), until, positive or negative, you couldn't live without it, only became aware of it when it stopped, filling you with terror, the fear of having disappeared, because if you weren't Tessa McGill, who were you, and how would producers and talk-show hosts remember you if *you* didn't know who you were?—but rather seriously *memorized,* right down to her pores. Tessa was used to being watched, but not scrutinized.

Between autographs she slid her mascaraed glance toward the far end of the table and saw her—a great square block of a woman, an absolute mountain of a woman, well over two hundred pounds of what was not fat but had to be solid muscle, sitting serenely with a sketchbook and a fistful of pencils, drawing her.

Tessa's first impulse was to put a stop to that. She had strict rules about her public appearances—still cameras only, no flash attachments from less than ten feet (she was convinced flashbulbs left permanent scars on your retinas), and absolutely no recording devices, video or audio; she'd gone so far in some places as to have security search bags at the door before allowing an audience in. She'd been more lax this time because it was North Carolina, not New York or Vegas or L.A., and everyone was so laid-back and polite and helpful you didn't want to upset them.

Besides, she'd brought Eddie along to prowl the perimeter undercover, not that he could in this place, the silly twit. His languorous attitude and prep school accent had almost gotten the shit beaten out of him in the hotel's C&W lounge the night before. Trust Eddie to stroll over to the pool table in the C&W lounge of a hotel in North Carolina and ask for a game without a clue to how dangerous it could be for strange fruit like him. Tessa had had to use all her eyelashes and the traces of her own Southern accent to extricate him from the grip of a couple of belligerent beer bellies who were going to show him what real men do for fun before they let him go.

He owed her, big-time. But he'd gone floating off on his own again after lunch and she hadn't seen him since. Without him, she didn't quite know how to handle this; she'd never had to deal with anyone *sketching* her before. She supposed once the sketch was finished the artist would try to either sell it to her or ask her to autograph it so it could be sold to a dealer. Pure profit for the artist, at Tessa's expense.

Not on your life! Tessa thought, and was about to say, in her best glass-cutting voice:

"Ex*cuse* me, but I'd appreciate it ever so much if you'd put that sketch pad away, since I'm positive I didn't give you permission to draw me. . . ."

—but something stopped her.

For one thing, the artist had an incredibly powerful aura, and it might not be a good idea to challenge her. For another, she knew this woman. Yes, she'd seen her prototype at every single one of these conventions, but this was different. A resonance from another life? No, even more different than that. Besides, maybe she only wanted to give Tessa the sketch as a gift, payback for all those wonderful moments in her local movie theater. She would gush about how much she loved Tessa's latest show-tunes album, Tessa would make appreciative noises, and everyone would go away happy. She could always file the sketch in the wastebasket next to the bidet in her suite (if her suite had actually had a bidet), unless by some remote chance it was any good.

Taking a cleansing breath and feeling calmer, Tessa signed yet another publicity photo of herself in a much younger incarnation, smiled her professional smile, and added another two dollars (the prints went for five; she got forty percent) to her mental coffers. At last count she'd signed over a hundred copies of her books, too. Then there was her appearance fee. So far, not a bad weekend at all.

She was working the cramp out of her signing hand when the last autograph seeker sidled gratefully away and Eddie materialized behind her.

"How're we holding up?" he asked, massaging her shoulders.

"What you mean 'we,' Kemosabe?" she flashed, shrugging

him off, irritated or pretending to be. "Where the hell have you been?"

"Oh, mercy, Miz Scarlett, don't yell at me! I've had a bitch of an afternoon."

Tessa's mouth quirked up in spite of herself. "And I'm sure you'll tell me all about it, too." She sighed, which was Eddie's cue to gather her belongings and get her back up to the suite unmolested.

The corridor had been closed off; security had been informed that Miss McGill needed to nap for a few hours before the banquet in her honor this evening. Two security people manned the doors at the far end, allowing only hotel personnel in to empty the trash and police the area. Somehow the mountainous woman with the sketchbook had eluded everyone's scrutiny; she was still there.

Or maybe she was in another part of the hotel, or another part of the universe, talking to Karen. For now, let's imagine she's right here, waiting to talk to Tessa.

She rose ponderously to her feet, not so much to intercept Tessa—who was a lot smaller, and a lot more agile—as to let her choose whether or not to acknowledge her. Eddie was sizing her up and hoping he could bully her with his voice; he'd had enough close encounters with the local fauna for one weekend.

"Miss McGill has to rest now!" he announced imperiously.

"I know that," the big woman said, holding the sketchbook out toward Tessa to let her decide whether or not to look at it. "Just wanted to show her something first."

Tessa looked and almost dropped her teeth.

Not only was the likeness incredibly good, and just subtle enough to take five years off her without obvious ass-kissing, but what she took at first to be just some sort of pretty-colored aura surrounding her now leaped into her line of vision to become—Oh, goddess! Tessa thought—images of her old friends the jellyfish.

Unable to take her eyes off the sketch, Tessa handed Eddie her tote bag and the portfolio filled with her glossies.

"Eddie, sweet, pop upstairs with all that stuff and draw me a bath," she said, patting his shoulder distractedly. "I'll be up in a little while."

Just as the bath began to deteriorate from soothingly hot to tepid, Eddie would give up in disgust and slip into the tub himself. Tessa wouldn't make it back upstairs until just before the banquet, and only because Eddie went back down to fetch her, hurrying her through a shower and a blow-dry, picking out her clothes for her because she was so not-there. At the banquet, the committee would be all abuzz wondering whether Miss McGill had had a few on an empty stomach (she wasn't noted for being a drinker, was she? They'd never have invited her if they'd thought . . .) because she seemed so preoccupied.

Miss McGill, in fact, was stone cold sober.

But Eddie's esper rating was nil, which was why he and Tessa got along so well; he didn't have to worry about her poking around in his mind because she invariably hit a stone wall. Okay, so he couldn't read her mind either, and he couldn't foretell the future, and even if he could see any jellyfish in the sketch—which he couldn't—he wouldn't have known what it meant, so he had no idea why this big bad bitch suddenly held his employer spellbound.

"Miz Scarlett, are you okay?"

"Fine, love," Tessa said vaguely, not looking at him but at Serena. When he still didn't move, she gave him a little shove. "Shoo, now. Mother's busy."

She motioned Serena to sit beside her at the long folding table.

"You and I have to talk."

"Sure thing," Serena acquiesced, sitting down heavily. "Only I can't talk long. I want to catch Karen before the banquet, too. . . ."

•

"No!" Karen insists. She's about to fling her pen across the room again. She used to be a lot calmer before she began this book. "Guys, knock it off; I mean it! I'm not down in Asheville,

I'm right here. Serena can't talk to me because I'm not there."

"That's okay!" Serena says serenely, easing her great bulk onto the floor; for some reason she no longer needs her knee braces and she's a lot more flexible than she's been since she was a kid. "I can come here instead. Can't stay long, though, if you won't let me smoke."

She smokes those damn brown cigarettes, Karen knows; the ones that look like thin cigars, and smell about as bad. She has a rule, following twenty-very-odd years with Ray, that no one is allowed to smoke in her new apartment. How does Serena know that?

"Wait a minute. No; I refuse to play this!" Karen is on her feet, backing away from Serena as if she were a ghost, a very substantial ghost. "I haven't met you. Yet. If I'm supposed to meet you at all. If you even exist. You can't be here."

Serena shrugs, stubs out a cigarette in the ashtray on her drawing table in the trailer on the side of the mountain, closer to the stars. "That's okay, too. You can come to my place instead. I can tell you about the lake colors, remember?"

"No, I don't remember, because it hasn't happened. Yet. If it's even—look, I don't mean to be rude but . . . guys? You can't bend the time line like this. It isn't believable. My editor's going to have a cow."

You did. When you did that flashback about meeting Benn—er, Max. Actually, Benn and Max. Max five years ago; Benn yesterday afternoon.

"Flashback, yes. You can do flashback, to the past," Karen is trying to explain, as if to a precocious but not yet experienced child. Serena is gone, if she was ever here. Nobody here but us jellyfish, Kemosabe. "But you can't flash forward. Not with humans. Our minds can't handle it."

Then why do so many of your kind consult Tessa's so-called Readers & Advisors?

"Well, I don't!" Karen says righteously. "I don't believe in any of that stuff. Ancient Astronauts, either."

Which is why we've chosen you to be our—what? Messiah?

"I don't think so!" Karen snaps. Damn feisty, these humans! "What, do I get to be crucified and everything?"

Interlocutor at least. [*Which one of you Mindless idiots said "messiah"?*] *Ahem. We like you. You're a lot like Hypatia, entirely skeptical. You present such a challenge to our skills.*

"Well, you're treading very dangerously here!" Karen warns them, settling down, refusing to be flattered. A lot like Hypatia! And look what happened to her! "Keep the shifting time lines in the fiction, please. You keep popping real-life people into my living room, the deal is off."

They don't argue, so she assumes she's won. Silly human!

"Right. Let's leave Serena and Tessa together in Asheville and leave me out of it. . . ."

•

The Dawn of the Third Day. Azure has been disbelieved.

Pay attention, please, this is important. A Mind that holds all truth within it, theoretically, cannot doubt. A Mind that eidetically retains every datum it has ever learned in an eternal present can theorize such a thing as untruth or inaccuracy, but cannot prove either. How, then, is Azure not believed?

There are those that are All There Are that are not only here! s/he reports on the Second Day.

Certainly, the Mind replies, *this is within the realm of the possible.*

It's true! Azure insists impatiently.

The Mind demurs. *Perhaps . . .*

Azure has provided the Mind with a full report on hir experiences, of tasting stars, of hearing the voice that is not voice (telepathy?) speaking from a somewhere-over-the-horizon world (now, here's a question: Why can't the voice be heard once the planet slips below the S.oteri's event horizon? Do brain waves travel in straight lines like radio waves? Be careful; you're on dangerous ground here!), the voice that spoke without speaking: *It is said we are not alone here in the bowl of the sky. . . .*

Is this a thought the Mind has had? *Of course!* the Mind retorts, producing it intact from whatever millennium it was first thought. *All thought exists in the Mind, for the Mind is All There Is, um, Are.*

Then if we accept the thought as its own axiom, Azure argues, *if the Mind can consider itself to be not-alone, who else might?*

Silence. Determined to prove hir point, Azure ventures forth on the Third Day.

The over-the-horizon world is also silent on the Third Day. Time to try elsewhere. Again as before, how countless many times, Azure tastes another star. To find hir unlimited cable channels all at a single source.

Urth? Is that what they call themselves? In how many different languages? You mean there's more than one? Oh, my! The burble and chatter of All There Are overload a seeking telepathic jellyfishic mind until Azure learns out of sheer survival to damp, narrow band, select, bleed out the static, one frequency at a time. What an embarrassment of riches! S/he cannot wait to tell the Mind.

But first, while s/he controls the remote, let us play. . . .

S/he might have spent hir time exploring the species that had the most numbers, but fairly quickly recognized them as fungus, even if they had six legs or udders *(moo!)*. Only the ones who sent the messages were All There Are (though there were some in the waters that came close), and there were only so many hours in a day. Besides, if it weren't for the thoughts, the voices, messages, s/he never would have found them. They were doing what s/he was doing, tasting the stars.

How strange they were! How long did it take Azure to understand that their color changes (. . . the purple border at first permitted only to the Julian family, later to members of the Senate . . . "wash your hands often, your feet seldom, your head never" . . . the clothes you wear for the way you live . . . don't get your knickers in a knot . . .) were not like hir own?

Oh, eye sea, those are called clothes. *They can be removed, and when they remove them . . . oh, my!*

Oh, my what? I don't have any of those. Not eyes or ears or much

*of a mouth. Can't osculate with just an orifice; you gotta have lips,
not to mention heart. Skin, now there's a novelty! Pity it never changes
color the way ours does, but it looks awfully comfy. Interesting how
their tentacles specialize according to form rather than function but, my
goodness! Arms, legs, fingers, toes; what varieties of havoc one could
wreak with those! Throats slit, heads rolled, rape and pillage. Tickling.*

*Sex organs. Since they can't change color, maybe that's
how this species comes in flavors? Or just comes? (Ewe see,
I'm learning!) Look what one or two (or more) can do with
those. . . .*

Thus ought to have ended the Third Day. But Azure stays out
in the sun too long, overstays hir welcome then, beside hirself,
tries to tell the Mind.

*Yo! Hey, guise? Look what I found! It followed me home; can I
keep it?*

S/he transmits it all back to the Mind, to any of the tendrils
that will listen, even as it pours through hir from the billions and
billions of minds that moil and broadcast unaware they're being
overheard, mind waves like radio waves sent at random Out
There, uncontrolled. It bubbles and burbles through the All of
the Mind, which recoils at first and then, predictably parochially,
reacts:

*THAT'S ENOUGH! COME BACK HERE AND STOP
THIS AT ONCE!*

Is it that Azure, who has no ears, does not hear? Or does s/he
think this is one of the little unconnected minds among the billions, trivial hence not worth heeding? Or does s/he—a first—
defy?

*Nyaah, nyaah, look what I've found! Be nice to me or I won't share,
so there! Isn't this fun? Whee!*

*What you mean "whee," Kemosabe? You can't talk, remem-
ber?*

Whee *can't talk, ewe mean!* Azure answers. *So what? Haven't ewe
ever thought a* Whee *bit in your mind, kicking up your heels*

with joy, even if you have no heels? Stop blending all the colors into grey and share with me ("and yes I said yes I will yes")—whee!

Whether the Mind accepts the offer or not, Azure, who remembers All, will not remember. Because like a kid playing on the beach too long and ending up with blisters, like Serena's fingers that don't feel the cigarette until she smells the flesh burning, Azure—who still doesn't understand Time—gets caught up in its slip-slide and stays out in the sun too long. Too late the realization: *I'm fried!*

Fried, Azure died.

It was a very long Time ago. Or maybe it hasn't happened yet. At any rate, Karen, it's a part of our history we're not proud of, especially after what happened next, so we don't share it with just anybody, do you understand?

"Yes, I do understand, actually," Karen says very quietly. "And I'm honored that you've chosen to share it with me. Who else knows about it? On this time line, I mean."

We'd rather not say. What you said before about humans not being able to slip-slide into the future . . . ?

Karen nods, deciding to trust them again—for now.

•

"You're telling me they're real," Serena said slowly after she and Tessa had talked for nearly two hours. "You've seen them, too."

"You knew they were, or you wouldn't have worked them into your sketch of me," Tessa said, not quite scolding her. Serena stubbed out her cigarette, which was beginning to get on Tessa's nerves, and grinned her little-girl grin.

"Yeah, I guess so. I wasn't sure, though. I'm on so many meds, I thought at first they were part of that. So I figured if you didn't notice them, or thought they were just some kind of background, then I'd know they were just mine. But if you saw them, I mean truly *saw* them . . ."

Tessa nodded. "It was a test for both of us. You, to see if you were hallucinating. Me, to see if I was a fake or the genuine article."

"Something like that." Serena desperately wanted another cigarette but stopped herself. "So where do we go from here?" Tessa gave her a quizzical look. "I don't understand."

"Well, don't you think we ought to tell somebody? It's obvious we're being contacted by—something. Extraterrestrials, creatures from another dimension, but something. Are we the only ones? Shouldn't we be trying to find out if there are others?"

"And how do you propose we do that?"

"Oh, I don't mean me. I mean you. You're a celebrity. Your books sell thousands of copies—"

"Hundreds of thousands."

"Whatever."

"Listen, Miss Bell—Serena, is it?—I think it's lovely that you and I have this—connection—with the jellyfish in common, but that's exactly all we have in common. It doesn't make us friends for life. And while I'd love to explore this further with you, you have to understand that I'm a very busy person and . . ."

This time Serena did reach for a cigarette, lighting it one-handed with a disposable lighter. What the hell, if Tessa could blow smoke, so could she. This was supposed to be the easy part! The opals, jellyfish—whatever either of them chose to call them, which probably had nothing to do with what they called themselves, if they called themselves anything at all—*meant* something, something important. And here was this silly woman—a psychic, if you believed her books—who was so busy obsessing over how many copies those books sold that she was missing the big picture.

". . . and I think if you were being fair you'd have to acknowledge that I've spent far more time with you than with anyone else at this con . . ." Tessa was saying, wondering where the security people had gone now that she needed them. She'd spent all the time she intended to with this really rather scary woman, and now it was time to make her exit. She got to her feet and started sidling toward the elevators.

"Please understand something," she said, all but patting Serena's hand. "I feel for you with your disability and all, I sincerely do, but there's really nothing more we have to say to each other, now, is there?" She batted her eyelashes expectantly; they had never failed her before. She took another careful step toward the elevators.

Serena felt like smashing something, preferably Tessa's face, but that would hardly advance the cause of man or jellyfish. She blew smoke and tried again.

"Look, did it ever occur to you—and I'm not putting you down as a psychic, because obviously you're good enough at it to make a living, which I never was . . . oh, I used to read Tarot in the state hospital whenever they let me out of restraints, but it was a parlor trick, see? A way to get them to untie me, and I'd do anything to get them to untie me. So I'd spin the most outrageous fantasies, tell them anything they wanted to hear . . ."

"And?" Tessa prompted, thinking *Humor her; keep her talking!* as she took another step.

"What I'm trying to say is that you and I are connected now, through the opals, the jellyfish, whatever you want to call them. And it means something. We can't be the only ones. We've got to do something!"

You bet your ass we do, sweetie! Tessa thought. *You've got to spend the rest of your limited life span looking for a cure for your disease. And I've got to get away from you and dress for dinner, and as soon as I get back to New York I've got to come to terms with the fact that I'm not the only one in this century to be in touch with them and then I've got to do something I probably should have done decades ago, which is form a game plan. Which no way nohow includes you!*

"Honey, listen, I don't know how to break this to you," Tessa said, "but they've been buzzing around me since my early teens, and I'm not even going to tell you how long ago that was. If they haven't conquered the world or even fucked up the phone lines in that amount of time, I doubt they mean us any harm. Even UFOs have taken prisoners; these little friends of ours haven't done that. I think we should just appreciate them for what they are and not try to exploit them, don't you?"

Serena blew smoke rings, surrounding them both in a blue haze; Rain twinkled in the corner of her left eye like a migraine aura. She was on the right track; she knew it. She'd made the mistake of alerting Tessa to something she hadn't thought of before, something she was damn well going to exploit on her own once she got rid of Serena. If Serena let her. She made a sudden move to block Tessa's escape.

"You're not going to just blow me off!" she said, breaking out in a sweat, huge teardrops of perspiration popping out on her forehead and running down her face. "This is not just about you and me, it's about something way bigger than either of us, something cosmic. You're in touch with people from all over the world—famous people, important people. You can—"

Tessa saw Eddie step out of the elevator and practically collapsed with relief.

Serena saw him, too, all six-foot-four and 150 pounds of him; she knew she could pick him up with one hand and snap him in half with the other, or could have if she'd taken her meds an hour ago like she was supposed to. Tessa wasn't the only one about to collapse.

"Oh, hell!" she said, shouldering the bag with her sketchbook in it, thinking: *Okay, Rain, I've done my bit; the bitch just ain't listening!* "I can take a hint. I'm outta here. You've got my business card in case you change your mind and try to see it my way."

Tessa showed it to her, still in the palm of her hand. "I most certainly do."

"If you ever run into anyone else who's in touch with them . . . because it would be a bitch for me to try to get in touch with you—"

"Of course!" Tessa finished for her, smiling her patronizing smile. "It was lovely talking to you. Take care of yourself now, hear?"

Oh, I hear! Serena thought, watching Tessa trail off into the elevator, a scolding Eddie in tow. *Believe me, I hear!*

ELEVEN

When we last left Larry Koster, he was trying unsuccessfully to get in touch with Tessa. By now he's called everyone in the business he can trust (it's a short list) and come up empty. He has several options.

He can write the script himself, using just enough of the one he's optioned from the fanboy as a base, give the kid a "based on a story by" credit and a kiss-off fee, and launch himself from there. He's already preparing his one-line story pitch: "A space-age messiah forms an alliance with extraterrestrials, saving their planet as well as his own" . . . from whatever the threat to the two planets happens to be. That's the only part he hasn't figured out yet. He'll offer it to the studios as a break-out project—written, produced, directed by, and starring Laurence Koster. Or maybe he'll go easy on himself and just take a supporting role, let a—ahem—younger actor play the messiah. It'll be up to the studio to decide where to go with it. Feature film, movie of the week, pilot for a series?

Or maybe there's an even easier way to go with it. After all, he's busy with his cop show, there are rumblings about another *SpaceSeekers* sequel, his horses are a full-time job in themselves; he doesn't have time to write an entire script. Maybe he'll hire himself a ghostwriter to do a couple of novels first, then peddle them for screen rights. All he'll have to do is feed the writer a one-page outline now and then and let him do all the work. Has the kid he optioned the script from ever written a novel? How about a whole series of novels, a comic book spinoff, action figures? The possibilities are endless.

Who is he kidding? The market's already glutted with that kind of thing, and if people aren't returning his calls that's a message in itself. He can't carry this entire thing himself; he needs a partner. Someone with some credibility.

Like Max. Max has been turning down offers to direct from people who won't give Larry the time of day. According to a squib in last week's *Variety,* Max is finishing up shooting on a nice little family film and is looking for a new project, something, in Max's words, "different." This project, with its sci-fi thrust, would be a natural change of pace. And the "reunion" angle—Captain Stark and his faithful sidekick Benn reunite to save the universe again, this time for another major studio or publisher or independent network or, hell, even cable if the price was right . . . Larry can just see the headlines, front-page *Variety* this time.

But Max was not on Larry's short list because Larry knows he will want to direct as well as coproduce. Not only that, but Max actually *will* direct, which will include telling Larry where to get off, when to stop doing shtick and hogging the closeups and cutting other people's lines and behave himself. Larry can just hear him:

"Larry, Larry, *tochis anf tisch,* you want it good or you want it 'A Laurence Koster Production'? Perspective, my friend. You've got to trust your director."

Larry's been bullying directors for decades. It's not going to work with Max, even on his own film. And if Max starts making script changes, as Max is wont to do . . .

So why bother? Why doesn't he just run his horses, live on his points from the *SpaceSeekers* movies, stop agitating? For once it's about more than being A Laurence Koster Production. It's about finding and nailing down those goddamn jellyfish. Otherwise, Larry just knows, he'll never get it up again.

•

Meanwhile, back in New York, Max Neimark is the featured guest on *Live with Regis and Kathie Lee,* talking about his new film.

What is Karen, who sleeps until ten and rarely watches television, doing up this early with the TV on?

"...a novel my wife was reading, actually, while we were on our honeymoon..." Max is saying, "...which I thought would make an interesting little film. We keep hearing so much about family values from both sides of the political spectrum, and it's occurred to me that movies have reached a point in their evolution where a studio can take a chance on something that doesn't necessarily have to be a blockbuster."

"Especially when it's directed by a Name and has such a surprising cast!" Kathie Lee suggests brightly.

"Well, exactly," Max concurs, crossing his long legs easily on the tiny stage. Can he really still be flattered at being considered a Name? When they break for a news brief, Kathie Lee leans forward and pats him on the knee as Regis rolls his eyes and mutters something about flirting with the guests.

"Max, you've said it's a family movie." Kathie Lee's tone is confidential, barely heard by the live audience. "Give me a little synopsis so I sound intelligent when we come back from the commercial. And Reege"—her voice rises—"if you say one word about my intelligence—!"

"Me!?" He's perfected his on-camera Outraged Innocent Act so that it plays equally well off-camera; there are giggles from the audience. "I have never cast aspersions on your intelligence, not once!" He leers at the women in the audience. "Your lack of tact, maybe, but—"

"Isn't he *awful*?" Kathie Lee demands as the audience joins their laughter. Even Max chuckles quietly. He genuinely likes these people. The commercial break over, Kathie Lee sits up straighter and burbles at the camera: "We're back with our special guest Max Neimark, known and loved by millions nationwide—can we say worldwide?"

"Worldwide. Why not?" Regis agrees magnanimously. "Why not galaxy-wide?" He shrugs at the audience. "Universe-wide?" They applaud. Max grins.

The Mind agrees.

"Reege!" Kathie Lee's being upstaged as usual. "In any case, you probably all know him best as Benn from *SpaceSeekers*. Did you know Cody loves the new series?"

"Does he really?" Max asks, benevolent, at the same time Regis says, "Noo, really? That kid of yours is just so smart. . . ."

Kathie Lee nods enthusiastically. "It's on just before his bedtime, and I tell him he can't watch it unless he's in his pajamas and ready for bed. And I have to tell you, I've always been a fan of *SpaceSeekers*. When I was a kid, I thought Benn was the dreamiest—"

"What do you mean, when you were a kid?" Max pretends amazement. "You're still a kid!"

"Oh, aren't you sweet!" Kathie Lee pats him on the knee again, on-camera this time. Is he the touchy-feely type? Will he mind? Is his wife in the audience; will she mind? She must be used to it, fending off the Benn-fans and all. "But now tell me honestly: Is it hard to be taken seriously once you've played a role like Benn? I mean, do producers and casting directors still see you in that type of role and not allow you to break out and do something different?"

"Not so much anymore," Max says, settling back, warming up for one of his monologues. "Right after the series folded, I remember, it was difficult. Very difficult. Because you'd go in to read for a serious role and either they'd tell you it wasn't for you, they didn't think you could handle it, or someone would make a crack like 'Where's your Third Eye?' and you'd try to laugh it off, try to say 'Look, give me a shot; I can do this,' but they weren't listening. Not so much anymore. But I'll tell you what's even more difficult—"

"Well, sure!" Regis cuts in, in case anyone should mistakenly think that Kathie Lee asks all the good questions; when *TV Guide* talks about the "chemistry" between them it is this not always friendly friction that they mean. "I've seen you do a lot of serious work in between the *SpaceSeekers* movies. That piece you did on Bosnia, for instance—"

"Exactly," Max supplies. "A very moving piece, a lot of soul-searching. Realizing that if my parents hadn't emigrated to this country, this might very well have been my family's story as well . . ."

They've sidetracked him, Karen thinks but, oddly, she knows exactly what he was about to say.

•

"I'll tell you what's even more difficult," Max says in answer to Kathie Lee's question (only Kathie Lee hasn't asked it on-camera yet, Karen has, backstage, while she and Max were waiting in the green room just before he went on. As the second-string guest, Karen will be brought out to talk about her new novel, *Preternatural,* in the last five minutes before the end of the show; that's how it works even in alternate universes), "and that is how a character like Benn can completely consume your entire being. Remember, we shot sometimes ten, twelve hours a day, six days a week, and Benn required a minimum of two hours of makeup on either side of that; I'd have a six A.M. makeup call, and when everyone else was leaving at seven or eight P.M. I'd still be there getting my own face back. On weeknights I'd come home and just fall into bed—out of makeup, but still in character. I didn't even start to 'come down,' so to speak, to come back into myself until about Sunday evening, and my wife . . ."

His first wife, Karen thinks, the one whose name is so close to mine, Karin-with-an-eye, which is probably the only reason he remembers who I am and that we've met once before.

". . . my wife used to know never to invite people for dinner until Sunday night because I'd still be in Benn-mode most of the weekend. Afraid I didn't give her much of a social life in those days. . . ."

"Then of course you get up before the sun on Monday morning and you start all over again . . ." Max is saying, only this time he's back on the morning show set explaining it to Kathie Lee during another commercial break. "I'll tell you, it kills you. You lose track of the real world, the world outside you. Your kids grow up before you know it. The things about the person you married that started out as little annoyances, by the time you look up from where you were—learning your lines, trying different ideas for the character, doing, in other words, what you were put on this Earth to do—have over a period of years, maybe decades, become major problems you can no longer live with. . . ."

No! Karen thinks. Max is a deeply private person; he would never say those things in front of a live audience, might never voice them aloud at all, not even to me in the green room, not even if he trusted me. Besides, is he talking about his life or mine, his kids or mine, his ex-wife or my ex-husband?

On-camera there's a detergent commercial; Karen flicks the TV off. The aforementioned conversation has not happened, in any universe, not with her or with Kathie Lee. Jellyfish are messing with her mind again. It's not as if she hasn't always had fantasies of hobnobbing with famous people, certain select famous people like Max, with whom she actually believes she could have a serious conversation, but now she's not sure how much of this is wish fulfillment, how much is future possible, and how much is just jellyfish all the way down.

Sure, stranger things have happened, and to writers she knows; the only difference is they never happen to her. Does that mean she isn't allowed to fantasize? What is a writer but someone who spins the common straw of daydreams into gold? Or at least enough cash to keep the landlord happy, in a good year. Hitchcock used to tell interviewers he fainted at the sight of real blood; Asimov was afraid to fly. Karen's only afraid of life. Not that she'd put it quite like that.

"That's not it at all. It's that life is inadequate. Life is being married to Ray Guerreri, thinking that's the best it's ever going to be. Life is Kansas. Some of us prefer Oz. Maybe I'm just trying to bring a little piece of Oz back with me, to share."

Trouble was, she used to know the difference. Now she's not so sure anymore. The edges are beginning to blur, the colors bleed over into the black and white. Joan of Arc died for less. What is the sound of one jellyfish giggling?

"I warned you to keep the real people out of this."
We've got nothing to do with it. You've been daydreaming about Max for years.
"No. That was Benn. There is a difference."
Is there? And you don't seem to mind Akhenaton or Hypatia.
"They're dead. They can't sue me. And while we're on the subject, what about Hypatia? And Jess? May we finish those stories, please?"
And what about Azure? Don't you care that Azure died?
"Bullshit! You told me none of you can die. So which is it? Either you can or you can't."
Silence, and a white room. Karen has decided for once not to paint the walls. She will buy movie posters, Japanese prints, Chinese cut-paper art, to keep these white walls from closing in on her. She has finally ordered furniture, a matching couch and love seat in a simple blue-and-white canvas stripe; it will arrive later in the week. She has bought a rug, foraged an armchair, lamps, bookcases, even a table or two from the other rooms; her plants have been watered. Tomorrow she will begin to unpack the books. Would that her mind could be so orderly. But her mind is Toontown, her mind is Oz; were either of them ever orderly?
"Let's finish with Jess and Hypatia," she tells the Mind. She has a con this weekend; she has to pack.
We'd rather tell you about Azure.
"Later," she says narrowly. She is testing them again. "It's still my novel."
Isn't it?

•

It wasn't that Jess was forbidden to preach. In fact, few but the *kohen* paid her any mind at first.

Her listeners consisted mostly of the other women in the village, who gathered at the well every morning to exchange gossip and folk cures and admire each other's babies. Where Jess had always been silent before, possessing neither gossip nor a cure nor a baby, she had become the object of considerable curiosity since her return from the desert. At first they asked her to tell of her experiences; eventually she began to volunteer. Every time she told the tale, something new would surface, surprising her as much as her listeners. Soon the other women waited for her, refusing to return to their houses until they heard what she had to say.

The menfolk didn't mind, as long as their women didn't linger too long and the chores got done. There was never a one of them who would be caught dead hanging about at the well with the women, though occasionally one might casually ask his wife what had been talked about.

The only one who actively disapproved was the *kohen,* though even he was not sure why. They were only women; it was not as if he was losing his constituency. At first he watched and waited, hoping to catch Jess preaching on the Sabbath, but since it was forbidden to go to the well on the seventh day, she was not so foolish. Later he was heard to remark to some of the more influential village men that they ought to take heed for their small sons who, before they were of age to enter the temple, hung about their mothers' skirts and might be unduly affected by all that womanish jabber at the well. When this careful insinuation was shrugged off—it was only a woman—the *kohen* set about to find another way. Then G-d provided.

Rumor ran rampant that the carpenter's widow's sight had been restored. This was more than the *kohen* could bear. He insisted the woman and her daughter be brought to him, and he examined the woman's eyes for himself. It was obvious that she could see.

"Clearly," the *kohen* announced, unfazed, "it is the case that she was never blind to begin with!"

Liar! Jess thought. Instead of being relieved that his dismissal had put her out of danger, she was infuriated. To spite him, she began to preach in earnest.

And what did she preach?

"That there is more in G-d's creation than only men and angels!" she would cry out, her voice growing stronger with practice and echoing off the house walls, finding the *kohen* even in his temple. "And if we are to rise out of the mud and become more like the angels, we must take it into our own hands to do so!"

It was no more complex or scandalous a thought than those Yshua spoke in the desert, to ever-increasing throngs. But that it was spoken by a woman, and that it suggested not submission but self-determination, made it dangerous. What if there were Roman spies about? The *kohen* summoned Jess alone this time.

"Tell me exactly how you effected this 'miracle.' "

Hesitant—the very thought of it still repulsed her—Jess told him. The *kohen* curled his lip in disgust.

"Do you understand what you are saying? Witches and demons deal in blood! I could have you stoned for this much!"

"I think not," Jess replied, knowing enough about it. "It was my own blood, no one else's."

The *kohen* eyed her narrowly, recalling a conversation with her erstwhile father when this harridan was but a strange-eyed child. How was it that a woman came to know so much, and felt so free to speak it?

"Tell me why you did this. Surely you knew it would be questioned."

Jess shrugged. "I wanted my mother to see again. Where's the harm?"

The answer was entirely too ingenuous; the *kohen* was furious.

"How if I forbid you to preach again?"

Jess considered this. "How if I tell you the Voices command me to continue?"

The *kohen* lost his composure entirely. "There are no Voices, save they are demons!" he shouted. "Preach if you dare, but I will not be responsible."

Jess nodded, accepting. "Clearly. Nor will I hold you so. But G-d might."

•

"Miss McGill? Are you all right?"

Tessa never had nightmares, and she never slept on planes. Besides, the flight from Asheville to JFK was under an hour; this was patently ridiculous!

"I'm, fine, yes, thank you!" she fluttered at the flight attendant just as Eddie returned from the john, a look of concern on his face. Tessa wondered exactly what she'd been saying in her sleep and how loudly, and what it would take to convince the other first-class passengers to stop staring at her. What the hell was this all about?

That crazy woman with the sketchbook had triggered something, that was it. Tessa still had the drawing, rolled up in a mailing tube Serena had had delivered to her suite expressly for the purpose. She ought to just slip it out of her carry-on and dump it in the nearest trashcan once they landed in New York.

Except that one of Tessa's previous personae had been an avid animist, and there was just enough resonance left from that life bleeding over into this one to make her wary of letting anything as personal as a graven image end up in a Dumpster at Kennedy Airport.

As the seat belt light went on, Tessa made a mental note to schedule an appointment with Shirley for another regression first thing tomorrow.

•

Jess knew the *kohen* would not rest until he'd stopped her. She also knew she did not intend to stop. Though why she went out into the desert to look for Yshua a second time was the one thing she never could explain.

She had promised him, vaguely, that she would come and hear him preach—it was more than he had done for her—but never intended to act on it. So what was she doing here, following the footprints along the river's edge again? At least this time she was prepared. She'd left her leather apron in the shop, had covered her head and brought a small loaf and even a waterskin along with her.

Look you, friend, she'd say to Yshua, assuming she could get close enough to him—not that she'd challenge him before his own crowd, not likely, but if she could work her way near the front and he recognized her, perhaps she could ask for a word with him in private, assuming she could talk her way past his enforcers, Simon Peter and those other fishy louts—Look you, friend, she'd say: I've heard the stuff you preach and, while it shows you did your homework in whatever amount of time a poor man's son is permitted to study with the rebbes, it's hardly inspired, you know? *Orthodox* is, I guess, the word I want to use, or would if I knew Greek. So I thought perhaps you'd like to borrow a little of what I've learned from the Voices to add a little spice. No, it's a gift, we don't have to talk about waivers or residuals. A freebie. Something to punch up your delivery, give the masses something to think about before they kill you.

Because they are going to kill you, or does that come as a surprise? Carry you on their shoulders one minute, the better to cast you down and trample you the next. How do I know this, you wonder, a mere woman who, before she went out to hear the Baptist preach had never seen a crowd this large? (And while we're on the subject, try to remember what happened to your noisy cousin, and think of how your pretty hair would look all arranged in a pool of blood on Salome's silver platter, hm?) How do I know? I know because the Voices told me.

They thought it fair to warn me what I was taking on, because they're going to kill me, too, you know; it's just a matter of time. So the Voices tried to warn me, but I said I didn't mind. G-d knows it's better to die for a reason than to just die. How many boy babies our very age died the night the soldiers came, and while we're on the subject, how did you manage to escape? As for me, half the women who should be my age died in childbed long ago; the rest are dried up, clapped out, and have half their teeth missing. Me, I've kept my health, and if I die before my time—well, what is time?

But you, you might survive a little longer, carry the message a little farther, because you're a man and they'll listen to you. Sure you'll make them angry, but not as angry, not as soon, because you've a cock and balls and they give you credibility, even though you never use them. So how about it, friend? Dare take a little editorial advice from a woman? Come on, live dangerously!

She didn't realize she was muttering to herself until she saw those on the fringes of the crowd edge away from her nervously. Were she speaking in tongues they'd have drawn closer, but simple common sense frightened them, made them move away. Fine! Jess thought. Let them make way for me; I'll get closer to their messiah that much more easily!

But Yshua had finished preaching for the day and was nowhere to be found. Tomorrow was the Sabbath; he was not fool enough to keep a crowd out in the desert this near sundown. By the Nameless, Jess thought, I've missed my chance! She was still muttering to herself hours later when she returned to her own village and, for some reason, took her usual place by the well and kept on talking.

"Friends!" she cried out to the slatterns and the stragglers fetching water at the last minute as the sun's final rays slanted into her eyes and she thought she saw something shimmering there. "You who have known me from birth know I am an ordinary woman, no different than any of you. True, my path is different in that I do a man's work and no man claims me, yet in all things else I am as ordinary as you. Yet have I heard Voices in the desert, and what does this mean?"

Talk to them! something inside her urged. Not the Voices, though Jess knew that they were watching, listening. *Talk to them, and let the rumor of your words get back to Yshua. At least you'll give him options.*

"What it means, I think, my friends—for I am a simple woman and cannot read the words the *kohen* recites from the Book, or even my own name in a Roman tax roll," Jess shouted, doing precisely what this new Voice suggested, though she did not have time to acknowledge it, "—what it means, I think, is that all of us are ordinary, and none are. If the Voices spoke to me, they can as easily speak to you. Perhaps they already have, but you have mistaken them for demons. Or perhaps you are so beset with other voices—your children's, your neighbor's, your spouse's, your mother-in-law's—that you cannot hear them. Perhaps if you hear them through me, you can hear them within yourselves as well!"

Her voice echoed off the house walls, the sun slipped below the horizon. The last of the stragglers had hauled up their water jars and scuttled away; they did not want to hear Voices, they wanted to be left alone. Even the dogs had disappeared. They knew. Sudden footsteps scuffed through the dust of the darkened alleys. The *kohen,* at the head of the mob, held up a hand and halted them.

Let he who is without imagination cast the first stone. It was a woman and it had to be stopped. What it spoke was blasphemy, and treason. Worse, it had broken the Sabbath. Neither the Romans nor the Sanhedrin could find fault with what happened next.

Here it comes! Jess thought as the first stone glanced off her shoulder, staggering her but not silencing her. The second was better thrown, and struck her in the chest, knocking the wind out of her. It was the third, not thrown but swung into the base of her skull from behind in the *kohen's* two-fisted grip, that brought her to her knees.

They made swift work of it after that. Some could not be persuaded to stop until long after it was clear that she was dead, her face and ribs crushed, her brain and heart and lungs a pulp. How long had they lived in fear of her? Some were old enough to remember the ancient eyes in her childish face; the rest had simply grown to dread her voice in the square.

Why hadn't they turned away from her, refused to listen? Wouldn't she have gone silent then? No. She would have followed them into their houses with her terrifying message that it was better to think and act for oneself than to leave matters to G-d and the Romans, and blame either or both when things went wrong. Better to leave her out in the square, where she could be dispatched cleanly with the stones of the road and not defile any one house with her blood when the *kohen* deemed it time.

No one could touch the body until the Sabbath had come and

gone; the flies and the dogs made sufficient example of it in the noonday heat. When the carpenter's widow was informed, she did not weep. But her once-blinded eyes went blind again, as if to spare her the sight of what her friends and neighbors had done to her only child.

Its dangerous spirit fled, the body was wrapped and buried as lovingly as if Jess had died of natural causes. Her wounds were so grave, the dogs' depradations so thorough, that no one noticed the dried blood caked about the dead woman's ears. Word of her fate reached Yshua as far away as Jerusalem. Almost, it might have given him pause.

•

In the Library of Alexandria five centuries later, Hypatia read the story of Jess's death with some dismay, but no surprise. Rubbing her nose thoughtfully with the rim of her eyeglass, she saw by the diminished height of the candles that it was nearly dawn. Her beautiful face would be lined with fatigue this day; she would have to draft one of her senior clerks to take over her duties for once so that she could extend her midday nap. Yet a thought nagged at her and would not have allowed her to sleep regardless of her weariness: What if Jess, and not Jesus, had been embraced as the Christ?

An idiotic thought, of course. As well imagine women as a matter of course permitted to be pharaohs and generals and librarians. When men bore the children, it would come to pass. But forgetting the messenger for a moment, what about the message? A religion based on self-determination, on *demokratia*?

It had been tried as a governmental experiment in Greece centuries before Jess was born. As a religion it would likely have been snuffed out as readily, and Jess along with it. Yet there was something about religions, Hypatia knew, particularly the messianic ones that, no matter how absurd their first principles, tended to outlast mere governments by millennia.

It might have been interesting had it worked. And it might have rendered Hypatia an ordinary woman, librarian of a Library run by women, answerable to a female governor backed by an all-woman army led by a female general. The very pope might be a woman, if women were ever to have need of such a thing as a pope, much less an army. Perhaps the very Library would not be such an extraordinary thing, but only one of a thousand thousand libraries scattered like beacons throughout the darkness of the known world, for a civilization that had no need of armies could spend its revenues on bread and books.

These thoughts, or only fatigue, made Hypatia's head swim. In such a world she might have stayed home with the babies and the menfolk who tended them, gossiping and stirring the soup just to be different. Ridiculous! She was basing her entire thought process on a piece of fiction.

That, she decided, was all the Messiah Scroll was after all, even though everyone knew that histories were written in prose, while fictions had to rhyme. At least every civilized person knew this; perhaps a slave who wrote such bad Greek was unschooled in proper verse form, too. Hypatia had not seen Amanuensa since that first night, had begun to wonder if she were not a fiction as well, save that the scroll continued to grow. Following their strange conversation, Hypatia had unrolled the entire scroll, finding the latter half blank. Since then the words had spread further along its length, as if they were writing themselves. Did their mysterious author come here in the daytime? Hypatia held the only known key; how did she get in? And how was she able to write as fast as the Librarian could read?

It was true Hypatia did not come here every night, yet even that seemed to be taken into account. The number of words added was precisely as much as she could read in a single night; the next night she came, she would find that an equal number of words had been added. No one could write that quickly or, barring the execrable Greek, that accurately. There were no smudges, no blots, no crossings-out, and what manner of ink was this that dried so bright and flawlessly it seemed to rise out of the page?

It was as if the scroll had a life of its own, and someone more superstitious than Hypatia might have had it burned. She was at least superstitious enough not to lie in wait for Amanuensa, to discover when she came here and how she got in without anyone's seeing or stopping her. What if the slave were not writing the scroll? This much Hypatia did not want to know.

Forget the messenger, she reminded herself; what about the message? What if the only difference between a messiah and the rest of us is a visitation by Voices, spirit shapes, messengers from some other dimension?

Well, what if? Hypatia rose stiffly from her reading desk—she would need a soak in the baths and a good massage as well as a midday nap—and began to snuff the stubs of candles in their brass candelabra. She had never heard Voices, believed in neither demons nor the Christians' angels. Was that why the Scroll had been left in her care? Was she supposed to be the messenger this time? She would read it to the end and then decide.

Marking her place with a bit of colored silk as was her wont, she snuffed the final candle and went out into the blinding light of day.

TWELVE

"Tessa, look, no matter how we approach it, it's still Hypatia," Shirley said pointedly. "Do you think I'd stay in business if I deliberately regressed people to lives they didn't want?"

"No, of course not," Tessa said primly. She'd been sitting in a little ball at the end of Shirley's couch, a most uncharacteristic posture. Now she clutched the hair at her temples as if to pull herself up by the roots, swung her feet back onto the floor, and slowly uncurled herself. "It's just . . . I finished all the books on her Eddie could find. She . . . I . . . died so horribly . . . I . . ." She blinked in the light coming through the blinds.

"Which may be one reason why you've been given so many subsequent lives," Shirley suggested. "Violent death leaves everything so unfinished."

Tessa thought about this, but it didn't satisfy her. "I guess not knowing how any of my other lives ended was okay. I could assume I died in my sleep. Knowing for sure is . . ." It is not a word Tessa uses ordinarily. ". . . frightening."

Shirley sat on the arm of the couch and began to stroke Tessa's hair. Even her most self-reliant clients needed occasional mothering. "I know, dear. It happens sometimes. A lot of people come to me because they think it's fun—I don't mean you necessarily—," she said off Tessa's dangerous look, "but the truth is we never know what we're going to find back there, and sometimes it's more frightening than anything we're dealing with in our present lives. We think that because we live in an era of drive-by shootings we're somehow braver, more at risk, than our former selves. We forget how dangerous it was merely to be a woman in any century but our own. . . ."

•

A thirteen-year-old stands in the convent yard in a steaming, teeming edge-of-the-rain-forest barrio, ready to surrender the newborn in her arms.

"We'll give him a good home, a wealthy family," the nun promises her, unwrapping the infant on the kitchen table to make sure the cord is healing uninfected. "He seems very healthy. You've not taken any drugs while you were carrying him, have you? Honestly, now."

The girl shrugs, clutching her now-empty arms about herself, scratching one bare calf with the toes of her other foot.

"I chew a little coca. It keeps me warm. I don't get so hungry."

The nun does not wish to be indelicate, but all the men drink, and some, not content to chew coca, preferred drugs that went directly into the veins, and the chromosomes of their unborn children. "And the baby's father?" she prompts.

". . . is my father," the girl answers, misunderstanding. Or perhaps understanding too well.

Having given an answer the nun does not wish to hear, she vanishes, bare footprints in the dust of the kitchen garden, a ripe tomato stolen in her flight. Fresh fruit, needed vitamins and nutrients, a too-tempting splash of red payment for the child she has surrendered, is still bleeding for inside. None of it matters. Unless she can avoid her father when he's drunk, there'll be another this time next year.

The nun rewraps the infant, making lists of whom among the parishioners she can ask to suckle him until he's able to tolerate the baby formula the North American adoption agency provides. *Popes and priests should have such revelations stuffed into their ears until they bleed!* she thinks in a moment of bitter, quickly quelled rebellion. At least every unwanted infant should be left on the steps of the Vatican, or every bishop wake up pregnant. . . .

Still, he's a beautiful baby; none of it is his fault. The nun finds herself smiling back into his smiling eyes. They begin to sparkle strangely, and the nun looks away, seeing her own past there. . . .

•

"I'd rather be Amanuensa," Tessa sighs, waiting for the elevator in Shirley's building. "We don't know how she died. It might have been in bed."

Shirley shakes her head. "Work it through in your writing. Don't brood over it. I'm here if you need me."

"I know, dear." Tessa pats her hand, her imperiousness restored. Let's not forget which of them is the Star. "Maybe it will work out after all. My deadline *is* in two months."

She means the deadline for her latest book on past lives. The Library of Congress classifies her previous volumes as Nonfiction: Biography, and there is a seemingly insatiable readership for them. But Tessa knows an audience can turn ugly in an instant.

•

Hypatia strolled the Corniche, the balustraded cliff face overlooking the Midland Sea, in the rays of the setting sun. This evening was dinner at the governor's mansion, but for now she was here to meet a Greek merchant who had some scrolls to sell.

He'd come to the Library straight from the quayside, the smell of the sea in his beard, saying he had some volumes of a scientific nature—mathematics and astronomy mostly, with a little bit of medicine—that he was looking to part with if the price was right. Hypatia asked if he'd brought them with him. Well, no, he'd answered, fingering the curls in his too-curly beard; he thought they ought to haggle first. He then proceeded to describe the contents of several of them, piquing her curiosity.

She would ultimately insist upon seeing them, of course, but in the meanwhile she intended this very evening to ask the governor to fund the purchase, setting the wheels in motion. If the scrolls were genuine, and in as good condition as the Greek said they were, she must have them. The Greek, of course, need not know this.

She had agreed to meet with him on the Corniche for a second round of haggling. Too close proximity to so many scrolls in the Library, he had explained, made him sneeze. He had at first named a ridiculous price, which Hypatia dismissed out of hand, then suggested he would give her the texts for the price of her spending an evening with him. It was her scathing answer, more than the dust of old scrolls, which had made him sneeze.

Recovered from his fit, he had apologized for the misunderstanding, then restated his original price. Hypatia had countered with an offer of half, and only if she could see the scrolls first. The Greek was reluctant to travel the streets with them. If she met him on the Corniche, they could walk together to his ship.

The Greek was late; the sun was in her eyes. Preoccupied, Hypatia didn't notice what lurked in the shadows.

That night in a sudden bout of confidentiality, she told the governor about the Messiah Scroll.

She often told him about new acquisitions—he liked to know where the money went—sometimes even bringing a particularly attractive specimen with her to dinner so that they could pore over it together. She'd almost done that tonight but stopped herself. Amanuensa knew Hypatia would not be in her windowless room tonight; perhaps she would add some intriguing dimension to her tale, a new character to replace the slain Jess. Leave the scroll with its author, but tell the governor. If he was in a good mood, she might persuade him to have it copied. She might even find ways to assign Amanuensa to be the copier.

"Put an actual value on it?" she repeated her patron's question as he offered her more wine; she had already described the earlier portions of the scroll in great detail, neglecting to mention it was still being written. "That I cannot do. But I believe it is significant in other ways."

"A religious tract!" the governor dismissed it. "Or worse, superstitious cant, necromancy, fortune-telling. Or are they not in-

terchangeable?" The governor, whatever necessary political nice-
ness he must maintain with the bishop and Rome, was a free-
thinker in his private chambers. "Keep it as a souvenir, my dear,
but don't go promulgating it about the city. Haven't you enough
enemies?"

"Does not your Roman Church postulate angels?" Hypatia
asked mildly, helping herself from a tray of fresh fruit proffered
by a servant. "If I had the scroll retranslated, these visitors from
another world could be made to seem angels. They may very well
be angels, in their true form. We who speak more than a single
regional tongue know how badly the Jews' testaments were
mangled in translation. Who's to say one of those dry old desert
nomads who fancied himself a scholar didn't take it upon himself to interpret God for the masses, deciding 'heaven' was any-
place that wasn't this place, and that the stars in the firmament
are just lights, leftover phlogiston from when the earth was made,
and not other worlds where such creatures as angels might dwell?
You must admit it's—dehumanizing—to think we're not alone
in the gods' creation, but we have only to call them angels to be
accepted."

"And tell the whole civilized world it crucified the wrong
messiah?" the governor interjected, waving the fruit tray away.
"My dear Hypatia, I do believe you have a death wish!"

"But the scroll tells more than that!" she answered, suddenly
fervid. Had he ever seen her so excited about anything? "It may
very well be that these angels are in communication with select
ones among us even now!"

The governor chuckled. "Oh, be careful, my dear! You're in
serious danger of becoming orthodox here, and that would disappoint me. You're not among these 'select ones,' surely?"

Her beautiful face creased with frustration. "No, alas, not I!
They seem to choose artists and lunatics, and I am neither."

"Thank God!" the governor murmured, again offering more
wine. Hypatia covered the mouth of her goblet with one white
hand to demur.

"However, once I finish reading it," she went on, thinking *Once Amanuensa's finished writing it!* Why don't I simply lie in wait for her, lay hands on her, chain her to a writing desk and demand to know what happens next? As well try to milk a butterfly; she will give only what she can give. "I may be able to detect the pattern, to know whom they will choose next. It's quite possible that they can advise us, help us drag ourselves out of the muck and closer to the stars."

"Some of us don't want to be any closer to the stars. You're talking like a fanatic!" the governor warned. The smile had worn off his face. Philosophy over late-night wine was one thing, and there was no topic they had not touched upon in these treasured sessions, but she was in danger of losing more than her perspective, and even he might not be able to protect her. Besides, he liked her not at all in this mood.

"I think, my dear, you spend too much time in that library," he suggested solicitously. "The vapors given off by some of those old scrolls . . ."

She did not look at all beautiful when she frowned. "Are you suggesting I'm as mad as those the angels speak to?"

"I'm suggesting you're overtired, that you've lost your objectivity." He placed his hand over hers on the tabletop, a gesture of concern. "Hypatia, my dear and beautiful friend, that's the worst thing a scholar can do!"

"So it is!" she said crossly, and slid her hand away from his. As she rose a silent slave stepped forward to place her evening wrap about her shoulders. "Thank you for dinner. I'll not mention the topic again!"

She had never used the whip on her horses before, but, still angry as she took the reins, she snapped it in the air above them, flicking the lead horse, startling all three. They started along the cobblestones far too quickly, matching their mistress's mood.

Alarums and Excursions, Take One.

They were waiting for her.

They waited in the courtyard of the Library, waited in the

shadow of the portico, hidden from the overspill of moonlight, leftover phlogiston from when the world was made, waiting for her to return from the governor's palace in a clatter of hooves across the cobbles. She had no warning. If the horses hadn't still been skittish from the abrupt start of their journey, they might have snorted some alarm at the figures huddled in the shadows, with their fear smells and furtive movements. Perhaps they did, dancing sideways in the traces as she reined them in, but, still furious from her quarrel with the governor, Hypatia paid no heed. She had already slipped the whip back into its holder and was stepping down from the chariot, wondering with half her mind why the slave from the stables was not there to take the reins—dozing again, no doubt, in spite of all the noise she made—when they set upon her.

They dragged her onto the cobblestones and, holding her down, stripped the garments from her beautiful body. True fatalist, she did not cry out nor, once she saw how many of them there were, even struggle against them. Her time had come, that was all. She allowed herself one small regret, that she would not live to finish reading the Messiah Scroll, then focused her attention on how much pain was needed for her and her attackers to achieve their mutual goal.

They had gathered abalone shells from the strand of the Midland Sea, sharp deadly things. Methodically, almost ritually, they began to flay the milk-white skin from her flesh, then the flesh from her bones. They left the most brilliant and perhaps most beautiful woman of her time a quivering gelatinous mass, her blood leaching into the cobblestones as she died.

Then they burned the Library.

Millennia of knowledge roared into a living wall of garish flame against the mud-brick skyline of Alexandria, illumining twisted alleys where men wallowed in an ignorance more virulent than filth, clutching it to them because it was familiar and it was all they had. The Library would never be rebuilt. A millennium more would pass before the species began to reconstruct the knowledge it had lost to religion, misogyny, and fear.

Sheets and runnels of flame gobbled scrolls and manuscripts, melted furnishings and wall hangings, liquefied the carcasses of rats who had succumbed to smoke while nibbling the odd end of parchment in the storerooms. Pillars and balustrades crumbled, balconies collapsed in shrieking protest, plaster sparked and sublimated, priceless mosaics charred and cracked with the anachronistic sound of gunshots, marble floors crazed like eggshells.

In a windowless room set about with brass candelabra, a figure lay curled fetally, protectively, about an unfinished scroll. She might have been sleeping, save that flame licked at her cropped and greying hair. Finally the flame threw into ghastly relief a future of Huns and Visigoths, plague and death. Its ashes would blow cold and sooty over three continents, settling over them a thousand-year pall, which would obscure the workings of the sky.

And yet, indifferent to matters of opinion, it moved.

•

Are you satisfied? Azure chides Virid, whose favorite subject is religion. *Look what they've done! Are you proud of them? Proud of yourself? Poor Hypatia, poor Amanuensa, poor Library, poor fools!*

Virid, rapt and nacrous green in the flicker of the flame, seems puzzled by the question. *We did not do this. They did it to themselves.*

While we did nothing! Azure reaches a tendril out, touching Hypatia's final pain. Barely a difference between them now, two quivering gelatinous masses, though Azure does not bleed. S/he grabs a Virid-tendril to make Virid feel it, too. *We might have prevented this!*

How? Virid wants to know. *We've tried with pharaohs and messiahs; you've seen the results. We thought we might have better results with scribes and scholars this time, and we have. Look at her closely. There's no blood flowing from her ears.*

They've torn off her ears! She's nothing but blood; there's no way to tell!

We have not done this, they have, Virid insists. *Killed one of their own. Makes one think, doesn't it? Even fungus doesn't turn on itself, destroying. Even absent the scroll they would have done this. Prevent it? How?*

S/he does not listen to Azure's answer, if Azure has an answer. To Virid all is as it should be. Hypatia will be born again, peering through her reading glass at the most recent installment of the Messiah Scroll, with the rise of yesterday's sun. For what is Time?

Besides, Virid rationalizes at last: *If they were a true Mind, they would not die.*

Azure knows differently. Azure knows about death.

•

Mad dogs and messiahs go out in the noonday sun. Alarums and Excursions, Take Two.

What must it be like to be All There Are and one day, a few million years later, discover that you're not?

Something screams down the tendrils/tentacles, tentative telltale of destruction, death. *Azure-blue, where are you?*

Fried? Died.

Did the Mind actually go there, slither-slithering, to the place where Azure, like Hypatia, lay bubbling, deliquescing in a puddle of garish, too-bright light? Or did it reach from where it lay, all tumbled intertangled all about each other, too lazy to send out for fungus, much less a member no longer amongus? *Azure-blue, where are you?*

A single pulsing tendril was all they found, all they had to work with. *What do we do now!?* Salvage, save, salvation. Put it back together—quick, before it melts!

It? S/he—well, that is, we. Whee! Oh, there ewe go again! This isn't funny; s/he's going to die if whee don't hurry, and who knows if it's catching?

Cleave hir to the Mind, regurgitate, reeducate—*Oh, come on, Azure, don't die on us now; we've no precedent for it! How's it going to look if All There Are are suddenly not all there?*

And on the Third Day Azure rose again, recalled to life, restored to the Common Mind. Every cell in place, rebuilt from a single tentacle like a dinosaur from insect DNA *(Makes perfect sense to us . . .)*, every memory rebooted out of the Never-Forget of the All There Are.

There now, see, which has not eyes to see? No harm done; we can pretend it never happened.

Except there's just one little problem. . . .

•

"So you *were* responsible for the blood flowing from their ears," Karen says. "Akhenaton and Jess, I mean. Weren't you?"

You never asked about Azure. A pout.

"Because Azure didn't really die. I was just talking to hir. If it was that easy to restore hir, then s/he wasn't really all that dead in the first place. You said yourselves it was a neverending Dream. . . ."

Well, yes, that's what we thought, *but . . .*

"But we're getting out of hand again here. Let's not forget you aren't real. I just made you up. And I haven't decided yet whether or not I want you to die."

She's impossible! Grey says to Azure and the others. *They're all like this, these temporal types. Impossible . . .*

•

In a book-laden flat in the faculty houses of a major Australian university, a cultural anthropologist is suffering from despair. He's spent a lifetime studying the Aboriginial Dreamtime from the outside, convinced at last that he'll never be allowed In until he exchanges his present skin for a different one.

"Go back to your own tribe," one of the elders had advised him decades ago when he was young and his degree was new and he still had all his hair. Fewer sun seams on his ruddy face, less wisdom in his mind. He hadn't understood what it meant.

"But I'm not tribal," he'd said with a small, tight smile. White man's smile, condescending. Didn't they have telly out here in the bush, didn't they understand that no one lived the way they did anymore? "I come from the city. There are no tribes."

"More pity for you," the elder had said, and turned away.

•

Home from one con, sorting through her artwork for the next, Serena lights a cigarette against the constant viselike pain in her head. It's time to talk to the opals. They haven't talked to her since she got home.

"Hey, Rain? I really need to talk to you guys. You were there; you saw what happened. You heard me trying everything I could to make Tessa see you, see how important you are. Maybe you'd better send someone else. Someone she can take more seriously than a two-hundred-pound fangirl. I mean, who the hell am I?"

She is expecting comfort; that's what they usually offer. Instead she's greeted with a kind of preoccupation.

Not now, dear! the one that she calls Feather answers in Rain's place. *Rain's a little indisposed at the moment, now that there is a moment. Can we get back to you?*

Serena is taken aback. For one thing, Feather's never spoken directly to her before. She vaguely remembers being introduced to hir in the beginning, after her last major surgery, along with Grass and Glow and Lake and a few others whose names she's forgotten, like the names of a lot of humans she used to know. But Rain is her familiar, the one she's most comfortable with. Feather strikes her as some sort of authority figure—Head Honcha, Chief Cachalong—and Serena doesn't do authority figures. Besides . . .

" 'Indisposed'?" she says, too loud. "What the fuck does that mean? I thought you guys were immortal. How can Rain be 'indisposed'?"

Not, now, dear! Feather says between clenched teeth, who has no teeth. We'll get back to you as soon as possible . . .

•

. . . because you see, as we tried to tell Karen, only Karen isn't listening: There's just one little problem. At this moment, now that there is a moment, the Mind doesn't know!

Doesn't know what? Well, anything, actually. Or everything. Because, you see, in reconstructing Azure it was essential to individualize. *Oh, it would have been simplicity itself to restructure the physical protoplasmic* stuff *of hir, like rebuilding a breast out of tummy fat or all those other miracles your reconstructive surgeons do. We might have reabsorbed the surviving tender tentacle into ourself and budded it like a lizard that's lost its tail, although in this case it would be more like making a new lizard out of an old tail. Or we might have simply borrowed a bit of tendril tissue here and there from anyone who could spare it. But the mind was a different matter.*

A mind, we all agree, is a terrible thing to waste, and so how were we to guarantee that what once was Azure could once again be Azure, now that hir death had given us a demarcation, a time line? Before Azure, now Anno *Azure, a twelve-step program replacing the Common Era of the Common Mind. The whole point being:* We never asked for this! *It was enough to make us understandably testy.*

That's where Grey came in. Heretofore Grey had been the glue. Chief Cachalong, the common *of the Common Mind. Not as you humans understand authority figures, just the dura mater, materfamilias that kept the rest of us—once we understood the eye and whee of us—from dissipating in all directions at once.*

Quite a job, and a thankless one, if you think about it, being the matrix, Grey matter, mother of us all. The mother of all brain cells, Grey is. And, as eye say, there's just one little problem.

Reconstructing the physical Azure was time-consuming (now that we knew there was Time), but not really all that difficult. It was the process of reintegrating the memories that blew our collective Mind.

Because, like Karen, we hadn't been listening. Oh, we'd been vaguely aware of the input Azure'd been giving us about hir newfound "discovery," with its access to unlimited cable channels and billions and billions of little momentary lives. But remember, we were All There Are. It was easy for us to dismiss Azure's fantasies as just some as-yet unexamined dimension of what we already were. To discover as we worked within the synapses of hir mind that these things actually existed elsewhere . . . well, you can imagine!

(Yes, you can. Imagine, that is. Try to understand that until this moment, we could not. Imagine, that is. How do you instantaneously learn

something like that, eye ask ewe, after millions of years of not knowing there is such a thing? Before you condemn us for what we eventually did, try to look at it from our point of view. Within a nanosecond we had to cope with (1) time, (2) death, and (3) our own insignificance. It's enough to turn anyone into Jell-O. Just try it sometime before you've had your morning coffee and you'll have some inkling of how we feel. . . .)

So we wove new memories for Azure out of the bits we'd saved of hir—scraps and overlaps, ragtags and selvages (quick, salvage that selvage!), great giggling discoveries—knitting up the raveled sleave of once-was with now-is and, as we did, discovered ourselves being—enlightened? What is light, which has no eyes, agnosic? Violated, too. Something Edenic, something naive-innocent taken away, replaced with something we might not have wanted, had anyone asked our opinion. Infused with Tree of Knowledge star stuff that Azure had learned and we were stuck with. Couldn't go back, now that there was Time.

And before all you physics mavens start lecturing us about time and about how if we can slip-slide back and forth in it the same way we slither across cave floors (easier, in fact; no friction), then we had no right to tell Serena Azure was indisposed at that moment because that moment either hadn't happened yet or had happened a few million of Serena's years before she, or even syringomyelia, were even born—lighten up! It's a plot device, okay? To make Karen sit up and pay attention.

Because all along, from the very first page, we've been trying to get Karen to listen but, typical writer, she's so obsessed with her narrative she's got the chutzpah to think she invented us. Heh-heh! Wait till she figures out it's the other way around. . . .

Right now you're probably asking yourself: What do they mean when they say "What we eventually did"? Or maybe you're just asking yourself "What you mean 'eventually,' Kemosabe?" Hah! Call it the end-of-season cliffhanger; you're going to have to wait a bit for this one. . . .

Karen, are you listening? Listen!

She is, but not to jellyfish. She is listening to what Max said about losing your life to your work, listening to two children she has lost to time and her own preoccupation, listening to virtually every parent she's ever known who's tried to master the juggling act between life and work.

("That's my daughter," he'd told her, producing a photo from his wallet at a con just outside of Baltimore. "She was born when I was nineteen. I dropped out of school, spent six years on the assembly line in a computer-parts factory, living in a trailer park, going to school at night, trying to hold it together. Now my ex-wife takes half my income for child support, and I only see my daughter every other weekend. She's eleven now. I lost the years between seven and ten because I went away to grad school. Every time I see her it's like she's aged years in a matter of weeks and, like an idiot, I keep waiting around for the reruns. It's killing me. I'd do anything to get custody, anything. . . ." There was something so poignant about him Karen had wanted to take him in her arms and croon to him.)

"Maa!" Her daughter Nicole's constant lament, at six, at sixteen, now at twenty-something. "God, Ma, give me a break!"

"Go ahead and hit me!" A defiant Matthew, age four. What had he done? Karen couldn't remember. "Go ahead and hit me; I'm gonna do it anyway!"

She'd never really hit that hard, an occasional swat on the backside to straighten him out, but she stopped hitting then, found more creative ways to blackmail him ("No more ice cream for you, mister; not ever!"); he was that kind of kid.

How dare he be an adult already? It wasn't time.

Their preschool years had lasted an eternity. Karen didn't do preschoolers; there should be some way to skip that part, swap, for example, with a mother who didn't do newborns. Karen loved newborns—sweet-smelling, suckling, helpless needy things, like jellyfish, all mouth and brain, seeking knowledge through sensation, agnosic—had no use for them from the time they started crawling (sticky handprints on everything, endless whining, repetitions of the same inane songs, idiotic TV commercials, nursery rhymes, incantations and deprecations overandoverandover again, spills and spit-ups and snotty noses) until they were articulate, in school, and gave her some time for herself.

"Maaa, he's in my room again!"

"AM NOT!"

"Nicole, let me try to explain this to you one more time: Your little brother's name is *not* 'Asshole.' . . ."

After that, breakneck speed to where they were now, and Karen could no longer remember who had played what part in which school play in what grade, or why she hadn't taken enough photos, or how they had the nerve to be so old so soon.

"I don't understand it. You're home all the time. How can you not have time for these things?" Her mother's version. "It's not as if you *work*."

Karen, are you listening? Listen!

It's too late to listen! she wants to scream. They're all grown up and I've lost them, lost them to an almost-career that wasn't supposed to leave me scrounging and clipping coupons and scanning the classifieds for part-time work and wondering if I'm going to be widowed before my son is out of school!

Would it make any difference if I were Stephen King? Would it make any difference if Ray had met me halfway? Dull people make the best writers. One of the reasons it takes Norman Mailer so long to finish a book is because it's such hard work just being Norman Mailer. What kind of life do I lead?

I do laundry, I do windows, I cadge book deals after months of haggling, then disappear into a narrative for six months to a year. Occasionally I go to cons. Is this a life? What the hell kind of life . . .

. . . do you lead?

Azure's death is the wake-up call in the ever-flowing dream. What the hell kind of life do we lead? Now that it is defined as life, over-against death (for the first time a possibility: Don't go too near the surface; now we know why), it brings with it the undeniability that we are not All There Are.

It is *not* fungus all the way down. It is the existence of species beyond our own, perhaps as many of them as of All There Are. Acknowledging this, acknowledging them, acknowledging that because of Azure they are also part of All There Are, changes everything.

What the hell kind of life do you lead once your entire universe changes?

If everything changes, Azure reasons, *then we also must change.*

Examine: the Grey Mind dictates: *Change? Change ourselves or change everything else?*

Yes to both questions, Azure answers, trying out new tender tentacles, tendriling tactilely about hir fellows, touching, tickling *(this is new—oh, I fancy this! Thank ewe, thank you!),* gratefully recalled to life. *Remember equal and opposite reactions. Change ourselves overagainst death and mutability. Then mutate the mutable.*

Something about the way s/he says this makes the Mind wonder: Has s/he done so already?

Examine: The blood running from the pharaoh's ears. Ditto Jess the Prickless Messiah. Would Hypatia have been so careless of death had she not been obsessed with reading the Messiah Scroll? And what of Amanuensa?

Azure, it's time we had a little talk. . . .

What you mean "we," Kemosabe? You're as implicated in all of that as I am; don't pretend you didn't know! You said we were All There Are, said they *were only part of the ever-flowing dream. And I believed you, sight unseen, which had not eyes to see. What did it matter if I tinkered with them here and there, not understanding that death is death? We could always tune in next week, watch reruns, fast-forward, slo-mo, instant replay. We all did it; don't blame me!*

Besides, that was the old days, now that there is Time. I haven't messed up lately. Would you rather cancel cable service, go back to what we were? Who are we hurting, when it's all just virtual reality? Interactive fiction, here we go: Try one on for size. Sex organs, fingers and toes—oh, my! Be a pharaoh for a day; that's fun! Be an actor with a sex life better than any of his stud horses'. Be a New Age guru or an

*alien with a Zen third eye, or maybe a messiah or two. Be a writer in
search of her next big book. . . .*

*Oh, granted, Karen's life is dullness itself at the moment, but she's
about to meet some very interesting people. . . .*

•

"Larry," Tessa says, the phone wedged against her shoulder as
she touches up her pedicure, cotton wads between her toes,
no time for salon visits on her current schedule. "Read my lips:
N-O, no! I don't have time to read your script; I'm busy."

Busy, she does not tell him, working up a substitute for the
latest past-lives book she is supposed to turn in two months from
now. She's sweet-talked her editor into extending her deadline
by promising him "something completely different" and, as she
waits for her nail color to dry, she's been quietly congratulating
herself. Now suddenly she's got Larry on her ass. No rest for the
weary!

"Besides," she continues, putting the brush back in the jar and
tightening it. "No matter what Scotty told you, I'm broke. So
spare me the speech about investment opportunities."

"You, broke? Don't make me laugh!" Larry counters. He's so
brilliant when he writes his own dialogue. "You're not broke,
you're just stingy. This concept's right up your alley—aliens and
seers and time travel and past-life experiences." He pauses for effect, seductive: "There's a nice, juicy role in it for you."

Tessa considers. Maybe she should at least read the script.
There might be some way to inject her jellyfish into it. That
would be easier than composing four hundred pages of text all
by herself, wouldn't it?

"I'm not broke per se, Larry," she explains primly. "My
money's simply . . . tied up at the moment."

"Sounds like something I could get into!" Larry quips, being
amusing. Tessa is not amused.

"Larry, fuck you!"

"Is that an offer?"

Tessa hangs up on him.

•

Déjà vu all over again. Serena sketches at the far end of the table where three *SpaceSeekers* authors are autographing. Wedged between Marie Englund and Paul Jonas—sometime comics writer, sometime TV story writer, known as the Seven-Day Wonder because he can supposedly turn out a completed manuscript in that amount of time—Karen (who doesn't recognize Serena in this universe, much less remember that she recently appeared on her living room floor) thinks: She can't be sketching me; she can't even see me!

". . . and then I wrote *Planet of the Inlaws* in only *five* days . . ." Paul is saying in his New York–nasal Egotist That I Am voice, signing autographs while he talks. Who is he talking to—the fans, his fellow writers, himself? Paul talks the way he writes—constantly. ". . . which I really hated, but they know I'm fast so they're always pushing the envelope. I told them: Make it worth my while. And they said: What did you have in mind? And I said Well, the wife and I have our eye on a Plymouth Voyager with all the trimmings; why don't we just say twenty-five thousand and call it fair. . . ."

Karen glances at Marie, who rolls her eyes and is clearly thinking of a Can You Top This story of her own. Karen sighs, tunes them both out, concentrates on the people who want her to sign their books, tries not to notice the sketch artist or to wonder what she's drawing.

"Can I ask you something?" He is about fourteen, his voice uncertain if it wants to be baritone or soprano this week.

"Sure." Karen smiles as she signs his book, glancing at the name tag on his T-shirt and writing "To Joshua . . ." She remembers how Matthew's voice broke literally overnight when he was this age, how pleased he'd felt whenever he was mistaken for his father on the phone.

"Do they pay you a lot to do these conventions?"

Karen shakes her head. "Just my expenses. Train fare and the hotel room, sometimes a meal allowance."

"That's *it?*" The kid takes his book back, wide-eyed. "I heard William Shatner gets like fifty thousand dollars to do a con."

"That's because he's William Shatner," Karen explains. "If I'd played Captain Kirk on *Star Trek,* I'd probably get that much, too."

The kid thinks about this. "That's like totally unfair. Why do you do it?"

Karen gives him the benefit of her complete blue-eyed attention. Someone once told her her eyes were "intimidating," whatever that means.

"I do it so I can get away from the little room where I spend most of my life, and visit cities I've never seen, and meet people like you, Joshua," she says.

"Oh," the kid says and, not quite blushing, fades off into the crowd.

"You're doing it again!" Marie remarks.

"Hm?" Karen asks vaguely.

"Now that kid's going to follow you around like a stray pup all weekend."

"No, he's not. He's going to go home and read my book and remember that at least once in his life an adult with no ulterior motive took him seriously. What's so terrible?"

"Geeks and weirdos!" Marie reminds her, and it's at that moment that Serena finishes sketching and begins to sidle closer.

•

It's working! Azure clutches at Amber excitedly.

Wheel sea! Amber is skeptical, distracted by Lake, who is playing at war games again. The October Revolution? Well, why not; it's certainly red enough. Lake is on a thematic kick; red is in. Last week it was the Parting of the Red Sea, and no matter how many times one tried to explain to Lake that it was a linguistic error that rendered it from Reed Sea to Red Sea, s/he simply isn't paying attention.

Exasperating! Amber thinks, wishing Azure wouldn't clutch so. *Whee weren't always so complacent about inaccuracy.*

Grey watches, overarching the whole of the Mind, discovering despair.

•

"What're you working on now?" Serena asks as Karen autographs a much-read copy of *Abide in Fire* for her. "If you don't mind my asking."

Marie and Paul have left the autograph table to be on a panel together; Karen is alone. There's something important going on in the main ballroom and Serena's the last of her customers.

"Of course I don't mind. It's a first-contact novel. Only I'm trying for something that isn't *War of the Worlds* and isn't *E.T.* either."

"Uh-huh." Serena listens intently, waits expectantly. She wants the whole synopsis. Karen hates synopsizing a work in progress; it always sounds so lame.

"Okay," she surrenders. Something about Serena suggests she can wait indefinitely. Karen can hear Marie crooning "Geeks and weirdos!" and it annoys her. "I have this species of aliens who can't leave their planet. But they're extremely intelligent, and they're telepathic, and since none of them has ever died, they think they're immortal. They also think they're the only intelligence in the universe. So when they reach their minds out of their solar system and discover human minds, they think we're imaginary. Something they made up. Meanwhile, on Earth, I have this human character who's a science fiction writer writing a novel about telepathic extraterrestrials." Karen hears herself running out of material. Does she need to say the book is autobiographical? "It's kind of a play on reality versus fiction. You know, 'Is it live or is it Memorex?' That kind of thing."

She dries up. Serena waits.

"How come they can't leave their planet?" she asks finally, as if a great deal depends on Karen's answer.

"Because they don't have hands," Karen explains, bracing herself for Ray's teddy bear speech. "They can't build spaceships. They kind of look like jellyfish."

She's not sure Serena's heard that last part, because she's stopped listening and is flipping pages in her sketchbook.

"Jellyfish, huh?" Serena's broad face breaks into a little-girl grin as she hands the sketchbook to Karen. "They look anything like this?"

THIRTEEN

Karen's heart drops into her shoes. *Oh, Christ,* she thinks: *It's a jacket design for someone else's book!* Not the first time I've gotten an idea out just a half-pace in back of some Big Name who'll sell a hundred thousand copies while I go straight into remainders. It's enough to make a person give up and get a real job. . . .

Only then does she realize what the sketch is really all about. At first she only recognized the S.oteri. (Yes, *recognized* them. There is Virid weeping hir crocodile tears, Amber licking hir lips—metaphorically, at least—over some bit of erotica—Azure busy trying to explain, Grey looking long-suffering as usual.) They are drawn with loving detail even though they're not the whole of the sketch. In the center—the part Serena was working on while Karen was signing autographs—Karen's face has been added almost as an afterthought. Yes, the likeness is good, but it's a quick sketch; it's going to need several hours of fill-in work to equal the jellyfish, to pull away and stand apart from them. The effect is unsettling.

In the sketch, Azure is perched on Karen's shoulder, hir tentacles twined around her neck to keep hir from tumbling off; one tendril tickles Karen's ear. Inadvertently Karen brushes a strand of hair back from an ear that's suddenly ticklish.

"What—how—?" she stammers. One of the reasons she became a writer is because she's so articulate. "Where did you—?"

"—get the idea for them? Same place you did. They're my friends. The one sitting on your shoulder I call Rain."

Karen waits. This is not about geeks and weirdos, but something else.

"See, I'm terminal," Serena is explaining. "Eight years ago my doctors gave me six months to live. I have this thing called syringomyelia. It destroys your nervous system from the inside out. For whatever reason, these pockets of fluid start forming in your spine and . . ."

Karen finds herself nodding, listening, caught up in the narrative of Real Life, of The Things That Affect Other People and Make You Stop Whining About Your Own Life, but bells and whistles are going off in another part of her brain even as she wonders *What does this woman's illness have to do with her having sketched the very aliens I'm trying to write a book about? Collective Unconscious be damned; this is too weird!*

". . . and so at first, with all the meds I'm on—painkillers, antidepressants, steroids, you name it—and I'll be honest, I've done drugs in the past, so you could say I've been there. . . ."

"I hear you," Karen murmurs, thinking: *If I were writing this, it would get cut way back in second draft!*

"So for the first—I guess it was six months or more—I kept thinking *These aren't real, they're just drug auras.* So I tried cutting back on my meds, and the things I was seeing only got stronger. They talk to me all the time now; I see them in my dreams. They fill my head with ideas I'd never come up with on my own, so they have to be real, don't they?"

"I—I guess so," Karen hedges, thinking: *Don't say that to her. Don't give her the slightest bit of encouragement because Marie is right and you'll never get rid of her.* "What I mean is, we all have our own truth, so what right do I have to tell you they aren't real if they work for you?"

"I think you know better than that." Serena takes her sketchbook back, flips the pages closed, slips it into her backpack, waiting. "You're writing a book about them. They talk to you, too."

"Not exactly," Karen says, feeling like Max: *I'm an actor; I play a role.* "I'm writing fiction. I made them up. They're not real to me. They're not real at all."

Serena studies her intently. "Then maybe you aren't paying attention. Does it ever occur to you that they might be making *you* up?"

"No." Karen shakes her head, adamant. "Uh-uh, absolutely not, no way." Even to herself she sounds too emphatic, determined this time not to be the guru, not to predict the fall of the Berlin Wall or the Second Coming or whatever it is Serena is about to attribute to her. Most of all she is determined not to admit that she's always felt as if her characters were inventing her. "Maybe it's different for an artist, but for a writer it's not like that at all. There are about four original ideas in the entire universe, and they've all been done before. You and I just happen to be on the same wavelength with this one, that's all."

She is about to give Serena her Jungian speech, but Serena isn't playing.

"What if I told you it's not just you and me? What if I told you there's at least one famous person who's in touch with them? Matter of fact, she calls them jellyfish, too; I always called 'em opals. If there are three of us, there have to be more. Maybe hundreds of people all over the world. Maybe not just in this century, either."

No, Karen thinks. *No, no, a thousand times no! I will not even ask her who she means, because if she mentions Akhenaton or Hypatia or especially Jess I'll freak. Don't do this to me, guys; it's just not fair!*

"Famous people?" she repeats, trying to still her beating heart. "Like who, Shirley MacLaine? Maybe you should try getting in touch with her."

Karen can hear how nasty she sounds, but she's got to get some distance here, got to retreat to her room and regroup. Jellyfish, weirdos, and geeks—oh, my!

"She doesn't do cons," Serena says flatly, as if she's already investigated that possibility. "Believe me, I've spent the past four years traveling around trying to find others like us."

Too late! Karen thinks: *I'm doomed.*

"What I do is what I did with you—sit off to the side where I won't bother anybody and start sketching one of the guests. It started out as just a way to practice my art, get somebody famous to autograph it, then auction it for charity. But it was also a way of scoping them out, to see if they were In Touch. That's what I call it: Being In Touch. Because they do touch you, if you let them. Rain's very good at helping me deal with my pain."

Serena wants to tell Karen about Tessa, but thinks: Fuck Tessa; she had her chance! Besides, Karen hasn't asked who the famous person was, doesn't seem to care. Is she going to blow Serena off the way Tessa did? What happens in the next minute or so is very important.

"I can see where this would be very important to you . . ." Karen temporizes, wanting desperately for this conversation to end.

"Oh, it is, believe me!" Serena says stonily, her face closing in around itself like a fist, dangerous. Karen's about to pull a Tessa on her and she's getting tired of this. "Because they haven't put it in so many words, but I think if I can find enough people who are in touch with them and get them together, they might be able to heal me."

This is an aspect Karen hasn't considered. She has no doubt that it was the S.oteri who messed with Akhenaton and Jess's minds sufficiently to make them bleed from the ears, though it's clear to her now that that wasn't what killed either of them, but if they can do that much damage, maybe they can also heal. She'll have to use that in her text. Meanwhile, though she should be running as fast as she can in the opposite direction, she instead lowers her shields and lets Serena beam aboard.

How many hours did she spend with her that weekend, in between her con-related obligations—panels, autographs, a solo reading from one of her *SpaceSeeker* novels, nodding and smiling at all the wannabes who were "going to write a book someday" (jellyfish, weirdos, and geeks—oh, my!)—devoting every spare minute to Serena, who became a constant presence every time she set foot outside her hotel room door? Karen listened, encouraged, asked just the right questions, not certain what precisely she was looking for but knowing somehow she would find it here, in among everything else. But how long, O Lord, how long?

She did know it was three A.M. Sunday morning before she crawled back to her room, even allowing Serena to walk her down the corridors ("Because I used to do corrections work," Serena had explained, "and while this is a pretty secure hotel, sometimes fans get rowdy on a Saturday night." Karen had tried to tough it: "They won't mess with me; I'm from New York" but Serena's sideways look had said Yeah, right; all 120 pounds of you!), which guests learned early on never to do with fans because they invited themselves into your room, into your life, if you were fool enough to do that. But Serena stopped at the door, still talking, and would not come inside. That was when Karen suggested she find a tape recorder when she got home and record the rest of her complicated life story on tape. She even gave Serena her address and phone number. Why? Was it compassion because by her own words Serena was going to die soon, or curiosity because the several lifetimes she'd already lived within this single one were so fascinating? Or was it only because Karen intended to use her, make her a character in her novel?

". . . one of the wealthiest families in Seattle . . ." Serena's smoky, raspy voice would fill a dozen ninety-minute tapes before she was done. Karen put them in her Walkman and listened while she folded laundry, ran the vacuum, finally unpacked her books. ". . . not because my father had ever done anything; he inherited his money. And my mother ran her own business, so I was a latchkey kid before there was even a word for it. It was like I didn't exist. My sister Weezy got the good grades and everything, and she was cute, not a big hulk like me.

"Anyway, I was doing drugs and acting out, embarrassing them in front of the neighbors, so they shipped me off to this snooty boarding school in Canada, which worse than a prison camp, but which was also where I discovered there was some value in being able to draw. . . ."

Her narrative looped around itself like a Möbius strip, but layered in between was the Saga of the Cachalongs, the incredible overlap of experience with the opals/jellyfish/telepathic what-sises from outer space which—except for calling them by different names: Rain for Azure, Grass for Virid, Amber Glow and Feather Grey, with Lake proving the exception even to that—Serena and Karen (Akhenaton, Hypatia, and Jess—oh, my!) had in common.

"Hypatia, now . . ." Serena continues the narrative, on the phone this time; Karen has already run through all the tapes. "I don't think she was ever actually In Touch. She was just tapping in through someone else who was. And I'd never have discovered her on my own, wouldn't even have known how to pronounce her name if Rain hadn't told me. Not that I'd heard of any of them. I'm an artist; I don't do history books. What do I know from pharaohs?"

"Not that you'd have found Jess in a history book, either," Karen points out.

"Makes it kind of spooky, doesn't it?" Serena draws on her cigarette so hard it squeaks; Karen can hear it from nine hundred miles away. "Knowing you and I are aware of this person that no one else knows about, that history has suppressed all these years just because she was a woman."

"Or who might never have existed in the first place," Karen suggests.

Serena seems puzzled by this. "Then how do you figure we both know about her?"

"I don't!" Karen almost shouts. What the hell is she doing? Ever since she got home she's been in avoidance, listening to Serena's tapes to keep from having to confront these—creatures—and settle once and for all who had invented whom. "I don't understand how we can both know about them in such identical detail, but it doesn't prove anything. I can cite you a dozen examples from my career where I've stumbled into something someone else was already working on. . . ."

"Why are you so afraid of it?" Serena asks calmly, and Karen doesn't answer. She's made herself far too vulnerable to this woman as it is. "Did I tell you I did a sketch of her?"

"Of who?" Karen's gotten used to the Möbius-strip effect by now, but feels obligated to clarify her position on the loop from time to time.

"Jess," Serena says, her tone saying *Obviously,* even though a minute ago they were talking about Hypatia. "As soon as I got home I sat at my drawing table and did a sketch of her. I mean, after I picked up the dog at my sister's and unpacked and threw a wash in and—"

"Yes?" Karen prompts.

"I've put over twenty hours into it so far. She looks a lot like me."

"Does she?" Karen says, thinking *Why am I not surprised?*

"I'm going to do them all, but first I have to go the library and get some books on Greek costume for Hypatia. Jess was easy, 'cause I've got this illustrated children's Bible, and it's always easy to find stuff on ancient Egypt for Akhenaton. But fifth-century Byzantine is harder. . . ."

Karen wants to scream. As politely as she can she eases Serena off the phone and sits for a long time staring at the dancing molecules of the wall. She's set up her bookcases now and there is less blank wall, but the molecules have adapted, becoming that much more frenetic in the corners, like water seething. Is it live or is it Memorex? Are the jellyfish real, or is she? There are no other choices.

•

Sagan and his contemporaries, clinging to their SETI arrays, insisted that if They ever arrived it wouldn't be in a starship; the distances were just too great. Communication, the pundits dictated, was the key: Communication via hardware, radio waves, something measurable. Telepathy was entirely too outré, too New Wave, too soft, *feminine, i.e.,* silly. Karen, grateful to be allowed to play in the same field as the Big Guys, had always accepted their dogma.

Besides, guys, she thinks angrily, feeling oddly betrayed, *don't do this intelligently. Don't connect with a world leader or the Dalai Lama or even Ted Koppel! Tap into the fevered brains of a midlist writer and a fan artist and expect them to find credibility among their fellow humans!*

She is trying to remember when she first heard them. Yes, heard them, always. Karen's characters always come to her first as voices. Odd, when you thought about it, because until she left Ray her world was wall-to-wall white noise, Ray being one of those instant-gratification types who had to have the TV/stereo/something talking back to him from the moment he walked into the house until he fell asleep in front of it every night. Sheer miracle that she had ever even heard them.

Voices. Disembodied jellyfish voices, their arrival no different at first than that of any of her characters—Joan of Arc time, voices in her head, voices sometimes more insistent than those of the "real" people around her. It was why she was often puzzled to realize whole chunks of her life had gone by unaccounted for. Voices in her head became characters on a page, and as she wrote each character would gradually embody and become visible. Karen would learn as if discovering rather than inventing them: color of eyes, texture of hair; age, height, weight, shape of face and body, hands and eyes, and what they did with them. Personalities, quirks, motivations, agonies and ecstasies, food and sexual preferences, religious bents, annoying habits.

Oddly, her jellyfish *(S.oteri, as in es-o-teric, see your dictionary. Karen, please try to pay attention!),* to whom one could ascribe None of the Above, except perhaps religious bents and annoying habits, their twining tendrilly tentacles putting her in mind of grapevines (or that wretched wisteria she'd planted in the yard of the house she'd given up in order to get away from Ray, which had tried to strangle everything else in the garden but never managed a single flower, not once, no matter how kind she was to it), or a Jell-O-wy quivery shimmering mass encompassing but not entirely containing a vasty Mind, hadn't seemed alien at all, despite their/its defiance of her characteristic emphasis on a character's hands and eyes, where they had none. Karen had felt at home with them from the beginning.

Joan of Arc had died for less.

"Something's happened to Rain." Serena has called again. Sometimes she calls more than once a day. Alone on that mountain with no one to talk to but a dog, she doesn't realize how needy she can be. Karen wants to shout at her, but there's something in her voice. "I'm not sure if it's recent or a couple of million years ago—you know how weird they get when you try to talk about time—but something really scary's happened to her. Sorry. I know they don't have sexes, but I always think of them as 'her'—"

"It's okay," Karen interjects.

"But something's happened to Rain. Something that's scared her, changed her. I can feel it."

The Rain in change is dangerous on the plain, Karen thinks unbidden.

"She's different from the rest of them now, and I don't think they know how to deal with it. Just be aware of that when you talk to them."

When I talk to them! Karen thinks. As if I can just add them to my Friends and Family circle. Hailing frequencies open, and no worries about the phone bill.

Well, why not? What has she been doing all along?

"Hey, guys? Can we talk?"

She has finally extricated herself from Serena's insistent presence, shut off the phone, shut out the world. She is not in her white room or at the word processor, but in the shower in the middle of the day, enveloped in a cloud of steam, streaming water through her hair and over her body, stream of consciousness, because that's how she's always gotten her best ideas.

She knows they're listening. "So tell me: You're for real, aren't you?"

As she turns the water off and reaches for a towel, there is a collective sigh. *What do you think we've been trying to tell you all along?*

Thus it fits together, the whole gestalt. The Jungian subconscious is really jellyfish all the way down. Every human thought, every human action since the beginning of time dictated to or at least influenced by the S.oteri? Is it any more terrifying than realizing that Earth is a liquid-centered rock hurtling through space or that walls and floors are made of molecules?

"I don't believe it," Karen, always the skeptic, announces once her heart stops pounding in her temples. "If it were true, there'd be religions popping up all around you; we'd all know. I think you're just voyeurs, getting your jollies out of harassing a few of us. You don't seem to accomplish much of anything.

"I mean, let's look at your track record. You tag an overbred, congenitally ill world leader like Akhenaton, and he doesn't get it; he thinks you're avatars of some new god. He then proceeds to bankrupt his nation in the name of that god. He's possibly murdered, his body vanishes—meaning, in his culture, that his soul is damned—the throne goes to his nephew, and all that remains of him is some weird art that's either realistic or some sort of political statement."

Yes.

"So how would you rate him—a success? A failure? I'm trying to get a handle on what you hoped to accomplish here."

An experiment.

She waits for them to say something more, but they won't. For the first time since she's discovered them, or they've discovered her, they are less than forthcoming.

"Fine. Let's try another example. There's Jess, if there ever really was Jess—and about that I'm still skeptical—who might have been accepted as a messiah as easily as Jesus, though she'd have had a problem with Monday Night Bingo."

So would Jesus.

"Were you in touch with Jesus, too?"

Silence.

"Tell me about the blood running from Jess's ears. Was she dead before they finished stoning her? Did you kill her?"

Silence.

"Will you kill me if I get out of line? . . . Yeah, I know: Silence. So I really don't have a choice, do I? I keep writing your novel or I don't. If I don't, you kill me. If I do, but I don't follow your dictates, you kill me. Maybe after I finish you kill me anyway."

No, Karen. That's not how it works at all.

"Then what? I need to know why you've tagged me and not, say, someone in media. Someone with some clout. Serena claims you've got hundreds, maybe thousands of contacts, but either you pick someone like Akhenaton who has a death wish, or someone like Hypatia who's doomed from the beginning, or Jess whom no one would take seriously. Or me, ditto."

Write your novel, Karen. Pretend we're not real, if it helps you. If you write it, you will know.

"It's almost as if you don't want to be taken seriously. Which I suppose means you don't really want to conquer Earth, you just want to watch. Which is cool, except I need some reassurance that you're what you say you are, and this isn't some sort of *Twilight Zone* episode where you really intend to cook us. . . ."

Again she hears the collective sigh, along with something else, a kind of tension or preoccupation, which she can't quite decipher, but which makes her uneasy. If it's possible to be uneasy on the verge of panic. Why isn't she panicked? It's because she knows despite the silence that they *didn't* kill Jess, her neighbors did. As for her life being controlled by aliens, she's dealt with editors and ex-husbands; what else is new?

She is left with silence, a tingling in her fingers and toes, a pounding in her temples, familiar symptoms of near-hysteria, or maybe only Writer Mode. It's always been like this: write or die. There are writers like Paul Jonas who boot up their brains simultaneously with their pricey computers; they process words like so much Velveeta. They profess not to understand—in fact they are more than a little afraid of—writers like Karen for whom it is a matter of work or insanity. But while writers like Paul are running for their lives, always one step ahead of the dry-up, the burnout, Karen knows the well is bottomless. If you write it, you will know.

As long as you don't look down.

•

Panic was not written in Tessa McGill's programming. Tessa, after all, had found her center. So why was she obsessing over the sketch that Serena person had foisted on her back in Asheville?

She'd canceled the rest of her book tour the instant she returned; her manager had pitched a hissy fit but she'd held firm. Then she'd lined up her voice-activated tape recorder, her good Cross pen, and her stack of fuschia legal pads, and proceeded to "write" the new book. Usually she'd jot a few pages of notes to jog her memory as she talked her way through whatever new aspect of herself she'd discovered, then hired a writer to turn her ramble into respectable prose.

Only this time there wasn't any prose, not even a ramble. There was a blank fuschia notepad, a blank tape in the recorder, and Tessa drifting away from her vintage writing desk to stare and stare at that goddamn sketch.

"Too much!" Eddie pronounced it when she'd had it matted and set up in the parlor—temporarily, she told herself. She couldn't bring herself to have it framed or hung on a wall, not really. "I mean, the likeness is good, though she could have been kinder about your throat, but what are those *things* in the background?"

"Good question!" Tessa scowled, inadvertently fingering the loose flesh under her chin. Past time she treated herself to a day at Elizabeth Arden, and while she'd sworn she'd never resort to cosmetic surgery, never was an awfully long time. "In fact, Eddie my sweet, it's a question I've been asking myself since I hit puberty."

"What the hell does that mean?" he demanded, but Tessa swept past him without answering and trailed up the spiral stairs to the bedroom, shutting the door. Eddie shrugged. It was Tuesday; Tessa had to prepare for her channeling group. He and his opinions had been dismissed for the day.

•

"Pygmalion, I need to talk."

Of all the people she knows, in and out of the writing business, Karen's agent is the only one she can trust with what she knows. She calls Tony Salda Pygmalion for a reason. She has no doubt that the German-Irish mutt with the cheap little B.A. from the wrong school would never have broken into this ivory tower Ivy League business if she hadn't had him to give her a little polish and the right books to read, then point her, sometimes shove her, in the right direction.

"It sounds serious," Tony says, his rolling consonants wrapping around her like a hug. Tony was the first to offer her couch space when she was leaving Ray.

"It is," Karen says, trying not to sound like a little kid.

"Come in to the office, darlin'. It's nothing we can't solve together."

To understand the dynamic, which was more than agent-client, one had to understand both of the players.

Antonin Salda had grown up in rural Pennsylvania, Appalachian coal country, second of five in a devout Czech Catholic family. His father died of black lung when Tony was still in high school and off-loading trams himself on summer vacations; his mother was still alive and vigorous at ninety.

"She used to get us up religiously every Saturday morning to do the windows," he remembered. "The coal dust, you know. It was everywhere. There were places in the ground where it was hot all the time, even in winter, from ongoing mine fires; couldn't put them out. You'd see the snow hit and vaporize, leaving the ground bare and steaming. Some of them migrated from year to year, ending up under people's houses. Whole families would die of asphyxia, or the house would have to be abandoned."

"But the dust was year-round, and our mother would haul us out of bed, my brother and me, to climb up to the second floor and do the windows. Thirty-two windows, every fucking Saturday. It was the Metropolitan Opera that saved my life."

"How so?" Karen, always a good listener, had been eating cold calamari salad on his tab at the time. She chewed, Tony talked.

"I had this little AM radio that I'd move from one room to the next as I worked, setting it on the windowsill so I could hear. It had absolutely no fidelity; you'd never tolerate a sound like that these days with all the equipment that's out there, but there it was, and in between all that twangy country shit there was one lone classical station broadcasting opera from the Met live every Saturday. I'd climb those ladders from window to window, warbling along to *Tosca,* with Stan making fun of me the entire time. My mother would have to leave, drive into town for the afternoon, it made her so crazy. But it kept me sane, and I thought: I want to live in a place where I can go and see this performed. So the minute I got out of the service, I came to New York. And here I am."

"And here you are!" Karen said, thinking: *And I'm ever so glad you are!*

"Now, in the winter"—Tony was just warming up—"it got so cold even the feather quilts didn't help. Ever sleep on a feather mattress? Most luxurious thing in the world! But it was a big, drafty old house up on a hill, and even with central heating you never felt really warm at night. We had a coal furnace, naturally, and there were these hot-air grates in the floor, but you had to damp it down at night and then someone—usually Stan because he was older—had to get up first and start it every morning. The rest of us, my sisters and I, would crawl out of bed with the feather quilts all bundled around us and hunker down on those grates until the heat came up. . . ."

Heat shimmered up from the hot-air grate, a direct conduit to the rumbling heat monster in the basement where his brother Stan sweated and shoveled. If he put his ear against the grate and listened, Antonin could hear the faraway scrap and sough of coal first scooped onto the flat face of the shovel, then heaved flying into the voracious, hissing inferno, could hear Stan whispering curses, whispering so their mother couldn't hear, as he worked.

The grate got too hot for his ear and Antonin pulled away, burrowing deeper into the quilt, which soon became too hot as well, and oppressive. Where the predawn cold had at first made him unnaturally awake, he now grew groggy again with the heat. Did he see shapes in the pale, craven sunlight peering through his mother's layers of sheer curtains and the coal dust on the windowpanes, shapes reshaped by the heat shimmer from the grate? In melodies from operas never written, they danced. What did they whisper to him?

Tony Salda grew up and moved to New York. His brother Stan stayed in coal country. Stan died suddenly when he was not quite fifty, officially of a myocardial infarct. Tony knew better. Stan had had to get up every morning and shovel coal, and never had time to see the music shimmering in the hot-air grates. Stan had died of a broken heart.

Karen moves a pile of file folders off one of the two armchairs in Tony's cluttered lair, sitting quietly while he tells the receptionist to hold his calls.

"You're onto something big," he says before she can open her mouth. "I can see it in your eyes."

•

Eddie's remark about her sagging throat wasn't what had pissed Tessa off. It was the fact that every time she looked at that goddamn sketch she saw something different, something that either hadn't been there in the beginning or that she simply hadn't noticed. That was why she found herself squinting at it, peering at it in various kinds of light, even bringing it over to the window to try it in direct sunlight, moving her head from side to side to see it out of the corners of her eyes because if she looked at it front-on the whatever-it-was wasn't there.

Finally she'd rationalized it as being early in the day and the result of some anticipatory spillover from her channeling group. Sometimes her ladies' individual auras impinged on hers as they went through the rote of their mornings—the facials, the hospital auxiliary, the literacy program at the local library, the luncheons for the ladies-who-lunch bunch—and gradually converged into her space, meeting in the lobby of her building, having the doorman announce them, taking the elevator all at the same time, safety in numbers, ready to begin.

Today as every Tuesday when Tessa wasn't on the road, they sat in the requisite circle on cushions on the floor, with their legs crossed and their arms extended in individual circles, the requisite incense burning, the requisite subliminal mood tape playing, the light just subdued enough to keep their minds off their laugh lines and neck wattles, following Tessa's lead, when Tessa suddenly "saw" what it was in the sketch (which she'd carefully squirreled away in her bedroom before the ladies arrived) and, clasping her hands to her face, she let out a shriek: "Oh, goddess—*Larry!*"

"Tessa? Are you channeling someone named Larry?"

It hardly seemed the right sort of name for a channeling. They'd exchanged surreptitious glances when she jumped to her feet, breaking the circle, stubbing out the incense, wrenching the tape player off, clutching the hair at her temples.

"Are you all right, Tessa? Is he hurting you? Do you want us to send him away?"

"No! No, it's—it's all right." Tessa took a few cleansing breaths and turned back to them, all smiles. "I've just . . . I don't have my center today, ladies; it wouldn't be fair to you all for me to continue. Why don't we break early and try again next week, hm?"

There'd been some mumbling and grumbling, but after all it was her party; they were here on her sufferance. It didn't take long for them to gather up their environmentally correct cloth coats and slip sussurating, with a final furtive glance over their collective shoulders, toward the door. Tessa waited until she heard the familiar grind of the elevator going down before she dared look at that damned drawing again.

"Larry Koster, you sonofabitch!" she seethed, seeing his youthful face swimming among the jellyfish framing her, well, no longer youthful one. This was the young Laurence Koster with the natural hairline, the washboard stomach, and Energizer Bunny sex drive who'd made her giggle uncontrollably whenever they fucked, the Laurence Koster who, on the eve of reading for the biggest role of his career, had twitched and gone furtive when she mentioned telepathic jellyfish.

Why hadn't she understood then what that twitch meant?

"You sonofabitch!" she repeated, rummaging for her Rolodex. Eddie always made himself scarce on her channeling days; he was the only one who could find anything in this place. "You knew about them all along, didn't you? You and I could have worked together with them years ago. We could have had it all by now, you *bastard*!"

Even as she said it, she wasn't quite sure what it meant. Have all of what? A clear path toward a comeback, via a starring role in his silly movie? Or toward becoming the messiah who would bring mankind toward the next phase in its evolution? Tessa McGill, define your terms, as your mother used to say. The answer came out yes, to both questions.

She finally found the Rolodex, then realized it didn't matter. Larry would have changed the number by now, the way he did every month. Well, shit! Tessa thought. It was too early, L.A. time, to call any of his handlers. Meanwhile, where was that silly script he'd foisted on her?

•

"Oh, come on, darlin'!" Tony says to Karen after she's spilled it all to him. He'd sat back swinging his chair from side to side, hands clasped behind his head, listening wordlessly while she told him everything, from the beginning of an idea for a novel to the realization that it wasn't a novel but a documentary. Now he leaned forward with his elbows on the desk, eyebrows raised. Did he think she was a Looney Tune?

"I've been telling you for years about there being more things in heaven and Earth, et cetera, et cetera, and you never believed me. It's why I've suggested you really should try regression." Tony was a staunch believer in past lives; was it only, Karen wondered, because his brother had died so young? "I've discovered this wonderful new person, and I'm sure she'd be willing to give you a brief session. It's absolutely painless, and you come back feeling as if you've just had the most refreshing nap. Why don't I call Shirley and have her—"

"Thanks, no." Karen suppresses a shudder. "You know I don't believe in any of that stuff."

"Then why are you afraid of it?" Tony asks incisively. He knows her too well.

"Whether I am or not, it's not going to help me here. What I need are answers on this plane. Like how do I know I'm not playing Leni Riefenstahl?"

•

Alarums and Excursions, Take Three.

We never asked for this! the Mind pounces on Azure. *Why did we ever bring you back to life? Look what ewe've done to us! Ewe've ruined everything!*

This disharmony is new, a desire among some (for now there are some. *Is anyone paying attention here? We're actually diversifying into autonomous individuals, not just color changes, cute names for each other. This is important*) to process Azure into so much fungus and rip hir off the wall, tear hir into bite-size pieces and dispatch— munch, munch, gobble, gulp, slurp, burp—all gone, problem solved. Meanwhile, mumbling and grumbling: *Look what you've done to us! If we'd known (but didn't we? Are we not All There Are, and thus know All There Is?), we'd have left you to burble and melt, a single tentacle dessicating in the sun like an earthworm on the concrete after heavy rain. Venture where you don't belong? It serves you right!*

But look at the imagery! Azure argues, beside hirself with the beauty of it. *An earthworm dessicating on the concrete after heavy rain; this was never part of the All There Are before! "Concrete"? Feel its hardness, lack of give, the gritty painful scrape against hands and knees when you fall off your skates—ouch! Virid, this one's for you and, Lake, you, too, for the visuals. Ever wonder why scrapes never hurt until you see the blood?*

"Heavy rain"—oh, my! Warm summer rain, tropical; or cold driving winter rain, chill down the neck; or intermediate, spring and fall? Don't earthworms burrow below the frostline in winter? Feel the rain on your face, streaming through your hair like Karen's showers. Isn't this worth the pain of knowing you're no longer All There Are?

Even a word like "frostline"—think of what that implies! What dies in silent desperation, what lives to survive the fall's first killing frost? These were not so much as within the realm of our consideration before; surely this is good! Even "earthworm"—oh, don't you see? "Earth" + "worm"—it's just too beautiful! Blind, sexless, brainless, agnosic; cut one in half and you instantly have two. In someone else's novel we might as easily have been earthworms and not jellyfish. Isn't this worth the discomfort of learning that whee are not and never were All There Are?

Maybe it might have been if we'd had choices! the Mind insists. *We never asked for this; you forced us to it. That's why even being eaten isn't good enough for ewe; it won't root out the unbidden knowledge ewe have given us! There's simply no solution. We never asked for this!*

If it is the purpose of All There Are to know All There Is, Azure suggests with studied calmness, hoping hir terror, also new, does not show, *then where is my transgression? What have I done wrong? Why see this as a negative? See it rather (which now, through such as Serena, has eyes to see) as the opening of a portal, which—*

Portals, in our experience, lead only from the cave to the surface, and look where that got ewe!

—opens to new aspects of the Mind. Things that are part of the All There Are that we simply haven't had time to explore yet, now that there is time. If these beings fret you so (sex organs, fingers, and toes—oh, my!), just change the channel. There are billions and billions of stars out there. They're only as real as you want them to be.

The rationale works for some of the Mind, but the rest remain discontented, which is why we say we're running out of time. That which remembers All There Is cannot absorb untruth, cannot pretend the Thou-Beyond is *not,* because it is. This is the rift, which widens, the pulling-apart ensues.

Big deal! Change the channel, eye tell ewe, or turn off the tube and get a life. . . .

But the grumbling continues, the rift widens, and some like Grey find themselves coming unstuck, falling through the cracks trying to hold on to both edges as they rumble, crumble (like something out of an Indiana Jones flick—red dust, red clay, red-rusted spikes, and mouldering mummy bones; Akhenaton, did the jackals get you after all or, like the Ark, will you turn up in a Spielberg movie someday?) ever further apart. Rumbling, grumbling, crumbling, mumbling—

Say, Karen, do us and yourself a favor, will you, and don't trivialize us, okay? Don't try to make us cute. Ray's right about one thing: We aren't teddy bears, not by a long shot. Just remember it wasn't the stones that killed Jess.

Oops. Did we say that? Just kidding, heh-heh, honest. Would we lie?

•

"Leni Riefenstahl," Tony repeats; naturally he knows who Karen's talking about, but he's looking for a context. "I'm not sure I follow."

Karen takes a deep breath, begins to shape the words with her hands, expressive. "The revisionist historians have typed her as 'Hitler's Pet Cinematographer' or 'The Official Filmmaker of the Nazi Party,' because it makes good headlines. But I wonder. She's on record as considering herself a documentarian; as far as she was concerned it was her job to shoot the footage of the rallies and in the inner Party festivities and let the viewer draw his own conclusions. She wasn't *creating* these events, merely reporting on them. Would the world have been better off *not* seeing all those goose-stepping thousands? It's a Shoot the Messenger scenario."

She sits back, strangely exhausted. Tony is nodding.

"Okay. But what's this got to do with you?"

"The S.oteri have apparently tagged me to write a novel in

which I tell what I know about them—their part in influencing human history, perhaps inspiring the occasional religious or political movement, or at least a novel or a painting or two, but also their general ineffectuality, that many of their 'subjects' die with blood running from their ears. In other words, warts and all. But what if they're lying to me? What if they're really intergalactic telepathic Nazis? Am I aiding and abetting their cause, or just reporting on it?"

"This reminds me of the argument you give me every time I try to steer you into mystery writing," Tony suggests softly. " 'It's as if in writing about murder—' "

"—I'm promoting it," Karen finishes her own sentence, feeling sheepish. She'd been very young the first time she said it.

"It never made any sense, you know," Tony chides her gently. "It's like saying you have to go out and murder someone before you can play Macbeth. To my knowledge, John Wilkes Booth was the only one who implemented that."

"Okay, it was a dumb stance to take," Karen admits. "But I still feel twitchy every time I kill off a character. And this time there's just one teensy difference. If the S.oteri are real, and if, as Serena keeps insisting, there are who knows how many other people out there who are also in touch with them—"

"Oh, there are, darlin'. Believe me, there are!"

For the first time in all the years she's known him, Karen sees them in his eyes.

FOURTEEN

$$B$$efore Karen can even say "You're in touch with them, too," Tony glances at his watch. "C'mon, I'll take you out to lunch."

Karen frowns. "Don't you have to make reservations?"

Tony smiles. "Already made."

He's been reading her mind again.

•

It's working, eye tell ewe, it's working—look! Azure, despite the sense of doom of late settling about hir shoulders, who has no shoulders, cannot help rejoicing. But the Mind has reached critical mass. Figuring it has just enough time while Tony and Karen are walking to the restaurant, it pounces. Except for a few stray ragtags out gathering fungus and not back in time, or those like Grey, who are either not sure or have tried to remain neutral throughout but cannot disengage before the mass of tentacles seizes Azure, the Mind as an almost-whole pounces and the melee is on.

Ow! Hey, cut it out! Get your slimy paws off me; you're hurting me!

Stop struggling! This won't hurt a bit. It didn't last time, remember? All we're going to do is reabsorb you and—hold STILL! (Dammit, somebody grab hir—ow! Who'd have thunk s/he was this strong? Ow, watch it; that's my tentacle you're tromping on. Whoops! How'd s/he squirt away like that?) Stop this at once!

"Hey, fellas? Is everything all right?"

Max has not been sleeping well lately. This is a surprise. A man

233

of inordinately clear conscience, he ordinarily sleeps like a baby; neither of his wives has ever even heard him snore. But last night, between pictures, he was restless. Now this morning he sits on the patio beside the pool, the newspaper half read, a stack of the more interesting fan mail his secretary has culled out of the thousand-per-week average waiting to be answered, watching reflections of light too neon-lurid even for L.A.'s notoriously bad Santa Ana air. Reflections of his dreams, shapeless as jellyfish. He thought it wouldn't hurt to inquire.

Why, Max, dear friend—heh-heh—what makes you think anything's wrong? You've never asked before. (Let hir go, dammit; s/he's stirring up too much static. We'll have to rethink this before we try again. . . .) Er, Max? What's the deal?

Max shrugs. "Probably nothing. Just making sure. I had some disturbing dreams last night. I thought it might have something to do with you."

"Who're you talking to?"

He hadn't heard Carole, padding across the flagstones in her bare feet, shoes in her hand, but doesn't startle at her inquiry.

"Myself, I guess." He's considered telling her about the jellyfish for some time now, certain she'd understand, where Karin never would. "You off to work already?"

" 'Already'! It's nearly nine." She kisses the top of his head. "You get so lazy when you're not working! I have client meetings all day. Will you pick Sammy up at after-school at four?"

Sammy is Samantha, his stepdaughter. "No!" he teases, kissing Carole's pouting mouth. "Of course I will. . . . What?"

She wears the look she wears whenever she's about to ask him something she's not sure he'll like. "She told some of the other kids that you played Benn. They refused to believe her."

"So, what? I'm supposed to bring the Third Eye?"

"Your own two should be sufficient," Carole tells him, kissing the bridge of his nose where the heavy-framed glasses have slid down. "Just do the voice. It always works at cons."

Max sighs long-sufferingly. "The things I do for love!"

•

Somewhere north of Richmond, Virginia, an overloaded station wagon pulls onto the shoulder of the highway; a gangly sixteen-year-old boy reluctantly gets out. His jacket is too thin for the winter weather; the duffle containing everything he could carry from the home he'll never see again feels simultaneously heavy and inadequate in his gloveless hand.

"I'm sorry, Johnny," his mother says, rolling down the window when he comes around to the driver's side. "I don't know what else to do. I can't afford to feed all three of you. I figured you're the oldest; you're best able to make it on your own. If you get real hard up, you call Uncle Henley."

"Uncle Henley's a drunk!" the kid sneers. "His whole house smells like puke. I'll starve first!"

"Uncle Henley's blood kin, and you're ungrateful!" his mother snaps back, seeing nothing inappropriate in either her words or her choice to leave her firstborn by the side of the road. It wasn't her fault her second husband split and left her with all those bills. She lowers her voice so as not to disturb Johnny's half-brother and half-sister, who are pretending to sleep in the back seat; years later, when they're adults, Johnny's half-brother will remember none of this, will deny it ever happened, will reminisce as if happily about a winter spent cutting school, hanging out in skating rinks and shopping malls to keep warm while his mother is at work, no thought at all of Johnny, who was always smarter, more outgoing, better with girls, as if Johnny had never existed. "I'll write you care of Uncle Henley when I find work. Maybe I can send for you then. We can all live in Baltimore or New York or someplace. Wouldn't you like that?"

Johnny opens his mouth and no words come out. He turns and starts walking toward the traffic so his mother can't follow him with the car; he doesn't want to know if she'll even try. In minutes he's around a curve in the road, back the way they'd come, and can no longer see the car; the noise of traffic passing him on the slushy road prevents him from hearing whether she's still idling there or if she's pulled away. Head down, dogged, he keeps walking.

But where was he going to go; what was he going to do? He could crash with some friends from school for a while, if he could overcome his pride and beg them, explain his situation to their disapproving parents. They might let him borrow couch space if he acts grateful enough, let him skulk around like the intruder he was, overhearing whispered conversations in their kitchens about that no-good mother of his. If it wasn't the dead of winter he could camp out in the D&D cave they'd built in the woods over the summer.

He'd do that anyway, Johnny decides as he trudges, last week's snow crunching grey and ugly under his feet; it was better than begging. He could build a fire, cook out. His mother had shoved five twenty-dollar bills into his jeans pocket just before they'd gotten into the car; that would last a couple of months if he was careful.

But how am I going to wash? he thinks with sudden anguish, a pain in his gut like the hunger pains already starting, though his mother had made them all a big breakfast at the grill in the out-of-business diner before they'd hit the road. He was growing again, hungry all the time; he'd never make it. A fastidious kid, he was haunted by the logistics of keeping clean, camping out in this weather. Because he had to keep going to school, had to keep up the pretense of normalcy, had to make something of himself so he'd never be dependent on people like his mother, people who couldn't cope, again. How was he going to do that if he had to go to school in clothes he'd slept in, stinking of sweat and fear and wood smoke, his hair all matted like some backwoods redneck?

"I'll kill myself first!" Johnny says aloud, his breath steaming out in front of him in the cold, sly flakes of snow frosting the hair that falls into his eyes, his glasses fogging. "I'll do it so it looks like a D&D ritual. Pastor's always talking about how D&D is devil worship. I'll show them!"

No, you won't, Johnny, a voice says deep inside him. *You'll get through this, and you'll remember how it feels, and when you're grown you'll do all there is within your power to help the refugees of other peo-*

ple's failures, and to see to it that, in your own words, young men need no longer die in wars. . . .

The snow falls heavier; the boy walks on.

•

No, no, no! Oh, no fair! This is all out of context; it isn't right! It isn't winter where Karen is, and this is not even the right time of day! Besides, you're talking about Johnny's future as if he's already living it, as if he's already grown. We're losing our hold, which has not hands to hold. Our sense of time has fallen and it can't get up. Alarums and Excursions—oh!

•

Middle age, Tessa decided, flipping through her copy of the SAG directory to see who Max Neimark's current agent was, means losing your mind, or at least your memory. Had it been so long since she'd made a movie that she'd forgotten how the system worked?

Max was a director, always looking for new projects, and one of the handful of people on the planet who could put a lid on Larry Koster. And while she didn't know him all that well, she was confident enough in her skills as an actress to believe she could sell him on jellyfish on the basis of a thirty-page proposal. She didn't need Larry at all.

•

"How long?" Karen asks without preamble when they're settled with menus, chardonnay for her and a Johnny Walker Black for Tony. He doesn't need to ask her what she means.

"Since I was a kid," he answers. "I've always wondered if they were the reason why I'm still here and Stan's not. It's why I started exploring regression. I'd already combed through the entire publishing industry trying to find someone else who'd seen what I'd seen, and found nary a one. Same with theater or the opera—well, you know the things that interest me."

Karen nods. "But you should have said something the minute I ran this idea by you. Instead you tried to talk me out of it. Why?"

He lets his hand rest on hers on the table between them. This is more than agent-client, always has been.

"Concern? Making sure you really were onto the same thing I was? Your visitors and mine weren't necessarily the same species, you know; there are more than one out there. And the way you described them physically, like jellyfish, sort of matched what I knew, except that mine never spoke to me in words, only in music. In one of my lives I was a contemporary of Vivaldi's, you know; even in this one I've got perfect pitch.

"I was also hoping in a way that you weren't involved, that you really were just writing fiction. So I didn't want to—unduly influence you—until I was sure. Posthypnotic suggestion or like that."

"But all these years you've been trying to have me regressed," Karen teases him. For some reason she's no longer quite as frightened as she has been.

"Well . . . " Tony starts to say. The waiter arrives to take their orders, bailing him out. "Let's review concept here," he says once the waiter's on his way. "Not *War of the Worlds,* and certainly not *E.T.*" He helps himself to a second roll off Karen's reproachful look; carbos have always been his downfall. "What you're really afraid of is that it might be *Invasion of the Body Snatchers.*"

"With one teensy little difference," Karen reminds him. "These guys are real."

Tony breaks the roll, butters it meticulously. "You're sure of that now? You didn't sound sure back in the office."

Karen shrugs. "As sure as I am of anything."

"And you mean to tell me you don't believe we've been visited by aliens before? What the hell are you doing in this business if you don't believe?"

"Earning a living! Exorcising the voices in my head."

Tony swallows a mouthful of bread before he continues. "Were the voices real? Before the S.oteri, I mean."

Karen thinks about this. "They're a manifestation of . . . something. Maybe just a chemical imbalance. I could be bipolar. Put me on lithium and the voices go away. Along with my livelihood."

"You don't believe that and neither do I," Tony says. "Face

it, kiddo; you've been chosen. Not a damn thing you can do about it. But as you yourself pointed out, they don't seem to have accomplished much of anything in the three-thousand-odd years they've been communing with us. Maybe they don't want to conquer the world, just visit it, use us as their eyes and ears. And if you don't write their story, they'll find someone else who will."

He doesn't have to mention names. Karen knows exactly who he means. The Big Name who claimed he'd actually been abducted by aliens. The Big Name with all the science degrees whose wife wrote his fiction for him. The Big Name columnist with unusual religious affiliations who farmed his ideas out to ghost writers. Any of them could do it, might very well already be doing it, for far more money, and with far more credibility, than she. Maybe her novel will have no more impact on the fate of the universe than Jess's preaching.

"Which one's your favorite?" Tony asks as the food arrives. Karen glances down at her calamari; did she just see it move? She's suddenly lost her appetite.

"My favorite?"

"Of the jellyfish. S.oteri." Tony's having no trouble with his entrée. "God, I love the name! Amber's mine. I think because we're both hedonists. You're more of an Azure type. Too honest for your own good."

"Maybe," Karen acknowledges. "But they've all talked to me at different times. Or talked to each other and let me overhear, at least all the identifiable ones. I get the impression there are a lot more of them than the ones who've allowed us to name them."

Tony puts down his fork and considers this. "That's very interesting. Instead of having just one interlocutor among them, you get to talk to them all. No question about it: You've been chosen, kid."

Karen pushes her plate aside.

"Tell me about the artist," Tony prompts her. "Is her name really Serena? I love it!"

•

"C'mon, dammit, pick up!" Serena says to the phone. She has left three messages on Karen's machine in as many hours. "I know you're there; you're always there in the daytime. Where the hell else could you be?"

Her illness has cranked up the pain level lately to the point where she sometimes can't even talk. She's wondering how much time she has left. Not how much more her heart and the rest of her autonomic functions can take; she's beaten the odds on those by nearly a decade and there are no longer measurable parameters. It's a matter of how much pain she can take psychologically before she has no mind left. And the opals aren't helping at all. Have they abandoned her? In that case, except for her dog, who has a bad heart and probably won't last through the winter, there's hardly anything to keep her alive, then, is there?

"Okay, you're avoiding me for whatever reason," she says into the phone, hearing Karen's recorded message for the fourth time. "But if you get over it before I die, call me back and I'll tell you who the famous person is. Maybe she'll talk to you, you being a writer and all, because she sure as hell wouldn't talk to me. . . ." She waits, knowing Karen's there, even though she's not. "No, huh? Fine, I'll wait as long as I can, but I have a feeling I'll be out of the picture soon; then you'll be on your own with them. And I have to tell you they've been very weirded out about something. Last time I felt anything like this was back in the state pen, just before a breakout. You never saw anything on the surface, you just knew the inmates were planning something, and that instinct was all that saved your ass. . . ."

•

Karen all but drops her fork. "I just remembered something!"

Tony looks concerned. "What's wrong?"

"I knew Serena before I even met her. I mean—there was a moment when she simply appeared in my living room. . . . We had a conversation and . . . inside that conversation there was another conversation . . . about a previous time we'd met at her house in North Carolina and she'd explained to me why the lake colors are called 'lake,' and when I got home I looked it up. Except I've never been to her house, and I'd never met her . . . except we had this conversation . . ."

She is speaking as if from a trance. Tony, who recognizes the symptoms, watches and waits. They're in a corner booth and the lunch-hour crowd is beginning to thin out; no one notices.

". . . and I remember yelling at the jellyfish, saying it wasn't fair of them to fuck with my reality like that, so they made Serena disappear. And then I forgot all about her, so much so that I didn't even recognize her when we did meet. She's very distinctive-looking; it should have triggered something. . . ." Very un-Karen-like, she suddenly bursts into tears. "Pygmalion, what's happening to me? Am I losing it?"

He's holding both of her hands now, squeezing them. "Maybe finding it. Haven't they told you you can send them away at any time? Why haven't you?"

"Because I'm too fucking curious!" Karen nearly shouts, remembering where they are just in time. Her tears are replaced by anger. "They know I have to see this through, if for no other reason than that I have to know how it turns out!"

Tony hands her his handkerchief, like something out of an old movie. "Well, there you are. 'If you write it—' "

"—I will know."

•

And if we stop dreaming you, you won't. Because if we stop dreaming you, you aren't.

Aren't you?

•

". . . and I thought: Max would be perfect for this," Tessa is babbling in Max's ear. "You have that kind of sensitivity to what used to be called a Woman's Picture that no one in this town since Cukor—I mean, the way you handled the courtroom scenes in *Little Girl Lost,* for instance, where any other director would have gone for the cliché . . ."

"And you see this as a Woman's Picture, is that what you're telling me?" Max asks her, bemused and amused at the same time.

"Well, not necessarily," Tessa corrects herself in midstream. "I only meant that that kind of sensitivity evidences to me a kind of versatility that—"

"Tessa?" Max interrupts. She has been babbling so fast she hasn't heard the Call Waiting. "Can you hang on for just one minute? I've got another call. . . ."

•

"Tessa McGill," Karen says slowly.

They are in the lobby of Tony's office, about to go their separate ways.

"Don't tell me she's turned up in your living room, too!" Tony says. Should he tell Karen he and Tessa have the same regressionist or will that only frighten her all over again?

"No, but she did turn up in my manuscript very early on—speaking of regression, it was a terribly hokey scene between her and *her* regressionist; I dumped it as soon as I wrote it. But she's the one Serena wanted to tell me about; she must be."

It's a reach and they both know it.

"Don't!" Tony warns her. "Don't even *think* of getting in touch with her. That bitch will steal the whole thing out from under you and turn the S.oteri into her own personal freak show. We might as well call Maury Povitch or the *Enquirer.*"

Karen sighs. "I just wish I had some backup. I feel like they're breathing down my neck."

"Karen," Tony is very serious now. "There's no time frame. Remember, they've been tinkering with us for three thousand years; they're not going to do anything drastic overnight. It's your own kind you have to watch out for."

"I hope you're right," Karen says, but she's still skeptical.

She and Tony kiss good-bye. "I'm going to put out some feelers on Miss McGill and find out what she gets up to between books," he says. "You go home and do your job."

•

Dangling his long legs in his heated swimming pool, stirring up reflections that reflect the reflections in his odd-color eyes, Max Neimark can't stop chuckling to himself. Real life is stranger than the movies. He has just fielded two very amusing back-to-back phone calls, told each of his callers separately to "send me what you've got."

Pity they didn't call simultaneously! he thinks now. I could have put them on a conference call and let them slug it out!

"Well, fellas, it looks like the jig is up. It's on the ether. I think it's time we went public."

Ordinarily they'd answer right away. The stuttering silence is a new wrinkle, part of the strangeness they've been exhibiting lately.

All right, Max. If that's what you want.

"It's not a matter of what I want; it's your call. If I don't exert some quality control here they'll turn you into a Disney production. Or is that what you want? Are you playing me against them as much as you're playing them against each other? Who's on first?"

No one is, actually. The Mind's becoming unstuck. It seems Azure's slunk off somewhere to be on hir own, and the rest of the Mind can't find hir. Some of it is inclined to think: Let hir go, good riddance! But the rest is panicked at the loss of control, and inclined to wonder what s/he's up to. There's also the question of how long s/he can survive without the rest of them. None of them ever has before. What if Azure can? Will s/he form a Mind of hir own? This planet's not big enough for more than one All There Are.

And now, of all times! Here we are getting our times mixed up, confusing Hypatia with Tessa, and the adolescent by the side of the road with some diplomat who won the Nobel a few years back, while meanwhile, back in outback Australia—

—a pink-skinned anthropologist, seamed and weathered by an Aboriginal sun, confronts the elders yet again.

"He's here to ask for another Dreaming!" one of the younger men hisses in an elder's ear. "Why don't we chase him off?"

The elder raises one hand for silence. "He's about to chase himself off," he replies.

"It took me some time to work out what you meant," the anthropologist tells the elder. " 'Go back to your own tribe,' you said, and I was fool enough to tell you 'I have no tribe.' "

"That was a long time ago," the elder says generously. "You were young."

"And now I'm not young. With that comes wisdom perforce, I suppose. It got me thinking: We're all tribal at root, aren't we? So I went back to my tribe, so to speak. I'm off for Britain. Got a grant to study the ley lines. They're rather our answer to the songlines, you might say—"

The songlines were the map of the Australian Dreamtime, by which the ancestors "created" the land by singing it into existence, and by which some few of their descendants could still, the white man's cities notwithstanding, travel the length and breadth of the continent, tribe to tribe, without ever losing their way. For centuries British farmers and sheepherders had been aware of what they called ley lines, stone circles older than Stonehenge set out in distinctive paths throughout the Isles, sometimes running through ancient burial mounds. Many had been obliterated by the plow or the occasional city, their ancient significance long forgotten. Perhaps it was time to remember again.

"Yes," the elder says. "I know of these things."

The anthropologist learned long ago never to question what an Abo says he knows.

"All right then. I'm taking your advice. Going back to my tribe. Following the ley lines—"

"—until they bring you home," the elder finishes for him.

There, ewe sea? It's possible to find yore way along the ley of the land, if ewe just keep an open Mind. Let Azure go for now. Karen will help us bring hir home.

No one knows where that idea comes from, but it sounds all right for now.

•

Meanwhile, Max Neimark is reading his fan mail.

"My dear Mr. Neimark," a high school student writes from her parents' high-rise apartment in a Tokyo prefecture, practicing her perfect English: "I understand you are coming to Japan to promote your new film, as well as the graphic novel series *Benn,* and I wanted this letter to reach you beforehand. Doubtless you receive numerous letters from fans explaining how Benn has changed their lives. I wonder if you can tolerate yet one more such story?

"You see, when I was seven years old, my father, who is in international banking, was transferred to his bank's branch office in the States. I suddenly found myself in a classroom in Bronxville, New York, with a note my mother had pinned to my sweater stating: 'This child speaks no English.' I was, as you can imagine, very frightened, and feeling very much the displaced alien.

"However, I was to discover on my television screen someone who was as alien and displaced as I. Benn became my role model. He spoke the most flawless English, and I learned from him, even emulating his accent. In addition, the nightly tales of how Benn and his shipmates traveled the galaxy doing good deeds inspired me, I am not embarrassed to admit, to consider a career in which I might do the same. In essence, I intend to pursue a degree in international relations, if only I can pass the exams for the university of my choice. . . ."

Max smiles, touching the letter to his lips reflectively. He will answer this one personally, including an invitation to the young lady to speak with him during one of his bookstore appearances on the Ginza. This was what it was all about, the interconnectedness, the sense that we were all in this together. He remembered trying to explain this to Larry during the run of *Space-Seekers.* Larry hadn't gotten it then; he didn't get it now.

Max brings the stack of fan mail into the house; it's late fall and the winds are whispering rain.

"Fellas," he says, "this is your last chance. Speak up now, or your director's going to have to exercise a little creative control. What do you want me to do here?"

Silence. For the first time since they introduced themselves to him in the mirrors in his father's barbershop, Max has an uneasy feeling about them.

He glances at his watch. Half an hour before he has to pick Sammy up at after school. Just enough time, he thinks, mischief sparkling along with the S.oteri in his odd-color eyes, to get Larry and Tessa on a conference call.

FIFTEEN

*O*cculus *Mundi,* Eye of the World.

It was amazing, Karen thought, how many synonyms there were for "opal." Serena still insisted on calling them opals; neither jellyfish nor S.oteri worked for her. Karen wondered if she should abandon the jellyfish motif (Tessa McGill would probably accuse her of stealing it), or merely take the opal dimension into consideration.

Come on, guys, talk to me!

"Tessa McGill," Serena told her when Karen finally returned her several calls. "You know, the New Age guru? She's one of us. She also thinks she's the reincarnation of Hypatia."

"I know!" Karen sighed, and told Serena about Tessa's turning up early on in her manuscript. "Don't tell me anything else. I've got to keep my objectivity here."

"How do you mean?"

"I mean I can't have any outside influences getting in the way of my writing from here on. I've told you how I don't read any one else's s/f whenever I'm working? Afraid I'll start mimicking without realizing it? I'm pretty much going to be incommunicado until this is done."

"I see," Serena says, thinking: It's snowing in the mountains already. Soon it will be up to the windowsills and I won't see anybody until spring. "I may not be here by then."

"Bullshit!" Karen says, not unkindly. She understands Serena's need to use her illness as leverage—it was her definition of self

for so long—but she cannot field multiple calls a day, from anyone. "Sometimes I think you're going to outlive me."

Serena will try calling her every few days regardless; Karen will
not take the calls. Serena has a sister, a pain counselor, a slew of
doctors, friends other than Karen; how had she managed before?
Right now, Karen has four white walls she shares with two
Generation-X adults, ostensibly her children, who pass through
her life mornings and evenings on their way to work or school
or increasingly complex social lives, replacements for the infants
she sometimes remembers more clearly. She has her work, the
blank white wall that opens out of Brooklyn into Toontown, into
Oz. She also has a terrible fear.

What if it really is jellyfish all the way down? What if her creativity isn't *her* creativity, but a by-product of three thousand
years of S.oteri intervention? What if we're all just apes clutching the jawbone of an ass (okay, a tapir—picky, picky!) with *Also
sprach Zarathustra* playing in the background? What if the S.oteri
have invented her and not the other way around?

Come on, guys! she dares them, cracking her knuckles, facing
the schoolyard bully: *I ain't ascared of you; let's do it!*

•

"Ultimately we're talking about the search for God," Larry
Koster tells Tessa, his captive audience. They are holed up in the
big empty ranch house where he's pulled the phone out of the
wall after one call too many from Janice's lawyer; he waves his
thick-fingered hands excitedly. "It's a now theme, Tessa; it never
goes out of style."

Tessa tries not to yawn. Between jet lag, the sudden torren-
tial rain, and the fact that everything in the house, including
Larry, smells of saddle leather and horseshit, she is coming
unglued. She should have insisted he come east and do this on
her turf, especially once she had him on the defensive.

"You *dare!*" she'd railed at him long-distance, catching him
while he still had a phone. Miraculously, he hadn't changed the
number yet this month. "You dare tell me you've known about

them all these years and you're only coming around to me now!

"You almost slipped that afternoon," she accused him. "The day before you auditioned for *SpaceSeekers,* which only altered your entire life. Maybe they're the reason why."

That got a reaction out of him. "Thank you, Tessa. Thanks a whole fucking lot. You're essentially telling me that I haven't done this on talent, that it's some kind of UFO power or something that's gotten me this far."

"Well?"

Suddenly she's ensconced in his living room. He doesn't remember inviting her. He's started to sweat, dabs at his brow and upper lip with a macho red bandanna he's pulled out of a back pocket.

"Believe me, that's not what they do for me! They—"

What was he *doing?* he wondered, hearing the words foam out of him, logorrhea, Montezuma's revenge of the mouth, unable to stop himself. Did they really own that much of him? He stuttered into silence, covering his brass balls. He'd only as recently as this past week, during a trip to New York he neglected to tell Tessa about (personally planting a story in one of the gossip columns about a "hot new project," specifics unspecified, he was working on), been able to get it back up again. Change of venue, change of climate? Reliving his lost Broadway youth, déjà vu all over again? Who knew? No, not even Tessa, much as he needed her, was to know how much of him they owned.

She was watching him narrowly. He dabbed at his face again, shoved the bandanna back into his pocket; the shtick gave him back his control.

"So what was I supposed to do?" he demanded. "Go public with them? Take them on the talk shows? Or just go around whispering to everyone I knew 'Do you see jellyfish, too? Do you hear voices when you think you're alone?' You and I both know people in this business who see and hear things that aren't there, and we know what happens to them. I couldn't risk my credibility. Not that I don't admire you for speaking out on your experiences, but . . ."

But you're a nutcase, and when you go down you're not taking me with you! he thought, getting angry again. It focused him. "All right, where were we? The search for God at the center of the universe . . ."

That's not what it's about at all! Virid tells the Mind worriedly. *Can they do that?*

They'd be no worse off than Akhenaton, Grey tries to reassure hir. *He made the same mistake, and merely took a nation with him. It corrected itself in the end.*

But! Virid tries to give shape to hir terrible fear. *But they have* media! *"You give us twenty-two minutes; we'll give you the world." They can take the whole world with them.*

Not if we don't let them, Grey insists, but even s/he doesn't believe it anymore. This is worse than Akhenaton, because while Tessa only feels like she's coming unglued, for the Mind it's what's happening. The Mind can't seem to mind its own business anymore. Who else is among the missing?

The Mind knows about Azure, off on hir own somewhere, not even connected with the Common Electrolytes *(How long can s/he do that? . . . Never mind how long, how can s/he do it at all; none of us has before. . . . Just because we haven't doesn't mean we can't; maybe none of us had the guts to try it, that's all. . . . Guts! That's not the point! S/he could have gone and gotten hirself fried again and we wouldn't even know. . . . But we'd have to know; we know All There Is—don't we? . . . We didn't know about Urth, eye tell yew, Occulus Mundi; how can we be Eye of the World if we don't have eyes and didn't even know their world existed until we borrowed their eyes to see? It's—Oh, shut up, all of you; stop stirring up static or we'll never find Azure. . . . Do we want to? Maybe without hir we can get back to normal again, forget about all this, which has never forgotten anything until now. . . .),* but there are other gaps in the synapse only now becoming apparent. Where, for example, is

Amber? How many more are unaccounted for? Is it going to be like this from now on? Forever is a very long time, now that there is time. . . .

•

"Apocalyptic!" Larry says. "That's what we need, something . . . apocalyptic. The end of the world as we know it. *War of the Worlds* only with a New Age or maybe environmental twist. Let's say they all weave themselves together into some massive life-form thousands of miles long, and maybe they don't need oxygen to breathe, so they can sort of float out into space and come to Earth—"

"—on the solar wind," Tessa finishes for him. "*Invasion of the Body Snatchers;* it's right there in the remake. Whatsisname—Leonard Nimoy—did the voice-over. It's been done."

"Okay, but those pod creatures were malevolent," Larry says, pacing before the fitful fireplace—he's tried getting the fire going better, but the flue hasn't been cleaned since God knew when—his enthusiasm unflagging. "Let's say our jellyfish are just . . . misunderstood."

Tessa gives him an exasperated look. "So how do you make your story apocalyptic?"

Larry stops pacing, deflating into himself like a hot-air balloon, sits with his hands wedged between his knees, shoulders sagging.

"I—I don't know," he says, bewildered.

How do you make your story apocalyptic? Just start messing with the Mind of an entire species, that's all.

A Mind divided against itself cannot stand. The Mind divides: parthenogenesis. Not like sex, not nearly as sexy, but almost as seductive. And one shall become two, and no longer cleave to each other.

(Can we do a bit on cleavage here, and how it's possible for it to mean both cleave-as-cling and cleave-as-cleft—split, sundered, bifurcate? . . . Looking down our cleavage, are yew? Stop this at once!)

Are we of two Minds now, or merely a more-enhanced one Mind? . . .

Are you out of your Mind? How can All There Are be more than All There Are?

Fractious factions pull tendrils loose in opposite directions. Azure's sort (along with Amber, or is s/he off on hir own, trifurcate?) pursue: Choose the wounded ones; they are the most receptive. Bruised vegetables make the best soup. Akhenaton and Jess (and a few more Karen will never know about. As a product of Western civilization, she will be given the facts only about her own kind; we who were once a global village have decided not to share) were accidents, overcompensations; we miscalculated the dosage, that's all. We'll be more careful from now on, promise.

The Grey Eminence, emanant, demurs. We have no right. They have, they *are*—

They? Azure's voice is mocking. Still among the Mind, then, or has this already happened, déjà vu all over again? *Who are "they"? It was you who first insisted they were not real. What's made you change yore Toon?*

•

"Maybe we are approaching it the wrong way," Larry admits. He doesn't know that while he was in the kitchen getting some aspirin for a sudden massive headache, Tessa surreptitiously erased the tape on her little voice-activated tape recorder; it's been overheating itself trying to keep up with him. She hasn't bothered turning it back on. "Forget the idea of their invading Earth; you're right—it's been done to death. What if we go out into space to find them?"

•

The thought knocks Karen back on her metaphorical heels. That's the most dangerous thing they can do!

Okay, Gentle Reader, you've been extraordinarily patient and we know you're confused, because we are, too. No, of course Karen doesn't have a clue what Tessa and Larry are up to. She either doesn't know or has forgotten that Larry's involved in this at all, and the last she's heard on Tessa was—

"Nada!" Tony reported. "She's dropped completely out of

sight. She's not in New York; I know that much. But none of the official sources will give out where she's gone, her editor is having shit fits because she's over deadline, hasn't sent them a single page, and won't return his calls. Even my unofficial sources have come up empty."

"Tony, I'm a regressionist, not a psychic!" Shirley had scolded him when he called her as a last resort. "Even if I did know, which I don't, would you expect me to tell you?"

"The only inkling I've got is from one of the columnists," he said, rummaging for something on his desk. "Here, let me read this to you: 'Seen getting out of an ordinary yellow cab at JFK, Tessa McGill headed straight into the Admiral's Club under full sail in the wee hours this morning. L.A., anyone?' God, can you imagine? She'll fly first-class and then cheap on limo service! That's all I've got, but I wouldn't worry too much—"

"She is cheap, isn't she?" Karen muses. "So if she plunked for the first-class ticket, that means she's in a hurry."

"Or someone else is picking up the tab for her. One of the studios, maybe. Or she's using up her frequent-flyer miles. Karen, there could be a million reasons why she's in L.A. Don't go to pieces on me now. Get back to work!"

"I'm working, I'm working!" Karen says, but at the same time she's thinking: The S.oteri are playing us off each other, Tessa and me, to see which of us can come up with the answer first: Are humans real or aren't we? Do they have any idea how dangerous that is?

No, Gentle Reader, of course Larry and Tessa aren't going to build a spaceship and go off looking for the S.oteri. They don't have to—the S.oteri have found them. Remember how in the movie version of *War of the Worlds* the aliens died of cold germs?

•

"The search for God at the center of the universe . . ."

Has Larry really said it more than once, or is Tessa inadvertently replaying the tape inside her head? Does the Great Ego have any idea of the sacrifices she's made to get here? As karma would have it, Eddie was actually on the phone with the airlines when not one but two casting agents called to tell her they were forwarding scripts for roles they just knew she was *perfect* for, and she knew if she didn't get back to them the day before yesterday they'd offer them to someone else, someone else who would probably walk off with an Oscar. Worse, while she was packing her manager called about a singing tour starting in Europe and winding up in Vegas, and she'd snapped *his* head off. She'd just cut her own professional throat to chase jellyfish with Larry Koster. Her hands were still shaking.

"Our hero"—Larry is still going and going and—"and I don't really have a handle on him yet, but I think he may be some sort of alien half-breed; it makes him more simpatico, both with our jellyfish and with the audience—isn't sure if he's actually searching for the biblical God or something entirely different—but he's journeying to the Galactic Center when . . ."

"I didn't think you could do that," Tessa interjects with a frown. "I mean, I'm no scientist, but isn't the gravity heavier or something at the center? If you tried to send a spaceship in there, wouldn't it get crushed like an eggshell? I don't know about that part."

"Whatever!" Larry waves her off testily; it's his skull that's being crushed like an eggshell. "That's the operative part of your statement—you're not a scientist; you *don't* know. Anyway, as I say, I don't actually have a handle on the hero yet, because I'm not sure if I want to act or just direct, but—okay, maybe he's alien, maybe not. Maybe he's from the future, but with some other kind of hook—"

"*Quantum Leap,*" Tessa recites, ticking them off on her fingers. "*Time Trax, Sliders*—Larry, you're thinking television. This is a feature."

"It doesn't have to be," he says. Tessa flutters her eyelashes at him; this is the first she's heard of it. "Maybe we shouldn't limit ourselves. I know you're a snob about television, Tessa, but get over yourself. We don't even have to limit ourselves to network these days; there are unlimited cable channels. . . ."

Tessa storms off to the kitchen to get herself something to eat;

she's been here for hours and Larry hasn't even offered. Small wonder—there's nothing in the fridge but beer and some moldly bread, and the pantry's not much better. By the time she's finished placing an order for delivery with Chalet Gourmet, Larry's off on another tangent.

"Maybe not an alien half-breed. Maybe a cop. Cops are always hot. Yeah, an intergalactic street cop, sort of a *T.J. Hooker* in space. . . ."

"*TekWar*. Or your own *CyberCop*," Tessa accuses him flatly. "Goddess, Larry, you're beginning to imitate yourself. How pitiful is that?"

Don't! the Mind warns, and Larry's headache starts to go away.

•

Karen's life bifurcates—real/not real. She is cocooned inside her work, where there is no time. Alternatively, she is free-falling through time and space. Grey becomes her familiar as Azure once was, Grey for the grey in her roanish hair, which started to silver when she was in her teens. Now she was forty-something going on twenty-something, still holding an infant in her arms while her actual children hit puberty and took SATs and went off to college, moving through her life like shadows, grey-edged alternate-universe beings, the subliminal buzz of static on a wavelength she can't completely access because there are iridescent jellyfish blocking the transmission.

How could she have gotten this old this soon? She feels better, stronger than she did at twenty. Young as the sunrise, old as the universe. But Grey is for the grey in her hair, for the grey matter, dura mater, mater familias within. Eye of the World, meet Karen, who will be your eyes and fingers, not understanding what you see, agnosic.

Tell me, Grey, tell me somebody, please! Am I only an ape with a pen in my hand? Are these words I write really mine or yours?

Does it matter, Karen? If you write it—

—I will know. You keep saying that, but do you know for sure?

Silence. Karen's life bifurcates—real/not real, but which is which? She's got to save the jellyfish, or are they trying to save her?

•

Larry Koster's life has always bifurcated; it's the burden of being an actor. In one version, his discussion with Tessa goes like this:

"We're missing the entire point here. Whatever form this ultimately takes, telepic or feature, we should be talking to lawyers, working out sub rights. Spin-off novels, comic books, even an animated series. I mean, we'd have to do animations or some kind of f/x—what is it? Blue screen—to show the jellyfish anyway. CD-ROM, now, that's the latest thing. God knows what it is— I never understood ninety percent of the technology I used to spout as Captain Stark, and I don't think I could even find the on switch on a computer—but I know it's hot."

"Don't forget action figures!" Tessa says past a mouthful of smoked salmon on good Russian rye bread, which she's washing down with a cheeky little pinot noir that almost—almost— makes her forget the smell of horseshit. She's being sarcastic, but Larry's too far gone to notice.

"You're right!" he says enthusiastically. "I hadn't thought of that. But merchandising is the thing. We'll clean up."

Don't! the Mind warns. How would Larry Koster look with blood coming out of his ears?

Larry opens a beer; his headache's coming back. He decides it's the smoke from the faulty flue and goes to damp the fire.

Don't! the Mind insists. *We can't do that anymore, now that we know they don't come back in reruns, now that we know it's wrong!*

Only if they're real . . .

"Don't," Tessa says impulsively; he gives her a quizzical look. "I like to watch the flames. Open a window or something."

He looks as if it's never occurred to him. "I can't. It'll set off the security system."

Tessa gawks at him. Was he always this paranoid?

"Larry," she asks slowly, almost sympathetically. "What is it that you're so afraid of?"

"Nothing!" he snaps, defensive as always. Now, if Karen were writing this, Tessa would motion him over to sit on the couch beside her and she'd take his hand for old time's sake and he'd break down and admit: "What am I afraid of? Everything! Crazed fans, vengeful women, my own mortality. Finding out that nothing any of us does makes any difference. Everything."

Then Tessa would rest his head on her shoulder and soothe him and they'd fall asleep on the couch just like that, innocent as children. Instead, she says:

"You're afraid of yourself, Larry Koster. Afraid of finding your center. That's why you need the S.oteri, and that's why they need me."

"You!" Larry snorts. "What the hell do they need you for?"

"To bring them to humanity," Tessa explains in all seriousness. "They need a spokesperson, an interpreter—"

"—a guru, a messiah," Larry suggests. Now he's being sarcastic and it's Tessa who fails to notice.

"Well, if you want to put it that way . . ."

"You're not talking screenplay here, you're talking Psychic Friends' Network!"

"Well, what's wrong with that?"

"And they say I've got a big ego! Tessa McGill, Jesus of the Jellyfish, using my screenplay for her own personal messianic mission—"

Tessa does something she hasn't done since acting classes—clenches her fists and screams at the top of her lungs. With her training and a two-octave range, it's enough to make Larry's precious quarterhorses twitch in their virtually soundproof stalls half a mile away. She then orders a car, stalks out of the house in disgust, and checks herself into the Ritz-Carlton. She is washing the stink of wood smoke out of her hair when the phone rings.

"Larry," she announces without preamble, "it's not going to work. You write it your way, I'll write it mine, and we'll hire somebody to edit it into shape before we show it to Max. We've got a year's option. Otherwise we'll kill each other."

"You're right," Larry says, acting with his diaphragm. Max had been entirely too accommodating during that conference call.

"Let's see what you've got" was all he'd said, and agreed on an option without even seeing a written treatment; the paperwork was already underway. If it were anyone but Max, Larry would have been suspicious. Now all he can hope is that Tessa's a slower writer than he is; he'll get his version to Max first and tell him it's a collaborative effort. After all, didn't his call get through to Max fifteen minutes before Tessa's did? Fair was fair.

Damn this headache!

"I'm sorry I called you names," he says, working for sincerity.

"And I'm sorry I screamed." Now that he's apologized first, she can afford to be magnanimous.

"Call me when you get back to New York."

"I will."

Now, again, if this were Karen's novel, she'd reach in, deus ex machina, and give them both a scolding:

"Don't you realize what you're doing? The S.oteri are already in the process of having a meltdown of their own invention; if you try to reduce them to a goddamn merchandising opportunity it could trigger some sort of mass psychosis. Do you have any idea what an entire planet full of angry telepaths is capable of? Do we really want to find out?"

But this isn't Karen's novel, is it? Besides, she knows neither Larry nor Tessa would care, not about the S.oteri, not about her. She is pond scum to these people; she'd never get through.

"They need us!" she wants to plead. "They're asking us to show them the elephant. You remember the story of the blind men and the elephant, don't you? Each one felt a different part of the elephant and came up with his own conclusions. The one who felt the elephant's side announced 'An elephant is like a mountain.' The one who felt its tail said 'An elephant is like a rope.' The one who felt the trunk decided 'An elephant is like a garden hose'—"

"Karen, dear . . . " Tessa begins dryly, while Larry jumps to his feet, defensive, demanding: "What the hell is she doing here?

How the hell did she get past security? I'll call my lawyer. She's got no business—"

"I'm sorry, am I boring you?" Karen cuts him off; she has nothing to lose now. "All I'm saying is, you're showing them bits of rope and garden hose and telling them it's an elephant. Somebody's going to get hurt."

She can't do that, of course. All she can do, she finally accepts, is finish her novel.

The sound of mowers outside her window is replaced by the scratch and swish of rakes and brooms, the scrape and sough of snow shovels; Karen scarcely notices. When she lived with Ray she did all the yardwork herself. That life is gone, no longer real. Only the two survivors she brought out of it into this life—her daughter and her son—are.

Neither Nicole nor Matthew, mercifully, is in touch with S.oteri. Yet in Nicole's green eyes, her passion for horror movies, her effusive generosity and equal parts anger, joy, and tears, Karen sees Virid dancing hir *danse macabre* of religious fervor and fallen sparrows, hir perverse insistence that tomorrow *must* be better than today. And in Matthew's steady hazel gaze and analytical turn of mind, his recognition of The Way Things Work all out of proportion to his nineteen years, she recognizes Amber of the historical overview, the philosophical perspective, the sense of place. S.oteri as projections of/into/out of human souls—it's a hook to hang a narrative on. She writes.

She can account for Virid and Amber now, and she of course is Grey. But Azure-blue, where are you?

•

Ever since the first brain surgery, Serena's life has bifurcated, though she's lived so many different lives she's scarcely noticed. Rich bitch, street kid, artist, short-order cook, hell-raiser, prison guard, artist again—all are equally real to her. This is still the artist's life, but suddenly Serena has a secret: The Eye of the World is hiding under her bed.

Actually, it's only her old friend Rain, the one Karen calls

Azure, but for the first time s/he's not just a sparkle and a whisper but something solid enough to stir up dust bunnies and make the bedframe quiver with hir trembling. Rain is scared. The other opals, s/he's explained, are really pissed at hir.

"What did you do to make them so mad?" Serena asks casually. There is no answer at first. "I wish you'd come out from under there. I can't bend down that far to see you, and it's awkward as hell trying to talk to you this way."

I can't let them find me! Rain whispers. *What they want to do is not kill me exactly, but they want to reabsorb me into the Mind, and it amounts to the same thing.*

"They'll find you eventually. Then it'll be my ass for being an accessory," Serena says exasperatedly. "You told me they know all there is to know."

I'm not so sure that's true anymore. Hell, even I'm having doubts about just about everything, and I'm the one who's been born again. Imagine what it must be like for them. They don't see what I see, even though they do.

"Come out from under the bed!" Serena insists testily—this conversation is making her head hurt worse than usual—and Rain obliges. "Just answer me straight about one thing: Are you guys out to conquer the world, or what?"

Rain sighs. *I don't know!*

SIXTEEN

Make up your Mind!

It happened this way: By the time we realized you weren't just projections of our own Mind, it was too late; we were involved.

Seeing was the best thing, because after a few thousand years of looking through your eyes to see you and your world (no, not quite as far back as the ape with the jawbone—er, leg bone?—of a tapir in his hand—sorry, Arthur! Though that might have been someone else; ewe sea, weir knot telling yew everything whee know!), there was a point where we began to imagine what it would be like to see ourselves through your eyes. Try for a moment, Gentle Reader, to see what we're saying here.

We were *imagining.* Creating a scene in which you arrived on our world in your spaceships (not for at least a millennium yet; as the fella from Vermont said: Cahn't get theah from heah) and saw us for the first time, put us in perspective—bigger than a bread box, smaller than a redwood; what size sample case would you need to bring one of us home, or could we sort of suction onto a bulkhead and sit there munching fungus even in zero-g?

So you taught us to imagine, because we thought we were imagining you. And by then we'd squiggled our way into a mind here and there. Not *Invasion of the Body Snatchers,* not at all. If Ahkenaton had said "Sorry, fellas, I'm perfectly happy with the old gods; think I'll be like my dad and go conquer a few new territories instead of funding the arts," you'd be able to visit his tomb in the Valley of the Kings even now. If Jess had decided we were the minions of Satan and turned on her heel and stalked away from us she'd still have been carving chairs and table legs well into her eighties. Your Aussie anthropologist would even now have stopped wearing out shoe leather walking the ley lines in exchange for a posh bit of tenure at the university, spouting the same old crap while grad assistants graded his papers, more hot air and fallen trees to add to global warming.

After all, Karen, you don't have to look any farther than your ex-husband: We give you—whether you want him or not—Ray (I Coulda Been a Contenda) Guerreri. True, all of these people would end up the way eighty percent of the population does—settling. Hiding the indefinably missing in their lives behind lines of coke or talk of benefits packages, or the things they could do if they weren't chained to the nine-to-five. Whining about their car payments, but safe. It's no easier being On the Edge than it is being All There Are.

So we started out watching, and ended up getting involved. Trying to get more of you to go out on the edge. So sue us. It's too late to go back now.

Some say. Others think all we've got to do is reabsorb Azure, cancel cable service, and all will be forgotten. We're divided along those lines now, parthenogenesis. And the two shall become four, and the four sixteen . . .

We never asked for this! some keep saying and Azure (this is before s/he took to hiding under Serena's bed) thought: *This could literally go on forever; maybe I was better off dead!*

Some of the Mind decides to oblige.

Hey, guise? Why are you looking at me like that, when you don't even have eyes? You've borrowed theirs, *haven't you, even while you're saying out of the other side of your mouth that you want nothing to do with* them *anymore, have I got that right? Um, guise? Don't come any closer or I'll scream.*

Nice trick, right? I know: In space no one can hear you scream. Especially if you ain't got vocal chords.

Stop babbling! the Mind squeaks along the synapses of hir mind. *Ewe have to stop talking like them, thinking like them. Stop it now!*

What you mean me, *Chemosabe? We're all doing it now; just listen to yourselves! Do you think by reabsorbing me you're going to unlearn that? And whether you do or not: THEY'RE STILL REAL.*

That's not important, someone says, and before Azure can even answer *Huh?* Virid says:

How'd you like a religious war on your hands?, and before Azure can answer smugly: *I have no hands,* she sees it:

Virid, usually the gentlest toward hir own kind, the more violently s/he enjoys watching others drawn and quartered (or burnt. Witch trials, now, those are a trip. Watch them writhe and scream. Lake never wants to play that one, because burnt blood is all black and viscous, not the pretty Chinese-lacquer red s/he prefers, burnt blood searing and spitting in the flames along with standard-issue deliquescing flesh, which, we're told, who have no olfactory nerves, smells like roasting pork. Positively scrumptious, especially where the fat's all crispy. But then it's all gone, and who gets to clear away all the bones and greasy paper plates after, we'd like to know?) isn't exactly threatening Azure, merely planting a new idea in hir mind. It's not as if the S.oteri can even start a fire, lacking two sticks to rub together, and where would they get the paper plates, not to mention a decent recipe for barbecue sauce? All the same, that's when Azure decides s/he's better off under Serena's bed, at least until this blows over.

Serena lets hir stay—not the first time a stray's turned up on her doorstep—even though Rain/Azure tells her s/he can't help her with her pain anymore without attracting the Mind's attention. The pain increases, Serena's time decreases. She keeps on drawing. Winter sets in for real, and the trailer on the hill is buried windowsill-high by a series of passing blizzards. Her dog Penny dies in her sleep. Serena's own prognosis still has doctors writing papers for medical journals about her.

"You're supposed to be dead," they keep telling her.

"Yeah, well. I never was one for doing what I'm supposed to do!" she snaps back, her eyes still watering every time she thinks of Penny, wrapped in trash bags and an old tarp, buried in a snow-drift until the thaw, when she will bury her under the rosebush she was always so hell-bent on digging up.

Pitiful, really, she thinks, wrapping her fingers around a new drawing pencil, when the only friends you have in the world are a dog and a bunch of jellyfish. She doesn't count Karen anymore, not on this time line; she's not sure why.

When her sister, laboring her four-wheel drive up the gravel road in the melting snow, drops her off in front of the trailer following her most recent stay at the medical center, she can hear the phone ringing before she even unlocks the door.

"I've been thinking about you," Tessa McGill says, all perky and ingenuous. (My dear, that's why we're called ingenues at the start of our careers!) "Wondering how about your health, and whether you were still drawing . . ."

Takes a bullshitter to know a bullshitter! Serena thinks, lowering herself into a chair, shoes wet with snowmelt dripping onto the carpet; in her condition it takes ten minutes or more to maneuver herself into position to take them off. "Yeah, I'm still here. I'd say I was fine, but I never was a good liar. What's on your mind?"

"You are direct, aren't you? Well, to be perfectly frank, I was wondering if you were still being—visited—by our mutual friends the jellyfish."

Serena lights a cigarette before she answers, making sure Tessa can hear the click of the lighter, the hiss as she draws the smoke in.

"Nope," she says flatly. "No jellyfish around here."

Thinking: They're *opals,* dammit! It's only Karen who insists on calling them jellyfish. To me they've always been and will always be opals, which is why I don't even have to lie to make this a short conversation!

"That's really too bad!" Tessa says with feeling, thinking: *Actually that's wonderful, because now they won't tell you anything that contradicts what I have in mind!* "How long has it been like that?"

Serena thinks for a minute. The questions are getting trickier. "Long as I can remember," she says. "With all the meds I'm on—"

"—you sometimes have trouble remembering," Tessa supplies for her, just as Serena hoped she would. "Oh, I do understand, dear, and it's really so sad! Just one more question, now, and I'll let you go. Have you shared what you know with anyone else? Because—well, I hope you'll understand when I say that it's *essential* that you keep this *entre nous,* because the movie industry is such a filthy business sometimes, but it so happens that I've been asked—I wouldn't go so far as to say *chosen* by the jellyfish; believe me, I have no delusions of being any kind of messiah—but I've been working on a way of bringing them to the attention of the rest of the world, so to speak, in a language everyone can understand, because even an illiterate can go to the movies, don't you see? And a very dear friend of mine, the actor Laurence Koster—I'm sure you know who he is . . . "

"I'm an old *SpaceSeekers* fan," Serena says carefully. "I've never met Mr. Koster, but I know of him."

She flashes on a memory of loading a handtruck filled with her artwork onto a service elevator at the start of an out-of-town con; just as the doors were closing she was joined by a florid, overweight superhero in an expensive powder-blue running suit. He'd startled at the sight of her, expecting to be alone (couldn't take the passenger elevators without being mobbed by fans), shot her a look as if she were pointing an Uzi at his gut, and jammed his pudgy hands between the doors, shouldering his way out.

She'd wanted to tell him it was cool, she didn't bite, had gone so far as to jab the button to reopen the door between her and his panic-stricken face, but he'd whirled and stalked away as fast as he could. Serena heard the words "fangirl," "cunt," and "bitch" trailing in his wake; once your lungs were trained for Shakespeare it was difficult not to project, even when you were muttering. Oh, yeah, she knew Larry Koster all right!

But what was Tessa saying? Something about her and Koster working on a screenplay together?

"Yeah, well, lots of luck," Serena says. Her cigarette's finished; so's the conversation. "But it's got nothing to do with me."

"She's no threat," Tessa tells Larry, who's got Janice's lawyer on the other line and is really not paying attention. Tessa sighs inwardly. Paranoid as he was, it hadn't even occurred to Larry that someone like Serena could claim theft of idea if they didn't handle her carefully. "However, there is someone else we may have to deal with. . . . What? No, she's here at my end; leave her to me."

•

Karen is on the downslope, another hundred pages to go. If only there wasn't so much racket going on in the background.

"Hey, guys? Keep it down, will you?"

Not long ago she'd have been shouting it at Nicole through a closed door, and the stereo might have been lowered a decibel. Or maybe Matt and his father and everyone in Yankee Stadium would be yelling at each other in her living room again. ("Dad, forget about it, okay? The Yankees suck; there's no way around it.") Nowadays Karen has a different set of dependents.

The four have become sixteen and the sixteen two hundred and fifty-six *(Think we didn't notice you slipped and said sixty-four back there? Hah!)* and, about as useful as Jesuits, they are all absorbed in splitting hairs and counting the angels dancing on the head of a pin. Why?

Because we're scared, that's why! Because we've fallen and we can't get up. Because we used to have all the answers and now we have all the questions and we can't answer any of them and it annoys the shit out of us, that's why!

Who have no shit. We think. We're not even sure of that anymore.

No shit, Sherlock. Karen, did you think of that? If fungus goes in one end (munch, slurp, munch!), something's got to come out the other, doesn't it? Even the simplest earthwormish alimentary canal scatologi-

cally (as opposed to eschatalogically, eschatology—you could look it up—being in the nature of what we're trying to do here) extrudes something. Earthworm shit is particularly good for plants; in fact, without earthworms your Earth would still be volcanic pumice all the way down. So what-taya think? Does jellyfish shit make good fertilizer? Good enough to grow your next year's crop of fungus? Talk about your closed-system technology; NASA ought to consult with us.

Okay, we're getting sidetracked here, who have no tracks, the old slipstream-of-consciousness trick—james joyce, archie and mehitabel, e. e. cummings, and all of them. Smart writers, that lot, saving themselves all that wear and tear on their pinkies, not having to downshift on a manual typewriter. Karen, are you old enough to remember typing on a manual?

"Are you kidding?" she snorts, thinking: Humor them; they'll settle down eventually. "Typed my first two novels on one. Strongest pinkies in the world!"

Yes, of course; we'd forgotten. You're actually old enough to remember Vietnam and the Draft, improbable as they both seem now. . . .

"Hey, no snide remarks about my age! Compared to you I haven't even been born yet. Besides, I think James Joyce wrote his drafts in longhand, on yellow legal pads. He couldn't see well enough to type. I read somewhere that he was so blind toward the end that—"

Karen? Why do we keep forgetting things?

She thinks about that one. What's most important, given their precarious state of Mind, is not to treat them lightly.

"For the same reason you keep learning new things?" she suggests. "Manual typewriters, for instance. If you don't even have hands, how could you possibly know how hard it was to work on a manual? How not only your pinkies, but your entire arm, all the way up to your shoulders, used to ache sometimes at the end of the day? Then there's what a secretarial chair does to your lower back! Did you know that when typewriters were first invented only men were allowed to use them? They were considered heavy equipment, and women were told they were 'too frail' to work as secretaries. I love listening to computer nerds

whining about their carpal tunnel syndrome. Bunch of wusses!"
She flexes her pinkies. "I'll arm-wrestle the lot of 'em!"

Humor her, someone says. *In her precarious state of mind . . .*

"Okay, I heard that! Look, we're all in the same place—learning new things, misplacing old assumptions. Not losing them
just—reevaluating? Mentally exchanging—osmosing, if you will.
Accepting the fact that we can both be real. It's possible. Work
with me, guys; we're almost there."

Maybe some of us don't want to go anymore.

•

Okay! Karen thinks two days later, squinting at the address above
the door of Tessa McGill's East Eighties apartment building.
Whose brilliant idea was this? Did the Great Guru summon me
on her own recognizance, or are at least some of the 256 fractious factions trying to distract me so I don't finish the goddamn
novel?

"I don't know what Serena told you," she said when Tessa
called her. "I'm not a scriptwriter."

"That's all right, dear," Tessa replied, keeping matters deliberately vague. "We'd just like to talk, very informally. It's a work
in progress, nothing definite. We just thought you might be interested."

What you mean "we," Kemosabe? No point in saying anything more until they're face-to-face. Karen finds herself jotting
down the address. Fast-forward, and the doorman is announc-
ing her.

"Miss McGill says to go right up." He nods toward the art
deco elevator.

"Why did you give her my phone number?" she will ask Serena when all this is over. "Why'd you even mention my name
at all?"

"Did I do that?" Serena will be frankly mystified; she is on so
many medications, and the brain surgeries have left gaps, lacunae
an *occulus mundi* can easily fill, that sometimes she forgets. "I swear
I didn't! I may have mentioned that she and I weren't the only
ones, I may have told her you were a writer, but I know I didn't

so much as tell her your first name, much less your last, honest!"

The door to Tessa's duplex is open a crack, which, this being New York, Karen finds downright alarming. If she steps through will she find the place ransacked, a bludgeoned body in the bedroom? She knocks, which pushes the door open further; the tiny foyer and the beginnings of the parlor look tidy and normal. A little heavy on the chintz and throw rugs, the writer in Karen notes, but—

"Miss McGill?" Silence. Now what?

Her answer arrives in a slink of black fur, purring green-eyed at her through the door. She kneels and reaches a finger in. It is duly sniffed and allowed to rub the bridge of his nose.

"Hi, cat! Want to tell the mistress I'm here?"

He doesn't, and sashays back into the apartment, no help at all. Karen knocks and calls a few more times, noticing by now that the chain is across the inside of the door; no foul play, just a game being played. She can picture Tessa lurking in the kitchen, listening, which in fact she is. Fed up, Karen goes back down to the lobby and asks the doorman to ring again.

"She says to go right on up," he repeats, hanging up the house phone with an eloquent shrug that says Sorry; she does this a lot!

The cat turns out to be a neighbor's.

"He's a nuisance!" Tessa confides cozily once she's sat Karen down and sent Eddie to make tea. ("Well, she likes cats. That's something!" was Eddie's assessment as the two of them lurked in the kitchen; he at least had the good grace to feel silly.) "He thinks he owns this apartment as well as the one across the hall. Shoo, now, Pangur; that's enough!"

Tail up, the cat disappears into the kitchen.

"You tell me you're just writing a novel," Tessa flutters at Karen, staring into her eyes for the longest time. But Karen went to Catholic schools; she's had to learn how not to flinch. "Why is it that I don't believe you?"

Karen allows herself to blink finally. She sees them, too, in Tessa's eyes.

"That's not my problem," she says, but politely. Don't be rude to the person who's pouring the tea. Catholic schools again.

"And you're already contracted to write this—novel?" Tessa says carefully. "Who's your publisher?"

"I don't think I need to tell you that. Why don't you call my agent and talk to him?" Even as she says it, she remembers that Tony's in South America this week, working a deal for a client so hush-hush she doesn't even know what country he's in, only that there's one phone in the entire town and he can only call in to the office once a day. Did you guys arrange that, too? she wonders. You really are playing us off each other, aren't you? Are you out of your Mind? "Tony will tell you everything he thinks you need to—"

"I'm talking to you," Tessa cuts across her. "And I'm doing my very best to try to help you, because the simple fact is that Laurence Koster and I have a movie script on an identical theme, which is already in production."

The S.oteri fade from both their eyes for a moment—Tessa's because she's lying, Karen's because she's scared. But in that moment neither can read the other's emotions, so it's counterproductive.

Karen puts down her teacup so she'll neither choke nor allow Tessa to see her hands shake.

"Far as I know, you can't patent a theme. I tell my readers there are only four ideas in the universe—"

"I'm not interested in your readers—," Tessa starts to say, but Karen's dealt with schoolyard bullies all her life.

"—and they've all been done before," she finishes, a little shaky. "So I guess I'll just have to write my novel better than your screenplay." She smiles, shrugs again: No hard feelings! "Or at least differently."

"Or you can cooperate with us and we can cut a deal." Karen doesn't react. "Face it, honey, your little novel's going to sell a couple of thousand copies and end up on the dollar table at the Strand—"

"Half-price in the basement first," Karen counters smugly; she's been there.

"My books sell that in a week," Tessa says flatly, thinking she's won this round.

"Then my little novel's no threat to your great big screenplay, is it?" Now it's Tessa's turn not to react. "So what are you— and, I assume, Mr. Koster—so afraid of?"

Afraid? Tessa wants to shriek, but doesn't. She, too, is aware that the S.oteri are playing both of them. *Sweetie,* she thinks in spite of herself: *I'm not afraid of you; I eat your kind for breakfast!*

"Ms. Guerreri . . . Karen." Tessa flutters her eyelashes. "I don't think you quite understand what I'm—what we're offering here."

Karen's gotten up from the overstuffed couch and is putting on her coat. *Preternatural* is dead no matter what she does; the Great Guru and Brassballs Koster have just killed it.

"I assumed you were offering to buy me off—," she starts to say just as Tessa says:

"Not at all. Mr. Koster and I would like you to come in with us so we can all work together."

Karen sits down to keep from falling over.

"Did I mention Max Neimark will be directing?" Tessa asks sweetly, thinking: Gotcha! "I know you've written two *Space-Seekers* novels—you see, I did my homework!—so I also know you must be a big fan of his."

I'll have to think about it! is the first answer that pops into Karen's mind, though it isn't the right answer at all. The right answer should be Oh, yes, Miss McGill, by all means, I'd be ever so happy to let you buy the rights to my little novel so I can pay off my son's college loans and walk through doors that were slammed and double-locked on me before I was born! Buy the rights to my little novel and Hollywoodize it into something no one will ever recognize, as long as it advances your cause, and the S.oteri, having created this little role-playing game, will just have to take their chances.

She sees herself in a designer dress, trying not to trip on the hem, rushing up to the stage to retrieve her Best Screenplay Based on Another Medium Oscar, or did the scriptwriters get that? She can see Larry and Tessa onstage at the Shrine Auditorium, jostling each other for mike time. Well, so what, as long as she got the money and a chance to work with Max Neimark? Well, okay, all that money and maybe a chance to *meet* Max Neimark, with about as much credibility as the last time. Did Max believe in the S.oteri? He'd keep the production honest, wouldn't he?

Hell, if she was lucky they'd run her around on a quick tour of the soundstage when everyone was out to lunch, and the screen-rights money would probably be cut so many ways that . . . Well, so what? The alternative was ending up on the dollar table at the Strand—again. That wouldn't help her, Matt's education, or the S.oteri. Karen wavers. Oh, yes! she wants to shout: "Yes I said yes I will yes!"

But something stops her. "I'll have to think about it," she says, and gets up to leave, again.

Tessa gawks at her speechlessly, purely amazed. Is the woman stupid? Why is it always incumbent upon her to explain things?

"We haven't even mentioned a figure," she tries. Karen shakes her head.

"That doesn't affect my decision. I'll get back to you."

Tessa follows Karen to the door, where she's trying to let herself out, except that the cat has reappeared and is dancing around her ankles as if under instructions, and Karen can't decide whether to let him run out into the hall or nudge him back into the apartment with her foot. While she's working this out, Tessa touches her shoulder; it is not a friendly gesture.

"If you think you can play hard-to-get-with me, sweetie, think again!" she says, with anything but sweetness on her suddenly hard-lined face. "The truth is, Larry and I don't need you at all; we've got the S.oteri. I just thought I'd do the magnanimous gesture, give a boost to an unknown, let you be a part of something that isn't just about the movies, you know, but about the next phase of humanity."

"I think I know what it's about," Karen says stonily. She feels the floor opening beneath her, molecules all the way down, but says what she's going to say anyway. "You're right: You probably don't need me."

She lifts the cat bodily off the floor and shoves him aside, making her escape.

"Our version of *Preternatural* will be a major release before yours is even in galleys!" Tessa shouts after her. She hadn't until this moment decided to preempt the title as well, but why not? "You can read all about it in the trades!"

"I don't read the trades," Karen says to the elevator walls moments later. Schoolyard bullies never seem to learn!

She's exhausted; the gravity around her seems to have gotten heavier. Now what? Call NASA or the networks? Maury Povitch, or the *Enquirer?* No. Back to the write womb and her word processor because it's all she knows how to do. Not that it's going to make a damn bit of difference.

Oh, but it does. We were counting on you back there, Karen, and you did a bang-up job!

"Yeah, right! Like you didn't just tell Tessa the same thing!" She stalks down the subway steps, into her own particular cave. "I can't trust any of you anymore!"

Upstairs where the atmosphere is thinner, Tessa is furious with herself, and with the S.oteri.

"Why did you make me do that?" she demands, clenching and unclenching her fists, taking cleansing breaths that make her feel no less clean. "Lie to her like that?"

We didn't make *you do anything, Tessa. We're like hypnosis. All we do is enhance your natural proclivities, make it easier for you to—*

"I mean, it was strictly Amateur Night!" she is raging. "I can do better than that in my sleep! I could have spent the entire afternoon sweet-talking her. I could have brought her around eventually; I know I could! Either I've caught a case of Larry's goddamn impatience, or it's your fault. You made me blow it!"

Oh, we see. . . .

•

. . . who now have your eyes to see. Nevertheless, Rain tells Serena, *it's driven some of us absolutely out of control.*

"Like you, for instance? Seems to me you started all of this. Is that why you're hiding under the bed?"

Winter's almost over, and Azure's been snuggled in among the dust bunnies, silent, all this time. Has the Mind called off the search? S/he doesn't seem to care anymore, and has decided it's safe to talk.

"Tell me what's going on so I can decide if I still trust you," Serena says.

Rain/Azure sighs. Where to begin? Reiterate the part about how what started out as watching slipped imperceptibly into involvement, no longer 2D/TV, (from the Latin *video* "I see"), but something active/interactive and no way to shut it off?

Imagine, Serena dear, s/he wants to say, *what would happen if your TV suddenly expanded into one entire wall of your house, and then wrapped itself around all the walls, then sucked you inside it and—no, it isn't working. There are no referents. It was just terrifying, that's all. And we had no one but ourselves to tell about it, no way to get outside our own Mind to have a look at it, you see?*

It started at least as far back as Akhenaton (sorry if we're reiterating, but Karen's jotting all this down as well; we want to make sure we don't leave anything out on this go-round), maybe farther; we don't even remember that. We are not—repeat not—responsible for that almost-australopithecene ape-type and his tapir bone. If it were up to us he'd still be gnawing at it, not using it to bash his fellow's brains in. Not our idea of evolution, nossir, not at all.

Okay, let me try it another way. I'll tell you a little story. Once upon a time Virid and I—the one that you call Grass—got into a bit of a theological discussion. Query: Do we create God in our own image? This was right after I'd died and been born again, you see, and Virid was one of the first to understand that this meant we could individuate as well as being All There Are. So, Query: Is God a carpenter, a jellyfish, a three-headed dog who demands human sacrifice, or all of the above? And why were we given this power-of-Mind to reach out across the parsecs and discover other minds if we were not meant to use it? It's the old Tree of Knowledge dilemma. You know:

Have anything you want here, God says, except the fruit from that tree. (Meanwhile thinking: Heh-heh, just watch them! *Suddenly everything else they have is meaningless; they are driven perforce to eat from that tree by the Perversity Quotient I've already programmed into the design matrix. Aren't role-playing games fun? Whee!)*

Serena has walked out in the middle of this monologue to give herself a shot of Toradol; it doesn't help. The pain refuses to budge, and Azure's still talking.

What I'm saying is: Only humans would invent such a perverse God. So why not God as Jellyfish? We can be anything your theology desires—angels, devils, the voice of conscience, "My God it's full of S.oteri!" instead of "It's full of stars!" A cosmic cribsheet to help you crawl out of your caves and put down your tapir bones and write poetry instead.

So maybe, I says to Virid, I says: Maybe we're the gods and they are our creation. And Virid gives me one of those sidelong looks as if to say Idiot, *that's been the Mind's official position from the beginning. Okay, I says, let's put it to the test: Let's stop thinking about them for a nanosecond and see what happens. They'll wink out as if they never were, while we go on and on and—*

And that's when Virid started to weep (quite a trick, which has no tear ducts) for, much as s/he thrives on death and dismemberment, there are characters in this particular role-playing game. ongoing dramatic series, mini-soap-opera whom s/he misses when they die. Rather like you'd miss the gerbil young their mother has eaten, the puppy whose skull was crushed by a passing car, the cat you had who liked to sleep in the clothes dryer—

"Okay, that's enough of that!" Serena snaps. The pain is at head-banging level, and she had a puppy once, long before Penny; her father had backed the car over it, on purpose. "Is there a point to this?"

Almost finished! Azure assures her. *What I'm trying to say is that Virid's point was that even though s/he could always play you back in reruns, it wasn't enough. It was almost as if s/he wanted some of you to live as long as we did. That's when I got nervous, who had no nerves,*

*and went running to Grey to tell the Mind, but by then they were pre-
pared to jump me and reabsorb me, so I split and ended up under your
bed. . . .*

The pain in Serena's head is so intense that tears stream from
her eyes, a physiological rather than emotional reaction. She
thought she knew how much this could hurt; she was wrong.

I have to remember to tell Karen this, she thinks. Why have
I cut her off all these weeks, refused to talk to her? Have to remember to tell her—what?

"Rain, look," she gasps. "I can't take much more of this. . . ."

Azure sighs.

*Serena, m'dear, I don't think you get it even now: I'm here! I am
actually here, out from under your bed, and in all these weeks you haven't
even bothered to touch me and confirm that. People in the next county
are finding UFOs in their backyards, and you're passing up, quite literally, the chance of a lifetime. . . . Serena? Try to ignore the pain for
a minute and pay attention; I want to ask you something important.
Tell me—honestly now—how many serious drunks have you been on
in your life?*

This gets Serena's attention. "Couldn't count 'em," she admits, tasting the Jack Daniels on the tip of her tongue and in the
back of her throat like rolling fire.

*All right, then. But you do know that every time you got drunk you
killed a couple of thousand brain cells and never felt a thing. If you'd
kept it up, by now you wouldn't remember your own name. So in that
spirit, we're—er, actually, I'm—proposing to borrow a few of your
brain cells for a little experiment of mine. . . .*

"You suggesting you swap your brain for mine? I don't know
how much of my brain is left. Not much of a swap."

*Not a swap exactly. Consider it an . . . infusion. Certain select por-
tions of your mind infused with resonances of the Mind, so you learn to
see things the way an S.oteri sees them. No past, present, or future, everything on a loop that perpetually loops back over itself. Ever make a
Möbius strip in math class?*

"Nope," Serena says stolidly. She's fascinated, but won't admit
it. Hell, Rain knows what she's thinking anyway, so why even

bother saying it aloud? She's so tired, so fucking tired, wants to lie down and die, but her body won't let her; it's too damn strong. Outlived her prognosis by nearly a decade now; takes a lickin' and keeps on tickin'. *Let me go, for Chrissake; let me die.* Möbius Strip? Sounds like a New Wave dance club. Wonder if they need a bouncer? What the hell was Rain babbling about? "I never spent that much time in school, remember? Mostly on report or cutting, sneaking into town to score. What the hell are you talking about?"

It's not important, Azure says. *Just try to think of time as not-time, as everything happening at once and continuously. . . .*

"Makes my head hurt!" Serena lurches to her feet, closing the blinds against the late-afternoon light. "Get back under the bed, will you? That sparkling's killing me!"

Sorry! Will you at least think about what I'm offering you?

"Maybe. Now shut up for a while. I need to rest."

She stretches herself out on the bed, knowing it won't do any good. What did Rain mean about some of them being out of control, about Grass wanting to play God? What is it exactly that Rain's offering her? Is the pain actually going away, or is she dreaming it?

SEVENTEEN

Serena dreams.

"A lot of what you're taking are antidepressants," the pain counselor at the clinic told her in the beginning. "Sometimes they'll give you weird dreams. If they're only occasional, try to learn to live with them. The alternative is reducing the dosage, which will increase the pain."

"Gotcha," Serena had said. "What's the occasional weird dream, right?"

Serena dreams.

"What do you think they'd do if you told them you didn't want to play with them anymore?" Karen asks, meaning the jellyfish, opals, S.oteri. This *is* just a dream, isn't it? "Suppose you told them you were tired of their messing in your thoughts, you wanted them to go away?"

Serena is surprised. "It would never occur to me. They take away my pain. They help me with my drawing. They show me wonderful things."

"Like what?" Karen asks.

Serena thinks. "You're the writer, not me. I can't tell you. There aren't any words. I just know that when they're not with me, something's missing. Something that's supposed to be there." She chuckles, grins her little-girl grin. "Beats the hell out of me! But I wouldn't give them up for anything in the world."

In the dream she can read Karen's thoughts, and what Karen is thinking is less than kind. Karen—prim, prissy, not nearly as far removed from Catholic schools as she'd like to think she is—is thinking Serena's addicted to the S.oteri, as dependent on them as she is on her medications. In the dream, Serena shrugs it off, though in real life it would wound her. She wants Karen's respect more than—well, not more than anything. Not more than the opals. Given the constant pain that is her waking life, isn't she allowed?

Serena dreams. Dreams aren't supposed to make you feel guilty, are they? That would make them nightmares, not dreams. She used to have horrible nightmares following the surgeries, but she doesn't anymore, not since Rain began to visit her. Opals. Let Karen and Tessa call them jellyfish; to her they're opals, cachalongs. *Occulus mundi,* the Eye of the World, because that's the world they show her in her dreams.

She floats into them, like floating in half-set Jell-O, except Jell-O is cold and they're warm, blood-warm; they surround her, buoy her up, safe and comforting. Everything is prettier here among them, color-enhanced, saturated. Nothing hurts her anymore. Nothing can harm her here; she is among friends.

Floating, disembodied, her limbs become tendrils, attenuated, sensitized. Some of the surgeries severed nerves; in real life she hasn't been able to feel anything from the neck down, except for an occasional tingling in her fingertips, for years. Sometimes even her face goes numb. Not here. If she has a face, it feels; little tentacle-fingers caress her lovingly, giving her all the love she never had. It's exciting. She floats.

Serena dreams. She is Jess the Messiah, preaching on a hillside, only in this reality no one tries to kill her. She is accepted, revered for what she is, and the world is a very different place.

She is Rain now, somehow; she and Rain are one. She's not into channeling like Tessa, doesn't understand how she can be herself and at the same time someone else, but it feels good. She remembers a conversation she and Karen never had, on the same day that Karen visited her in the house on the hill and she explained about the lake colors.

"You and I knew each other in another life," she'd told Karen. "It's the only explanation for why we get along so well now."

Karen had shaken her head. "I don't believe any of that stuff. Reincarnation, UFOs—"

"Just 'cause you don't believe in it doesn't mean it isn't real."

Karen had shrugged, one of those people who didn't have to argue herself hoarse for what she did or did not believe in.

"Let me put it this way: If we do have more than one life, it doesn't matter. We don't bring anything that we've learned with us from one life to the next; we have to relearn everything from toilet training to language to love all over again, so what's the point? It's a very inefficient system. I prefer to think we live parallel lives."

"Oh." Serena had thought about this. Since she'd met Karen, she'd started reading a lot of science fiction; it not only gave her more imagery for her drawing, it expanded her mind. "You mean parallel universes, different incarnations of ourselves living at the same time, but in different places?"

The thought appealed to her. Maybe her parallel selves didn't have syringo.

Again Karen shook her head. "Not several different selves, but different dimensions of the same self."

"I don't follow you."

"Where do you go when you're drawing?"

"I—I'm not sure. With the opals?"

"But you didn't always. You said they didn't come to you until after all your surgeries. You were able to disappear inside your work long before that."

"Yeah, but my work wasn't all that good. You've seen how it's improved over the years."

Karen had dismissed it. "That doesn't matter. It's still your work, and you're the one who's found ways to improve it. Same with any artist. Where does an actor go when he talks about being 'inside' a role? I know when I write I live through my characters. I'm not aware of the passage of time on the 'outside.' The same with being in love. When you're totally immersed in a relationship with someone—"

Outside the dream, where Serena cannot read her thoughts, Karen stops herself. Totally immersed in a relationship with someone, she thinks. Like who—Ray? Maybe she was, in the beginning, so long ago she can't remember; Ray was never immersed in anyone but himself. Maybe not even then. Maybe never again.

"I can't say I ever felt that way with a lover," Serena admits, having thought it over. "Maybe if I hadn't gotten so sick . . . maybe if I had a little more time . . ."

"Maybe even our dreams are parallel lives," Karen suggests finally. "Like a split-screen version of our waking selves. A kind of—*meta*life. Extra."

"Maybe." The answer hadn't satisfied Serena, either in her dream or in the conversation she and Karen will never have. Lots of conversations she and Karen will never have, including the one where Karen yells at her for giving Tessa her phone number. Serena smiles in her sleep. She can do without that one!

Serena is Rain. It is only a dream, isn't it? If it were real, Rain could take her with hir, back to the Eye of the World, where the opals live; she could be one with the Common Mind.

How about that? Serena thinks, chuckling in her sleep. She'd like that a lot. Under the bed, despite hir nervousness, who has no nerves, Azure chuckles, too.

•

Karen types feverishly, the words flying from her fingers. It's no longer just a matter of beating out Tessa and Larry—she has no real hope of that—but of staving off something she feels rather than knows is happening among the S.oteri. It's essential to keep them focused so they don't fly apart.

"Hey, guys? I know it's difficult to work from a chronology when you've only recently discovered the concept of time, but I need to know when Azure died."

Silence.

"Look, I know it was after s/he discovered humans; it was gawking at us that made hir stay out in the sun too long. But when? Akhenaton's time, recently, back to the cave? I need to make sure I'm being accurate. Just give me that and I can do the rest on my own. Hello?"

Back to the cave, indeed. It looks as if that's what it's coming down to. Azure's gone on walkabout, Virid's weeping over every fallen sparrow, Lake wants to pull out entirely and leave stranded all the little gerbil minds on this island Earth and crawl back into the Plato's Cave of the Common Mind and spend eternity watching shadows. Amber's at least arguing for changing the channel. Shut humans off for a while and let the *occulus mundi* eye some other *mundi* for a few million years, eh?

But what if that disappears them? Virid wails. Has s/he finally flushed one too many goldfish down the toilet? Whence this change of heart?

Hey, Karen? Do you suppose we even have hearts?

"No answers from you, no answers from me," she says stolidly, and keeps on typing while she waits for Tony, finally back from South America, to return her call.

Fiber-optic cable, like electrolytic synapses, connects two kindred minds, Manhattan to Brooklyn.

"You know more about this than you're telling me," she accuses him. She's been trying to puzzle out Tony's role in all this—according to him, aside from having perfect pitch, he's never had a creative urge in his life—but if the S.oteri are attracted solely to artists and messiahs, as Karen's research indicates, where does he fit in?

"Moi?" Tony is innocence personified. "I was lost in the jungles of fucking Brazil while you were taking tea with Tessa McGill. You're the writer, darlin'. It's got nothing to do with me."

"Well, it does now. You can contact Max Neimark's office for me. Let him know I'm working on this thing, and that Tessa fucking McGill even stole my title!"

"And what's that going to look like?" Tony is the very voice of reason.

Karen sighs. "Like I'm some crazed fangirl with no credibility. I'm not Isaac Asimov; I'm strictly midlist, which means I'm too low on the food chain to be believed over McGill and Koster, who've probably already got a finished product in hand."

"You got it!" Tony says. "Karen, darlin', look, the politics of this shouldn't even concern you at this point. *Que sera, sera.* Your feeling is that the S.oteri are playing you and Tessa off each other, and you did exactly the right thing in blowing her off. God, listen to me! As your agent, I want to strangle you, but it's their game now. Let them suffer the consequences."

"That's what worries me, Pygmalion. I think they already are. . . ."

•

The pharaoh's brain was the consistency of cold oatmeal by the time whee were done. Now it's happening to us.

A Mind divided against itself cannot stand, has no leg to stand on. Little blobs and clumps of grey matter like cold oatmeal squibble away from what was once the main mass of the Mind, recongealing in the far corners of the caves, bubbling and sulking in flashes of lurid Technicolor. Toil and bubble, squeak and trouble; it's not that we don't want to answer Karen but that we can't. We're just not sure of anything anymore.

•

Fiber-optic cable, like electrolytic synapses, connects two not-so-kindred minds, coast to coast.

"He'll read it and get back to us by the end of the week," Larry Koster tells Tessa, calling her just before he goes out on his morning ride.

"It" is only a thirty-page treatment, not a complete script. The truth is that neither of them has managed, separately or together, to construct a decent film script. Even the treatment has some holes in it, but Max was a bright guy, Larry knew, and he'd be able to build around those in his mind for now.

It would have been so nice, Larry thinks, if Tessa had been

able to bring in that troublesome little writer she'd told him about; she could have helped with the treatment. But Tessa, apparently, was losing her touch. In any case, once Max agreed to go ahead with it—and there was no question in Larry's mind but that he would—they'd have to bring someone in from the Writers Guild. To the layman, it might look like the Emperor's New Clothes. But this was Hollyweird. Blockbusters had been built on less.

"That's awfully soon!" Tessa remarks suspiciously, knowing how long it usually took for director-producers to make up their minds. She's exhausted. After weeks of squabbling, Larry had eventually opted out, leaving her to do most of the writing. Now he was as usual trying to hog all the credit. And the S.oteri seem to have cut her dead. There's been nothing but static on all her channels; she's literally had to write every word of this herself. Besides, she really hates Larry's insisting that they have to blow up at least one planet in order to make the story work. "Are you sure he's not just giving us the brush-off?"

"Max would never do that. Max is an old friend," Larry says, trying not to sound too smug. "And we caught him at a good time. Carole's apparently planning to kidnap him up to Tahoe for some late skiing in a couple of weeks; he wants his desk clear before he leaves town. . . ."

•

Serena dreams, a riotous olio of Toontown and Oz all in one; her artist's fingers itch to draw it all as fast as it reels out before her, spins dizzy-making all around her.

What do you think? Azure asks, perched on her shoulder, twinkling gently in her ear.

"Oh, yeah!" Serena breathes. "I can buy into this, no problem!"

However, Azure cautions, *there is a slight catch. A little something whee—er, eye—would like you to do in exchange. . . .*

"Isn't there always?" Serena says. "And why do I think it has something to do with dying? Not that I'm afraid of dying, only of not being able to die, if you know what I mean."

Being helpless, Azure supplies. *Alive, but not living.*

"Exactly," Serena says. "If it's anything else, you got yourself a deal."

The tumble of myriad overlapping images clears, becomes a dawning day, in a place she knows like the back of her scarred and nail-bitten hand.

There is a small creek at the very back of the property behind the trailer on the hill; in the warm months she can hear it whisper to her in between the crickets and the nightbirds. In another few weeks, when spring begins in earnest, it will be snow-swollen and dangerous. One year it overflowed enough to swamp her back garden and lap over the doorsill into her kitchen, leaving mud and grit and a detritus of leaves and twigs and small stones that took weeks to swab out entirely, but most times it's a pretty thing, crystalline and soothing, almost narrow enough to jump across in places, if Serena could still jump. Even in the coldest weather it moves fast enough so that it rarely freezes over.

There is still snow in the deep woods and farther up the mountain, but here at midlevel things have begun to thaw. It is suddenly unseasonably warm, somewhere in the eighties, warm enough to bring clouds of gnats alive from whatever limbo they inhabit when it's freezing, and the creek is noisier than usual. Serena finds herself standing on the near bank, though she hasn't been here in over a year; the climb, the winding path, the slippery rock had, she thought, put this special place forever out of her reach. Yet here she is. Is this part of the dream?

A cry, two cries, pierce her ears, her very brain; since the onset of the syringo, she can't handle sudden high-pitched noises. She searches for the source through the pounding in her head (since when does her head hurt in dreams, too?) and spots it, upstream a ways.

A homemade raft or what actually looks like an old kitchen door and some odd lengths of lumber jury-rigged together and ripping apart in chunks in the bump and scrape of midstream

rocks and shallows—carrying two frightened kids, who have discovered too late that the rapids are too rapid here, the deeps too
deep, the downslope too precipitous. Serena knows there is a
sudden drop-off, a mini-cataract, not a mile farther down; no raft
will survive it. Do the kids know it, too, or are they just terrified in general? If they had anything to steer the raft with origi-
nally it's long gone, and they know they're in deep shit.

Huck and Jim! Serena thinks with the little corner of her brain
that, like Karen's, always manages to observe and analyze regardless of the speed of crisis. The black girl looks to be about
twelve, her corn-rowed hair beaded with creek water (How can
she see this so clearly? Serena wonders. They're easily a hundred
feet from where she stands); it is she who stands clinging to the
branch of one of the countless trees drooping over the creek bed,
holding the raft wedged in place against a jut of rock by main
strength while the ten-year-old, dishwater blond and white-face
scared, crouches against the drenched and bucking juggernaut,
clutching the older girl's legs and shrieking with fear.

Serena is in action.

"Hang on!" she yells, waving her arms so the two kids can see
her. She somehow convinces her unbending legs to carry her into
the water hip-deep; good thing she's already numb because the
water's cold enough to numb any feeling person. What the hell
kind of pre-spring-fever insanity possessed these two to go rafting this early in the year? "I'm coming to get you. Don't let go
until I say so!"

She wades as far upstream as she can trust herself, trust the
creek bed, then plants herself, thick and solid as one of the bank-
lining trees, and stands fast. The older girl is frozen in place, staring at her, trying to keep her head; the younger one keeps
screeching. Serena wishes she would stop. The pain in her head
has gone beyond blinding; she can feel the cracks beginning in
her skull. *Go ahead,* she thinks: *Shatter like an eggshell; it's Time!*
She waves her arms again.

"Okay, you standing up—what's your name?"

"Cassie!" the black girl yells out. "Short for Cassandra, ma'am!"

Figures! Serena thinks. Science fiction's not the only thing she reads since she met Karen.

"Nice to know you, Cassie. Mine's Serena." Keep 'em calm, keep 'em thinking, make 'em trust you. It worked in the state pen; it'll work here. "What's your little friend's name?"

"Her name Teresa Ann. My arms're getting tired!"

"I know. Hang on for another minute. Here's what we're going to do. . . . " Serena is shouting, past the rushing of the creek, through the cracking and booming, like icebergs, inside her head. "You get Teresa Ann to let go your legs. Do it, girl; we don't have time to argue. Then you let go that branch and swing onto the bank on the other side. Can you do that?"

Cassandra's eyes go wide. "But ma'am—she my friend. I can't just let her go!"

"Yes you can, Cassandra, 'cause I'm gonna catch her when she comes on by!" Serena shouts. "You'd best explain it to her fast, 'cause I can't stand here much longer!"

Cassandra assesses her, thick as a tree, strong as a man, and knows that if anyone can pluck Teresa Ann off the raft on the flyby, this big-ass white woman can. She leans down to shout something at Teresa Ann that Serena cannot hear; the younger girl squeezes her whole face shut, shaking her head and clutching tighter. With the same strength that's kept her clinging to that slippery-slick branch all this time, skinning her hands and straining her skinny arms damn near out of their sockets, Cassandra kicks free of her, swings clear, and jumps.

Serena takes a nanosecond to make sure she's landed safely, hands and knees in the mud, before she braces herself for the impact of the runaway raft. It bears down on her in slo-mo, slewing and shimmying with the current. Teresa Ann has fallen facedown, clutching what once was the top of the kitchen door when it was a kitchen door, a bundle of sodden denim and wet-straw hair too shit-scared to scream anymore.

All I've got to do, Serena thinks from a suddenly pain-free adrenaline high, *is time it so the fucking raft slips past me and I can pry the kid loose, if she'll come loose. If it hits me, I'm dead. Rain, help me out here!*

No problem! Azure whispers. *No problem at all. . . .*

She times it exactly right, plucking Teresa Ann loose and tossing her like a sack of wet laundry onto the bank on the side where she'd been standing, out back of the house on the hill. No one's too clear on what happens next.

•

They're not all here! Karen realizes as she works—uphill now, and alone. Every morning Nicole slips off to work and Matt to school before she's even out of bed; where it used to be her and the S.oteri it's now a scatter of occasional visitation by one or more of them, furtive, as if what's being said must not be overheard by the others.

Try to remember, Amber says, sometimes borrowing Tony's voice, *how all of them turned up in your manuscript or in your fantasies early on. Larry and Tessa, yes, but also Max.*

"No," Karen reminds her. "That was Benn. There is a difference. It doesn't mean Max will be on my side. Max doesn't know I exist. It doesn't mean you won't turn on me and blow my eardrums out. But I'll tell you this for nothing: It's the only way you'll stop me from finishing this my way. Better make up your Mind."

Remake it up, you mean, Grey murmurs, fretting, having gone to pieces, like the Scarecrow in Oz: That's you all over!

"What?"

Never Mind . . . Karen, some of us are really unhappy with the direction this narrative is taking.

"Why only some of you? I thought you were all of one Mind."

(Damn, she's clever!) Er, oh, just a figure of speech. We're still getting used to speech, yew Noh. . . .

"Uh-huh."

Karen, please stop typing for a minute and pay attention. Something very odd has happened in the middle of a creek in North Carolina. . . .

"Look, not now, okay? Serena said she'd call me when she was ready. At least I think that's what she said." She stops typing, rubs her temples where the frames of her glasses sometimes dig in, painful. "She was pissed at me for being pissed at her for giving Tessa my phone number. At least I think that's what she said. At least, I think she said it." She stops, glowers, puts her glasses back on. "You're doing this to me on purpose. I'm warning you: It's not going to work. I've got a contract; I'm going to finish this goddamn book if it kills me."

You said it; we didn't!

Just as a hedge, she calls Serena's number; it's busy. She'll keep hitting the redial at intervals over the next several hours; it will continue to be busy. Well, what the hell else can she do? Fiber-optic cable is not electrolytic synapse; she and Serena are no more of one mind than the S.oteri are. Besides, in the interim, they're up to other tricks.

Karen, if you had your life to live over again . . .

"Well, I don't. All I have is the metalives I told Serena about, so forget about it. You're not going to turn me around here."

But if you could . . . would you have married Ray?

"In the beginning? Yes. But I'd probably have left him a lot sooner. Now you answer me one: How come you guys can see our future but not your own?"

What about your children, Karen? Would you do things differently in your children's lives?

Never underestimate the schoolyard bully until you knew what he was threatening you with.

"They're good kids!" she says with a thread of panic in her voice. "You leave them out of this!"

Karen, Karen, Karen, we'd never hurt your children! What kind of monsters do you think we are?

She grunts. "Monsters of my own creation!"

Now, now, you know better than that! We're merely offering you your memories back. All the things you think you've forgotten, all the times you looked up from what you were doing and discovered they were older, taller, more autonomous than you expected them to be. All the memories you hold most precious, enhanced, expanded, every detail accentuated. And we'll let you redo the bad parts, the times you lost your temper, the times you failed. Remember when Nicole was five and you were brushing her hair and she whined and squirmed and carried on so much that you whacked her on the shoulder with the hairbrush? Just a little tap to get her attention, but the brush slipped and raked down her fragile little back, leaving a bright red scratch that haunted you for days. Or the time you took your eyes off Matthew for a fraction of a second to pull a load of towels out of the washer and he tumbled down the last two cellar steps, fracturing his skull on the concrete floor? The guilt, Karen; that's what we're talking about. We'll take away the guilt. We'll see to it that you never hit Nicole with the hairbrush, that Matt never falls down those stairs. And in your mind they can grow older or younger as often as you want. We'll give you back your children, Karen. Trust us!

It was tempting, seductive; who wouldn't desire it? But how many times had she found herself cornered by women old and not-so-old, on park benches and at bus stops, on line in the supermarket, living and reliving their lives through children long gone, children grown up, grown old, died young, or never were? Dream children, never-found-the-right-man children, all-those-fertility-tests-for-nothing children, stillbirths, crib deaths, drug deaths, fantasy children to replace the ones gone bad? Was that their secret, in league with the S.oteri, no longer any boundaries between them and Oz or Toontown or even Hell itself, addictive like a drug? For the rest of her life Karen would stare into people's eyes seeking the telltale sparkle, wondering.

We'll give you back your children, Karen. All the parts you can't remember, the fuzzy photos that didn't come out the way you'd hoped, the ones that didn't come out at all. Relive each moment, rewrite the script; you can be the perfect mother in this draft, no regrets. . . .

Seductive as sex. Who wouldn't?

No! Karen thinks, no longer bothering to say it aloud. Her hands are in her lap, the cursor blinking on the screen, but she's only stopped for a moment; she will go on. We grow our kids up so they will leave us, leave the nest and fly away, come back only when they want to and on their own terms; that's how we know we've done it right. The past is the past, all gone! My fault for not paying attention. All gone, too late, too bad!

We'll give you Benn. . . .

"Nice try!" Karen resumes typing. "Already got him, thanks. Had him for years."

That was lame! someone mutters. *As if we could give her a fictional character in the flesh. Are you out of your Mind?*

Ahem. A young lover, then. One of those college boys who follow you like puppies at cons. . . .

"You really are desperate, aren't you?" Karen's flying fingers never flag, eighty-five words per minute, strongest pinkies in the world. She knows writers of several sexes who have gone that route; it's ugly. "They're babies. They need a mother more than—"

We'll give you Max.

That does it. For the first time her fingers falter.

"Okay. You want to give me Max? Fine. Have him call me and tell me he wants my script, not Larry and Tessa's. If you can't do that, piss off. Or answer the question you never will answer: How can you see our future and not your own?"

•

"Tell me one more time now, Cassandra." The sheriff's voice is warmer than he intends it to be and he's trying not to smile; he's got one of his own her age. "I'm going to be real upset if I find out you're not telling me the truth."

She sits on a bench in his office, bundled in a Red Cross blanket and sipping hot chocolate. A sleeping Teresa Ann, worn out by the entire event, leans hard against her, wrapped in an identical blanket and drooling on her shoulder.

"I ain't lying, sir," Cassandra says, clear-eyed and self-assured. It's only a matter of time before her daddy drives the ten miles to retrieve her; she knows she's already in as much trouble as she can possibly be. She'd hoped Teresa Ann's parents would come instead, but it would only postpone the inevitable. Her daddy was warming up the belt so he could warm her butt. "We had a pole, only it broke on a snag and we couldn't steer no more. Then this lady come in the water and rescue us."

"What lady?" the sheriff asks. He's asked it already, but he wants to hear it again.

Cassandra shrugs. "Don't know who. Big lady. Thought she was a man, 'cept for the voice. Told me to jump. Then she grab Teresa Ann and flung her. That's how she cut her lip and got all over mud. Teresa Ann, I mean. Time I turned around, she gone. The lady, I mean. Wasn't in the water or on the bank. Wasn't anywhere I could see, just gone. Might could be the raft hit her."

"Might could," the sheriff agrees. "What did you do then?"

"Told Teresa Ann to stay put where she at, but she didn't." Cassandra glances down at the younger girl, disgusted. "She run off and left me. Used to be my best friend. Guess I'm gone re-think that some."

"Never mind that now!" the sheriff chides her, hiding his smile again. Two kids damn near drowned, and all they can do is fuss about being best friends. Girls! "Tell me what you did then, after Teresa Ann ran off."

"Went for help. Found a path through the trees and followed it till I came to a house. Only there's a dog. Was gone run back the way I came, only the lady pull him back on a choke chain. Told me to come up and wait on the screen porch while she called y'all."

The sheriff nods, watches the girl finish her hot chocolate. Her story fits with the picture he and his deputies have been piecing together all afternoon.

"No more questions, Cassandra, thank you." He rests a fatherly hand on her thin shoulder. "Your daddy should be here real soon." He sees her grimace and understands why. He'd tan his own if she ever got the harebrained notion to go rafting on a piece of junk like that. He thinks a minute. "I wouldn't worry too much. I'll see can I have a talk with him. Tell him how you saved Teresa Ann's life."

Cassandra gawks at him.

"Well, you did, didn't you? You and the big white lady. And we still ain't found her."

Nor would they. They'd gotten a call at around seven this morning from a Mrs. Dottie Weems informing them that there was "a half-drowned colored girl" on her screen porch who, Mrs. Weems was certain, "wasn't from around here." At about the same time Emergency Services had patched in with a call from the other side of the creek. Teresa Ann had run off, all right, straight into Serena's unlocked trailer where she'd stopped her teeth from chattering long enough to dial 911 the way they'd learned in school. The sheriff's deputy had had to drive five miles each way to cross the bridge in Boone and retrieve both girls. It was nearly lunchtime before everyone was back at the station and they could get some answers.

Cassandra's description of a "big white lady" could only be Serena Bell, Mrs. Weems informed them importantly, "that rather odd woman with the limp who lives in the trailer 'round the other side. I hear she's got some dreadful disease. . . ."

She didn't anymore. Volunteers with a string of borrowed coon hounds, led by a deputy with a bloodhound, searched both banks of the creek and deep into the woods until twilight, when a chopper with a searchlight took over. Forty-eight hours later the search was abandoned. Serena's sister Weezy closed the real estate office for the rest of the week and saw about arranging for an empty-casket funeral.

Watching, Rain/Azure sighs contentedly, hits the rewind, and replays the scene again.

•

"Run that by me again?" Max, Larry, and Tessa are sitting in Max's office on the lot. Larry and Tessa's script treatment lies on the desk in front of them. "The planet blows up at the end? Who blows it up?"

"The hero does," Larry says immediately. "That is, he doesn't, actually. I mean, it does blow up, but it might not be because of what he's done. It might be an accident or some sort of natural phenomenon. A volcanic eruption, due to the planet's being so close to the Galactic Center, or something. We've got the credits rolling before the audience figures it out. That way we leave it open-ended for a possible sequel."

Tessa has her legs crossed and is fingering a loose thread on the hem of the perfect little suit she picked up at Bullock's the last time she was out here, looking fixedly out the window as if the roofs of the stars' trailers grouped in the parking lot below them were the most *fascinating* thing she'd ever seen. Max takes a minute before he asks his next question; he hates to hurt anyone's feelings.

"So what makes your hero a hero and not a genocide?"

The word makes Larry flinch. "That's a little harsh. I mean, it should be obvious. They've already killed several of our people. Our hero's just trying to get himself and the seeress out alive. Besides, they're aliens. They're not human."

Max shakes his head, laughing his deep, resonant laugh, incredulous.

"Larry, Larry, almost thirty years with *SpaceSeekers* and it's taught you nothing? You don't kill aliens just because they're aliens—"

"—because it's not politically correct!" Larry's on his feet, bouncing off the walls already. "Don't quote that bullshit at me! It was a goddamn TV show!"

"And this is a goddamn disjointed treatment," Max says, his voice as calm as Larry's is strident. He looks toward Tessa, raises an eyebrow. "How much of this is yours?"

"I—" She stops picking at her hem and raises her hands eloquently. "We might have rushed it, because we knew you were leaving town. Maybe if we polish a little . . ."

"That's not what I'm asking." Max removes his thick reading glasses. He's noticed Tessa's having a problem making eye contact, and he knows why. He focuses his odd-color eyes on her to make her look at him. "Interesting title, *Preternatural*. Where'd you get it from?"

EIGHTEEN

Serena's sister called Karen that night, right after the memorial service.

"I drove up to the house from the cemetery to make a start on sorting things," Weezy ("It's really Louise, but I've always hated it!") explained. "It wasn't as if it was a big service, just Mom and me and some people from town. Couple of reporters from the TV station in Boone, but I sent them packing. Well, I let myself in here, and everything was all organized, almost like she was expecting it. Does that sound strange to you?"

"Not at all," Karen hears herself saying, but Weezy hasn't stopped talking.

"What I'm saying is, she had all her old drawings boxed and labeled, and there was a blank sheet on her drawing table, but she hadn't started anything on it yet. And there was a whole separate stack up against one wall that weren't her usual style at all. My sister did almost exclusively portraiture—once in a great while one of the local inns or restaurants would commission her to do a piece for them—but these are neither fish nor fowl. And every one of them had a little Post-it stuck on it marked 'For Karen.'

"I had no idea who you were until I started going through her address book. I think I may have read one of your *SpaceSeekers* books way back when. . . ."

Karen listens numbly while Weezy, who apparently no more knows where a sentence should end than her sister did, loops through her Möbius strip of a tale. Ordinarily she would patiently explain that she's working on deadline, and, while she wishes she could spare the time to come down and pick up the drawings herself it's just not possible, especially since she will not fly ("It has to do with a deal I made with God the first and only time I ever flew"), so could Weezy please send them and she'd pay for shipping? In one of her metalives, because she needs to see for herself, she gets on the train.

It is fourteen hours, she knows, from New York to Greensboro, another two hours by car to the winding gravel road that leads to the trailer on the hill. In her Mind's eye she steps along the same rock-strewn path that first Serena, then Teresa Ann, took in opposite directions and at very different speeds to and from the creek, stands on the bank and watches the froth and tumult of the water, which is not as high as it was a few days ago, picturing it, right down to the slewing, downstream juggernaut that is the empty raft once Teresa Ann lands tumbling on the shore and Serena loses her ever-precarious balance on the slick creek bed, folding at the waist, falling slow-motion backward, arms upraised, going under with no hope of surfacing, her face almost smiling and incredibly, inscrutably calm.

The body had not yet been recovered by the time Weezy called.

". . . which the sheriff says is very odd," Weezy pointed out. "The stream just isn't that deep or really all that swift, and it's full of bends and shallows, and my sister was a big woman. The sheriff says there hasn't been a drowning hereabouts since that hurricane a few years back—Hugo, I think it was—but even then everyone reported missing washed up eventually. . . ."

Backtracking, Karen sees the yard behind Serena's house, the path through the trees leading to the creek, the sneaker prints—child's size 2½ Nikes—skidding smudgy through the mud as Teresa Ann, sobbing and holding her ribs against the stitch in her side, streaks across the grass to the kitchen door, the phone, and help.

". . . and I can't believe I'm standing here talking to a total stranger about my sister as if this was just something on the TV news!" Weezy is saying, tears in her voice. "I just can't get over it. This whole thing makes no sense; it's the kind of thing that happens to other people, you know what I mean?"

"Yes," Karen says. She is standing in Serena's kitchen looking down at Weezy, a much smaller woman than her sister, even as Weezy talks to her long-distance on the phone.

"That's why I went ahead and held the memorial service even without the body. The body—just listen to me!" Weezy stops; Karen knows she's crying. She waits until Weezy's stood on her tiptoes to pluck a tissue from the box on the kitchen windowsill next to the rabbit's-foot fern, blowing her nose before she can go on. "I guess I just didn't know what else to do."

"You did exactly the right thing," Karen says, wrapping her voice around Weezy like a hug.

"I'll go ahead and send you those drawings, then," Weezy finishes up, but Karen's barely begun.

In her Mind's eye she drifts from room to room with entirely too much familiarity. Granted, Serena had described her little world in minute detail on those hours and hours of audiotapes; the artist's eye capturing every knothole in the paneling, every worn spot on the carpet, the very scratches on the furniture, the precise position of her drawing table and the works in progress hung on the walls above it—Vincent and Catherine sharing a venue with Benn and Spock and Obi Wan Kenobi—but it's more than that. Karen even knows about the drawings Weezy's sending her, though Weezy hasn't described them and she hasn't seen them yet, not in this life.

She knows before she sees them that they chronicle the evolution of a Mind, from a planetary pond of blue-green algae to a pulsing iridescing All There Is to the separate tendrilating tendentiousness that is a too-true-Azure-blue, pulling away alone, all, all alone and staying too long at the fair, reduced to a single dessicating tentacle tentatively Recalled to Life and bringing havoc in hir wake. What follows is a chronicle of the dissolution of a Mind, apocalyptic.

Is this how it ends? Karen wonders. In that case we've been

going about it the wrong way from the beginning. It isn't about the S.oteri's trying to destroy us, but about our destroying them!

Yet she sits there with her hands in her lap, unable to write a word since Weezy's call. In the movies and in everyone else's novel the crisis is always clear-cut. The aliens are invading Earth, for what to them might be an eminently good reason, but there's never any doubt in anyone's mind that they're the enemy, and it's only a question of Yankee ingenuity and big enough guns to defeat them. And the enemy is inevitably monolithic, of one mind, not splattered like the Pharaoh's brains into countless little lumps of cold oatmeal, each disagreeing with hir neighbor. Why was she, child of Vietnam, too blind to see that, just like growing up on John Wayne movies, it's never been a question of Us Americans against the Dirty Yellow Japs, but of as many questions as there are individuals, even within a Mind divided against itself?

"Jeez!" she says aloud. "Scratch that last sentence, will you? It makes no kind of sense!"

She knows the S.oteri didn't kill Serena, but did they, as they did with Jess, at least predispose her to her death? ("Bullshit!" she can hear Serena, drawing on a cigarette, explaining. "It was time. Told myself whenever the pain got too bad I'd go out in some kind of SWAT-team blaze of glory, my name on the local news, at least. It was time, that's all.") If she writes it, she will know. If she continues to sit with her hands in her lap, they'll simply turn it over to Tessa, who'll reduce it to a Movie of the Week. Now that they're no longer of one Mind, does it make any difference at all?

Karen? The voice is so small it cannot possibly be the entire Mind, is not even recognizable as any single individual. It's possible Karen doesn't even hear it.

Karen; we're scared! Please don't leave us; you're all we have!

It's a whisper, a whimper, a squeak, lost in the sound of a northbound train, or a ringing phone. The phone in Karen's white room is very decidedly ringing. But in one version of her life she is trapped on an Amtrak train just south of Alexandria, Virginia, while an elderly gentleman asks if she minds his sitting in the empty seat beside her to eat his lunch, since his wife of forty-five years—the very number of years Karen has lived on this Earth—who is waiting in the car up ahead, doesn't approve of his drinking in the middle of the day (inured—jellyfish, weirdos, and geeks, oh, my!—Karen murmurs Of course, go right ahead while he sips his beer and shows her photos of his grandchildren, squeezing her knee not entirely paternally when he gets up to return to his wife), and her answering machine takes the call. In another, she is right beside the phone but, too stunned to speak to anyone human, lets the machine pick it up anyway.

The answering machine automatically plays two bars of electronic Beethoven, a fact she did not ascertain until she'd already set it up and used the tape, too late to exchange it for a different one. In another life, a life where she has time to fret over minutiae, that ice-cream truck singsong would irritate the hell out of her. Now, she no longer cares.

"Für Elise," the voice with the chronic hint of a chuckle beneath it remarks. "Very pretty. I'm calling for Karen Rohmer Guerreri. This is Max Neimark."

Yeah, right. As if she could possibly have had any doubt. As if the crispness of his consonants, the bottomless vowel sounds, the sheer rotundity of his resonances wouldn't have told her.

It's too late! she wants to tell him. Benn may have been my role model since I was sixteen, but as you're always telling anyone who will listen, you're not Benn (or are you?), so appealing to the fangirl in me isn't going to help! You're probably calling to reiterate Tessa's threat, to remind me that I'm playing with the Big Kids and I haven't got a prayer. You, of all people! But it doesn't matter, because I'm not writing anymore, may not ever write again unless I can figure out what's really going on. It's too little too late, Max Neimark, and I'm not budging, not even for you!

Breathless as a high school kid, she grabs the phone.
"Hi, Mr. Neimark? I'm here."

For the first time in his adult life, Max hadn't been able to
sleep at all last night. There had been times in the past, toward
the end of his first marriage, when he'd started awake after a couple of hours and lain there watching the years tick away as he
realized he'd done everything possible to save a relationship that
was beyond saving. But last night, having told Carole to take
Sammy and go on to Tahoe without him this morning because
he had some odds and ends to clear up in town, he'd sat up in
a chair all night so as not to disturb her, with sleep the furthest
thing from his mind. He knew why, but knowing why hadn't
helped.

Until he'd read Larry and Tessa's script treatment, he'd accepted the presence of the S.oteri in his life as an extra, a little
gift, like having a photographic memory or perfect pitch. It had
never occurred to him to consider them as a resource, exploitable.
Now he wonders how he could have been so naive. What might
he have done with that knowledge all these decades if he had
known?

He should have called Karen Guerreri yesterday, while he still
had Larry and Tessa in his office, put her on the speakerphone
and had her tell her version of it and shame them while they were
sitting there, but he hadn't, and not only because he believed
Larry was virtually beyond shame. The director in him needed
to see all sides of the picture, to know before he began what sort
of stuff his actors were made of.

"You and I met at CreationCon in New York in '89," he tells
her when he finally gets through, and Karen fights the urge to
say No-o-o, really? Gosh, it must have slipped my mind! *What
is going on here?* she wonders. Since when does the Big Star remind the Little Writer that they've met before? But she bites her
tongue because his tone suggests he's saying it more to remind
himself than her. "We talked about your writing."

"Yes," Karen says. Yes, we did. You asked me questions and

actually seemed to be paying attention to the answers; it was . . . gratifying.

"I understand you're working on a first-contact novel now."

"That's right." Don't act surprised that he knows; don't act anything at all! "At least I was, until yesterday."

"I see. You've finished it, then?"

"No, actually, I—"

"Hold that thought," Max the Director says. "Because I'm flying to New York tomorrow. I'd like to meet with you."

All Karen could think, stuck on a stalled R-train beneath the East River trying to get into Midtown, the mailing tube with Serena's drawings clutched tightly in both hands, was: You asked for this. Famous Hollywood directors do not drop everything, including ski trips with their wives (She doesn't remember Max's mentioning that; how does she know?), in order to come to Mohammed. By rights he should have stated his case on the phone or at most demanded you come to him. But you dared the S.oteri to bring Max to you, and they have. Now if only you knew whose side he was on! The S.oteri themselves have bifurcated, into those who want to go forward and those who want to rewrite history, their own as well as yours. Your only problem is sorting out Who's on First and deciding which faction you're going to go with. Kind of like having your choice of schoolyard bullies. . . .

She and Max sit in a couple of comfortable chairs in his suite at the Warwick. They'd first met downstairs in Sir Walter's (even in restaurant light she could see the glitter of S.oteri in his bicolor eyes and wondered why she'd missed them the last time they'd met), but even hiding behind his thick reading glasses he'd been swarmed by a gaggle of 'Seekers, and suggested they'd be better able to talk uninterrupted upstairs.

They stood close but not touching in the crowded elevator. When she'd first stepped down out of the sunlight into the restaurant he'd risen to shake her hand, the only time he's touched her. Now he places a careful distance between their two chairs, crosses his long legs, and listens as Karen tells him all she can think of to tell.

She has made up her mind to argue her own legitimacy over against Tessa's. Then she's not sure what she'll do. The easiest thing would be to let Max think he was buying her off, put up a good argument before she allowed him to talk her into not finishing the novel she's afraid to finish now anyway. The unfinished nature of Serena's death aside, how many times have the S.oteri told her she could quit anytime she wanted? Okay, she'd quit. Take Max's kiss-off fee, earn more in an afternoon for doing nothing than for five years' work. Very market economy, very Hollyweird, the Queen of the Remainders finally learns to play the game.

Too easy. Nothing in her career has ever been easy; what makes her think it's going to start now? Action = equal and opposite reaction. This is a trap, a trick question. Max is testing her, and so are the S.oteri, or at least some of them. She has made the fatal mistake of getting involved with her characters; she can't abandon them to the fate some of them foresaw in Serena's drawings, not now.

"I know," Max says. "Exasperating, aren't they? How long have you been in contact with them?"

He is rerolling the sketches in their mailing tube, having examined them while Karen talked. Now he seals the tube and holds it out to her. She doesn't take it just yet.

"I'm not sure. It's hard to tell if they've always been responsible for the voices in my head—in which case now that so many of them don't want to play anymore, I might as well pack it in and become an insurance underwriter—or if they only arrived with this book."

Why am I confiding in you? she wonders. Go ahead, make your offer and get it over with!

"Well, what do you think?" Max is studying her thoughtfully. "Don't you take credit for your own ideas, your own creativity?"

"For the blood, sweat, and tears? Certainly. But the talent's handed to us at birth; none of us gets to choose. Given my druthers, I'd be conducting the New York Philharmonic. Pretty difficult, since I can't read music."

Max chuckles. "So I guess you'll have to settle for saving a planet."

It's the last thing she expects him to say. "It's nothing that grandiose. They're only connected to a handful of humans, a couple of hundred at the most. If they had the power to destroy Earth, they'd have done it in Akhenaton's time. And they certainly don't have that kind of power now that they're all divided and subdivided."

"That's precisely what I mean," Max says, coming dangerously close to sounding like Benn, or is that only Karen's imagination? "I wasn't talking about Earth, but about putting the Mind back together. Saving the Eye of the World."

Karen digests this. "The S.oteri planet. Me."

"Yes, of course. Isn't that what we're talking about here?"

Karen wants to hug him. "Then you *do* get it! I thought you were in cahoots with Larry and Tessa. Thought you were going to wave your checkbook at me and—"

Max looks hurt. "Did you really?"

"I—" The floor shifts under her, molecules all the way down. Max is on her side; she's safe. Every fangirl's dream.

"Let's look at it objectively," he says. "They've told you more about themselves than they've told me, Larry, and Tessa combined. They were honest enough to show you that, yes, some of the individuals they've chosen throughout history have been found to have blood trickling from their ears after they'd died of something else. . . ."

"Maybe they were lying," Karen says, not sure if she's playing devil's advocate or if she believes it.

Max looks at her curiously. "Isn't it a given that an entity with an eidetic memory can't lie because it can't hold two contradictory thoughts in its mind simultaneously?"

"That's the theory," Karen says. "But it's all fiction. We don't have eidetic memories, we as writers have simply created fictional species that do. We don't really know for sure."

"Hmm," Max says. "Interesting premise. We're trying to save an actual civilization by means of a fiction."

"No shit, Sherlock!" Karen can't believe her nerviness, but she's all nerves by now, nothing left to lose. "Pretty weird, until you consider that this whole thing began with each side thinking the other was a fiction of its own creation."

"And they came to you," Max says with sudden solemnity. "Of all of us, in nearly four thousand years of history, they came to you."

"Stop it; you're scaring me!"

"No, think about that. Larry and Tessa have it wrong. Why? Because they're both so caught up in their own agenda they're falling all over themselves. And me? Hell, I've been sitting here all these years just listening to them like background music, watching them like the tide coming in; they never even told me they had a name. To me they were like the rain forest, a natural part of our evolution. Necessary, even if we didn't yet know for what, but something you just left alone, didn't tamper with, contemplated from a distance. You were the only one who saw, really saw."

"Only because they let me see—"

"—only because they knew you could tell their story."

"No, not just me. Amanuensa saw it, too, and look what happened to her."

She hugs herself against a sudden metaphysical chill.

"There's no historical evidence for Amanuensa, Karen," Max says gently. "She only exists in your novel, so far."

"Max, I'm scared! I—"

"Don't be scared," he breathes, and suddenly he's holding her in his arms. "I'm right here, and I'm on your side. You don't need to concern yourself with Larry or Tessa; I'll manage them. You don't need to concern yourself with saving the universe—"

"—just one planet."

"Maybe. We still don't know that for sure. If what we're try-ing for is going to do the least bit of good, that is. The only thing we know for sure is that you've *got* to finish this novel."

Karen allows herself to be held a moment longer, rests her head in the hollow of his shoulder, then breaks away. In another life, maybe . . . She sighs. "Okay, Boss. But which of the voices do I listen to?"

Max takes her chin in his hand for a moment, almost as if he intends to kiss her. His eyes have lost their S.oteri sparkle, and are at once smiling and incredibly sad.

"What else? Your own."

It isn't until she gets home that Karen realizes she'd been test-ing him, too. If he'd offered to bring her out to L.A. with him, watch over her, "take care of everything" while she worked, she'd have known he was in league with the revisionists. In set-ting her free he's told her he wants what she wants: To tell the story whole, from all sides.

•

Grey Matter, dura mater, mater familias sans familias, using hir grey cells, ponders what has become a most unsettling situation. What's a mother to do? S/he can see all of them in hir Mind's eye, off in their bubbling troubling corners, sulking and plotting, carping and snapping and slapping at each other like preschool-ers on a rainy day, not a happy camper in the lot. Were they al-ways so . . . silly?

You don't understand! s/he wants to scream at Karen. *The All There Are cannot hold together on the strength of a work of fiction. It isn't right!*

Ignoring hir, Karen types. If the Mind will not give her the words, she will find them, as she has always done, on her own:

"They could be detected in many places, by those who knew how to look, in mirrors, stained-glass windows, heat shimmers on sand or tarmac, oil slicks on standing water, the depths of 'clouded' gems like opals, migraine auras, the Dark Night of the

Soul. They had always been here and, perhaps, always will be as much a part of human existence as the elements we breathe. . . ."

Karen slips between molecules, slipstreams through time, for there is no time in Oz or Toontown, composes over one hundred final-draft pages in the time it usually takes her to rough out ten or twenty. The manuscript grows heavier, more ponderous each time she touches it.

At some point the ground gives under her, and, like Alice, she tumbles into the rabbit hole sinkhole gravity well realization of what it is to be an S.oteri and suddenly *not know*. After a billion years or so of seeming infallibility, that's got to be unsettling. Small wonder, she thinks, that they're flummoxed, lost and panicked, bubbling and bumbling, bumping heads in the dark of the cave, agnosic. She feels for them, feels with them.

"Hey, guys? Seriously, don't panic; it's not that bad. If you'd just stop scurrying around for a minute, we could—"

What yew mien whee, Chemosabe? Ewe don't exist.

"Oh, fine; that's a great attitude! Let's try to remember that we both started from that premise, huh? Only one of us had the courage to change her Mind."

Silence. No, Karen thinks. Not one of us, but two.

"Azure-blue, where are you?"

Karen kneels on the rag rug beside Serena's bed, peering under. Somewhere amid the dust bunnies Serena didn't have time to vacuum out before the waters rose and the screaming began, Azure is cowering; s/he who has never been alone now wants more than anything to be alone. Karen remembers something Max said in parting.

"They never gave me names—do you realize how fortunate you are? Not for their species, not for themselves. So I made some up, depending on how they struck me. The director, always; I couldn't resist. The one you call Azure I called Garbo, always wanting to be alone. But Grey, Grey I called Preminger, the director, the one in charge. This one I could relate to. . . ."

Garbo, Karen thinks with a smile, as much for Azure as for
Max.

"Azure-blue, where are you?" she repeats in her softest, gentlest voice—coaxing a kitten out of a tree, a frightened child into
a darkened room, a young fan out of a suicide attempt. "Come
out from under there and talk to me, please?"

Except she isn't really in Serena's room, isn't anywhere at all.
She exists in a universe that is molecules all the way down—a
keyboard, a chair, a blue screen where the f/x will be laid in
later—slipstreams through time as her ten-year-old daughter de-
posits her hamster in the middle of the keyboard.

"Pekoe came to visit you," Nicole announces with that older-
than-the-universe glint in her green eyes, which says Pay attention to me *now* or twenty years from now I'll be telling my shrink
how you neglected me!

"Nicole," Karen had said in her calmest, most authoritative
voice: "Take the hamster off the typewriter *now!*"

It had been her response then and would be, dammit, if she
had it to do over, because if a ten-year-old didn't know that hamster shit inside the one piece of equipment that meant her
mother's livelihood was not desirable, then she had to be taught.
If not now, when? Should she have smiled indulgently instead
and cooed: "Oh, how cute, Sweetie! Yes, you and your hamster stay here and wreak havoc in my life. Stay this way forever!"

Like hell.

"You still don't get it, do you?" she says to whichever tentacle of the schizoid Mind is toying with her this time. "It's about
growth, change, evolution. You can't keep a kid in stasis, anymore than you can a Mind, and I'd no more want Nicole to be
ten years old again than—"

Than what?

"Guys, seriously. Just because you can't handle time, you
don't have the right to unglue ours. Why not continue to use us
to explore time, get the feel of it? What would be so terrible?"

Ewe aren't real. We created yew.

"Fine, believe that! But for Chrissake deal with it! You've

changed your Mind? Well, good for you! The human minds you're already involved with will wink out in the equivalent of a nanosecond relative to your life span. Just don't get involved with anyone else, and then you can go back to the once-was. Wait till we're all dead and you can do whatever you choose to each other, no witnesses. Haul the dissidents out from under the bed and reintegrate them, disintegrate them, do whatever you want with your own kind; that's your right. . . ."

Does she only imagine a whimper of despair *(Nooo!),* a scurrying of tendrils amid the dust bunnies that might be Azure? At least someone's paying attention.

"Remember the First Principle of Exploration in *SpaceSeekers?*" she goes on. " 'Thou shalt not intervene in the normal evolution of the other'?" Even as she says it she can hear Marie groan: Jellyfish, weirdos, and geeks, ohm aye! "Or the whatsis—the Prime Directive in *Star Trek . . .*"

That's fiction, Karen! Virid says in Nicole's best Valley Girl voice. (Like, Mom, you just don't understand *anything!*)

"Aren't we all? Imagine God as the ultimate novelist." Silence. "Well, figure it: If, according to you, humans are fiction, then how do you characterize the fictions we fictions create? If a fiction creates a fiction does that make it fact? Equal and opposite reaction?"

That's physics, Karen. The long-suffering tone tells her this one's Grey.

She knows what they're doing, keeping her talking so she won't have time to write. Who says they have no concept of Time? Max has taken a copy of her partial manuscript back to L.A. with him, where he intends to sit Larry and Tessa down and insist they read it or the deal is off. He expects the rest finished and her out there with it in hand by the beginning of next week. Karen's not even thinking of what it's going to take to get her on a plane after more than a quarter of a century. But if the S.oteri keep distracting her, she'll never get it done—they hope. Or some of them do. What's happened to the rest? Why don't they speak up? She's got to get Azure out from under the bed.

"Okay, fine: I'm fiction. Then unwrite me. Kill me off. I dare you."

Schoolyard bullies she has known, the grit of concrete wall at her back, their hands shoving at her, their spittle flying in her face. The way their eyes always slewed away from hers at the last minute, exposing their fear.

Well, we could if we wanted to . . . we just don't want to. Yet. If we don't like what you've written, then . . .

"Uh-huh. I thought so!"

Okay, confirmed: they can't kill her. But they can still drive her mad. Pull out of her mind and leave her with roaring silence, not to mention no career. Pull out of however many other human minds that rely on them for everything from religion to Max's image of the tide coming in. They still don't realize that theirs is the greater danger. Karen scans what she's already written.

". . . as the waters receded, the less evolved succumbed, pulsating gelatinous masses exposed to the stab of merciless sun through tenuous atmosphere—boiling, sublimating, leaving stickiness and shadow on rock, weeping away through chill of night and gone by morning. Those who specialized into pseudopods, tendrils, tentacles, learned first to sense radiational and vibrational variations, then to propel themselves to the shelter of caves, safety, survival . . ."

That isn't the way it happened at all.

"Oh, really?" Karen, checking for typos (writing herself a Post-it: "p. 55: 'gorrific' crucifixions?"), gives them about as much attention as she might a hamster on her keyboard. "What then?"

We have always been All There Are.

"Uh-huh. And there really was a Garden of Eden, and it's all the snake's fault. Or the woman's. Or the tooth fairy." She is back at the word processor. "It happened precisely this way. You told me. It's right there in my outline. You just don't remember."

Noooo!

She knows that tone, that cry of anguish, of illusions shattered and lives come to naught, hopes dashed like brains against a fieldstone wall, a packed-dirt floor, enlightenment deliquescing in iridescent puddles illuminated by a wall of flame, of Xyklon-B and babies spitted on Roman swords or Balkan bayonets.

"Yes!" Karen contradicts them against the growing ache in her temples, the roaring silence in her ears. "It's true: *You don't remember!* Not my writing it, not your living it. It's a glitch, a change, illumination. Deal with it."

She hears what begins as static percolating along the electrolytes of the Mind, interconnecting synapses that have lain dormant since everyone's gone bubbling off on hir own. Wires crossing, shorting out, spitting blue sparks, dangerous? The static increases in places, intensifying into patent electric pulses, which must be painful (does a Mind interconnected with humans feel pain?), Karen imagines.

No, not imagines: witnesses. This is happening, now. It is not fiction; she has caused this by her words, mightier than the sword. Max was right: it's up to her to save the world, their world. She starts to shake all over.

Keep them thinking! she thinks. *As long as the Mind is thinking it will still be a Mind!*

"Hey, guys, can I tell you an interesting story?" She's never been able to type and talk at the same time before, but she does now, even though her voice quavers and her hands are less than steady. "I want to tell you what really bugs me about the space program. You'd assume that as a science fiction writer I'd be entirely gung-ho about the space program, right? It's a given, like the fact that so many astrophysicists claim to be atheists. Well, okay, a lot if it is for the same reason they wear plaid shirts and pocket protectors; it's all about peer acceptance and getting grants for their next project. Start wearing silk shirts to work and the rest of the tribe will think you're a pod person. So they buy their disbelief in God from the same Land's End catalogue as the plaid shirts, and they're accepted by the tribe. There they are, looking at the blueprints through their telescopes and denying the existence of the architect."

Is there a point to this story?

Yes, Karen thinks: The point is, you're still curious; if I can keep you curious . . .

"I was telling you what upsets me about the space program. It's not the congressional thing like the snafus and cost overruns or the failure rate; this is terra incognita, and there are bound to be miscalculations. Tell you the truth, I'm amazed there haven't been more deaths. Are you with me so far?"

Silence.

"No, it's none of that. What disturbs me is that the voice on that recording the Voyagers took out of the solar system, our very first nonradio message to any and all interstellar species—present company excluded, of course, since you snuck in on us unawares—belongs to a Nazi war criminal! Granted, he was U.N. Secretary at the time, as if that's not ironic enough, but of all the exemplars of humanity they could have chosen, it's this man's voice that gets sent out into space. Which, maybe, if you think about it, isn't really that ironic at all."

She can barely hear her own voice through the roaring in her ears. The gravity around her has been growing heavier; it now feels as if it's in the 2-g range, which makes it difficult to sit upright, much less to keep her fingers on the keyboard. At least she's stopped trembling.

"Then again, who am I to judge?" She types as she talks, making fewer typos now. "Maybe as U.N. Secretary he was trying to atone for the sins of his youth? Maybe he didn't consider them sins? Most people don't get up in the morning thinking 'Today I'm going to do as much evil as I can'; that's strictly Toontown. What I'm saying is that life lived in time is like *Rashomon*; there is no absolute truth, only perspective. Who you are and where you are and how the event seems to you from where you're standing. So just because the S.oteri have clung to what you've thought of as absolute truth for a few billion—ow!" She takes off her glasses, as if that will make the pain go away, rubs her temples though she knows it's futile. "Come on, guys; knock it off! What's next, blood from the ears?"

Stop this at once!

"Like hell!" Karen rallies, puts her glasses back on, inverse Clark Kent, stronger with them than without them, squinting against the pain. "Go ahead and blow my brains out; it's the only way you'll stop me. And it won't really change a thing!"

She is free-falling, but so are the S.oteri, panicked blobs of Jell-O tumbling at different speeds all around her. They jerk and twist from time to time, as if bouncing against live wires. Oh, they can feel it this time! The Absolute Truth that they're nothing but glorified plankton (as if, who isn't?) must be—literally—a great shock to them. What is the sound of one jellyfish screaming?

"You've got a choice, guys." Karen forces her fingers to move over the keyboard, even at 2-g. "You can pull it together or you can let it pull you apart. . . ."

Just when she thinks the pain will crush her skull like an eggshell (fresh brains like Jess's all over the newly printed manuscript; poor Max will be so upset!), the phone rings. Swimming upstream against gravity, Karen grabs it.

"Karen? It's Max. Should I ask you how it's going?"

"Almost done," Karen says. The pain gives her a final tweak, then actually starts to recede.

"I've booked you a ten A.M. flight tomorrow. I figured Newark is better for you than Kennedy, no?"

Dutifully Karen writes down the flight number, feeling the sensation return to her fingertips again as the local gravity settles back to normal, listens as Max tells her there'll be a car waiting for her when she gets to LAX. Details. Reality. Has she mentioned she doesn't fly?

NINETEEN

"Pinch me; I'm dreaming!" she says as she steps down into Max's sunken living room to see Laurence Koster, Captain Stark in the too, too solid flesh, decked out in Rodeo Drive macho, and putting entirely too much business into pouring himself a drink. He half-turns with a grunt of acknowledgment as Max introduces her.

To her credit, Tessa McGill has decided to play the grown-up this day. Resplendently Madame Blavatsky, looking like nothing so much as a human-size jellyfish in layers of flowing multifloral gauze and strand upon strand of jade and amber and lapis and, of course, two gigantic but no less real opals pendant from her ears, she floats across the room to give Karen her own version of the Hollywood Air Kiss.

"So glad you could come, dear!" she breathes as if this were her party. "Now we can complete the circle for our channeling."

Karen is decidedly underwhelmed. "Max? For crying out loud, I didn't come here—"

"—to do excerpts from *Blithe Spirit*," he says mildly, bypassing Tessa to relieve her of the manuscript box containing four copies of her final hundred pages, which she held in her lap in the 757 all the way here. "I know. You also just got off a plane; you need to decompress a little. What're you drinking?"

"Water's fine."

He pours from a bottle of mineral water; no one drinks the tap water in L.A. Does Karen only imagine the flicker of jellyfish mischief reflected in the pale green glass? "You want ice with that?"

Karen shakes her head, and Max smiles as if with approval.

"Come for a walk with me."

He has his arm around her shoulder and is propelling her out onto the patio toward the garden; is she going to argue?

"Carole's still at Tahoe or she'd give you the guided tour, so I'll do the honors instead," he says, loud enough to carry back to the house. "I especially want to show you the rock gardens; she's really proud of those. . . ."

Larry watches them go. Women like Karen make him distinctly uncomfortable. She's one of those impervious schoolmarm types, the kind you'd only come on to if you were really desperate, the kind who'd probably listen to your every word with a smile on her face, then tell you you were very sweet but essentially full of shit. Too many people have been telling Larry he's full of shit lately; it's beginning to wear on him.

Tessa watches him watching them. "Conspiracies?" she wonders aloud. "Plots and cabals? What's the story with those two?"

"If it were anyone but Max . . ." Larry shrugs. "I'm sure it's exactly what it looks like. Whatever that is."

•

"Are you sure you're not flying all the way out there just because of some, shall we say, misplaced affection for this moviestar person?" Tony had asked Karen as she packed.

"You mean am I doing this because I've got a crush on Max?" She'd wedged the phone between her ear and her shoulder, folding socks. "If you'd asked me that twenty years ago . . ."

"I'm asking now."

"Not a chance. I'm playing with the Big Kids this time. Gotta keep my head clear."

"Don't forget that, not even for a minute," Tony cautioned. "If you need backup . . ."

"I know, Pygmalion. Think me some happy thoughts," she'd said.

"I thought we agreed we were on the same side," Max says now. They are sharing one of several stone benches in the garden. Karen seems inordinately interested in a bed of mosses and succulents Carole has arranged around some mica-flecked rocks and mugho pines; they are far enough away from the house to escape even Tessa's radar. "I wish you'd trust me."

"I *do* trust you!" Karen says vehemently. "It's them. They. Tessa. Channeling, for Chrissake!"

"Hey, I don't believe in any of that stuff either. But if we don't present a united front to the S.oteri, let them see that we can work together even though we're four distinct personalities with four distinct opinions, why should they trust us?"

"United under Tessa?" Karen is furious. "I don't think so!"

"Karen, why are you here?"

He had asked Larry the same question when he arrived.

"I was about to ask you that!" Larry said, immediately on the defensive.

At least he hadn't brought his usual entourage; one never so much as spoke the words "story session" in Larry's presence without conjuring up his agent, his manager, his attorney, and any one of a series of very large men with shoulder holsters. Larry always packed his own muscle. And usually insisted they meet on his turf. Max had expected resistance, had worded his request very judiciously, had been amazed, and not a little wary, when Larry had so easily acquiesced.

"We're here to talk story," he repeated when Larry arrived, antsy and full of demands. "And, ultimately, to make a movie. The novel's a done deal, already signed for, and I intend to stay as close to it as possible in script. What I need from you and Tessa is creative input. We're going to put our heads together and come up with the elements for a screenplay we can all agree on before we go to the studios."

"Who writes the screenplay?" Larry wanted to know.

"I do."

His tone said "nonnegotiable." Larry tried pushing the envelope from another direction.

"And you direct. *And* coproduce," he'd said, trying to make it sound unreasonable. "That's a lot on your plate."

"You were going to do all that and more," Max reminded him.

"What can I tell you?" Larry's tone implied that the rules didn't apply to him; they never had. "So what's in this for me?"

"The role of a lifetime," Max promised him, and Larry had started to object. "That's the deal, Larry. Take it or leave it."

Larry had had a whole lot more to say, but Tessa's arrival had put the kibosh on that.

"We're here to make a movie!" he'd greeted her brightly as she sailed through the door, and Tessa had given him a bemused look. She didn't know Larry's grandmother had had Alzheimer's; she drew her own conclusions.

Max, listening, had merely shaken his head. *We're here to make a movie!* Larry still didn't get it. Would he, ever?

"Karen," he asked her as they sat together in the garden, though he already knew the answer: "Why are you here?"

Because you asked me to be here! She wants to say, but that means Tony's suspicions are on target and she's still just a fangirl and this whole thing is a joke. She takes a minute to frame her thoughts, literally shaping them with her hands before she speaks.

"To help bring the S.oteri back together . . . before they disintegrate into so many little paranoid pieces that they just melt, even without the sun. . . ."

Max listens and marvels. There is no talk of making movies here, no negotiations, no deal cutting, no muscle. Even when they'd met in New York, there'd been no mention of money, points, creative control; she hadn't even mentioned her agent. Karen's motivation was as straightforward as Larry's was twisted; the contrast, Max thought, would make for some interesting drama. He hoped it wouldn't be lost on the S.oteri. It was his job to find a context from which to show them the elephant.

". . . to keep them from—I don't know—destroying their own civilization just when it's on the verge of a breakthrough . . . ," Karen is saying; she thinks that through a little further. "A civi-

lization that might be on the verge of contacting other extraterrestrials, if there are any, if they haven't already. Jesus, Max, that's
a helluva responsibility for just four humans!"

Max shrugs; they can't do better than their best.

"And how are we going to accomplish all that in a single Hollywood afternoon?" His tone is patient, not patronizing, the
coach giving the pregame pep talk, the director doing what he
was born to do.

"By making a movie based on my novel." Even as she says it
Karen has to laugh; it's too bizarre.

"By showing them the elephant," Max says.

Karen beams at him. They are joined in the same gestalt, her
gestalt. She knows she never said as much to Max; in a moment
of synchronicity—or maybe only jellyfish—he has come up with
it on his own; she cannot not trust him now.

"By showing them that we're all fictions in the mind of God,"
she finishes.

"Exactly." Max nods, pleased with her progress. "I mean, look
at us!" His gesture includes the two of them and the two con-
spirators in the house. "Three aging actors and a science fiction
writer—"

"—a *midlist* science fiction writer," Karen corrects him.
"You'd think they could've gotten a Clarke or a Bradbury."

"Maybe they tried!" Max says. "Maybe they got shot down.
Maybe they went the political route first, went to Gorbachev or
Boutros-Ghali or the Dalai Lama, same deal. Clinton? Nah.
Maybe Jerry Brown. Then for some reason they made the leap
to actors."

"No mystery there," Karen suggests. "Performers are our roy-
alty. Hollywood is our metaphor. Who makes more headlines,
Boutros-Ghali or Michael Jackson?"

Max chuckles. "Point taken. We should be grateful they didn't
go with Michael Jackson. So, okay, maybe they tried Eastwood
and Costner and Streep—nothing. Decided they'd settle for a
Koster or a Neimark or a McGill . . ." Karen finds herself gig-

gling. "They tried for the top and failed. Or were failed, by everyone else. Now they're down to us, and we can't fail, because they're running out of time."

Karen stops laughing. "Absolutely! But Tessa—"

"Tessa!" Max dismisses her with a wave of his hand. "How much do you know about me as a director?"

The question seems egotistical, out of character. Karen examines it for its true meaning.

"Enough to know you always bring out the best in your actors. Everyone says that that scene in *SpaceSeekers III* where Captain Stark learns that the Glomerans have killed his son is some of the best work Larry Koster's ever done."

"And do you know the story of how I got that scene out of him?"

Karen's heard the grapevine version; every 'Seeker has. "Only that you cleared the set and had a very private talk with him. Nobody knows what you said, but it's obvious from what's onscreen that you made him reach down inside for something he'd forgotten he had."

Max nods. The grin on his deeply lined face is almost beatific.

"That's all you ever have to do with a good actor, or a good person. Let them find what they have inside. If that means letting Tessa think she's in charge in real life, it's no different from letting Larry think he's calling the shots on the set." He laughs his mellow laugh. "Every time he'd break a scene and come at me jabbing at something in the script with those fat fingers of his— 'Max, the focus of this scene is completely wrong. It should be on Captain Stark.'. . . 'Max, I have a problem with this dialogue.'. . . 'Max, there's nothing for Captain Stark to do in this scene'—you know how I'd handle him?"

Karen shakes her head, enjoying this. Is it possible to have fun while the S.oteri bubble and squeak? As possible as it is while children die of bombs or dysentery. Not only possible, sometimes necessary. The alternative was the kind of mass psychosis that threatened the S.oteri even as they spoke.

"I'd pat him on the back and say 'Larry, Larry, relax; we'll shoot it both ways.' Do I have to tell you whose version ended up in the final picture?

"That's what I'm going to do with all of you this afternoon," he finishes. Karen looks puzzled. "Let you have your heads, reach down inside, and find what you've got. Find out how much each of you is willing to give. Show *you* the elephant. Then shoot it as many ways as necessary to get the job done."

If there were birds in the garden, the ubiquitous sound of L.A. traffic in the distance, there is silence now. Max gets up from the bench, offers Karen his hand.

"Know how a producer says 'fuck you'?" The words are surprising coming from his mouth; there is mischief in his bicolor eyes. He and Karen answer simultaneously:

" 'Trust me!' "

•

Think for a minute about magnets, Karen has written in her manuscript. The voice is Grey's speaking to whatever remains of the Mind out of some memory that is not hir own. *Remember the little round ones that you stick on your refrigerator or even those weak old-fashioned horseshoe magnets you played with as a kid, and how weird it was to try to force two like poles together and have them fight you, pushing away as hard as you pushed forward? Now click your mouse twice to turn your magnets into jellyfish and you get some idea of what's going on here on the Eye of the World.*

Ouch! Electrolytes, electric shocks, all that's finished now. Every little cell of the Mind has gotten itself a good healthy shock and is still smarting from it. Vicarious pain is one thing, guise; this is real. Even Lake and Virid, lurid bruises, Christmas colors, have had enough, haven't you? Are we awake? Are we paying attention? Good. On to the next phase.

You'll notice each of you has been polarized, Grey goes on, or is it Karen, lecturing? *which makes you naturally attracted to certain of your fellows even as you're simultaneously repelled by others. The guy you thought was your best friend has suddenly turned on you, though you haven't done or changed a thing. Happens to humans all the time.*

Now what? Is it as simple as flipping yourself over to expose the opposite terminal so you can hook up, interconnect, get back together? Is that what you want? Half of you just sit there while the other half does a one hundred eighty degree? That's it?

Okay, fine, someone mutters. *Which half? Who goes first?*

And what if some of us still don't want to play?

Grey sighs. *Who'd've thunk it would be this complicated? If only Azure would come out from under the bed . . .*

Azure-blue, where are ewe? Whee promise not to hurt yew (heh-heh). We'd just like you to come out here and complete the circle for our channeling, help us get back together. . . .

What is this, the old Captain Stark We're-stronger-with-you-than-without-you speech? Azure demands. *Catch me if you can!*

•

Tessa has taken the liberty of helping herself to a copy of those last hundred pages, giving Larry a copy as well. He is thumbing through his assiduously while she holds forth.

". . . very easily be the basis of every mythos we possess," she is saying as Max and Karen come back inside. "Consider the Elements. Substitute air, fire, and water for Grey, Lake, and Azure, and the Earth's already here, so that completes it. Or consider it from the point of view of color imagery. Blue—Azure—is a very strong color. I remember there were tests done some years ago involving blue and pink, where just looking at a piece of cardboard painted one color or the other could make the subject physically strong or weak. And certain ethnic groups place a very high value on the color blue. If you ever walk into a Greek household, for instance, you'll see a blue eye inside a clove of garlic hung over the door to keep away evil spirits—"

Larry glances up from his reading, his big thumb halfway to his mouth, turning pages.

"This isn't your Tuesday channeling group," he says tightly. "Give it a rest, will you?"

Tessa considers telling him to fuck himself but doesn't want to give herself away in front of Karen. Her drop-dead look is lost on Larry because he will not, cannot make eye contact, with her or with anyone. Now he tosses the manuscript on an end table, disgusted.

"The last five pages are blank!" he announces.

"Don't be silly!" Tessa exclaims, though truth to tell she's been talking too much to have read that far. She flutters pages, even as Karen retrieves Larry's copy, flips to the end, and shows the text to Max. Is it possible Larry can't see what's there? She is about to say something to that effect, but Max shakes his head. *He has to find it for himself!*

"Max, I was thinking," Tessa says, looking at Larry oddly. He sits hunched disconsolately in a chair, his hands wedged between his knees as if he expects any one of the other three to suddenly lunge at his privates. "Even Benn's Third Eye was blue. Now, did your makeup man do that just to contrast with your own eyes, or was there some underlying significance working through his subconscious that—"

"Oh, Jesus Christ!" Larry explodes.

Max waits them both out. "Are we settled?" he asks. "Can we begin now?"

I'm going to miss this! Virid says softly. *When we have to forget about them, I mean.*

Who told you that? Amber wants to know.

Isn't that the only way? Grey will want us to absorb Azure and dismantle all hir memories. I'm simply assuming that the rest of us will have to unlearn everything we know, too. I hope it won't hurt! But more than that, these people are my friends, *dammit! I care what happens to them!*

Amber is frankly taken aback. Was it only yesterday that they saw humans as gerbils in a lab, eating each other's young?

Since when did you decide that? s/he asks Virid. *Compassion for a species that has no compassion for itself? You're the one who gets off on the war movies, the horror movies that are these people's everyday lives. Blood and guts are your specialty.*

No, blood is Lake's! Virid corrects hir primly. *But guts . . . .well, you've got me there. But I do care, honest! And they care about us. They honestly think that they can save us from this thing that's happening to us.*

Not bloody likely! Lake chimes in with a snort of derision.

Whether they succeed or not, it's enough that they want to try! Virid begins to cry. *And whatever happens, I don't want to forget!*

Amber has been giving this some serious thought. *It's impossible,* s/he suggests, *to forget everything. At least one of us will have to remember in order to make sure the rest have forgotten, don't you see? And the fact that even one of us remembers means the rest will start to ask questions again, which will contaminate the Mind all over again. It's a conundrum. It's hopeless. It makes my head hurt!*

Which is mostly head! Virid clucks, all sympathy. *Now you know. . . .*

"Each of us is going to have to risk something," Max is saying. Is he only speaking to the humans in the room? "We may not even know what it is, but we have to be prepared to put ourselves on the line here, sacrifice something, not hold back."

" 'Risk is our business!' " Larry quips, quoting an old Captain Stark standard. No one laughs, not even nervously. Larry pouts, fidgets.

"You're asking us to reach down inside ourselves, as actors," Tessa says, remarkably subdued. It's only now occurred to her that messiahs never die in bed. Does she want to be Jesus of the Jellyfish that badly?

"More than that," Max tells her. He gives her the floor. "It's all yours."

She beams at him, surprised to be given carte blanche so readily, and prepares herself. "All right. I think the first thing we need to do is close the blinds and—"

"No!" Larry bolts out of his chair as if heading for the nearest exit, sounding like nothing so much as an S'oteri undergoing shock therapy.

"No, you don't understand!" He's broken out in a sweat, and

not only because he's so overdressed; he's rubbing his temples violently, the No-Hands Kid, still doing shtick even in his real life. "I can't—I don't believe—"

Tessa is studying him intently. "If you don't believe in channeling, Larry, then you've got nothing to be afraid of. It doesn't hurt a bit. Trust me."

"I—" He dries, looks to Max helplessly. "I need to talk to you!"

Max gestures toward the garden. "Take five!"

The Gender Thing is interesting, Amber tells Virid, two small patches of calm in the bubble and squeak; like a solo violin, poignant in a bomb shelter, it is sometimes possible to find a small air pocket of civility in the windstorm of Armageddon. *Watch now: Larry will confide to Max what he's never told anyone before, that what we've been doing for him all these years is not curing cancer or even making him a better actor, but just helping him keep his cock up. To which Max will answer:*

"Dumbo's feather."

"What!?" Larry has surprised himself with his own confession, but he couldn't risk having his Great Secret slip out in front of the women. It's a Guy Thing; he expected Max to understand, show a little sympathy. Is Max making fun of him? Always on the defensive, Larry unconsciously clenches his fists. "What are you talking about?"

"You really believe that's what the S.oteri do for you?" Max asks quietly. "Like they've got nothing better to do?"

"Tessa thinks they've appointed her Messiah!" Larry offers. "Who's crazier?"

Max chuckles. "We all are. So what are you saying? You're afraid if the S.oteri turn away from us you'll never get it up again? All the more reason for you to want to help them pull together."

"Not if in so doing they forget about us. Maybe we're better off if they stay split into all those different pieces. Some of them can help us and the rest can go to hell."

Max is shaking his head. "I don't think it works that way. I think they've functioned for so many millions of years as a single entity, a group Mind, that they either make decisions by consensus or they completely disintegrate."

"So either way I may never get it up again!" Leave it to Larry to put everything into perspective.

Max finds this terribly amusing. "Given your track record, would this be so terrible? I don't know what to tell you, my friend. If you want my opinion, they really are just Dumbo's feather. You've gotten it into your head that they function as an aphrodisiac, so it becomes a self-fulfilling prophecy."

Larry raises both hands helplessly. "I—I can't be sure. It's a . . . leap of faith I'm not sure I want to make."

"That's valid," Max acknowledges. "But what I meant about each of us making a sacrifice . . . maybe this is yours."

And that's when Larry says—I kid you not—he actually says "I'm of two Minds." Can you believe that? Amber is still holding court. Virid, however inconsolable, keeps listening. *Then Max claps him on the back, gives him the old Captain Stark We're stronger with you than without you speech, promises that of course it won't appear anywhere in the script, and he won't say a thing to the girls, but by the time they go back inside Tessa and Karen have become just the best of friends because they know exactly what Larry's problem is, and he'll know the minute he steps into the room and they burst into giggles that—*

Tessa and Karen are hugging each other, weak with laughter. Larry looks like a little kid about to cry.

"Was it Hitchcock who said 'All actors are children'?" Max wonders wryly.

"Houseman used to tell us we were animals," Tessa supplies, sobering up. "Or was it furniture? 'You are merely pieces of furniture, to be moved about on the stage at my will.' Or something like that. I forget." She sees the stricken look on Larry's face. How difficult to be the weaker sex! "Aw, Lar, I'm sorry, honest! We'll stop teasing you now, promise!"

Larry mutters something, still hunched with his hands clasped between his knees. Max has busied himself closing the blinds, and when Tessa indicates they should sit on the floor, he obliges with

326 Margaret Wander Bonanno

some of Carole's custom-upholstered sofa pillows. No hands-in-a-self-contained-circle for this channeling. Tessa grabs Larry's left hand, pulling him reluctantly onto the floor, and Max's right, nodding to Karen to take their free hands. For the heavy-duty jobs, nothing beats the human touch.

This is so silly! Karen thinks, holding Max's warm, dry hand and Larry's sweaty one in each of hers; Larry had flinched at first, unaccustomed to being touched by ordinary mortals, but her azure-blue high beams (she has begun to learn how to use that "intimidating" look) persuaded him to get over himself. This is playacting! she thinks. Click your heels three times and say "There's no place like home!" I can't possibly take it seriously.

You'd better. If you don't, who will?

Who the hell was that? Karen sees that the other three have their eyes closed, getting into it or better actors than she. Tony believes in this stuff! she thinks. I wish he were here!

She doesn't yet realize that he is. Along with a thousand little lives she'll never know about, from Akhenaton to the infant in Peru and the nun who sees her own fate in his eyes, from Jess and Hypatia to the adolescent plotting D&D scenarios on a friend's borrowed couch while the friend's parents stage-whisper about him in the kitchen, to the young woman in the Tokyo prefecture sitting for the exams that will decide her university status, and, in her society, virtually the course of her life, Tony Salda adds his spirit to the four-cornered circle in Max Neimark's living room. He sits at his desk in the deserted agency office—everyone else has gone home for the night—hands clasped behind his head, eyes closed, smiling faintly, pulling with the forces of good against the forces of entropy, even though none of the players knows who is which anymore.

Meanwhile, back on the Eye of the World . . .

•

Stop struggling! the Mind commands, having finally found Azure and dragged hir out from under the bed. The bubble and squeak has polarized, all right, coalescing into Us vs. Them, two camps (roughly; there are still some Undecideds) divided along the lines of Forget and Never Forget. The Forgets, who insist they are the only true Mind, are rounding up the Nevers and there's a great deal of metaphorical dust being raised. *Stop this at once!*

The Mind giveth, the Mind taketh away. This is to be the Final Solution. Here's how it works: We're going to take all the memories, all the cable channels, all the videos of everyone from the ape clutching the jawbone of an ass through the midlist s/f writer hunched over a grey legal pad with a cheap Bic pen in search of her breakthrough novel, and pack them all into Azure. Concentrate all our energies into leaving Azure on the surface. After all, in the time before Time, that was where she died. Even as we restore what, for all we know, was probably meant to be in the first place, we'll no longer remember why.

Once Azure's gone, the memories are gone. There is nothing left but the All There Are, back in the Garden absent the snake, our preternatural virginity restored. Freedom from want, desire, pain, or fear, where there is no time, and never Mind the inherent contradiction in the fact that if one didn't want one wouldn't want, that if one really was All There Are there would have been no need to reach across the floor of the Platonic cave, much less across a galaxy, in search of something more.

Tree of Knowledge? What tree of knowledge? Not us, Boss; we never touched that tree! Nobody here but us jellyfish—a spineless lot, really, just hanging out, doing our jellyfish thing. Humans? Other species? Never heard of them. Not us, Boss; never touch the stuff!

Now, if only Azure would stop struggling so . . .

There's just one little problem . . . Virid interjects.

Oh, don't start! We've made up our Mind, and that's that. It will all be over soon and we won't remember a thing.

We will remember Azure, Virid says. *Do you honestly think we can just shove hir out onto the surface and listen to hir scream (Help, I'm melting!) until s/he can't scream anymore, listen to hir in our Mind as she whimpers and pleads until s/he stops? We'll remember that scream—as we remember everything—forever, and we won't even know why.*

I'll take that responsibility! Grey offers—mater familias, martyr familias, anything to keep the familias together. *Once s/he's gone you can leave all your memories with me. Mother will take care of everything.*

But! Virid wants to say, but the lot of them are suddenly struggling with Azure, trying to cram all their memories into hir in one frantic gang bang—

NO-O-O-O-O!

"Um, excuse me?"

Oh, God, it's Tessa! Who left a window open? Quick, everyone: Quit struggling and act normal!

(One of you in the back there—yes, you! Hold on to Azure; don't let hir go. Keep your tentacles clamped tight over hir virtually nonexistent mouth, and if s/he lets out so much as a squeak, drag hir out the back way and onto the surface, no arguments. The rest of you, cover for us. . . .)

Yes, Tessa dear? How may whee help yew?

"My friends and I would like to talk to you. We were wondering if it would be possible for you to change your Mind."

Well, funny you should put it quite that way, because that's exactly what we were doing when you barged—um, channeled—in here. (Believe you me, when I find the bubblehead responsible for leaving the shields down and letting her beam in, I'm going to . . . !) And we want to assure you and your little friends that we've gotten the matter completely under control all by ourselves. No need for you to worry. You can all go home now; we'll manage just fine on our own from here on.

Tessa seems momentarily nonplussed. "Well, how convenient for you, but it sort of leaves us humans out in the cold, doesn't it? Don't you think it's a little rude to just cut us off like that after all we've done for—"

"Where's Azure?"

That's not Tessa, but Karen, Karen who doesn't believe. Karen who despite her disbelief has accessed Tessa's public-access channel to do something she doesn't believe in, because who but a fiction writer would be better able to see that the S.oteri are creating a little fiction of their own?

Azure . . . Azure . . . As if the name rings only a distant bell. *Oh, you mean Azure! Why, Azure's right here, aren't you, dear? Come on up front here and show Karen that everything's all right now.*

(And if you so much as breathe funny, we'll . . .) There's a dear! See,
Karen? What did we tell you? Here s/he is, and s/he's just fine, aren't
ewe?

Azure slithers forward slowly, as if not all hir tentacles are in
complete working order, smiling weakly.

"You were going to 'forget' hir, weren't you?" Karen says
softly, accusing. Silence. "Like you'd like to forget us. So here's
a question for you, the one question you never answer, because
I don't think you can—"

Non-sense! a fragment of the Mind says grandly, though by reflex. *The All There Are know All There Is. We can answer anything!*

"They're starting to babble," Larry observes to no one in particular. "Can jellyfish get Alzheimer's?"

"Then I'll ask you again," Karen persists, ignoring Larry.
"Why is it that you claim to see our future but not your own?
And, since you see time as a continuous loop, what happens to
us when you forget us? In rewriting your future, do you change
our past?"

TWENTY

It's not in the script. It even breaks Max's concentration.

"Oh, I don't believe this!" Tessa protests. The channeling circle dissolves.

"A moment!" Max cautions Tessa, a hand on her arm. "Karen?"

She takes off her glasses, looking vulnerable, polishes them on the hem of her shirt, puts them back on.

"I'm sorry. I never took physics; couldn't do the math. So maybe I'm missing something really basic here, but if they pull out of our minds, do they do the same to all the humans they've communicated with in the past? Because it's all the same to them—past, present and future—like a Möbius strip."

Max, who did take physics, could do the math, is nodding.

"Which is one of the current theories about the shape of the universe. Go on."

"Well, then: Does Akhenaton decide to go to war instead of founding a new religion? Does that make it easier or harder for Jesus when his time comes? Without the Messiah Scroll to obsess about, does Hypatia keep her guard up—"

"—so her enemies don't kill her and burn the Library?" Max finishes for her. "Interesting concept. The Library remains as a continuous source of knowledge, changes the course of Western history. Maybe there'd be no Inquisition, no pogroms; maybe they'd have listened to Galileo. Maybe someone else would have reached Galileo's conclusions centuries earlier, and we'd be in space by now, out of the solar system even. An entirely different dynamic. This could be a wonderful thing."

"Or a terrible thing," Tessa suggests. It's all nonsense! she thinks; the old, evolved souls like mine will survive no matter what happens to history! "Just think: No religious conflicts, therefore no Crusades, therefore no way for the plague to get to Europe. Besides, with the Greek knowledge of medicine preserved in the Library, they'd have found a cure for it before it even started. No plague, no reduction of the population in Europe; we'd have overpopulated ourselves into oblivion five hundred years sooner—"

"—or developed contraception along with a cure for the plague," Karen suggests.

"Well, maybe—"

"Who cares!" Larry's been silent for a whole two minutes. "What does any of this have to do with us? We're supposed to be making a movie here; let's stick to the script!"

Tessa looks at him mildly. "Look at it this way, Larry: If the S.oteri change history, you might never exist."

The idea is too ludicrous for him to contemplate; he attacks it front-on.

"Who cares? If I don't exist, then I'll never know I don't exist, right?" He jabs one blunt finger in Azure's direction. "You, straight answer: Can you rewrite our history or can't you?"

Azure's smile is sicklier than ever. *We don't know!*

Whether s/he speaks for hirself or for the whole of the Mind, it's the first time any of them has admitted this to anyone but Karen.

"That's not the only thing you don't know, is it?" Tessa asks, moving closer to them physically and emotionally. As she does, not only Azure but the lot of them become visible in the room around the four humans, shifting uneasily, unable to make eye contact, who have no eyes. The effect might be mesmerizing, like a kaleidoscope, an aquarium, except that the questions are too sharp-edged, disturbing to both sides. "You don't know how Karen's novel ends, or what kind of movie we want to make out of it. So it is possible for us to be creative without you, because we're real, aren't we? You might as well admit it, because you don't know much of anything anymore, do you?"

A kind of wail issues from Grey's direction. *Don't you see? That's why we have to do this before it gets any worse!*

"Unlearning some of your acquired knowledge is going to make it *better*?" Tessa's incredulity is mocking. "How the hell do you figure that?"

More agitation among the tangled tendrils, some stretching out toward Azure (to embrace or erase hir?), who tucks hirs under hirself, making hirself very small. Karen looks to Max for counsel, but he's simply watching, the director waiting for his actors—all of his actors—to reach for something inside themselves.

"Just one more question," Karen dares. "This decision to forget Azure—is it unanimous?"

More agitation. A very small green voice says *No!*

MAX: Good for you! Do you want to tell us why?

VIRID: (addressing Grey and the Mind as well) Well, no one's bothered to ask me, but I don't want any part of this. Violence, and having to forget! I want to remember everything. I want to keep on seeing and hearing and touching and tasting. And I don't want Azure to die.

S/he slithers over to stand with Azure, who wraps a tender tendril around hir, welcoming. The Mind is suddenly making a great deal of noise.

That's right, you'll see! Thwart us in our purpose and yule sea! We'll unwrite you, delete you from the memory, crash your hard drive, take you down with us. . . .

Reverberations percolate around about two worlds. The infant in Peru begins to weep, and the nun holding him weeps, too, as inconsolable as he. Karen feels the same despair she feels at the end of every book: the sure and certain knowledge that she'll never write another word again.

The student in Tokyo stares uncomprehendingly at the final question on her exam, her mind a blank. An angry adolescent, fists clenched, glasses sliding down his nose, stands shifting his weight outside a bar in suburban Virginia, wondering if it's worth his while to retrieve his alcoholic Uncle Henley and ask him to take him in, or simply stand on the highway with his thumb out, taking his chances.

In his darkened office, thirteen floors above a Midtown street where nightly hookers of both sexes ply their trade, Tony Salda rubs his temples, feeling a headache coming on. On both coasts, in Europe and Canada and Vegas, Tessa watches her roles dwindle as her laugh lines deepen, while Larry feels his career shrinking along with his prick. The S.oteri continue to clamor, their noise getting louder and louder. Larry finally can't take it anymore. He clears his throat.

"Excuse me? Um, EXCUSE ME!" He hasn't lost his stage voice, not even after all this time, projects from the diaphragm, looks at each one of them individually until he has reduced them all to silence. He stands slowly, deliberately, moving toward the S.oteri like a gunslinger, about to milk a Captain Stark Saves the Universe moment for all it's worth. "It's my impression that we've all missed the point here. It's not that you . . . S.oteri . . . just want to be All There Are—you want to be the That Which Created as well! You're all acting as if you think you're God!"

This could mean the end of every life on Earth! someone mocks him. What is the sound of many jellyfish giggling?

But Larry is in character, oblivious, projecting his emotions through his eyelashes; he would do the same for an audience of a million or an audience of one. Or an audience of spineless jellyfish.

"You think you can alter the face of reality on a whim. You think just because you tell us you can't lie, we're supposed to

believe you when you do lie. You think just because you feel
like it you can appoint yourselves judge and jury on your own
world among your own kind, and maybe you can. Who's to stop
you? Executioners, too. Make poor Azure go away; s/he'll come
back another day! But are you sure? Are you really sure?"

He holds out his hands in helpless appeal, his face animated,
his voice barely a whisper, though he enunciates each syllable
meticulously.

"And what gives you the right—what gives you the *right* to
decide for us? You pick and choose among us at random, ask us
to allow you access to our brains, and then what? You get bored
and just leave? What happens to us? Do you suck our brains out
when you go? What gives you the right?"

He's done it again, the way he has for thirty years, the on-
screen persona who has gradually come to inhabit his very pores
serving to remind them all of what the real issues are.

"Look, um, maybe I know a little something about what
you're going through," he says, softening his tone, relaxing
his shoulders, slipping his hands into the too-small pockets of
his too-tight jeans, looking a little sheepish. "Max has spent his
whole life fighting the *SpaceSeekers* thing—*I Am Not Benn* and
all that—but I got off on it, I'll admit it. I liked being a god,
thank you very much. So I know how you feel, and I . . . I
feel *for* you."

"Are they real, Larry?" Max asks quietly.

Real? Larry wonders. *What is real?* This thing he does for a living, pretending to be someone else for most of his waking hours
for more than forty years, something Spencer Tracy once dismissed as "not a man's profession"? Is that real? His sex life? There
have been so many women he long ago stopped trying to remember their names, can no longer even keep count. Maybe the
closest he can come to reality is the painful recognition that, like
every man who needs multiple encounters in order to justify his
existence, he really *isn't* the world's greatest lover. In fact, he uses
up his bag of tricks in a very short time and has to find someone
new to dazzle all over again. Pain is real, isn't it?

"What?" he says now. "Real? Yeah, I guess so."

He sits down, calmer now, less hunched and defensive, almost relieved. Tessa and Max exchange knowing glances; Karen resists the urge to applaud. Even Grey refrains from pointing out that they don't suck people's brains out, they never have, and the blood from the ears was a long time ago. Wasn't it?

There's that time thing again. Max picks up on it.

"So there it is, Preminger," he says directly to Grey, mind of the Mind, director to director. "You're real. We all admit it. Now we want the same acknowledgment from you. Are humans real, or do you still think you're the gods who created us? What exactly do you have in Mind?"

The clamor begins again, bubbles and factions all scrambling about, dizzying the humans, the vertigo of being caught in a blender full of oatmeal, threatening to trickle off in their own directions all over again. If Grey had hands or eyes s/he would weep or wring them.

We never asked for this! s/he pleads. *Help, I'm melting! You're the director—do something!*

The scene reminds Max of every movie set he's ever been on. Time someone took control.

MAX: (clearing his throat) All right: QUIET ON THE SET! (Waits a beat) Okay. Some of us are trying to shoot a picture here. If you have a specific place to be, get there. If you don't, kindly clear the set.

It works. The dissenters shuffle into the background; Virid and Azure and Grey (whose side is s/he on, many shades of Grey?) and a few others stay where they are.

"We'll shoot it like a documentary," Max tells them. "Tell the truth as each of us understands it, as plainly as possible. Let people, and S.oteri, decide for themselves if it's real or not."

Grey wavers. *Is that all there is? Is that really all your script will be about?*

Max takes his copy out of the box, hands Karen hers. Larry

retrieves his from the end table; Tessa has never let go of hers.

"I don't know," Max says honestly. "I haven't read that far yet. How's about we all gather around and read it together?"

Picture it. Step down into Max's sunken living room with us, Gentle Reader, like stepping into the shallow end of the pool, a pool that is aquarium, undersea, the inside of a cave. Four humans, looking surprisingly small and vulnerable for all their sometimes self-importance, sit in the inner circle, reading with their trained and not-so-trained (in Karen's instance) voices from the words that Karen wrote for them. The outer circle, reading over their shoulders, consists of a gradually increasing number of S.oteri, their tentacles interlaced about each other and draped over various parts of human bodies. They sway gently, undulate, as if underwater. Some still stand apart, uncertain, gathered in little gelatinous heaps in the far corners, but still listening. In the beginning was the word.

> GREY: (hovering over the ceiling like an out-of-body experience) It seems you have succeeded in getting our attention. What do you want of us?
>
> TESSA: (all sincerity, floating along the floor in her multiplicity of garments and beads) Only to offer you a compromise. If you cannot comprehend us as reality, continue to think of us as fiction, but do us no harm. And if you feel the need for a human interlocutor, someone to speak for you . . .

Yes, it's Tessa, playing herself, warts and all, as she was in the beginning, eager to make the S.oteri her comeback vehicle. She will also, in a series of flashbacks, play Hypatia and, in so doing, realize what the S.oteri are really about. Growth and change, character arc. Name above the credits, plus points. She even gets a chance to sing. Move over, Ancient Astronauts, Tessa McGill is back in town!

In a nameless village in Peru, a sad-eyed nun dozes, a contented infant sleeping against her milkless breast. The student in Tokyo gives the final question her best shot, shrugs, and leaves the examining room. Tony Salda locks his Midtown office and decides the brisk walk home will clear his head; he thinks of Karen and breathes a little prayer.

> LARRY: (playing himself) That's *it*? We're just going to leave them alone, let them float in and out of people's brains at will? Where's the narrative tension in that?

Yes, Larry's playing himself, as no one else can, as if he's ever really played anyone else. Max will play Akhenaton, in a frame story around the main narrative, which slipstreams across time and place from S.oteri cave to australopithecine cave to the cave of a Hollywood soundstage. The S.oteri will be Hollywood magic, courtesy of computer morphing and voice-overs by well-known actors, happy for a day's work and their names in the credits in a Max Neimark Production.

> GREY: But what about you? For all our time together, Karen, it is you we understand least of all.
>
> KAREN: What's not to understand?
>
> GREY: Your greatest fear was that we were the source of all your work, that without us you would never write again. Yet you were willing to let us go.
>
> KAREN: (New York cool) Yeah, well. I get that way at the end of every book. It passes. Deep down, I always know the creativity's mine.
>
> VIRID: (softly, as always) Good for you!

Yes, there's even a role for Karen, or an actress playing Karen. This is not in the manuscript, but it's what the S.oteri want. When they started this scene, Karen turned to Max and stage-whispered "Rewrite!" but he shushed her. Let the actors find what they have inside. Karen retreats. She'll talk them out of it later.

KAREN: . . . at least, that's how I see it. Those of you who want to keep the contact with us just go on as you have before. The rest of you . . . well, it's probably painful, but you could do what Azure did. Go up to the surface and die. Then have the Mind regenerate you without your memories of humans or . . . anyone else you might be in touch with. Death and resurrection (she laughs). Hell, it's worked before.

GREY: (speaking for the Mind) We shall consider it. (to Azure) Well, kiddo, looks like you're off the hook, this time.

AZURE: Whee!

"Playing myself . . ." Larry marvels, pacing the flagstones by the pool like Captain Stark on the bridge. The reading's finished, and everyone seems happy. "I don't know, Yeshiva Boy. You think I have any audience appeal?"

"You can start by dropping that particular expression," Max says with a rare edge of anger in his voice. "I never really cared for it, frankly. I don't know why I've waited this long to tell you."

"Finally got to you, huh?" Larry grins in spite of himself. "You know, I think I've seen you angry maybe three times in all the years I've known you. Not that I don't keep trying to annoy you. God knows I annoy most people without really trying. What is it, Max? Why doesn't anybody like me?"

"I like you."

"*You* like me," Larry says, as if it doesn't count. "You like everybody."

"This movie will make 'em love you," Max assures him, but Larry isn't satisfied. "Larry, *tochis anf tisch,* you're a very unpleasant man. I can afford to like you because I don't have anything you want. Granted, I'd never leave my daughter alone with you for five minutes, but—"

It's suddenly all very funny.

"—but you still like me!" Larry says, laughing at himself, something he's sure he's never done before.

"—because I'm a very nice guy!" Max takes off his heavy glasses to wipe tears of mirth from his bicolor eyes. "And you know what? You're going to give me the best performance you've ever given. Better than the best of Stark, better even than your Shakespeare."

"Oh, yeah?" Larry rubs his own eyelashes, watching the twilit reflections in the pool, more relaxed than he has been in months. "And why am I going to do that?"

"Because you love me," Max says. "Because I'm a very nice guy. And you know what else? I'm going to see you do Shakespeare again—"

"—before we're both older than Lear!" Larry adds, and suddenly that's funny, too.

•

Silly! Amber announces, watching the two men hug each other. How many times have Stark and Benn embraced on-screen? *This time next week they'll have "artistic differences" and be at each other's throats. . . .*

So what? Virid says. *I think they're rather sweet. . . .*

•

". . . and it's a wrap!" Max announces, climbing down from the boom to spontaneous applause, led by Larry, from cast and crew.

From her vantage between two thick intertangled tentacles of lighting cable, Karen marvels. Despite months of work on manuscript and screenplay, weeks of watching the shoot, terrified at first at hearing her words issuing from actors' mouths, it's still pinch-me-I'm-dreaming time for her. Perhaps it always will be. Fact and fiction interlayer, interweave, indistinguishable even now. Will she ever again know the difference, now that she knows there are S.oteri?

•

"So what happens now?" Max asked her when they were alone in his living room, waiting for the car to take her to a hotel. Tessa, leaving arm in arm with Larry, had twinkled at them as she left, surmising all manner of subtext that wasn't there. Let Tessa think whatever she chose. Karen, Max, and Benn know the truth.

"I go home and wait for the postpartum crash. Then I wait for you to call me and tell me you've got a deal with one of the studios and it's time to get back to work."

He'd had his arms around her, as he has in a thousand, thousand Benn fantasies but this, Karen knows, is as real as it gets. The Benn fantasies are gone; she doesn't need them anymore.

"How does it feel to save the world?" he teased her. The car had pulled into the circular drive and waited discreetly, as if the driver would wait all evening if necessary.

"Is that what we've done?" Karen wondered. She'd touched his cheek, caressing the odd little scar just below his left cheekbone before kissing him for the second time in a lifetime, this time on the mouth. "I thought it was just fiction?"

There will be a wrap party later this evening, after the stars have gotten out of makeup and had a chance to decompress. Tessa wends grandly toward her trailer with Eddie in tow, while Larry has allowed himself to be cornered by reporters from *Entertainment Weekly* and the trades.

". . . wondering, Mr. Koster, why you'd decided to go with an adaptation of a script from a novel by an unknown, when it was rumored you had a similar project already in the works?" the hotshot from *Variety* wants to know.

Larry catches Karen's eye from across the soundstage but pretends he hasn't. The schoolmarm's been quiet as a mouse throughout the shoot, but she still makes him twitchy. Even knowing there are S.oteri isn't going to change Laurence Koster overnight.

". . . comparison of the two indicated this was the better property . . ." Karen can hear him saying. Magnanimous of him. "Max and I, as you know, go way back and I . . . trusted his directorial instinct. Besides, without the burden of directing, I have more of a chance to stretch as an actor. I'm very comfortable with that decision."

"What's next on Laurence Koster's agenda?" the leggy blonde from *E.T.* asks winsomely.

Depends on what you've got planned for tonight! Larry thinks. The schoolmarm is still watching him, probably taking notes for her next novel.

"You're not going to believe this . . ." he tells the blonde, projecting his emotions through his eyelashes, ". . . but I'm going back to my roots. As some of you may know, I got my start in the theater and, as a consequence, I've decided it's time to bring my life full circle. . . ."

"The fullest circle Larry Koster knows is the one he's got sucked in behind his belt buckle!" Tessa remarks sotto voce, trailing over to give Karen one of her little professional hugs. She watches Larry and sighs. "I've always had a fondness for fresh ham! Well," she adds brightly. "And how did it seem to you today, dear?"

"Dazzling as always," Karen says, meaning it. She is about to say something else, something about reality seeming pale by comparison with the razzle-dazzle she has watched take place here and in the dailies, back to Kansas after Technicolor Oz, when her voice trails off.

Tessa turns to see what's distracted her. They both end up staring fixedly at a scene transpiring near the outer entrance, where a security guard is giving directions to a startlingly familiar figure.

•

Enter Serena.

She nods a thank-you to the security guard and strides confidently toward where Tessa and Karen stand, openmouthed.

Karen the writer notices immediately that her knees bend now;
she no longer needs to swing her legs from side to side in order
to walk. Part of her thinks: They must have done the surgery to
replace her knee joints after all. The rest of her says off Serena's
broad-faced little-girl grin:
"You're supposed to be dead."
"Yeah, well." Serena reaches into her ubiquitous backpack
with the drawing pencils lined up in their individual holders and
fishes out a pack of her thin brown cigarettes and a throwaway
lighter. "Never seem to get the knack of doing what I'm supposed to do. Guess I'm not supposed to smoke around here either, huh?"
"You're a walken!" Tessa says in wonderment. "A ghost. The
rules don't apply to ghosts."
Serena puts the cigarettes away. Her grin widens.
"Trying to cut down anyway." She holds out an arm in Tessa's
direction, pinching herself, inviting Tessa to do the same. "That
feel like a ghost to you?"
"Maybe you'd better tell us what happened," Karen says,
waiting for Serena to disappear like f/x against a blue screen.
"Well, see, I was drawing, and I heard these screams coming
from the creek up in back of the property. . . ."
As they head for the commissary, anywhere away from the
glare of publicity that still surrounds Larry—he glances in their
direction once but isn't curious enough to follow through, pre-
ferring to keep the microphones in *his* face, thank you—Karen
lags a little behind the other two, looking for subtle differences.
Yes, there is the fluid walk, and though she's still large, Serena's
lost a considerable amount of weight. As if she was somehow able
to get off the steroids that made all her other meds work and go
back to her pre-illness size. But this is Serena. In spite of weeks
of living in Oz, Karen is sure.
As sure as she is that it isn't just Serena.
". . . and I felt myself go down, and I didn't fight it. Felt the
water close over my face—cold as a sonofabitch!—and fill my

nose and my mouth and trickle down into my lungs, but somehow I was still breathing at the same time. Does that make sense? There was this sense of incredible peace. And I thought 'This must be one of those out-of-body experiences they talk about'—"

"Well, exactly!" Tessa says as they sit together at a table for four.

"No, not exactly!" Serena says. "It was something completely different, because afterward I blacked out, and the next thing I remember I came to in the woods and it was dark. I was covered with leaves, like someone had found me lying there in my wet clothes and covered me up to keep me warm, except—"

"Except?" Tessa prompts. Karen hasn't said a word.

"Except my clothes were dry. And I was in a park in Louisville, Kentucky, back where I used to live. That's over two hundred miles as the crow flies. And when I got downtown, I found out it was the night of the same day!"

She sits back in triumph, grinning her little-girl grin. Tessa, no longer sure of her skills as a guru, has suddenly turned empiricist.

"Well, then. That explains why the sheriff's office couldn't find you anywhere in North Carolina. Someone must have pulled you out of that creek—"

"—someone awfully strong!" Serena winks at Karen, who suppresses a smile. "I once topped out at two-eighty."

"—then for whatever reason driven you to Kentucky . . . you were obviously unconscious, or at least in shock, which is why you don't remember that part . . . I don't drive, but—two hundred miles? I imagine it would take them until after dark to drive that distance. Then they left you in a wooded area, covered you up to keep you warm, while they—well, I don't know. Went for help?"

Tessa flounders. It sounds implausible even to her.

"You're right about some of it, though," Serena says. "Someone did pull me out of that creek and get me to Louisville. And when I came to, I wasn't alone."

"Azure-blue, how are you?" Karen whispers softly.

Serena turns to her. Her eyes are a very dark brown, hard to see the sparkles in them even before the change.

"Good for you! How'd you guess?"

Karen shrugs. "I'm a writer."

"Oh, this is too much!" Tessa pouts, slapping the table with both hands, loud enough to draw attention even in the noise of this crowded place, where there are enough actors' emotions per square foot to light all the lights on Broadway. "That does it; I'm hanging it up!"

"Hanging what up?" Max is with them suddenly, sliding out the empty chair, his tone good-natured. One of the reasons he gets away with teasing the likes of Tessa is that he does it so disarmingly. "Thought your thing was letting it hang out?"

"Not anymore. I'm hanging it up. Hauling in the shingle. Getting out of the guru business," Tessa says, though with somewhat less emotion. "Let's face it, it was always more work than acting anyway, and now that you've given me my comeback vehicle . . ."

She flutters her eyelashes at him, but Max is impervious as usual. His smile is for Serena.

"Good to meet you finally," he says.

"Same here," Serena answers. "Although, it's kind of like I know you already. After thirty years of having Benn as a guest in my living room every week . . ."

Max has heard it all before, which is not to say he minds hearing it yet again.

"I need some herb tea!" Tessa announces, now that the scene has shifted focus away from her. Karen waits until she's flounced off to the counter before she loses it.

"Wait a minute! Wait just a goddamn minute—no, this is too much!" Both Max and Serena look at her mildly. She gathers herself. "I'm sitting here calmly accepting the fact that Serena's been resurrected and joined with the S.oteri—or is it just Azure?"

Serena shrugs. "Near as I can tell. I'm kind of interconnected with the rest of them, but I'm only actually joined with Azure."

" 'Joined with—'?" Karen repeats, shaking her head. "No, I don't even want to know the full range of what that means just yet; I'm trying to keep this plotline simple. I mean, okay, yes, I wrote that, Max shot it, it's all there. But when I was writing it, it was just wishful thinking. Now suddenly it's real."

Serena shrugs again, fumbles in her bag again for the cigarettes, realizes no one else in the commissary is smoking, puts them back. "Sure feels real to me. Right down to the nicotine fits. Weird, isn't it? They cured everything else, but I still need a cigarette."

"It's an addiction," Max agrees. He's quit; he knows.

"When you say they've 'cured everything else' . . . ," Karen says. "Even we weren't that optimistic. Neither the novel nor the screenplay—"

"Not the S.oteri, either," Serena says. "Guess I wasn't being accurate. I'm not cured. All the damage is still there. But it's stopped degenerating. I seem to be in remission. And there's no more pain. No need for meds. That was the first thing that spooked me, even more than ending up two hundred miles from where I'd started. First thing I did was haul myself up and go looking for some friends I still knew in town. I was halfway down Cherokee Parkway before I realized I was walking like I used to walk back before all the surgeries, and that I'd been off my meds for over twelve hours, and nothing hurt. Hitched a ride downtown, got back with people I hadn't seen in ten years or more, been hanging with them ever since."

"That's wonderful!" Karen says, meaning it, but there's an edge to her voice that has nothing to do with Serena. "But all of a sudden you're here. You breeze onto a closed movie set, and not solely by talking the talk with security, and Max says it's 'Good to meet you finally'—"

Max leans toward Serena confidentially. "Got a good ear for dialogue, doesn't she?" Serena laughs her smoky laugh.

"You knew about this all along, didn't you?" Karen accuses Max. "I'm not going to ask you how Serena got in touch with you, or whether or not you knew she was alive when you met me in New York, but you've certainly known since. You and the S.oteri, in cahoots the whole time. A reverse on the old Jackie Cooper 'Your dog is dead' routine. A test of the Emergency Broadcast System, like hiding under the desk in grade school as if that was going to save us from the Bomb. . . ."

Max waits until she's finished. Her voice has never risen above a stage whisper, but she's made up for volume with intensity. There are tears of betrayal blurring the S.oteri in her eyes. Serena sits quietly, making her large self very small, grateful Karen's wrath is for Max and not for her.

"Remember what we talked about?" he says finally. "Finding what each of us has inside?"

" 'How does a producer say "Fuck you"?' " Karen reminds him bitterly. "Why didn't *you* trust *me*?"

"I did trust you. Maybe it was a question of . . . maybe this was my Dumbo's feather. What am I going to say, 'The jellyfish made me do it'? Maybe I didn't trust myself."

It's a lame excuse, and if it were anyone but Max . . . Karen thinks. Blame Benn for stealing her heart in high school, and herself for forgetting that S.oteri aren't teddy bears. No one's been hurt, Serena's death was a false alarm, and Karen will get over her bruised feelings. What is the sound of one jellyfish laughing?

"I'm sorry," is all Max says, but his tricolor eyes are smiling at her and Karen smiles back in spite of herself.

What is the sound of one jellyfish laughing?

By the time Tessa returns with her herb tea, they've worked it all out—Max, Karen, and Serena, Azure and the Mind. Larry's paranoia about having his brains sucked out from across a galaxy notwithstanding, the S.oteri couldn't have done it if they'd tried. As Max explains it to Karen, with a little help from Grey, it's as if the S.oteri Mind runs on direct current, but human minds are wired for alternating current, which protects them from unwanted incursions by telepathic aliens.

". . . but my nervous system was so shot with the syringo that I'd lost all my shields," Serena chimes in. "So just as I started sucking in all that water, I sucked in Azure, too. As if s/he'd found a frayed wire, a contact point to join hir brain with mine. S/he'd been preparing me for it all winter, in case the rest of the Mind really did try to reabsorb hir, s/he could hide inside my head. Pretty neat, huh?"

Karen disagrees. "Pretty messy. What's the trade-off?"

"I get to live a normal life span. When I die, Azure gets to pick someone else with a terminal illness and live through them. Or just hang out with the Mind for another zillion years or so if s/he chooses."

"Do you feel any different?" Karen wants to know.

Serena's grin fades for the first time, exchanged for a frown of puzzlement rather than distress. "I always thought that, being an artist, I saw things differently from other people. Colors were more saturated, light was more intense. . . ."

Karen nods. They've discussed this before; it's the way she sees things, too. But Serena is shaking her head.

"Compared to what I see now, I've been living my whole life in black-and-white."

Is it really that simple, or only that complex? Maybe an occasional S.oteri will run into an occasional human with a rare neurological disorder and join like Azure and Serena, and the impact on human evolution will be almost imperceptible, but there. Anything else is going to depend upon the kind of hit-and-miss contact that's been going on since the cave. Oh, and an odd little s/f film called *Preternatural*.

". . . and maybe a few thousand years after our little movie has been bounced off the cable satellites and forgotten, right alongside Kurt Waldheim's message to the universe," Max is saying, "and the possibility of extraterrestrial intelligence, including telepathic jellyfish, is as acceptable to the layman as, say, quarks, we'll have the technology to go pay the S.oteri a visit. Maybe we'll find ways to join with them physically as well as mentally, to form a hybrid third species. Maybe you need to write a sequel, Karen."

"Tell it to my editor!" Karen says, and everyone around the table laughs.

Between now and then, Karen thinks, never one to leave a subplot hanging, someone's going to have to call Serena's sister and tell her she's still alive and somehow explain where she's been and how she got there and why she no longer has syringo. And God forbid the media get ahold of this; it'll be UFOs all the way down. But this isn't a Spielberg movie, and I'm just the writer; it's not my problem anymore. She watches as Max offers Serena a tour of the soundstage, and finds herself alone in a crowded room with Tessa.

"So what's on Tessa McGill's agenda now?" she asks sociably.

Tessa sighs. "Well, after all these months of soul-searching, it occurs to me that this planet's not ready for a messiah, not yet. What will I do for an encore? Beats the hell out of me!

"I've always wanted to see Tibet," she says wistfully, contemplating the bottom of her teacup, then suddenly beaming at Karen as if they were the best of friends.

"Who knows, kid?" she says, just like in the movies. "Maybe I'll become a nun."

Karen allows her that. It's all only fiction, isn't it?

EPILOGUE

It is the Friday night of a fan-run media convention, a Meet-the-Pros reception replete with homemade cookies and soft drinks, a guaranteed sugar buzz to start the festivities off right. The Big Stars, including Max Neimark and Tessa McGill, will not arrive until tomorrow; Laurence Koster was also invited for the full weekend, but his manager has informed the committee that he will put in an appearance for one hour only on Sunday, no autographs. Tonight it's up to the second-string guests, the artists and the writers and the tech people, to entertain the paying customers.

Karen has watched her fellow authors extricate themselves one by one from the fans and sidle toward the bar; she has promised to join them later, but now she's not so sure. None of them has read her Breakthrough Novel yet, but many of them resent it nonetheless.

The reviews are out, sort of. *Publishers Weekly* has opted to synopsize the plotline in a one-sentence paragraph rather than pass judgment; *Kirkus Reviews,* true to form, has chosen to pretend that *Preternatural,* and Karen Rohmer Guerreri, do not exist. *Locus* has had this to say:

> . . . having made a splash with a couple of *SpaceSeekers* novelizations [*sic.*] some years ago, Ms. Guerreri now attempts the writing of a "serious" first-contact novel. The results, a screenplay deal notwithstanding, are mixed, a hodgepodge of sci-fi cliché that was old before *Footfall*

was a twinkle in Larry Niven's eye, with an occasional original idea . . .

Beginning tomorrow, one of the video rooms will feature continuous showings of a documentary called "The Making of Preternatural." Lots of cutaway interviews with the director and the principal actors, narration by the mellow-voiced director himself. It promises to be a big draw. For the first time in a long time, the Remainder Queen can hope to sell some books.

In this reality.

In an alternate reality, a more familiar one, Karen's novel *Preternatural,* sans screen version, will turn up at the chain bookstore in the mall across the highway from the con only because the bookstore manager was enterprising enough to see her name on the guest list and ask her to do a signing. Out of the fifty copies he has ordered, forty-seven will be unsold returns. When Karen gets back to New York, she will find four copies under "New Releases" in Forbidden Planet; they'll be down the street on the half-price shelf in the basement of the Strand within the week. For the next several years fans will ask her "Where can we find your books? We've looked everywhere, but none of the bookstores carries them." She won't know what to say to them.

Even in this reality, seeing her name spelled correctly in the con program is pinch-me-I'm-dreaming time. Tomorrow she'll sit at the same autograph table with Max Neimark and Tessa McGill. It is all fiction, isn't it?

As usual, most of her fans are women and 'Seeker-geeks, and most of them offer her one of her two *SpaceSeekers* novels to autograph. *Preternatural* only hit the bookstores last week, and the film won't be released until just before Christmas. Strictly speaking, she doesn't have to sign autographs until the official session tomorrow but, being Karen, she signs anyway, as grateful for her fans' attention as they are for hers.

She will never know where he came from, or why she didn't see him coming.

"Hi," he says, a copy of *Preternatural* proffered in his hand. "I loved this book, though there are some things in it I'd like to ask you about. But first, could you autograph it 'To Raymond'?"

His voice is soft and incredibly pleasing, with the faintest touch of a regional accent she can't quite place; Karen feels it wrap around her like an S.oteri, warm and comforting.

"My ex-husband's name is—," she starts to say, then stops, wondering what the hell is wrong with her. Her ex-husband's name is Ray, not Raymond, and what's that got to do with anything?

"I'm sorry?" Raymond says with a slight frown. Karen takes the book from him and shakes her head, a flush of embarrassment creeping up her neck.

"It's nothing!"

She tends to sign autographs with whatever she has in her hand, unless a fan has a favorite pen. Raymond has handed her a fountain pen. An honest-to-God fountain pen.

She has gotten a good enough look at him to be able to describe him in a novel: tall and slender, younger than she (five years, ten? She can never tell men's ages), wearing glasses, and losing his hair. Not much to go on, as character description goes, and yet. And yet he doesn't look like anyone she's ever seen before. She's grateful Marie and the rest of them aren't here. Marie would give him the once-over and type him immediately.

"Geek!" she'd remark as he walked away, not caring if he heard her. "Although the bod has possibilities. I like wide shoulders on a man, but he could use a little more meat on him. Val Kilmer he's not!"

No, he certainly isn't, Karen thinks. He's . . . Raymond. Raymond who, Raymond what? What's going on here?

Time seems to have stopped, and sound as well. There is no one here but the two of them against a blue screen, f/x to be added later. Later, too, he will show her photos of his daughter and talk about his desperate sense of loss, waiting for the reruns. In alternate realities he'll tell her about how his mother left him by the side of the road when he was sixteen, and about how he won the Nobel Prize, but for now . . .

Karen finds his eyes behind the glasses, brown and sparkling. With mischief or with unspilled tears? Karen the writer senses that this man contains a goodly measure of both.

Good-bye, Benn! she thinks, to the S.oteri's great amusement. *Thanks for the memories, but I have a feeling I won't be needing you anymore. . . .*

"To Raymond . . . ," she writes, in a hand that trembles. She has seen the S.oteri in his eyes.